The Ethiopian

JP O'Connell

To Kelley + Jesus

DEDICATION

To my father, who gave me my first taste of travel when just a young teenager, to faraway Egypt. To my mother who listened to my many musings and read every word more than once. To my sisters and brother who lent me their patient ears on more than one occasion, and to my many friends scattered far and wide who encourage and inspire me.

CONTENTS

ACKNOWLEDGMENTS

I often ask myself, what manner of imagination must writers have had before the era of the internet? I flew via Google Earth to places I have never visited to investigate the lay of the land. I watched boats as they approached Tyre, caravans cross the desert, trucks trundle along the Khyber Pass and travelers swim in the Indus on You Tube. I read entire novels from the first and second centuries via various online libraries and scoured maps of ancient cities on a myriad of webpages. I plotted distances by land and by sea calculating wind and currents, miles and knots. Traveling vicariously on my computer screen, I was able to assuage for the most part my desire for accuracy in this book. Imagination played a great role, but the multitude of details I required would have been absolutely inaccessible in the short amount of time it took to gather them if I were not a child of this computer age.

PART ONE

ALEXANDRIA, EGYPT

Gregorian Calendar – January 1ˢᵗ, 162
Alexandrian Calendar – Koiak 21ˢᵗ, Fourth Akhet
The Season of the Inundation
1ˢᵗ year of Marcus Aurelius

"The inhabited part of our earth is bounded on the east by the Unknown Land which lies along the region occupied by the easternmost nations of Asia Major, the Sinae and the nations of Serice"
(Ptolemaios, *Geographia*, ca 150)

CHAPTER ONE

Aware. The space between sleep and consciousness was very fine. I could hear movement in the far recesses of the house, as well as on the street outside the small, high window of my room, where what seemed just a moment ago I had observed the moon's passage before ascending into unconsciousness. I lay on my bed, an alcove really, built directly into the wall at knee height. I wondered if this were not how it felt inside of a sarcophagus. It was just barely long enough to accommodate my long frame. If I bent my toes just so, I could touch the base while at the same time feel my closely shaven scalp brushing against the head. Keeping my eyes closed, I took a deep breath, inhaling the morning smell of bread mixed with the wet, green aroma of the dew on the reeds by the lake. I sat up and stepped down off my bed. I stretched. Naked but for a short linen kilt hanging around my waist, I stumbled in the dark to the small table in the corner opposite the front door. The tiny flame of the oil lamp was extinguished. In the pitch dark I fumbled my way to the kitchen where I heard hushed talking behind the reed door through which streaks of light cut Zebra stripes across the black earthen floor. I stood just outside the door identifying the voices before abruptly swinging the door wide and making a low, quiet growling noise. Abebe and Abeba both squealed, and my sister dropped the loaf of bread she had just taken from the oven.

"Quieten it down out there!" my father's voice boomed from where he and my mother slept on the other side of the kitchen.

I laughed silently. My sister picked up the loaf she had dropped and hurled it at me. "Imbecile!" she shouted in a whisper. The girls giggled under their breaths.

"My lamp has gone out," and before I had finished my sentence, Abeba, the older of the two girls had run out of the room whispering that she would bring Zos.

"You are up early," I said yawning.

"No more than usual," she threw back at me, still recovering from my scare.

"Oh, pour me some tea and stop pouting," I said stretching. I could just touch the open thatch roof of the kitchen. The tiniest piece of thatch floated down and lodged in my eye. Zos brushed past me at that very moment almost causing me to fall over the urn full of grain soaking in water someone had left in the middle of the floor. Abeba came back in behind him.

"Pour the tiger a cup of hibiscus tea Abeba," my sister said as she continued taking small, triangular loaves of bread from the oven.

"Mmm. That smells good," I whispered.

"If you're lucky, there will be enough for you. Why don't you eat the one that hit you in the head?"

"You're lamp is lit sir," Zos said peaking back in the kitchen. I had not even seen him leave. Abeba handed me a steaming cup of tea. I balanced it gingerly as I made my way back to my room.

"Is everybody up," Seth grumbled from his pallet in the common room.

"Everybody but the old folk," I said as I passed. Seth and my sister slept in the common room. My room was too small for them they said, even though it would have surely given them more privacy. I was not bothered. I liked having space to myself. I never had to worry about people roaming in and out of my room on their way to somewhere else while I slept. During the day I was scarcely at the house, preferring to spend all of my time at the Library. I took a sip of the tea now in my dimly lit room. The sky was still dark through my tiny window. I took another sip of my tea and sat on the floor against the alcove that was my bed, the brick cold against my bare back. The tea was bitter but warmed my insides as I sat on the smooth earth floor. I needed a bath. I downed the rest of my tea and stepped outside. There was a short dock directly opposite our home reaching out about two paces into the water of the lake. This was my favorite time, when the sky was just beginning to change color from night to day, when the papyrus of the new day was still fresh and clean. Stars hung on the western horizon while a faint yellow ribbon quivered like a mirage to the east. I walked to the end of the dock, dropped my kilt and dived into the cool brackish water of the lake. It seemed as big as the sea, impossible to see the opposite shore. I swam out some distance before turning back toward the dock. I pulled myself up out of the water and toweled off with my kilt before tying it back round my waist, wishing a good morning to those already up and on their way to somewhere important. I looked up and saw Zos, his short mop of hair sticking up in every direction, looking over the edge of the roof of the house. I waved. He gave me a big smile and waved back.

I was unable to imagine life without my servant Zos. He was always there, like this morning, taking care of the little details of my life, the things I had no time for, like lighting my lamp, making my bed, cleaning my room, fetching anything I ever needed. I held my arms straight out from my sides and flapped them, walking back to the house. I heard Zos giggle from over my head. I looked up. "I do not know why I cannot fly up there Zos… try as I might these wings just do not seem to have the right angle." His head disappeared.

CHAPTER TWO

It was the end of First Proyet, the Season of Emergence. My finger hovered over the teardrop that was the Caspian Sea, the centerpiece of Strabo's map of the world, strangely analogous to what I had always imagined as the body of a legless squid. I was finding it hard to concentrate with the knowledge that at the eleventh hour, before sunset, I was to be officially betrothed. Zos, currently standing at attention to my side, had not ceased to remind me of the fact all day long. Before I was aware of what was happening, he held his hand under the reed pen just as a yellow drop of ink splashed into his palm. "The color of imperishability, like the union you are about to form sir."

"Zoskalis, where do you come up with these things? No ten-year-old should sound like a Delphian Oracle." I blotted the pen on the scrap of soiled papyrus he offered. Zos smiled enigmatically, most assuredly contemplating his next pearl of wisdom.

What was I worried about? Arranged marriages obviously worked. Look at my own parents, happily married their whole lives, they met for the first time the day they were joined in matrimony. Their parents were much stricter about that sort of thing than they were being with me. The last I had seen of Silara was at the Festival of the Entrance into Egypt. Silara was Mary and I, Joseph as we re-enacted their escape from Herod to save the baby Jesus. We had hardly spoken to each other except to read our lines, my mind more occupied with work at the Library. My parents and her parents thought we looked good together, a perfect match. Me, an up-and-coming scribe, though only 23 years old, already promoted to the post of Director of Religious Acquisitions of the Library of Alexandria, the foremost library in all the world. Silara, daughter of one of the seven deacons in our Ethiopian church. One thing led to another, and here the day had arrived for the engagement ceremony. I touched the pen to the dry scroll. The ink was gone. Exasperated, I handed the empty reed to Zos. He refilled it with yellow ink.

It was not that I was against marrying. Who was? But to be honest, I really did not even know Silara. We had grown up in the same community, attended the same church, but she sat with the girls and I with the boys. Besides, since I was young enough to talk, I spent all of my time at the Library with my father or in classes; whereas she, well, who knew where she spent her time. But according to my mother, none of that was important. We would learn about each other over time, the way it was meant to be. Who would ever tie themselves to someone they knew too well? There would be too many reasons to avoid union. This was a decision that must be made objectively, by third parties, ones who could see the whole picture, the grand scheme. If I trusted my parents, which I did implicitly, I could be confident that they were making the right decision for me. So why was I still worried?

CHAPTER THREE

The street was quiet, the shadows long at this hour of the evening. I had avoided coming as long as possible, feeling in the pit of my stomach that each step I took today was irreversible, etching another glyph in the stone that was my destiny. Both our parents had chosen this neutral location, the home of the head deacon of our church, to formalize the engagement. Before I knocked on the door, Zos opened it, most likely having spied me from his perch on the roof. He raised his eyebrows and glanced to his right where my mother sat, visibly annoyed at my late arrival. Chairs were lined up along each bare wall. Silara sat between her parents on one side of the room and my mother and father were seated on the opposite side, leaving the middle chair open for me. Other family and servants stood in the doorways watching in silence. I felt that I had walked into a wake. Rubbing the back of my head, I quickly walked to my chair and took a seat. The deacon, standing between the two groups spoke.

"We are gathered here to recognize in the sight of God and these two families the formal engagement of Scribe Kaleb of Adulis, son of Yakub and Miriam and Silara of Berenice, daughter of Moses and Silkenas." Silara's face was set in stone. I set mine accordingly. The deacon, after a long and thorough prayer, delivered a timely and moving discourse on marriage and family, drawing parallels to the patriarchs, to the apostles and even to our own parents. Throughout, I struggled to find a place to rest my eyes. Silara sat directly in front of me, her dark hair wild and thick, her eyebrows graceful on her wide, smooth forehead, and her almond shaped eyes inscrutable, her full lips pursed ever so slightly whether in concentration or frustration, I could not tell. Her mother and father had no trouble finding where to rest their gaze. It was firmly fixed on me. I looked at the floor. A beetle fell from the ceiling into the middle of the room on its back. I watched it struggle to right itself. My father coughed. I looked up at the deacon, at the wall above Silara's head, back at the deacon. Twice our eyes crashed into one another, held for an instant and then continued the search for where to land safely.

The meal after the ceremony was a welcome relief. Strangely enough, however, I later had no recollection of what we talked about, of what we ate or of what time we left; the only thing I remembered afterwards was the briefest of moments when, in the bustle of getting seated for the meal, my bare arm and Silara's met, from the forearm to the back of our hands. In my memory, we stood frozen, attached by the backs of our arms for an interminable amount of time before sounds started filtering back into my consciousness, and she and I were directed to our seats of honor. Again opposite each other. Again struggling to keep my eyes from wandering back to her face.

CHAPTER FOUR

Being called to the offices of Klaudios Ptolemaios was not an infrequent occurrence. Although his time was primarily occupied with research for his next treatise, he maintained tight control over the workings of the Library. Nevertheless, the summons had interrupted me in the middle of retouching a 250-year-old copy of *The Histories* that I had been studying. Normally, I would have called someone from the Department of Restorations to handle this, but there was little to do at the moment, and I liked to keep up my skills with the more menial tasks above which I had not so long ago risen. I had come across a section of the scroll where the ink was flaking, and it just needed a tiny bit of retouching. Voila. I raised my hand in a flourish. Leaving it drying, held down at each end by translucent alabaster paperweights and under Zos' supervisory eyes, I proceeded down the well-lit corridor to Ptolemaios' office.

I stood silent, waiting for him to finish what he was doing. What was he doing anyway? He was holding a piece of glass up to a high window, prismatically casting painted scenes into the dark corners of his office. As his hand twisted, the scenes distorted and changed. It was magical.

"Oh! What are you doing standing there?" he said, looking over at me with eyebrows creased and a slightly perturbed expression masking the fact that I had startled him.

"I was told you wanted to see me," I said, rubbing the back of my clean-shaven head with my right hand.

"Of course I did. So, what are you standing there for? Have a seat, have a seat," he waved his hand in the general direction of the two ornately carved ebony chairs that stood opposite his desk where he now took a seat.

His eccentricities had long since ceased to disturb me. When I had first begun working at the Library, I would tremble at the mere thought of being addressed by this iconic man of learning. I was a miserable insect dwarfed before his monumental intellect and fame. For the first year of my employment, he thought I stuttered. "Out with it nka-Kaleb," he would insist, as I stood staring at the floor searching for my misplaced tongue. But I felt that those days were now ancient history. I was as at home in the Library and in Ptolemaios' presence as in my own home in the presence of my father. In fact, at this point, I think my father made me more nervous than Ptolemaios.

"What took you so long to get here?" he asked, his voice absent of annoyance, more curious than anything.

"I was repairing the ink in a copy of Herodotus' *Histories*," I said.

"Why were you doing that? We possess an entire department dedicated to that type of thing." If nothing else, Ptolemaios wanted people to stick to their respective departments. It got messy when everybody was doing everything. What happened most of the time when that was the case, he liked to remind us, is nobody ended up doing anything.

"I was reading and noticed the ink. I certainly do not want my hands to get rusty," I quickly added.

"Hands get rusty, as if that were even a possibility. So why did I call you here... oh yes! I have a new mission for you."

My heart skipped a beat. Since being promoted to Religious Acquisitions, I had been sent on two missions. My first was to obtain the writings of the Pythagorean Mathematics Cult. That particular venture had stirred up quite a bit of disturbingly dangerous antagonism from the elusive members of the secret society. Initially Ptolemaios had received veiled anonymous threats, but that problem seemed to have dissipated once his *Almagest* was published. After all, he had only wanted to see if there was anything that he could use to add to his latest work, which had since become the standard in astronomy and the study of cosmology. That mission left me with a thirst for travel that would not be quenched. It was all I could think of, the next assignment. But they came less frequently than I would have liked. My last trip was much less exciting. I traveled the length of the Nile gathering Egyptian religious texts to be copied. It was better than being cooped up in the Library every day, but it was too close to home. I wanted to see the world, visit places I read about in the scrolls that surrounded me, taunting me with glimpses of faraway, exotic smells, colors, customs and languages. I was already 23. If I were going to see the world, I must start moving. "A mission?"

I feigned dispassion, not very effectively evidently since Ptolemaios shot back, "Oh wipe that foolish look off your face. Is that supposed to be a look of indifference? It looks more like you bit the peel of a lemon and discovered a pearl inside."

"Tell me about the mission!" I said, throwing decorum to the wind. I sat on the edge of the hard wooden chair, my eyes surely popping out of my head.

"I offer you a clue," he said slyly, looking at me now out of the corner of his eyes. "What lies between Samarkand and Babylon?"

"The Caspian Sea!" I shouted, immediately covering my mouth with the back of my hand and sucking in my breath. I was far too excited.

"Right area," he laughed, enjoying my discomfiture. I must have looked like a child dancing around trying to take the candy from the hand of his father.

"Rhagae, Hecatompylos… am I closer?"

"Precisely!" he exclaimed, pleased. You have obviously spent some time in the Department of Cartographic Studies.

"Reading Strabo, and of course your masterpiece, the *Geographia*."

He waved his hand impatiently. He accepted compliments like a sommelier with an inferior wine. He had no time for it. "Enough of that. What do you know about Rhagae?"

"It is the spring residence of King Vologases IV, king of the Parthian Empire. It lies just south of the Caspian Sea and sits directly on the Silk Road route between Ecbatana and Hecatompylos, autumn capital of the king. The people speak Pahlavi. Beyond that, nothing."

"Not bad my good scribe Kaleb. You might want to do some more reading up on it, and everything between here and there while you are at it. You leave in a month."

Before I left his office, he explained to me that what the Library lacked in its Department of Religious Archives was writings from the East. We had encyclopedias of the gods from Babylon to Spain, but we had nothing from further east. We needed to expand our horizons. A month ago, a Parthian had spent some time in the Library, and Ptolemaios had gotten to know him. "He was a Zoroastrian," he told me.

"A Zoro… what?" I asked.

He went on to explain a bit about the religion and the fact that the writings of their religion were scattered all across the empire of Parthia. There was no single text. My job was going to entail collecting as many of the texts as I could and bringing them back here to add to our collection. When I left his office, I could hardly breathe.

Next I knew, I found myself standing at the north end of the Library at the top of the white marble stairs leading down to the harbor. A faint breeze blew the smell of the sea up the stairs. The Pharos, tallest lighthouse in the world, stood directly in front of me, on the opposite side of the harbor, blazing white against the flawless blue of the Alexandrian sky. Blue and white, the colors of this city, blue sky, blue sea, blue Nile, and leagues of white marble, white streets, white columns, even the clothes of the Egyptians, spotless white. The lighthouse was a sentinel, announcing to one and all, "You are in Alexandria, most glorious city in Egypt, in the Roman Empire, in all the world!" but to me it was an arrow, pointing out to sea, out to lands I had never seen, a stylus, etching adventures in the ever changing parchment of the sea.

One month. Walking now with purpose, I made my way back down the wide open corridor to the cross hall leading to the Department of History where I had left Zoskalis and Herodotus. Zoskalis stood where I had left him, straight as a statue. The document was dry. Zos moved the paperweights to the side, and I carefully rolled the scroll back up, slipped it into its cylindrical pouch and returned it to its place. "Zos, I need fresh ink and papyrus." I paced the room while waiting. One month. There was much to do, not the least of which would involve postponing the wedding, and I was sure that would make no-one happy, including, now that I took a moment to think on it, me.

CHAPTER FIVE

The sun was setting; leaving the road we walked bathed in pink. Mareotis Way was about a Roman mile long, the width of my adoptive city. This was a familiar road, my daily path, from water's edge to water's edge. I worked on the banks of the Great Sea or the Mare Nostrum as the Roman's liked to call it, and I lived on the banks of Lake Mareotis. I was never more than a stone's throw from water. I had even been born on the water, well, not literally, but my family was from Adulis, a port city far south in the Kingdom of Axum. Nevertheless, I had lived here now for most of my life. My entire family immigrated to Alexandria when I was seven, three years younger than Zos.

The streets were deserted at this hour. We both walked barefoot, Zos because he had no shoes, me because I carried my sandals. I really only had them for special occasions anyway. They were far too fragile to wear all the time. The smooth marble of the street was warm to my feet. The quiet smack, smack of our feet on the marble interrupted the calls of the water rail from the marshes of the lake welcoming us home, growing louder as we neared the end of the road and the edge of the lake. We turned right towards the Necropolis, which fortunately was still some distance away. My house was the second entrance on the right; the door faced the lake. The final dark orange spray of the dying sun painted the long wall broken only by the doors of each home. Once inside, I called out to announce our arrival. It smelled of lentils, onions and garlic. My mouth watered. We walked through the first small room, my bedroom, black as pitch now that the sun had gone down, to the main room of the house. Zos' sisters had already laid out the freshly beaten carpet and arranged the flat floor cushions for my family. They scurried back and forth from the kitchen bringing shallow bowls of water and cups of beer. I ruffled Zos' head and he disappeared behind the open doorway to his family's rooms. The door was hung with beads strung on cords, and they rattled and clinked after him. My father sat in the corner of the room reading, his chair slightly elevated on a dais. I went to him first and kissed his hand. "You arrive later than usual," he said, not taking his eyes off the scroll he was reading.

"I have news," I said. "But I prefer to wait till all are seated for dinner."

At that he looked up, searching my eyes. "Hmm. I suppose I must wait then." He went back to his scroll.

CHAPTER SIX

"Where?" my mother asked again, her hand suspended in mid-air clasping a dripping piece of bread that had just pinched up a generous portion of lentils. The circular piece of bread placed in the midst of my father, mother, sister Gabra, her husband and me was being rapidly devoured. My brother-in-law Seth had hardly waited for my father's interminable blessing of the food to end before he had eagerly begun stuffing his mouth. Zos' two sisters, Abebe and

Abeba, walked languidly in circles around us, slowly fanning the air to keep the flies away while we ate.

"Rhagae," I repeated slowly between bites. "It is a city just south of the Caspian Sea in Parthia."

"That's the end of the world!" she gasped after taking a drink to wash down the last bite. "You can't seriously be planning to go there! And your wedding?" she looked desperately at my father who continued methodically chewing his food. His eyes were impenetrable. I could never tell what he was thinking, or if his mind were even on what we were discussing.

"It is not the end of the world mother," I said, trying to keep the exasperation from my voice. "Ptolemaios has once again confirmed that the earth is a sphere. And Parthia is not even halfway."

"What's a sphere?" my sister asked as she waved to one of the girls to bring more beer. I patiently explained what a sphere was and how that related to the one we inhabited. I could tell my sister had lost interest as soon as I started explaining, but my mother hung on every word. She was not entirely uneducated. After all, she had married my father who had been a member of the Royal Council of Scribes of the Kingdom of Axum. He had been sent to Alexandria to learn all he could and bring that learning back to the capital of the kingdom, but in the end had settled in Alexandria, bringing up his family and starting a small school for young Ethiopian scribes who would take their learning back to Axum. It had taken some time to convince the council in the royal capital that the opportunities for an education here far outweighed anything he could start back home. Besides, with his connections, forged after many years here in the city, he could guarantee his country a better-rounded group of intellectuals for having studied in what he regarded as the capital of erudition.

As usual, my grand news, once delivered at home, was depressingly anti-climactic. After the initial announcement, and my sister's question, which I knew she only asked to say at least something, conversation quickly turned to mundane topics. The exterior wall needed painting again due to the infernal humidity so near the lake. Seth had made his biggest sale yet, an agate encrusted gold necklace. He was a goldsmith and had a small shop on the edge of the Jewish quarter nearest the theater. His jewelry had achieved some fame throughout the city, with a combination of Puntic flair and Egyptian ostentation which was quite original. That brought cheers all around the circle. My father said very little. Interspersed with the conversation was the sound of flies, laughter from the other side of the door where Zos' family lived, chewing and cups being refilled. I excused myself after thanking my mother for a delicious meal. She gave me a big, white-toothed smile, her eyes tender, seeming to understand my sudden despondency.

Watching the moon over the lake from the roof of our home, I considered the upcoming journey. In a way my mother was right. It was practically the end of the world. Even Ptolemaios' book of geography gave very scant detail on anything beyond India or further north than the Caspian. It truly was near the limits of the known world. As I stared out at the reflection of the moon, I heard footsteps ascending the narrow stairs from between the common room and the kitchen. My father took a seat next to me, dangling his legs over the edge as I was. Up here, there was a soft, warm breeze on our backs, blowing in from the Sea. The leaves of the fig tree on the edge of the lake in front of me whispered. My father's voice broke the silence. "I am proud of you son. This is a great opportunity for you. Forgive your mother. She did not want to encourage you until she knew my mind. But she is also very proud of you, though fearful. Like Solomon said, 'the lot is cast into the lap, but its every decision is from the Lord.' You are embarking on an adventure whose outcome you cannot even imagine, but all is in God's hands. I am reminded of when I was commissioned to come to Alexandria. I was a young man, much like you though a bit older and with a family." He laughed, "I had never been further than the capital at Axum. My parents were not enthusiastic. They knew it was a great opportunity, but I was the eldest son, and they were not happy about not seeing their grandchildren for who knew how long. But we prayed over it, and they sent me off with their blessings in the end. I never expected to settle here. One never knows the outcome of a venture."

"I am not going away for good," I said. "The whole purpose of this mission is to return with the documents."

"I understand that, but only God can see our future. Arrangements will have to be made with Silara's parents. We must have the wedding sooner."

"I would rather postpone it. It would not be fair to Silara for me to leave immediately after our marriage."

"As you wish. Your mother will not be happy."

We sat in silence for some time after that. Eventually my father rose to leave. "Thank you father," I said as I looked out over the water. I listened to his footsteps as they receded down the earthen steps.

CHAPTER SEVEN

Fourteen days had passed. Passage had been booked on a Greek merchant ship leaving the 4th of Paremhat. I had copied any maps of relevance to my journey and was reading all I could find on anyplace there was any chance I might travel, taking copious notes. I had also employed the young scribes-in-training under my supervision in copying books I thought might prove useful on the trip, particularly anything medical. I was summoned to Ptolemaios' inner sanctum again. We had had many discussions since the day he announced my mission to me. He had given me names of contacts, abundant advice on precautions to take, foods to avoid, protocol to be observed in the different cultures I would encounter, and I hung on every word of it, imagining myself already on the ship, on my way to the great unknown.

But this visit involved a much more practical matter, money. "Our accountant has doubtless included the expected expenditures of food and lodging along the way as well as the hiring of dromedaries, donkeys, camels and ferry passages, round trip from here to Tyre, incidentals and a travel stipend to buy gifts and such of course," he said in one long breath. "We would fain have you make a trip of that magnitude and find yourself unable to bring at least something back for your family now would we? I have estimated that the entire trip should take anywhere from six months to a year." A year. How exciting! I could hardly wait. "Here is a belt that has been specially designed to cause the least discomfort but provide the tightest security for the amount of money you will be carrying on your person." He handed me what looked like a girdle that fit snuggly to the hips and fastened with a clasp, fitting my form so as not to be discerned under other clothing. And it contained 14 gold aurei. Each aureus was worth 25 denarii, and my salary was only 15 denarii a month. This was a veritable fortune, more than a full year's salary.

"I would rather not take it till the day I leave, if you do not mind sir," I said, politely refusing to even touch it. "That is so much money. I have never seen so much money at once in my life."

"Nonsense," Ptolemaios snorted. "The rooms you work in, the scrolls you study, the chairs you sit in, they are priceless. This is nothing."

"I beg to differ sir. This is gold. I would be a nervous wreck for the rest of my days here if I had to keep up with that."

"As you wish," he said as he waved his hand in the air. "You will be wearing it soon enough I imagine." I looked at it again; that girdle was going to be hot. I was not looking forward to keeping up with that everywhere I went. Money made me nervous. I dealt with it as little as possible. My father handled my salary. I never saw money except when my mother sent me out to buy something, and that almost never happened since I was never home. The last time I handled any amount of money was on my last mission, but the total came nowhere near what I would be handling now. "And just so you are aware, anything you conserve from your trip will be yours to keep. If it turns out you have to pay a price for the documents you seek, you can speak with our contact Yonas in Ecbatana. He will furnish what you need."

The last thing I heard was "yours to keep." As a scribe, I knew I could earn my keep anywhere I found myself. I almost determined then and there to not even take that girdle with me. I could earn what I needed on the road itself. But what if there were an emergency? What if I needed money quickly? The money belt would come with me, like it or not.

"You should change out the gold coins in the bigger cities as you need them. It will be hard to find anyone that handles such large sums in the towns you will pass through, plus it will draw attention to yourself. Be discreet."

"Right. Discreet." With a year's salary jingling around my waist like a dowry girdle. And did he say Yonas was in Ecbatana?

CHAPTER EIGHT

Zos and I did not normally talk much on our way home in the evenings. I did not know what went on in that 10-year-old head of his nor was I that bothered to find out. I had plenty to occupy my thoughts without adding his to them. But he had been even more silent than usual these last few days.

"What is on your mind, Zos? You have hardly spoken a word in three days."

"What can I say sir? There's nothing to say. You're leaving and will be gone for who knows how long. What will I do? There will be nothing for me to do. I'll probably be sent to the countryside to work in the fields with my brothers." He looked so despondent, staring at the ground as he spoke in a hushed voice.

I knew not what to respond, so I said nothing. It was true. There would be no reason for Zos to keep living here in Alexandria. His sole job was looking after me, and if I were not here, there would be no need to keep him here. We did not speak again before reaching the house. It was still light. The sun had not dipped below the horizon yet. The blue doors along the wall front facing the lake reflected the blue of the lake. Red hibiscus was brilliant against the white of the freshly painted front of the house. From the sounds of it, everyone was on the roof. Zos opened the door for me and then ran past me up the stairs. I shut the door behind me, following Zos up to the roof.

Everyone was there. The flat expanse took in the area above my room, the common room and the roof of Zos' family's house which was a mirror image of ours. The roof was swept clean, and there was a clay pot with a fire in it between where my parents and Zos' parents sat on short stools. There were other stools scattered about. Abeba and Abebe were chasing each other from one end of the roof to the other, giggling and calling to each other, but not too loudly so as not to disturb the adults. My sister and her husband were not present. Zos' father, filling my father's cup from the pitcher of beer said calmly, "Abeba, Abebe, stop making such a racket and go downstairs for a bit. We'll call you when you can come back up." The girls immediately ran down the stairs, giggling as they went. Zos looked up expecting to be sent down as well. "Zos, you sit there," his father motioned to a stool. I joined the circle, suspecting some announcement or other, suspecting it had something to do with me... and something to do with Zos. I could tell Zos had no idea what was going on.

"Kaleb," my father began, "Zos' father and I have already discussed this. It is entirely up to you. I will not try to convince you one way or the other. Of course, I speak for myself. Your mother may have other plans."

"Hush!" my mother swatted at my father's arm. "I'm sure he'll make the right decision," she said, looking at me anxiously.

The sun was just beginning to drop below the horizon, casting a pale pink and yellow over the vast expanse of the lake to my left. Ahead of me spread out the rooftops of hundreds of homes. One could practically cross Alexandria jumping from one rooftop to the next. I looked expectantly at Zos' father, curious but half guessing already what this would be about, some type of compensation for Zos for the time I was away. "I haven't even spoken of this to my son, Kaleb sir, but I know he would agree in an instant. Have you given any thought to taking nka-Zos with you, to be your servant on the long journey?" Before I could respond, my father interrupted.

"Let the man finish Kaleb." Zos seemed to have stopped breathing.

"We are a humble family, of humble origins. Your parents, in their great kindness, brought us here to live and have provided for us ever since. Our two oldest sons got some schooling and manage their own farm now on the other side of the lake. Our two oldest daughters are married and were supplied with an enviable dowry by your parents. And now we've got our two youngest daughters, Zos and the baby to prepare for the world. Zos loves you. Without it being said, he decided to be your servant, and only yours from the time he could reason." I looked at Zos. His eyes were wet. He saw me looking and looked at the floor. "You are going to need an extra pair of eyes on the caravan. How will you ever separate from the dromedaries and your things if there isn't someone there to keep watch? You're going to need someone to do the thousand small errands that must be done every day while you're taking care of your more important business. Where will you find someone more trustworthy and careful than my son? It will be like having family with you. Your parents tell me you could be gone for as long as a year. Zos could learn from you. He could learn to read and write, to speak other languages. Don't answer immediately. Think on it. Tell us tomorrow. But no matter what you decide, we will not harbor hard feelings, right Zos?"

"Right," whispered Zos without lifting his eyes.

My head was whirling. This was the last thing I expected them to say. I had not thought once about bringing Zos along with me.

This was *my* adventure, and I was planning it to be a solo trip. The thought of having to take care of Zos was almost overwhelming. I looked at Zos, staring at the floor. I looked at his parents, looking down as well. I looked at my mother who was nodding her head yes. So at least I knew where she stood.

"I will do it. I will take you Zos." The words were out of my mouth before I knew what I was saying. Where did that come from? Zos got up, ran to me and hugged me. He had never hugged me before.

"Thank you, thank you." His mother caught her breath, her eyes glistening. My mother as well. They hugged each other. Zos stood back apart from me, looking at the floor and said, "I will be the best servant in the world sir. You'll see," and with that he ran down the stairs to the interior of the house.

"I knew you'd make the right decision Kaleb," my mother said.

"I could see the wheels turning in your head son," my father smiled. "I am sorry we surprised you like this, but it was something that had to be addressed, and your mother and I were both in agreement that you needed to take Zos. But we did not want to pressure you. It needed to be your decision."

Zos' father filled all the cups with beer, and we drank to the adventure that awaited me and his young son, to the road ahead. "Two are better than one," my father quoted, "because they have a good return for their work. If one falls down, his friend can help him up. But pity the man who falls and has no one to help him up! You cannot dismiss the wisdom of Solomon, son."

CHAPTER NINE

When spider webs unite, they can tie up a lion.
(Ethiopian proverb)

Although somewhat protected by high walls and the absorptive qualities of the acacia trees vaguely casting careless shade over the wooden tables and stools scattered across the courtyard, the din of the market rose and fell lethargically over the men seated near the entry arch.

The three men sat in silence, staring at the table in the midst of them as if it bore some inscrutable glyph that had yet to be deciphered. A tamarind pod spun heedlessly in the direction of the

Pythagorean cabal. Its click on the table, like a beetle on dried parchment, roused the oldest of the three out of his stupor. "There is nothing to be done at this point. Avoidance of revenge is a virtue, and regardless, the exposure is three years old."

"The key word being avoidance Nerva. Serving up punishment for a crime is also virtuous. Acts such as this cry out for retribution which is very different from revenge. Besides, the passing of time has made him careless. This is precisely why we have taken other steps." The youngest of the three lifted his head to look at the sky, a dingy blue, and continued speaking, "We had two choices, to eliminate the source of the exposure or aid in his exposure of something equally significant to overshadow our own disaster."

"You disregard a third option." Both men turned to look at the golden haired Teuton. "We could do both." Silence. All three returned to the invisible glyph on the table.

"But that would require getting a message to our contact in the East," Nerva, weathered forehead creased, continued looking at the table. The vibrations of his deep voice disturbed the tamarind pod. "Kaleb leaves on the next ship bound for Tyre."

"We do not even know what he seeks. How could we influence his finding what we are unaware of?" The youngest said this while rubbing the top of his head, as if a genie in his mind would reveal the secret if caressed sufficiently.

"Oh ye of little faith," the Teuton chided. "Suppose I told you I have already taken care of that."

"What do you mean?" Both men looked wide-eyed at the Teuton. "How could you act without bringing this before the council?"

"Who says I did not bring it before them? In any event, we need only observe how things unfold. But we must remain unified; after all, after unity, number commences, and fragmentation. Above all, we must not divide ourselves. We will wait and watch, and in the end, we will wreak our retribution on the revelator."

PART TWO

THE GREAT SEA

Gregorian Calendar – February 20th, 162
Alexandrian Calendar – Meshir 12th, 2nd Proyet
The Season of the Emergence
1st year of Marcus Aurelius

"I fly up as a bird and alight as a beetle on the empty throne which is on your
bark, O Re!"
(The Book of the Amduat, ca 1426 BC)

"On learning that the sides of the ship were four fingers, think: The passengers
are just that distance from death."
(Diogenes Laertius, *Anacharsis, Lives of Eminent Philosophers*, ca 250 BC)

CHAPTER TEN

Sun, glorious sun. The water sparkled so brightly it was hard to
regard. Like the harmonic note behind the main chord, the dull
whish of the small waves splashing against the stone wall of the pier
played counterpoint to the chaotic noises of the harbor. Birds cried
as they flew overhead; shouts crashed from deck to dock and back
again. I took a deep breath, inhaling the heat on the marble, the faint
smell of fish and salt water and my mother's perfume. My family was
with me as well as Ptolemaios and a few of my colleagues from the
Library. My meager belongings had already been loaded on board
the Greek cargo ship: one change of clothes, one drinking cup, water
skin, wine skin, wool mantle, leather sandals, small supply of papyrus,
palette containing pigment and writing reeds, documents for the
journey including maps, instruments for grooming and a supply of
hibiscus for tea, food for the voyage and finally the even fewer
belongings of my servant Zos. I was wearing my golden girdle under
my white linen kilt. How uncomfortable it was. Would I ever get

used to it? My white scribe's skullcap was planted firmly on my freshly shaven head, ready for travel.

I had taken my time this morning with my bath in the lake. It would likely be the last bath I had for some days, unthinkable for an Egyptian. I had swum out further than was my wont while Zos splashed around closer to shore. The low white houses rose up graceful and white against the morning sky. To the left the red Aswan granite of the Pillar of Pompey rose majestically from the midst of the colonnaded route to the stadium and the necropolis beyond. The water, a mirror of onyx, reflected the date, fig and palm trees lining the shore. Alongside the warm currents that swirled around me, a brief wave of premature nostalgia washed over me, a presage of the longings I was to feel remembering this moment, my heart carefree and happy, the wide world before me.

My mother had carefully pleated my kilt the evening before, desirous that her son cast the most presentable figure on this auspicious day. My father gathered us around him along with Zos' family, his mother in tears since the moment she had first appeared this morning. My father lifted his hands, and we bowed our heads as he commended us into God's hands. "Amen" we said in unison. Zos had turned out in his finest as well, and his mother had obviously made him oil himself. He shone like a mahogany statue. All but the crown of his head was shaved clean, his small ears standing out making him look vulnerable and younger than his ten years. He wore a plain white kilt and a thin gold necklace that Seth had given him as a parting gift. It was the most precious thing Zos had ever owned. He wore it with great pride this morning, the gold gleaming against his bare dark neck.

I did not favor jewelry, never wearing any except the brass bracelet on my left forearm with my name etched across it in broad hieroglyphs, a gift from Ptolemaios when I was promoted to Director of Religious Acquisitions. Nevertheless, I too wore a necklace that had just been given me. Silara and her parents had visited our home yesterday evening. As they left, Silara surreptitiously slipped a small package into my hand. After everyone was in bed, by the dimmed wick of the lamp in my room, I unwrapped the gift. It was a tiny-beaded necklace with a flat bronze oval pendant inlaid with a single smooth piece of ivory which, upon inspection, bore a painted likeness of Silara. I stared at it for a long time before laying it beside the lamp. A brief pang of guilt pierced me at the thought that I should have thought of something for her. I mentally ran through my belongings. No, I would have to send something later.

A horn sounded. The time for departure had arrived. Unfamiliar with having to say goodbye, my first inclination was to be done with it and head for the ship straight away. That would have been too easy. Again, I had to embrace everyone present, my mother finally breaking into tears. I could see that Zos was as ready as I to escape this maudlin scene and head for the deck of the waiting ship. Finally, after more well wishing and last minute advice, we mounted the ladder to the upper deck amidst shouts of "Careful! Watch your step! You're almost there!" A deckhand was waiting at the top of the ladder to help us with the last step. We waved once at the top. Oh that the ship would make a move and fast. How long would we be compelled to stand here waving? How long could I take it? I was ready to hit the high seas, feel the wind in my face, see the sails unfurl and Alexandria disappear in the distance, towering Pharos behind us, the open sea ahead. How many times would I look back at that scene in my mind and wish I had been more patient. Little did I know how much time would pass before I saw my beloved Alexandria again, yet even then, it would never be the same.

CHAPTER ELEVEN

The crew cast loose the hawsers. The captain shouted exhortations, "Be brisk with it!" as the sailors prepared the tackle and reared the pine-tree mast which was quickly lodged firmly in its deep socket. Straining the cordage and with well-twisted thongs, they drew the shining sail aloft. With all of the rigging set, a land breeze whipped the canvas full, and the ship plowed into the surf, the prow effortlessly cleaving the colliding breakers that raced to the Alexandrian shoreline.

Half an arpent long and two perch wide, the ship left little to the imagination. There were ten crew plus twelve passengers, including Zos and me. We slept atop deck under a massive canvas that had been stretched across the majority of the rear deck, allowing for freedom of movement around the one giant mast from which billowed the huge white sail. As night fell, I spread out my wool robe which I had brought for cooler weather on which Zos and I could sleep. I found it difficult the first night to find the unconsciousness that came so easily at home. In a very short time, an impenetrable blackness had invaded. I could not discern if my eyes were open or closed. I experimented a few times. Open. Closed. No difference. The canvas that protected not only us but the merchandise that would not fit below deck also impeded any breezes from reaching the floor where we lay. The stagnant air smelled of tar, brine and a faint hint of urine and made my skin feel sticky. I moaned at the thought of not being able to bathe for three days. My girdle of coins made lying down on a hard surface acutely uncomfortable. No matter in which direction I lay, I could feel the hard cold coins pressing into my flesh like the thick scales of a monster fish. It seemed that any time I was close to drifting off, I would hear something scurry past my head on the floor. Ships were notorious for transporting all manner of vermin, and here I was lying on the floor eye level with them. Zos was out in minutes. I could hear his steady breathing next to me along with the jagged stertor around us. None of it however drowned out the sounds of the waves beating monotonously against the hull of the ship. Nevertheless, despite the distinct discomfort, I was still full of the thrill of finally being on the journey. In the end, it was the water, was it not always the water, my familiar friend, that lulled me into a fitful sleep.

CHAPTER TWELVE

The winds kept us moving at a fast clip; the operators of the sail stationed port and starboard, adjusted the multiple forestays keeping the sail constantly full. One entire day of nothing but water in all directions. It was projected that if the weather continued cooperating, the following day we would sight land and could arrive in Tyre by as early as that evening or at the latest, the following morning.

I spent the morning explaining to Zos what we were doing, where we were going and what the plan was. I did not go into details about the Zoroastrian writings. Suffice it that he knew I was a scribe on a journey. I bound him by a promise not to let anyone know I worked for the Library of Alexandria. The story was that I was a scribe from the Kingdom of Axum on a trip to visit relatives in Ecbatana. Using a piece of chalk from my writing materials, I drew a map out on the deck floor showing Zos where we were and where we were going. He sat rapt. Of course, there were not many distractions on board. Many passengers were dozing in the fore of the ship where the breeze was more tangible. Evidently I was not the only one that failed to sleep last night. Others leaned over the sides aft and watched the trail of foam created by the ship's passing fade into the distance like a forgotten memory. A heavy torpor had descended over the entire ship. One passenger was standing apart from the rest, facing Zos and me. I had noticed him several times since we boarded, looking in our direction, only to look quickly away when he saw that I had caught him staring. "Do I know you?" I called out in Greek, looking him full in his narrow birdlike face. He was unkempt and wore a soiled Greek toga that hung loosely on his thin frame, evidence of more than just a bad night's sleep. He looked quickly away and moved towards where the crew was lounging near the mast, leaving me with an uneasy feeling in the pit of my stomach.

Feigning indifference to what had just occurred, I turned back to Zos. "Your parents mentioned studying language. Does that interest you Zos?"

"Yes sir," he said, eyes bulging. "Would you be my teacher?"

"Will you be an obedient pupil?" I was not a teacher, and if Zos were unwilling to put forth enthusiastic effort, I could not bother myself to teach him.

"I will do everything you say Teacher," he smiled. He had never called me teacher. I liked the ring of it.

"Excellent then Zoskalis of Adulis, we will begin the lessons forthwith. There is nothing else to occupy our time on this forlorn ship." I thought for a moment. What should I teach him? What would serve him best initially, give him the greatest advantage at this early stage of his life? "You speak Greek as well as Ge'ez and Egyptian right Zos?"

"Right Teacher."

"Can you read and write?"

"I can read a bit Teacher. After all, I do spend all day watching you."

"Right. How about we start you off with reading Greek?"

"You will teach me to read?" Zos asked excitedly. He was only one year past the normal age a boy would begin his studies, but the chances that he would ever get to study were slim to none.

"I think I will also teach you Aramaic."

"Who speaks that language Teacher?"

"Most people where we are going Zos, and it is a language that will serve you well. If you know Aramaic, it will be easier to learn many of the languages of many of Rome's eastern provinces. The only important language you would lack then is Latin."

"Do you speak Latin also Teacher?"

"Yes, among others. But for now, we will focus on Aramaic. Repeat after me…"

CHAPTER THIRTEEN

It was the Hour of the Depths, the gloomy waterhole of dwellers of the underworld according to the Egyptian clock, on our second night at sea. Evidently I was so tired from the lack of sleep the night before that I was unconscious before I closed my eyes. Nevertheless, I was to be denied sleep again. A deluge of cold sea brine doused me from head to foot wrenching me from the silence of sleep to the violent raging of wind and tossing of the ship. Zos held tightly to my arm as we crawled out from under the tarp, popping as it strained against the gales that ripped at it like a kite caught in a sandstorm. The squall ploughing up the sea blew directly into our teeth. We crawled under the flooded bulwarks for protection though they were being continually washed over by the waves. Herculean billows tumbled one over the other in quick succession, almost touching, as they did, the clouds. The most formidable were those which broke against the sides and made their way over the bulwarks, flooding all the vessel. When they neared and broke, I was sure that they would inevitably swallow up our ship which they first lifted high up as if upon a mountain, and on retiring plunged into an abyss. We could scarcely keep our feet, so violent was the rolling of the vessel, and a confused din of sounds was heard; the sea roared, the wind blustered, the women shrieked, the men shouted, the sailors called to one another; all was wailing and lamentation. There was no middle space left between sky and sea. The clouds touched the waves and the waves were all mingled by the bluster of the wind.

The pilot yelled, "Bring the yard round!" The sailors speedily obeyed, pulling on the ropes to keep the sail opposite the wind. The vehemence of the gusts, however, compelled them to leave one half unfurled, resulting in the vessel heeling to one side. We expected to be capsized as the gale continued to blow with undiminished fury. To prevent this, and to restore, if possible, the vessel's equilibrium, we all scrambled to the side highest out of water, but it was to no avail. We ourselves were raised, but the position of the ship was in no way altered; after long and vain endeavors to right her, the wind suddenly shifted, almost submerging the side which had been elevated. In concert with the mighty trumpet call of discordant winds, a universal shriek arose from those on board, and nothing remained but to hurry back to our former station. We repeated this several times, our movements keeping pace with the shifting of the vessel; indeed, we had scarcely succeeded in hurrying to one side, before we were obliged to hurry back in the contrary direction, backwards and forwards like the runners at the stadium running round the goal. We continued these alternate movements during a great part of the night, blinded by the dark and the spray, flashes of fiery lightning granting frozen glimpses of the roiling sea and terrified faces. Reflecting the strife of the waters below, echoes of rolling thunder filled the sky.

Zos and I held tight to a post securing a bulwark and prayed loudly, commending ourselves into God's hands. All at once, the wind began to abate and the ship emerged as if from the gates of Hades into calmer water, the lightning and thunder receding into the background. The shouts turned from shrieks of fear to cries of rejoicing. The sailors began bailing the copious amounts of water trapped on deck back into the deep. Zos and I rose to help, praising God for delivering us from certain death. I recalled the accounts of Paul's shipwrecks and marveled that he had the wherewithal to testify to the men on board his ship in the midst of a storm of this magnitude. The untattered half of the sail was unfurled and fresh rigging pulled taut to take fullest advantage of the wind the storm continued to blow in our direction, as we aimed to get as far away from it as possible. Stars had reappeared in the sky to the northeast. Zos and I withdrew to the rear of the ship and stripped off our dripping tunics, wringing them out and drying ourselves as best we could before donning them again. "I did feel I was in need of a bath, but that was not what I had envisioned!" Zos laughed. Joining him, we laughed until our sides hurt, expelling the last of the tension we had felt for the past several hours. The wind to our backs, and the length of the entire deck before us, I raised my hands and again offered our thanks to God for saving us and the entire crew.

CHAPTER FOURTEEN

Land! I could smell it. Mingled with the dominant aroma of salt, mildew and urine I detected an indefinable addition. Perhaps it was dust, or the scent of cedar and olives wafting towards us from the coast. Whatever it was, it had invaded my nap the way a mosquito inserts itself under a net. I was propelled from the hard deck to the bulwarks to confirm the suspicions of my nose. Only the endless sea lay spread out on all sides, a steady breeze keeping the sails full. I found Zos playing temples and tombs with a piece of chalk on deck. I joined him for a while to pass the time, and then we spent the rest of the day in lessons, trying not to scratch our itchy, ashy skin, blanched from the saltwater and sun.

Tyre was sighted before the sun entirely disappeared beyond the watery horizon. The blackness felt distinctly different from the first night. Lit lanterns glowing orange in the dusk hung round the ship so we could be easily seen. These were well-trafficked waters. Twinkling lights glittered along the shoreline where Tyre must be. The rest of the coastline was black, a more profound black than the sky overhead which after some time began to take on the quality of day. I had observed the bird-man skulking around the deck over the course of the day. I never caught him looking in my direction again. It was almost as if he were going out of his way to avoid me, a feeling that did not sit well with me. I would have to be on my guard till we were safe with our contact in Tyre.

The moonlight cast my form in shadow on the floor. As I turned to inspect it, I saw Zos approaching.

"Describe what you see out there in Aramaic," I said, the sweep of my hand encompassing the space between our ship and the sparkling coast. I had him repeat the phrase, "I see," and then give me a few sentences.

"This is a light," I said in Aramaic, pointing to a lantern nearby. "Do you see a light?" I then asked, continuing in Aramaic.

"Yes," Zos answered enthusiastically.

"Complete sentence please."

"Yes, I see a light," he said somewhat more hesitantly.

"Excellent! Do you see water?" I asked, using vocabulary we had practiced earlier in the day.

"Yes, I see water," Zos responded more confidently. And the lesson had begun, under the starry host of the Lebanese coast.

PART THREE

TYRE

Gregorian Calendar – February 23ʳᵈ, 162
Alexandrian Calendar – Meshir 15ᵗʰ, Second Proyet
The Season of the Inundation
1ˢᵗ year of Marcus Aurelius

"In every vital activity it is the path that matters."
(From the walls of the temple of Luxor)

CHAPTER FIFTEEN

Crystal clear blue sky, blue sea and the towering fortress walls of
the island of Tyre. The city was almost 3,000 years old. Often called
the carrier of civilization, this capital of ancient Phoenicia had settled
colonies all over the Great Sea as far away as Spain. Hanno had
navigated the entire continent of Africa 600 years ago. Most of the
alphabets of the modern world could trace their origins to
Phoenician script. Even after their destruction by Alexander,
founder of my own city, they had risen from the ashes and developed
once again into a pearl of the Great Sea, rivaled only by Alexandria,
city of half a million souls. And just five years ago, Anicitus, born
near Tyre was named a bishop at Rome. With sea spray in our faces,
Zos and I leaned far over the prow watching as the city grew closer.
Although Alexandria was on a much grander scale, colonnaded
avenues, the towering Pharos, the royal palace and harbor facing the
sea, Tyre commanded a distinctive presence. The heavy stone walls
of the city surrounded the island as if the city itself had been built on
the foaming tips of the waves. Our ship made its way around the left
side of the island and into the harbor known as the Port of Egypt.
Here arriving vessels from the south cast anchor. The northern Port
of Sidon, on the other side of Alexander's causeway, built when he
laid siege to Tyre four hundred years ago, was primarily for receiving
ships from the northern shores of the Empire.

As we were in no hurry, Zos and I positioned ourselves where we could watch all the activity from the deck. The sails were furled and stowed, like scrolls returned to their pouches, and the mast was lowered by the forestays and quickly brought to the crutch where it was secured. Once the rowers had brought us safely alongside the pier to the place of anchorage, the sailors cast out the mooring stones and made fast the stern cables.

What little Zos and I had brought was on deck. I requested that our things be unloaded last. Three large ladders, almost like stairs, were laid against the ship's side and hooked over the bulwark. The other passengers' things were unloaded promptly, and they all disappeared in the mass of humanity that scurried hither and thither on shore. An army of slaves boarded the ship and began extracting the cargo from the hold. Barrels of Egyptian wine, hundreds of bags of wheat and barley, crates carrying precious jars of coveted Egyptian perfume, crates of other Egyptian craftsmanship, glass wear, vases, furniture and rolls of bleached white linen. Several accountants stood at the base of the ladders ticking off each bundle that descended on the backs of the slaves. Further down the pier, other ships were also unloading. Was that a leopard being carried in a cage down the ladder of the neighbor ship? And it was followed by two more. The men descending and ascending the ladders scarcely cast us a glance. There were people of every shape, size and color, but we were definitely in the minority with our mahogany skin and now not so crisp white linen kilts. Finally, when most of the excitement on our ship was past, I called over a couple of slaves and bid them carry our things. They were happy to earn an extra couple of quadrans for a moment's labor.

"We'll carry it into town for you for one *as* each. We're done for now." Zos looked at me. They were speaking Punic.

"Excellent," I replied in Punic. "Follow me." I told Zos in Ge'ez to follow behind them and keep an eye on them. It was already proving advantageous to have Zos along, and the trip had hardly begun. I was anxious to remove my golden girdle and have a proper bath. I felt disgusting, and my kilt was stained from three days sleeping and eating in that ship. No matter how hard I tried, I could not keep it clean, and there was definitely no water to spare for the luxury of washing clothes on board. Zos looked worse than I did. His skin was not as ashy as mine and vaguely glowed from the humidity in the air, but his kilt was more brown than white. As we passed the three leopards I had seen earlier, I could hear their low growls. I looked back to make sure the slaves and Zos were still behind me. Zos had his eyes glued to the two slaves. I smiled. With so many distractions in this new city – Zos had never been out of Alexandria – he was more concerned about keeping an eye on these two than checking out the surroundings. We had pretty much taken in all there was to see anyway while standing on board the ship.

Just as we were reaching the steps to the city at the end of the pier, a rather portly young man in an orange tunic came running in our general direction. I stopped when I saw it was actually me he was running towards. "I am so sorry. My sincerest apologies," he gasped as he approached. He slowed to a fast walk when he realized I had stopped walking. "I meant to be here sooner but was delayed. I am sure you know how it is," his hands flailing around as he talked as if they would help deliver the meaning in the event I did not understand his words. "But of course, you wonder who I am." I must not have disguised my bewilderment very well. "Ptolemaios sent word that you would be arriving on this vessel. I posted my slave to inform me of when you reached the port." The two men behind me carrying our things grunted. "Of course, let us walk and talk. I will guide you to your quarters. Everything on this end has been arranged. Would you like for my boys to take your things now?" he said, indicating the slaves behind me. Four fair skinned boys in plain brown kilts appeared beside us, about the same age as my Zos.

"No thank you, I think these men have it under control." The two men with our things looked relieved that they had not just lost a job. How thoughtful of Ptolemaios. Why though had he not said anything to me about this? A surprise? What other surprises had he arranged?

"Is that your boy in the back there?" he asked looking back at Zos.

"He is my servant boy," I said. The four boys that had come with our guide fell back to where Zos was walking, keeping a suspicious eye on the goings on up ahead. "So, what did you say your name was?"

"Oh, of course, how rude of me. I was in such a hurry you see." Again the flurry of hands. His face was no longer pink from the exertion of running. He brushed the long, curly brown hair out of his round pudgy face. He was definitely not Greek. He had a pronounced Phoenician nose and thick eyebrows. "Scribe Sikarbaal of Sidon at your service," he announced as he took a bow. "I pray your voyage was smooth and uneventful."

"For the most part," I replied vaguely. "And I am…"

"Scribe Kaleb of Adulis," he said before I could finish. "Yes, yes, Ptolemaios told us all about you and," in a suddenly very hushed voice, "your mission," he finished, his eyes fairly popping. "It is all very exciting, I am sure."

"Right. And you know Ptolemaios because…"

"That sly Ptolemaios, he did not enlighten you at all, did he?"

"Evidently not," I said, my curiosity peaked.

"Let us get you installed and cleaned up before we reveal all, shall we?" he said as we climbed yet another set of stairs to a three tiered stone building set right into the outer wall of the city. "Here we are. A room on the top floor has been prepared for you. There is a commanding view of the port and the old city from the terrace up there, quite spectacular really. Your boy can stay with mine or with you, as you wish."

"I will keep Zos with me," I said. Zos heard his name and looked at me with his eyebrows raised.

"Yes Teacher?" he asked in Ge'ez.

"Why, can he not speak Punic?" Sikarbaal asked shocked.

"Only Greek, Egyptian and Ge'ez," I replied, immediately regretting the unintended insult to the Punic language which was no longer the lingua franca it once was. "We plan to study Punic however. It is next on his list."

"Oh, I see. My boys here speak only Greek and Aramaic."

"Splendid," I said. "Maybe they can teach him a thing or two in Aramaic. That is also on the list."

The slaves carrying our things were looking a bit exasperated at all this conversation in front of the door of our host. "Up we go then," Sikarbaal said as he pulled a large ring of keys from his belt. After fiddling for some time to open the door, it swung open wide, revealing a small stone foyer entrance with yet two more doors and a staircase running along the right wall. "No need for me to climb up with you. Just follow the stairs to the very top and you have the entire top floor to yourselves. There should be a bath drawn already and fresh clothes laid out on the bed. I will return before nightfall to take you to dinner."

"I do not know what to say," I said flabbergasted. "Thank you on behalf of myself and Ptolemaios. You have been very generous."

"Yes, yes, now I must hurry. Another appointment awaits me on the other side of town. Until this evening then. If you need anything, let one of my boys know. I will leave two of them with you." With that, Sikarbaal left in as big a hurry as he had appeared.

The two hired slaves deposited our things in the center of the large open room at the top of the stairs past a narrow hallway. I gave each of them ten quadrans, a bit more than we had bargained for, but I was feeling generous. They bowed, thanked me and departed. One of Sikarbaal's boys followed them down to make sure the door was securely fastened when they left. Zos was already running in and out of the rooms off the narrow hall, exploring every corner of our latest stop. "It's huge!" he said in Ge'ez. Sikarbaal's boys sat by the door to the stairs.

"Let us know if you need anything," the taller one said.

"And look at the view Teacher!" he said as he walked slowly to the balcony overlooking the harbor. Half of this level of the building was taken up with the rooms we had passed on entering. The other half however was entirely open with couches and carpets scattered comfortably throughout. The room ended as a balcony, the entire east side of the room open to the sky, thick cedar columns supporting the roof. I followed Zos past the columns to the balcony. As Sikarbaal had said, we had an unobstructed view of the port and the old city of Tyre. "There's the ship we came in on," said Zos pointing.

"I need a bath," I said turning around. "I cannot enjoy all of this properly till I am clean. He said there was a bath ready for us. I guess that means we can bathe all the way up here." I looked around but all I saw were couches, hassocks, cushions and carpets. The walls were smooth grey stone, and the floor and ceiling were polished cedar. Near where Zos and I had been standing, there was a curiously shaped object, large and circular and covered by what looked to be a piece of canvas. "What is this?" I muttered as I got closer. I pulled the canvas back revealing a huge tub of steaming water.

"An entire tub of hot water," Zos exclaimed almost reverently. "I've never seen anything like it."

"This is the way people inland bathe, when there is no river nearby. We do not have these in Alexandria. We are surrounded by water." I immediately began to remove my kilt, remembering the golden girdle just in time, before giving it away to Sikarbaal's boys by the door. Feigning modesty, I stood behind one of the columns and undressed, wrapping the girdle in my kilt, and then walked back to the tub. Zos was already naked but had not gotten in yet.

"I'm waiting for you Teacher. I don't know what to do exactly."

I laughed. "You will have many tales to tell after this trip. Follow my lead." I called over the boys by the door. "I need you to pour water over us as we wash," I said. "We need to wash before entering the tub."

Confused, the younger boy said, "But that's what the tub's for... to wash."

"I have no wish to soak in the dirt and grime that come off my body. I need to remove that first and then enjoy a good soaking. Now where is there a spot for water to drain off? Perhaps over here on the balcony?" I inspected the balcony and found small holes in the short wall with spouts for draining rainwater. "Here will work just fine," I said. The boys looked incredulous, but followed my instructions. They used the buckets that had been used to haul the water up the stairs, filled them up and brought them to where Zos and I had installed ourselves with a bar of soap from the side of the tub. We squatted. "Now pour the water over us slowly, just so..." I splashed the water over my head and body and stood, rubbing soap into my dirty skin and hair. They repeated the motion with Zos, and I passed him the soap. One boy went for more water. "Now pour slowly so I can wash off the soap," I said, squatting again so he could reach my head. "Ahh, delicious," I said as I scrubbed the soap from my body. I stood to scour the rest of myself as the boy continued to pour water over me. The other boy was doing the same to Zos. Clean, we both splashed over to the tub into which we enthusiastically jumped. Sikarbaal's boys looked on as if we were lunatics. "Now clean that soap up why don't you?" I called as I slid under the water.

CHAPTER SIXTEEN

Candlelight reflected from the blue-green and beige tiled walls and sparkled off the water of the fountain in the center of the dining hall like fireflies. The air hummed with conversation from the myriad of tables, and music from the small group of singers and musicians filled the empty spaces and arched alcoves. Plants hung from the ceiling, giving the impression of being in a garden. Trays of aubergine in sesame oil, okra with onion and garlic, prawn marinated in butter and garlic, lamb cubes marinated in lemon juice, olive oil and spices and innumerable sweet pastries of nuts and honey were constantly being set on the tables and then replaced with yet more intricate delicacies. I had never eaten in such extravagance in my life. Sikarbaal was sitting to my right, an attractive Greek woman to my left and four other guests filled the remaining four chairs at the round table. All were scribes like me, from different points of the empire.

"So it is true that Claudius Galenus is back in Pergamum?" asked Jabnit, the young scribe from Gades, the southernmost Punic colony on the coast of Spain. "His advances in the medicine of sports is legendary."

"Actually, he has gone to Rome. He gained considerable experience in his post as physician to the gladiators in Pergamum, but he felt the opportunities in Rome were greater. He passed through Alexandria on his way to read from the works of Aristotle that are housed in the Library. I was able to talk with him on a few occasions. He is a brilliant man."

"How fortunate for you to work in such a temple of knowledge," said the woman to my left. "I work in the Library of Athens. It is still quite new, so the collection there is quite small, but it is growing. I would love someday to visit Alexandria though."

"That is actually where I am headed," said the large, fair-skinned, balding man across the table from me. "My patron has just died at the ripe age of eighty, and I am taking to the Library of Alexandria a copy of his memoirs that he dictated to me. A copy is already housed in the Library at Rome, but Ptolemaios has requested a copy for your library as well."

"And who might I ask was your patron," I asked, intrigued.

"Favorinus of Arelata, the orator and philosopher."

"A courageous man with a biting wit," exclaimed the thick-haired patrician Roman woman next to him. "I was in the employ of Aspasia Annia Regilla, my patroness, until her death last year. She related an anecdote from her youth to me."

"Please, let us here it," the biographer of the late Favorinus raised his glass, "perhaps I will have to amend my copy of the memoirs."

"Yes, do share your story madam," Sikarbaal seconded.

She slowly looked around the table. All eyes were on her. She took a delicate sip of wine and began. "Favorinus and his arch-opponent Polemon of Smyrna were debating in Athens in the presence of the Emperor Hadrian. Hundreds of the most prominent Athenians were in attendance, including my patroness and her husband Herodes Atticus who were entertaining the emperor during his visit. The topic of the debate, which I cannot now remember, was announced, and Polemon had the first turn. As is usually the case, the first exchanges involved the prodding and poking of those skilled in rhetoric. Nothing of any import was said until Polemon defended a point that caused the emperor to frown. My patroness said that a hush fell over the assembly. Favorinus made to reply, but Hadrian silenced him. There is no doubt that Favorinus could have soundly defeated his opponent who had just committed a mortal gaffe. However, perturbed that he would not have the last word with Polemon yet determined to respond somehow, he said, 'It would be foolish to criticize the logic of the master of thirty legions.' Rather than laugh, which is what Favorinus had hoped, Hadrian's frown darkened. The Athenians in attendance, feigning empathy with the emperor, proceeded to pull down a statue that had recently been erected in Favorinus' honor. Favorinus, in a stunning show of indifference and disdain stated it was a pity that Socrates had not had a statue for the public to vent its anger on or he might have been spared the hemlock. Soon after this he was banished by Hadrian to Chios, where he spent the next eight years."

"The power of the word, that frequent Hydra of delinquencies. How effortlessly it twists the hand of fate," muttered Sikarbaal. "It is said that he who keeps his mouth and his tongue keeps his soul from troubles. If only Favorinus had held his tongue at that moment, it would have been Polemon, not he, that was exiled."

"And yet, our profession is doubly powerful in that we are recorders, not only of the spoken word but of thoughts and events. One speaks, and it is heard only by those who are in earshot. Once written, it continues to speak for as long as the written record remains." The young Jabnit's intense eyes scanned our faces.

"Truly said by the progeny of the inventors of modern writing. It is no surprise that we inhabit a social stratum that allows us to mingle with everyone from kings to the common man. No other vocation allows such flexibility of movement or commands such universal respect. To scribes, workers of the greatest profession on earth!" Sikarbaal raised his glass as did we all.

"Were you in Rome last year when Polycarp was killed?" I asked the bald biographer.

"As a matter of fact, I was," he replied. "I even attended the event. It was unforgettable. Word had gotten out that a famous follower of the increasingly popular Judean religion was to be tried. I did not know till later who he was. In my living memory, Christians have not been fed to the beasts in the coliseum, though it is no mean thing to be accused of being a Christian. The punishment is quite brutal at times. It has been over fifty years though, since the time of Emperor Trajan, so this was an important occasion." I winced. I would not have said *important*, more like tragic. It was said that the new emperor, Marcus Aurelius, was not friendly to Christians. The biographer had our attention. "So I was sitting there, in the maenianum secundum imum with Favorinus.

"What is that?" asked young Jabnit.

"The tier of seating for the wealthy plebeians. It is as close as someone like us can ever come to the action. The senators, officials, patricians, top priests and vestal virgins with the emperor, they all claim the really good seats. We were quite close though to the spot where he was brought in. It was quite an event. The noise of the crowds was deafening, the vendors selling everything from wine and food to fans and cushions. A crier walked to the center of the arena and held up his hand. A hush came over the entire crowd. They say the coliseum can seat 50,000 people. The crier shouted, 'Polycarp has been arrested!' The stands erupted in shouts, and an old, white-haired man was led out, his hands bound behind him. The pro-consul met him in the center of the arena. The crier held up his hand again. Again, the hush over the crowd. The proconsul shouted in a loud voice, holding his hand out in the direction of the emperor, 'Swear by the genius of Caesar. Say "Away with those who deny the gods."' I swear by Jupiter, everyone there was sitting on the edge of his seat craning his neck to hear what that pitiful old man would say. And do you know what he said, this old man that I almost felt sorry for?"

"What?" we all asked in unison.

"He waved his hands toward the crowd and cried, 'Away with the godless!'"

I heard the woman to my left gasp. I gripped the arms of my chair, my stomach suddenly in a knot.

"Well, that really got the crowd going. The roar was deafening. The proconsul was saying something else, but no one could hear anything for the shouting. Finally, the proconsul held up his hand. The shouting stopped almost immediately. The proconsul said, 'I have wild beasts.'

'For 86 years I have served Jesus, and he has never wronged me. How can I now blaspheme my King who saved me? Call the beasts,' he calmly replied. I tell you, that old man's courage made the hair on the back of my neck stand on end. Favorinus and I looked at each other, amazed. I think the same thing was going on all over the coliseum. The shouting had stopped. Now there was just a low rumbling. The proconsul began to speak again in a loud voice. I missed the first part of what he said, but I caught, 'I'll have you destroyed by fire.'"

The young Greek lady gasped again. I began to wonder if she were not a Christian as well.

"I will never forget what Polycarp said next in his heavy Lidian accent. He said 'The fire you threaten burns for a time and is soon extinguished. In the judgment to come there is a fire of eternal punishment reserved for the wicked.' The stands rocked with shouts for the lions. But the time being passed for the lions, men emerged onto the arena with bundles of wood. A pyre was built in the middle of the arena and the old man bound and laid on top. The fire was lit and quickly roared into the air. It seemed the old man's body was protected from the flames. I swear by Zeus it did. And just as the crowd began to murmur at the apparent miracle, the executioner rushed forward and thrust a sword into the man's body."

I felt a bit dizzy having heard a first-hand account of the death of the most venerable Christian in the empire. Bishop of Smyrna and student of Ignatius, protégé of John the Apostle, he was a precious link to the first apostles. And he had been burned alive at the age of 86. How barbaric.

"And they call *Christianity* a barbarian religion," I said quietly. No one spoke.

The biographer broke the silence. "I have since become a Christian," he said.

"But you still swear by Jupiter and Zeus," Jabnit said raising his dark eyebrows.

"Habit," he replied. "Soon after the spectacle of Polycarp's death, I got hold of some of the writings of a philosopher from near here named Justin."

"I have read some of his writings," I said.

"I stopped here on my way to Alexandria purposely to find him. His writings have profoundly affected my thinking. I hope to make my own copy of the Septuagint, the Gospels and the letters once I get to Alexandria."

"Perhaps I will have returned by then and can facilitate your endeavor," I said. "I work in that department of the Library."

"You honor me."

"Not at all. It would be my great pleasure. I should not be hard to find. Besides my father, I am the only Ethiopian working there."

"It seems there will be a return to the persecutions of Trajan's time," said the young Athenian librarian.

"Rome is the epicenter," I said. "The issue is not so serious in Alexandria. There is quite a large Christian population there, as there is in my native country, the Kingdom of Axum. The incredible thing is that the mere fact of calling oneself a Christian is a crime. For what other crime can one be exonerated by merely denying a name? It is quite mind-boggling. If I am a thief, proof of my crime must be brought to bear. I cannot say to the judge, 'No, I am not a thief; I deny that I have ever been a thief,' and expect him to free me. If I am a traitor, witnesses must be brought to confirm my treachery. And my denial will not secure my freedom. However, when one is accused of being a Christian, the crime is in the name only. If I were to deny that I was a Christian, I would be released. What other crime can compare to this?"

"The crime is in professing belief in a barbaric religion that the state does not recognize," Jabnit said.

"The same state that recognizes everything from a woman with a cat's head that is supposed to protect us to a man who ate his own children to keep anyone from usurping his throne? Ironic that it is a crime to say one worships a creator who made us in his own image, valuing and honoring the life he has created, a crime to believe that honesty, virtue and right living are worthy pursuits, a crime to love others as one loves oneself. The Romans, profligate in the number of gods and goddesses they worship have turned the state into the supreme god, Caesar as its representative. He is the one god that must be worshipped or else, the one absolute that denies all other absolutes. It is not surprising that Polycarp refused to deny what he believed to be true. It would be a denial of everything beautiful, of everything God is and an admission that the state is god."

"A denial that could have saved his life. He could always have recanted his denial. I cannot imagine being willing to lose everything for the sake of a name, particularly the name of Christian from what I know of it."

"And tell us, what do you know of it?" the biographer asked, alert and curious to hear Jabnit's answer.

Looking around at us, he began to speak in a low voice, in the tone of one telling a frightening tale for children, one that would end with a shout to elicit shrieks. "I hear adherents know each other by secret marks and insignia, and they love one another almost before they know one another. Everywhere also there is mingled among them a certain religion of lust, and they call one another promiscuously brothers and sisters, that even a not unusual debauchery may, when Jesus is mentioned, become incestuous. Intelligent reports would not speak of such a variety of goings on unless truth were at the bottom of it. It is well known what transpires at their banquets; all men speak of it everywhere; even the speech of Fronto the Cirtensian testifies to it. On a solemn day they assemble at the feast, with all their children, sisters, mothers, people of every sex and of every age. There, after much feasting, when the fellowship has grown warm, and the fervor of incestuous lust has grown hot with drunkenness, a dog that has been tied to the chandelier is provoked, by throwing a small piece of offal beyond the length of a line by which he is bound, to rush and spring, and thus the light being overturned and extinguished in the shameless darkness, the connections of abominable lust involve them in the uncertainty of fate." Everyone at the table had listened in patience, the biographer and the Greek lady to my left were looking more indignant with every phrase that proceeded from Jabnit's mouth. The others sat in rapt attention, as if hearing again a favorite story. Sikarbaal was practically drooling, his eyes moist, obviously titillated by the story.

"Quite a tale," I said, "and one not unfamiliar to my ears. My question to you Jabnit, is if you have investigated this claim yourself or do you merely proceed from hearsay? You have two Christians sitting here before you. Do you propose that we take part in such practices?"

Sikarbaal leaned forward, a lascivious look in his eyes. "Who can tell?"

"But that is not the end of it," continued Jabnit. "I hear that they adore the head of an ass, that basest of creatures. I know not whether these things are false; certainly there is ample suspicion of secret and nocturnal rites, and their ceremonies are in honor of a man punished by extreme suffering for his wickedness. They venerate the wood of the cross, a fitting altar for reprobate and wicked men who worship what they deserve." He paused to take a drink, looking at me, daring me to answer the latest calumny.

"You say that you hear the donkey's head is esteemed among us a divine thing," I responded. "Who would be so ridiculous as to worship that? Who is foolish enough to believe that it is an object of worship except those who consecrate whole asses in their stables in honor of the goddess Epona, who according to Plutarch is the progeny of a man's coupling with a mare? Do you not offer up and worship the heads of oxen and of sheep, and you dedicate to gods half goat and half man, and gods with the faces of dogs and lions. Do you not adore and feed Apis the ox with the Egyptians? I do not see you condemning *their* sacred rites instituted in honor of serpents, crocodiles, birds and fish, and if any one were to kill one of these gods, he is punished with death. It is most ironic, however, that though you say they are gods, you are not more afraid of Isis nor of Serapis than of the pungency of onions."

Jabnit was not to be deterred. In an even lower and somewhat secretive voice, he proceeded. "Say what you may, but you cannot deny the stories regarding the initiation of young novices. It is as much to be detested as it is well known. From what I gather, an infant is covered over with meal, that it may deceive the unwary. This infant is then slain by the young pupil, who has been urged on to deliver seemingly harmless blows on the surface of the meal, in reality inflicting dark and secret wounds. Thirstily they lick up its blood; eagerly they divide its limbs. By this victim they are pledged together; with this consciousness of wickedness they are covenanted to mutual silence. Such sacred rites as these are fouler than any sacrileges."

"If that is true of all who claim the name of Christian, then it must also pertain to us," I said.

"We are not saying that!" Sikarbaal stuttered.

"How unjust it is, Sikarbaal, to form a judgment on things unknown and unexamined, as you and Jabnit do!" the biographer said indignant. "Are we not supposed to be purveyors of knowledge, recorders of events and history? Do we not have an obligation to investigate a claim before publishing it?"

The young woman to my left spoke for the first time since the debate had begun. "And now I should wish to meet him who says or believes that we three at this table who call ourselves Christians are initiated by the slaughter and blood of an infant. Do you honestly think it possible for anyone but the most sadistic brute to shed, pour forth, and drain that new blood of a baby, of a child scarcely come into existence? No one can believe this, except one who can dare to do it. On the other hand, it is not uncommon to hear how you expose your newborns to wild beasts and birds, or if that is not expedient, you crush or strangle them with a miserable kind of death. There are some women who, by drinking medical preparations, extinguish the source of the future man in their very bowels, and thus commit a parricide before they bring forth. And these things assuredly come down from the teaching of your gods. For Saturn did not expose his children, but devoured them. With reason are infants sacrificed to him by parents in some parts of Africa, repressing the babe's crying with caresses and kisses, assuring the god a smiling sacrifice. Moreover, among the Tauri of Pontus, and to the Egyptian Busiris, it is a sacred rite to immolate their guests, and for the Galli to slaughter to Mercury human, or rather inhuman, sacrifices. You have surely heard how the Roman sacrificers buried living a Greek man and a Greek woman, a Gallic man and a Gallic woman. To this very day, Jupiter Latiaris is worshipped by them with murder, and worthily of the son of Saturn, he is gorged with the blood of an evil and criminal man. I believe that Jupiter himself taught Catiline to conspire under a compact of blood, and Bellona to steep her sacred rites with a draught of human gore, teaching men to heal epilepsy with the blood of a man, that is, with a worse disease. What difference is there between these rites and him who devours the wild beasts from the arena, besmeared and stained with blood, or fattened with the limbs or the entrails of men? To us as Christians, it is not only unlawful to commit homicide but to even see or hear of it, and we value human blood to the extent that we do not even use the blood of edible animals in our food."

"Believe us, Jabnit", I said, "that many Christians also were the same as you, and formerly, while yet blind and lacking understanding, thought the same things as you, namely, that Christians worshipped monsters, devoured infants, and mingled in incestuous banquets. Who would believe that such fables as these are always set afloat by malicious rumormongers and are neither ever inquired into nor proved? Why does no one think it strange that in so long a time no one has appeared to betray the doings of this nefarious sect in order to obtain not only pardon for their crime, but also favor for its discovery? Why does no one question why a Christian, when accused, neither blushes nor fears, and that he repents, not for being a Christian but that he had not been one sooner?"

The biographer interjected, "If reason were truly to judge in these cases, they should rather have been pressed not to disavow themselves Christians, but to confess themselves guilty of incests, of abominations, of sacred rites polluted, of infants immolated."

"Indeed," I said. "That is precisely what I said earlier." I looked at Jabnit.

CHAPTER SEVENTEEN

My head was still swimming with the images of Polycarp's martyrdom when I laid my head down to sleep. It was already the hour of the Sokar serpent by the time Sikarbaal deposited me at the tower door. Everyone was reticent for the evening and the conversation that had started to end. Though Jabnit may have seemed antagonistic to Christians, he was only repeating what he had heard. As scribes, we grappled with ideas, not with each other like the barbarians. And Polycarp. How would I handle myself in his position? Would I be that brave? I had read his writings. He went to his martyrdom almost joyfully, anticipating it with something akin to pleasure, knowing that he was going to be put to the ultimate test, to lay his life down in the service of our Lord and Savior. Pulling the blanket closer under my chin to ward off the chill of the night, I lay awake for what seemed a long time before drifting into troubled dreams.

PART FOUR

BOUND FOR PALMYRA VIA DAMASCUS

Gregorian Calendar – February 24th, 162
Alexandrian Calendar – Meshir 16th, Second Proyet
The Season of the Emergence
1st year of Marcus Aurelius

He found him in a desert land, and in the waste howling wilderness; he led him
about, he instructed him, he kept him as the apple of his eye.
(Moses, *Deuteronomy 32:10*, ca 1,500 BC)

CHAPTER EIGHTEEN

Silver light cast porch-pillar shadows against the stone wall. Water washing against the ramparts of the city below augmented the chill of wet air. I shivered under my cloak. Zos had our belongings packed and ready to take down. Sikarbaal's boys that had slept outside the door of our apartment were already carrying down the first load. Walking me back last night, Sikarbaal had explained that a caravan was leaving today. We must either go with this one, or wait till the end of Paremhat for the next one. It was not far, only three days' journey to Damascus, but the road was not safe to travel alone. I opted to leave today. The sooner we got to Ecbatana, the better. I was reticent to say goodbye to the sea, but the allure of the city beyond the Euphrates was irresistible. I planned to spend more time here on the return trip. I wanted to learn more about who exactly Sikarbaal was and how he knew Ptolemaios. His role in our journey had not been satisfactorily explained, although he was an unparalleled host, regardless of the position he took in last night's conversation and the glimpses of perversion I saw in his eyes. No one was beyond redemption. The dinner conversation last night had been extremely stimulating, not least owing to the common profession of all at the table who hailed from the far reaches of the empire, from Gades to Tyre, Athens to Alexandria. How small the world was.

Zos and I followed the boys down on the last trip, the steps dark and narrow, the walls cold and slippery, and met Sikarbaal just as he was arriving with two donkeys, led by the two slaves he had with him yesterday at the port. The two boys who had stayed with us loaded the donkeys with our things, and we set off, the donkeys led by the young boys in animated conversation, no doubt recounting the strange behavior of these two black Alexandrians. Zos was quiet, too excited to talk I imagine. There was much to keep his attention.

After winding through several narrow streets, the cool morning air crisp on my face and unprotected ears, we came out to a wide paved Roman road. We followed this road lined with arcades out of the city, past the coliseum, several stately buildings and finally the enormous hippodrome to the caravan depot. The snow of Mount Hermon, far in the distance, glowed the color of a budding pink hibiscus in the dim morning light. How Sikarbaal had organized everything on such short notice, I would never know, but our dromedaries were waiting, and the entire cost of the journey from Tyre to Dura had been paid for. We would skirt Damascus, picking up additional travelers and a Palmyran guard detail which would be hired for the journey to Palmyra where we would stop briefly before heading for Dura on the Euphrates.

"How can I ever thank you Sikarbaal," I said as I mounted my dromedary, its stiff hair prickly under my fingers. Zos had also mounted his. The third dromedary was loosely tied to mine, loaded with furniture for the tent, folding cots for sleeping, low tables, basins for washing, two short three-legged stools and rolled carpets for the flooring of the tent. Two large bladders of water, sewn down the middle, hung over the hump of each animal.

"Thank Ptolemaios when you arrive back home," he said. "Now off with you, and may the gods grant you a safe journey."

"May God in heaven repay you for your kindness to us," I replied. Zos and I simultaneously made our dromedaries rise, and with a final farewell, we turned and lumbered in the awkward gait of our beasts to the center of the caravan where I had read was the safest place to be.

CHAPTER NINETEEN

Because we focused on the snake, we missed the scorpion.
(Ancient Egyptian)

A dark hood pulled over his head hiding his entire face, the figure sat atop his dromedary watching Kaleb and Zos make their way to the center of the caravan. He shifted uncomfortably. Blast these brutes. Why did he have to be the one to follow Kaleb? Hadn't he done his part already?

He had been given his instructions; follow them without giving himself away. Kaleb had noticed him on the ship, but what was he supposed to do? In such a confined space with a limited number of people, it was impossible not to be noticed. He should have played it off better though when Kaleb called to him. He had panicked. He was pretty sure that he had not aroused any lasting suspicions, but he couldn't shake the gnawing sensation in his gut that he had committed an irreparable mistake, putting Kaleb on his guard. In any event, he had left that part of the story out when he recounted his courage in the face of the storm at sea and laid out what he had discovered to the mathematicus at the emergency meeting of the Pythagorean Cult of Tyre. They had praised him for his discretion and given him the money necessary to complete the journey to Dura.

Nonetheless, he would be keeping a wide berth between himself and Kaleb from this moment forward. He knew from the chalk drawings on the deck of the Tyre-bound vessel when Kaleb explained their route to his servant boy that Ecbatana was the final destination, and that was really all he needed to know. He had already sent word ahead to Dura to arrange for the second part of the journey and prepare the instructions for his next move. Until they knew what Kaleb was after, they could not make a final decision. Meanwhile, he would stay away from Kaleb entirely. He did not want to be recognized and approached again. Maybe he should come up with a good cover in the event that happened.

CHAPTER TWENTY

Five days from Tyre, one from Damascus and about eight to go before reaching Palmyra. The first part of the journey from Tyre was interesting enough. The landscape was constantly changing. The road was straight, paved and in good repair, with regular road markers to indicate how many Roman miles we had traveled. Mount Hermon's white peaks dominated the northern horizon, winter vineyards on its terraced hills, while what little was left of the famed cedar forests of Lebanon provided a break in the monotonous landscape to the south. By the third day out of Tyre, the hilly terrain grew flatter until we were passing through a dry waste broken by olive trees as far as the eye could see in every direction.

Each day, once the caravan was underway, it continued till evening. We had learned after the first day that we would need to prepare food for mid-day in the morning to have something to eat before the evening. The first day I had begun to feel the first pangs of hunger when the sun was high overhead. I expected the caravan to stop for a break, but the sun continued its path across the dusty blue sky and the caravan continued its relentless march toward the horizon. By evening, we were both famished. We discovered that first night that being in the center had another advantage. It seemed that was where the food vendors had positioned themselves as well. Within minutes of stopping, the smell of roasted goat, fried onions and garlic and boiled lentils filled the air. Zos and I could barely set up the tent before seeking something to eat.

"Are you a cook?" A neighbor I had not seen before asked.

My dromedary which I had named Fang, was hung all over with basil plants. In fact, Fang's name came from Aramaic for garden since I had begun to refer to him as the hanging gardens of Babylon. I leaned far back as Fang's front legs buckled before completely sitting.

"Not a cook. A scribe," I said as I dismounted, feeling the same unsteadiness of legs I felt every evening when first touching the ground again.

"So why all the herbs on your camel?"

"I read in a document from India that the smell of basil keeps away mosquitoes. And actually, the basil plants keep the more foul odors that waft this way at bay."

"Something to keep in mind," he said as he dismounted his camel.

Zos, wiry and energetic, pulled the tent off my camel where I used it as padding for the long rides. We were close to the exact center of the caravan for many reasons. Embracing my new persona as a traveling scribe, I was more easily accessible in the middle. Also,

every point in the camp was equidistant, but most importantly, it was
the safest spot to be in case of attack by bandits, important not only
for my own safety but that of Zos whose parents would never
forgive me if anything happened to him on this trip.

The noise from the rest of the thousand plus camels all over the
camp was deafening. Amongst the lengthening shadows of the late
afternoon sun, Zos began to set up the tent. First he pulled a short
broom from a bag that hung at Fang's back end and swept the area
we would use to avoid ending up with a rock in the middle of the
back if either of us decided to take a little nap.

"I am becoming more efficient, eh?" said Zos carefully
sweeping as if he were raking the ground, keeping the rising dust to a
minimum.

I collected the posts that formed the skeleton of the tent. They
were placed strategically all over Fang, easy access but out of the way
during the day.

"Thank God in heaven for that. Nevertheless, I am ready to
stay put for at least a few days in a decent inn where I can bathe and
sleep in a real bed." In less time than it takes a beetle to slide off the
nose of the Sphinx, we had the dusty white tent in place, with a flap
in front that formed a porch, the largest area, where I could sit and
work. We left the sides down to prevent what few breezes did blow
by from making their way through unimpeded as night brought
cooler temperatures. This tent, from Tarsus, was one of the best
money could buy. Sikarbaal had helped me pick it out for our trip.
We would be spending many a night in it before we found ourselves
back in Alexandria. I took my back-rest from in front of Fang's
hump and set it up for the low table where I would write. Zos
unburdened Fang and the other two camels of the various bags and
hanging pots, putting the bags in the U formed by the camels, the
rugs and cots inside the tent and the basil pots around the porch area.

"These rugs need a good beating. They are so dusty, I get caked
in it every time I lay them out," Zos complained as he spread the
rugs to create a floor for the tent.

"You are welcome to take them to the edge of the camp and
beat them," I said. "I can deal with the dust for a few more days if
you can. It is a long hot walk to the camp's border, especially
covered in carpets." I bent over and brushed my head, suddenly
aware that I was covered in the dust to which Zos was referring.

I lifted my water skin and tilting my head back took a long satisfying draught of lukewarm water, feeling it drip down my chin and onto my neck. "Zos?" I offered him the skin. He swallowed long and hard, his Adam's apple bobbing up and down before settling in to groom the camels. They would drink no water till Damascus.

The voice of a vendor arrived long before she appeared in person. "Bread, cheese, olives!" she shouted repeatedly. Another voice competed with hers calling out "Goat's milk! Goat's milk!" My ear had quickly become trained after only a few days to hear the calls of food over the din of other voices shouting when camp was being set up for the evening.

"Three pieces of flat bread, two portions of cheese, and, let us see your olives." The woman took the huge basket from her head and set it on the ground. She lifted the cover off the clay jar her boy was carrying, one on each end of a short pole he had balanced across his shoulders. Zos came over and stuck his nose into the pot.

"These smell great!" he said as I smacked the back of his head.

"Take your dirty hands back to the camels."

"I didn't touch anything. I was just smelling," he complained.

"Do not be impudent," I snapped.

Zos finished with the camels. I set up the table with dinner. Goat's milk in clay cups, cheese, olives and flat bread. Zos held his hands out as I poured water from a large skin over them to clean them. An Egyptian would never touch his food without washing his hands first.

I raised my hands and prayed, "Stretch forth your right hand and bless this food set before us for the nourishment of our bodies. Teach us to seek your pleasure in all things so that when eating, drinking or laboring, we do it all for the glory of your holy name. For yours is the glory forever and ever. Amen."

"Did you sleep well last night?" Zos spoke first.

"Relatively. And you?"

"Like a rock." This was the first real conversation we could indulge in each day. The mornings came very early, and there was no time to spend over hot tea and conversation before the caravan was on the move. I would often fall back asleep on my dromedary before our morning language lessons, rocked by the constant swaying and tinkling of bells.

"How wonderful to be young and sound." For the hundredth time, I thanked God and my and Zos' parents for convincing me to bring Zos along. Traveling alone was outrageously boring, and there was no end to the little things that had to be done.

"What did you dream of last night Zos," I asked in Aramaic, picking up my cup, the smooth clay warm with fresh goat's milk. This trip was proving to be a great opportunity for him to learn Aramaic, and he was an apt student.

"Last night, no dream."

"You are not going to escape that easily," I laughed, continuing in Aramaic.

Zos got up and cleared the table. I cleaned the table top. Just as I began to call for Zos, he appeared at my side with my palette. He sat beside me and took a reed pen in his hand, holding it with confidence. When we first began, he was afraid to even touch the pen. I began to dictate in Greek, and Zos wrote on the scraps of used papyrus I had gathered for this purpose.

We had finished one page of dictation when the first client of the evening arrived. Zos laid down the reed pen and cleaned the table. I stood and greeted the newcomer. "Health and peace to you," I said in Aramaic as I motioned for the guest to sit on the opposite side of the table, where Zos had placed a cushion.

"Health to you," replied the prospective client. "I hear you are a scribe in many languages."

"Indeed. What language do you require?"

"Pahlavi."

"That will not be a problem, but it will cost a bit more since the script is different from Greek. Letters in Greek are at base cost, and other languages range in cost depending on how common they are. Here is my menu of prices." I passed the client a tablet where languages and prices were listed in order from most expensive to Greek. The edges were cracking and the thought went through my mind that I could have Zos copy me out another. It would be good practice.

"Considering I cannot read Greek, this tablet is of no use to me. Perhaps you could interpret it for me."

"Of course, my apologies. Pahlavi is one *as* per 15 words."

"That's outrageous!"

"Greek is about nine times cheaper. I could write it in Greek for you if you would prefer. I am actually offering you a very competitive price. If you would rather have a look around elsewhere to find something better, be my guest. But I guarantee the quality will not be as good as mine. I tell you what. I will give you a discount since you are my first customer of the day." Actually my Parthian was not that great, but I was not about to announce that fact. I had begun teaching it to myself along with the sacred Zoroastrian language of Avestan on this journey to prepare me for what was to come in Ecbatana.

"How much then?" asked the man, more interested now that he felt he was getting a deal.

"Shall we say one *as* per 30 words? That is a real bargain… what I usually charge for Latin."

"I guess that will do."

"Before we begin, can I offer you a cup of goat's milk?" I asked as Zos set a cup in front of the man and reached for the clay thermos where we cooled the milk.

"You are very kind," the man replied, touching his hand to his heart in a gesture of thanks. "My sister's husband lives in Ecbatana. I need to inform him of our progress. He is originally from a village in Sogdia. He unfortunately does not speak Greek; otherwise, I could save some money."

I took up my pen. Zos rolled out a fresh leaf of papyrus, setting an alabaster rectangular block at the top of the sheet. I held the bottom closest to me with my left hand. I was transported ever so briefly to the Library, the feel of the pen between my fingers, the papyrus spread under my hand. I shook my head and focused, hand poised over the document waiting for instructions. "When you are ready," I said, looking up at the man.

"Begin with…"

I interrupted, "Imagine you are dictating. I will write every word that proceeds from your mouth from this point onwards. Do not feel you have to give instructions. Just speak as you want the letter written."

"Of course. Here I go then."

To the noble lord of Bukhara, son of Kish of the family Qarshi. One thousand and ten thousand times blessing and homage on bended knee, as is offered to the gods, sent by his servant Manzer. Sir, it would be a good day for him who might see you happy and free from illness. News of your good health being heard by me, I consider myself immortal!

Your servants are safe and the journey is peaceful. There are currently 25 members of our party. All that you requested has been obtained, including goods acquired in Tyre, and all are well guarded. The caravan is immense and moves slowly; nonetheless, we project to arrive in Damascus tomorrow, the 1ˢᵗ year of Marcus Aurelius, the 21ˢᵗ day of Meshir."

The client paused. My eyes rose from the papyrus. "That is it then." I read the letter back to him to confirm that I had it right. I then counted the words. "That will be one sestertii and one *as*."

"I thought you counted 127 words. That would only be four *as* since four times 30 is 120."

"You cannot read Greek but you can certainly calculate. What are you thinking? Seven words are a gift? Anything under 30 words is also counted as one unit of 30. If your letter had been two words long, I would have charged you one *as*. And what of the papyrus? Do you think it is free? This is precious papyrus, almost impossible to find outside Egypt. Did you provide it or did I? Have you never had a scribe write a letter for you before?" I acted indignant, took the letter and acted as if I were going to tear it in half.

Zos stood to the side barely concealing a smile.

"Stop, stop! Here are five *as*. And thank you for the goat's milk. Might your business prosper."

"And yours," I called as the client disappeared into the sea of tents. I shook the coins in my open palm, feeling their weight, enjoying the feel of security they brought before dropping them into my purse.

"Teacher, has our lesson finished for the day?" Zos asked a little too eagerly. He was ready to stretch his legs and roam for a bit.

"For now anyway. I need to write for a while. Locate the public tent for me, so I can go there when I am done?" The last vestiges of heat in the air dissipated. The overwhelming din of arrival was calming down to occasional shouts or camel moans as many were now taking a mid-evening nap. I took out my journal from the bag that never left my side and set to chronicling the events of the past night and day up to this particular point in time. Ptolemaios demanded that I keep a detailed diary of every event on this and my previous trips which I then archived in the travel section of the Library. He insisted that it was very useful information for anyone else planning to make a similar journey besides the usefulness of chronicling the mode of life in different parts of the world. I heartily agreed since I myself had made use of such journals before embarking on this particular quest.

Although I intended to also write a letter home, and perhaps one to Silara, my hand unconsciously reaching for the necklace, my eyes began to feel heavy. I returned my journal to the bag and extracted Zos', a mismatch of scrap papyrus and parchment cobbled together into the semblance of a book. I knew it would be a while before he was back, but I wanted to leave it out so he would know what I wanted him to do. I left a note tucked half under it and his pen lying to one side.

The camels were asleep in a U pattern, the goods that had been unloaded nestling in the middle. I stretched out along the open side completing the square, effectively surrounding our things. The carpet that covered our things was sown with hundreds of little bells which would awaken me in an instant if anything were amiss. I stared for some time at the ruffling roof of the tent against the sky. The steady breathing of Fang and the other two camels lulled me into a trancelike sleep.

CHAPTER TWENTY-ONE

I opened my eyes to see Zos lying next to me, sound asleep. I sat up and scanned my surroundings. It was dusk. Everything was as it had been when I lay down, except the note under Zos' journal was gone. I got up carefully so as not to disturb Zos and after a long luxurious stretch, sat down at the table. The note was marking a page of the journal. I opened it and saw that he had indeed chronicled the past day. He had written on the note, "Teacher, my journal is ready for you to correct." I began to read it.

Yesterday afternoon, the caravan stopped just before dinner for the millionth time. For the millionth time, Teecher and I dismounted the cammels and walked for the first few steps bowlegged and wobbly. Our rutine never changes. Teecher always stays in the center of the caravan. I swept the area where the tent would go and spread out the tent. Teecher bilt the tent. We washed and cleened our teeth. I unloaded the cammels and groomed them while teecher organized our things and bought diner.

After we ate, Teecher tought me more Aramaic and made me practice writing. I'm getting better every day. After lessons I went to the tent of my friend Amun. He is also ten years old like me and is servant to an old couple

*from Thebes. They allow him freedom like my teecher in the evenings after the
initial chores are done, and we wander around the camp waching and lisening.
When our shadows are as long as we are tall, we return. The rest of the evening
was long and boring. I took a nap, sat on the pile of things in the middle of the
tent and stared at the ground, walked in circles around the tent, carved a grave
good for Amun, a little dog that would keep him company in the afterlife, played
a game of Odd and Even with myself, and red the book Teecher gave me.
Finally, in the morning, it was time to load the cammels and start the journey, my
favorite time.*

I looked up at Zos sleeping. His journal writing was becoming
more descriptive and his spelling was much better. He had very few
mistakes in fact. The formation of his letters was still childish, but it
was also improving. Boring. I smiled. Yes, if it was boring for me, it
must be a hundred times more boring for ten-year-old Zos. It was
good he had a friend, but I must talk to him about the grave goods. I
drew a small mark to the left of each line that contained errors. Zos
would attempt to discover the errors and explain them to me.

I carefully removed a compact scroll I kept in my bag. It was a
copy but valuable nonetheless. It was the only reference our library
had of the writings of Zoroaster, or Zarthosht as he was known in
Persia. His religion was quite popular in this area of the world and
had even spread further east and to parts of the west as the cult of
Mithras. For now I was just familiarizing myself with this religion,
but my real work would begin once we crossed into the gates of the
great city of Ecbatana, still so far away. It was one of the centers of
Zoroastrianism. From all appearances, it was a very secretive
religion. It seemed that only its followers really knew its ins and outs,
and it was very difficult to obtain the scriptures. Very few copies
were made and were held in strict secrecy, not available to the
uninitiated. That was my job. Locate and secure a copy of every
piece of writing available on the subject, preferably the actual sacred
scriptures themselves. No one knew what I was doing except the
director of the Library and me. I thought of Sikarbaal. He knew too.
Who else had Ptolemaios told? Zos knew I worked at the Library
and that being a scribe was my cover and means of making extra
money, but even he did not know the true nature of this mission. It
could often be very dangerous to try to reveal what others wanted to
keep secret. I believed truth was light, and to obscure the truth was
to hide the light. In my opinion, any religion that had hidden secrets

hid them for a reason, namely, their untruth. If the claims of a religion could not withstand the light of day, they were not worth believing, although more often than not, it was that very secrecy which attracted people the most, the idea that they knew something that no one else knew, that they were among the chosen, the elite, the initiated. In every case though, in my experience, what was guarded as the magic secret, the great powerful hidden word, ended up being either absolutely ludicrous and unbelievable or incredibly mundane. It was incredible to me that people could allow themselves to be so duped. I was determined to expose truth, or untruth. Knowledge was power and truth was light. Knowledge should not be kept secret, especially if it were knowledge about the meaning of life. What was more important?

Zos surprised me in my ruminations. I had not even had time to read my scroll. He caught me staring out at the ground deep in thought. He put his hand on my shoulder. "What did you think of my journal?" he asked yawning.

Though I had many compliments to give him, what came out of my mouth was "you still spell teacher with two 'e's' and I have told you a hundred and one times it is 'ea.'" He immediately looked down, dejected.

"I'm sorry Teacher. I'm so stupid. I'll never get it right. I'm a worthless student. You shouldn't even waste your time on me."

"Forgive me Zos. That was a minor problem. Your writing today truly impressed me. I was primarily interested in your increased use of detail, a very important ingredient in journal writing. So tell me about Amun and these grave goods."

Zos sat across from me and began to tell me about Amun, his friend. Zos used his hands as he talked, his skinny arms gesticulating to emphasize what he was saying. His dark eyes sparkled as he talked. He waved away a fly without annoyance, fingered his necklace and clapped his hands. I watched and listened to him, imagining my own children and… Silara. I was beginning to feel as if Zos were my own son. I had had plenty of servants growing up in Ethiopia, and now living in Alexandria, but I had never become close to them. They were invisible for the most part. Zos' parents were servants in my parents' home. They were Ethiopian as well and had immigrated to Egypt with my family. If not for my parents' urging, I would not even have considered taking along their son as a servant. Yet here I was, sitting across from this young boy, listening to his adventures with his friend Amun. "So that is why I made him the dog. He says he needs a dog to keep him company in the afterlife."

"Right," I said. "Show me the dog." Zos pulled it from the pouch he always had around his neck along with the gold necklace my brother-in-law Seth had given him. It was quite a good carving, half the size of his own small fist. The wood was light brown, but he had used charcoal to give it black spots and little eyes. I turned it around in my hands. "Nice job Zos. But tell me, what is this made from?"

"Wood of course," he cocked his head to one side.

"And what happens to wood when it is buried in the ground."

"It rots," now he was wrinkling his forehead.

"So how do you propose a wooden dog that rots when buried is going to keep your friend Amun company when he dies?"

"Well…"

"One of the prophets said 'woe to him who says to a wooden thing, "Awake;" to a silent stone, "Arise!" Can this teach? Behold, it is overlaid with gold and silver, and there is no breath at all in it.' What do you believe Zos? I know your parents are Christians, like my family, but you have grown up in Egypt. So what do you think happens when one dies?"

"Well…" Zos now not only had a wrinkled forehead but pursed lips and was staring off to the left.

"We will come back to this conversation. I want you to think on it. I have work to do in the gathering tent. So where is it great Zos the explorer?"

Zos opened his mouth in a wide smile. "It's very close Teacher spelled 'ea.' I'll take you. I can be back in a flash. I know you do not like to leave the tent unattended, but Fang and the other two camels are here."

It was dark now. There was a soft orange glow hovering over the camp from the hundreds of campfires. I picked up my palette and motioned for him to lead me. This was a city of tents. There were most likely over three thousand people camping here. The camp extended forever on all sides. The air on the ground was stifling and flies outnumbered people a hundred to one. But at this stage in the journey, I hardly noticed the flies anymore. It was either that or be driven insane. Within less than a hundred paces, we were at the gathering tent. Zos saluted, turned and disappeared behind a tent on his way back to our site.

CHAPTER TWENTY-TWO

Malice drinketh its own poison.
(Ancient Egyptian)

Bored to distraction with lurking in the periphery of the camp, the lone Carpathian spy decided to take action. He had pitched his tent at an oblique angle to Kaleb's where he could observe the goings on without calling attention to himself. Scratching the blistered scab on his arm where a scorpion bite refused to heal, he grew increasingly agitated watching closely the serious conversation between Kaleb and his servant boy. He treated that boy more like a son than a servant. Yet more evidence that the man he followed was a fool. His dislike of Kaleb grew with each passing day. After all, it was Kaleb's fault he found himself on this horribly uncomfortable caravan in the first place. He fantasized about sneaking into Kaleb's tent and finishing him off once and for all, ending this torturous trip with one well-placed knife thrust. He had spent the last two days feverish and itching from the scorpion bite. He caught himself scratching at the scab again.

And then his chance came. Both Kaleb and the boy left their tent unguarded. He pulled the hood of his cape over his head and made his way quickly to their tent, ducking inside before anybody could see him. He scanned the tent quickly, looking for the scroll he had seen Kaleb writing in earlier. Perhaps the scribe had written something regarding the purpose of his trip. In the dark interior he could only make out two empty cots. He stepped back outside the tent and turned towards the covered area between the sleeping camels. Just as he lifted the corner of the bell encrusted blanket covering their belongings, the boy rounded the tent and caught him in the act.

"Who are you?" he shouted. "Thief!"

Again he panicked. He leapt passed the boy as a rod in the boy's hand made contact with his legs. He did not stop running till he was near the edge of the camp and sure he was not being chased. Twice he had tripped over tent pegs, stubbing his toes badly and scratching his knees. Sweating heavily, he pulled the hood off his head and stood still to catch his breath. He touched his knees and felt blood. Campers all around stared at him suspiciously. He kept moving. At least the boy had not seen his face. He would have to dispose of his cape. The boy might recognize him in it. Reluctantly, he found someone willing to buy it off him. Now what would he do? That was his only protection against the chill in the evenings, plus the hood provided him cover when he was watching Kaleb from a distance. He would have to find another one, buy one off somebody if he could. What was wrong with him? Now Kaleb would be doubly on guard. Damn that boy! Berating himself, he made his way back to his tent fighting off a wave of nausea. He could feel the fever coming back. Blast it all.

CHAPTER TWENTY-THREE

There were already a large number of men gathered at the low tables scattered across the floor of the tent. Though high ceilinged, the lamplight from the lanterns at each table gave the place a feeling of intimacy. The air moved more freely here since the tent was so expansive and the roof so high above the ground. All of the walls had been rolled up to the ceiling. There was a flurry of activity as waiters carried wine, tea and small dishes to and from tables.

I sat to one side where I had a good view of the whole place and set my palette next to me. A waiter rushed to my table and knelt down beside it to take my order. "Bring me a cup of cinnamon wine, cheese, bread and a bowl of dates." I closed my eyes to relish the breeze on my face and hands, the smells of grilled onions and garlic that hid, even for the space of time it takes to swallow, the foul smells of the camp, to imagine I was back in Alexandria, in my favorite restaurant, with friends. There was really nothing like spending whole afternoons or evenings with friends, lost in conversation about every topic under the sun.

A smell, not of the kitchen, invaded my reverie. I opened my eyes and there, just beyond my table, walking directly towards me, was a most lovely sight, preceded by a delicious aroma of pressed roses and jasmine. She was dressed entirely in a robe the color of the desert sky on a cloudless day. She wore a tall, immaculately white turban and a thin, transparent veil that could not cover the night black skin, flawless features and long eyelashes. She was looking directly at me. I was so taken by her eyes, I failed to notice she was surrounded on both sides by older women, each studying me warily and steering her towards a table at some distance from mine. I knew it was rude to stare, but I could not help myself. Fortunately I was rescued by the arrival of the waiter, bringing me my order and fussing about my table. I focused my attention squarely on the food and drink before me. It was not recommendable to show undue attention to a woman one knew nothing about, especially one as obviously well positioned as the beauty who had just sat three tables away from mine at a perfect angle to maintain in view without appearing obvious. She could be married, probably was, to a man just waiting for an excuse to show his prowess. I had only just begun this particular journey and was not willing to risk my entire mission for a spectacularly beautiful woman. Besides, I was engaged. I should not even be looking at her. It was amazing how well my peripheral vision was working. If I looked straight ahead, from all appearances focusing on the men at the table playing cards, I could make out everything that was going on at the beauty's table. It was a good thing I could control myself. Only trouble lurked behind another man's wife. It was shocking he would even allow her to come under this tent, accompanied or not. In the midst of my attempts to appear that I was not watching her every move, one of the old women, wrapped head to foot in a white robe and with a white shawl over her head, stood and walked purposefully towards me. I looked down and picked a particularly succulent date, seemingly oblivious that she was approaching my table.

"And what brings you, fellow Ethiopian, on this journey to Damascus?"

"Excuse me?" I said, slowly looking up to see her staring down at me. "What makes you think I am Ethiopian?" realizing as the words came out of my mouth that I had responded automatically in the same language she had addressed me with, my native tongue of Ge'ez, the language of Ethiopia.

"Well, for one, you speak like one," she laughed without smiling. "My mistress would like to speak with you. You may approach our table, but sit where I indicate."

"Although I am quite occupied here, I will happily submit to such a gracious invitation offered by such a charming lady, regardless of who the envoy of such an invitation is," I smiled politely as I slowly stood.

An attentive waiter was beside me immediately. "Shall I bring your things to your new table, sir?"

"That will not be necessary," the cronish old woman said. "He will be back shortly." I looked at the waiter and raising my eyebrows, shrugged.

"Keep an eye on my box if you would," I asked, passing him a coin, one I had just earned this morning. Easy come, easy go.

On arriving at the table, my guide indicated where I was to sit. "Scribe Kaleb of Adulis at your service lady," I bowed and then sat directly across from the veiled beauty. "How can I be of service?"

The veil was held to her turban by delicate, simple silver clasps at each end and by a slender silver chain elegantly attached to the veil at the top of her aquiline nose and suspended from the center of her forehead from a clasp framing an oval ruby, the whole of which left her almond eyes, black as onyx, completely liberated, free to gaze and to be gazed upon. "You do not know me, but I certainly am aware of you, Scribe Kaleb of Adulis," she whispered, putting special emphasis on the word scribe. My late husband, secretary to Lucius Munacius Felix, the governor of the Province of Egypt, was a close friend of Klaudios Ptolemaios, Director of the Library of Alexandria. We have had occasion to speak of you. I know you by your reputation if not by sight."

"And how, pray tell, did you know it was me sitting there just now?" Not only was my secret out, but I had been discovered by one of the most influential people in Egypt. And did she say 'late' husband?

"There has been quite a stir among the Pythagorean religious community about the recent publication of Ptolemaios' latest treatise on mathematics, the *Almagest*. The most zealous among them speak out against you personally as the one that brought many of their most secret documents to light after acquiring them under what they believe to be underhanded means, thus permitting Ptolemaios to draw conclusions they believe would have been impossible without you. Your daring and fearless quest to bring all truth to light has made you something of a hero among many of the more enlightened in the Alexandrian Greek community."

"I am only doing my job madam. I am certainly no hero."

"Please, call me Mihret. As for how I knew it was you sitting there just now, I have my ways. As I said, I have heard much about you and have had a keen interest in meeting you. Your servant boy has befriended one of the boys in my entourage, and he mentioned your name. I investigated and inferred you could be none other than the much talked of librarian. What I did not expect was for you to be so young and so, how should I say, charming."

She looked me directly in the eyes when she said this. "The pleasure is mutual, madam. Nothing but praise for your husband and for your works of charity among the poor of Alexandria have reached my ears. Would that more of the influential of our blessed city follow your example."

"You are too kind. Sekhet, bid the waiter bring our scribe friend's things to our table. We have much to discuss, and very little time as we are within sight of Damascus."

Sekhet, the woman that had so kindly shown me to the table, gave me a very suspicious stare and rose to call the waiter.

CHAPTER TWENTY-FOUR

"And then I whacked him across the legs as he ran off!" Zos reenacted his movements with excitement.

"What did he look like?" I asked, impressed with Zos' quick thinking and courage.

"He was covered head to foot in a dark hooded cape. He ran away so fast that the people around our tent weren't able to react. I'm sorry Teacher. I should have caught him, but I was afraid to chase him and leave our things unattended."

"Lesson learned Zos. One of us will have to keep watch over our things at all times from this point forward." An image of the man on the ship popped into my head. "Did he seem unusually thin Zos?"

"It was hard to tell with the cape covering him," he said, obviously wishing he could tell me more. "I should have caught him. If I had hit him harder…"

"Forget it Zos. You could have been hurt. I am amazed that you handled it so well. Was anything taken that you could tell?"

"No, Teacher. I checked everything, and it seemed that nothing had been touched."

"Well, we escaped lightly this time, thanks be to God. We will just have to be more careful in future. Let us move all of our things into our tent, and from now on, we will keep them in there instead of outside."

CHAPTER TWENTY-FIVE

We arrived at Damascus late the following afternoon, bought provisions for the next leg of the journey and camped outside the gates of the ancient city for a night before continuing on toward Palmyra. I had probably seen the last of Mihret since she was spending time in Damascus before continuing on to Ecbatana. She had spoken of hiring me to handle her accounts and documents, but I did not want to delay the journey any more than necessary, and, tempting though the job was, I had declined. Zos and I had made inventory of what we had failed to plan for on the caravan. I thought we had all we needed, but it soon became apparent that to maintain a modicum of civilized cleanliness, we were going to need a few indispensible items. For one, it was becoming obvious that Egyptians were among the minority when it came to brushing teeth and maintaining basic hygiene. The paste we had brought from Egypt was running low, so in Damascus, leaving Zos on guard at our campsite, I made a foray to the marketplace in Damascus and bought enough from an Egyptian vendor to last for months, one more bag to hang from my dromedary. While searching for the toothpaste, I happened upon a vendor selling skull caps, and I thought of Zos. I should buy him a white skull cap since he was a scribe in the making. In the same shop, I bought Zos a diptych which he could use for his journal writing. My final and most important purchase was a parasol, two in fact, one for me and one for Zos. Riding all day in the sun was turning us black as soot. One boiling afternoon as the sun beat relentlessly down on my turbaned head, I remembered pictures I had seen in the Library of Indians on elephants with parasols protecting them from the sun. I determined then and there to buy each of us one in Damascus, and if I could not find them, I would have them constructed. Fortunately, I found them because there was not enough time to have them made.

Palmyran archers, famed for their skill at protecting caravans in these parts, had been hired and now surrounded the camp on their camels and horses upon leaving Damascus. Zos and I fell quickly back into the routine we had established since leaving Tyre. Mornings, once camp had broken, normally at daybreak, were spent in Aramaic lessons from the back of the dromedaries. We were wrapped against the cool morning air in our cloaks, dry and brown like the earth. The white skull cap I had given Zos never left his head. He had put it on as soon as I gave it to him, bowing and kissing my hand. He would have even worn it to bed had I not insisted he take it off to sleep.

Zos loved the parasols. From the first day with his, he began to carve little figures to hang from the edges. By the time we reached Palmyra, they were complete with bells and figurines dancing with every movement of the dromedary.

Sage green scrub trees that might provide enough shade for a lizard like lonely sentinels in the otherwise barren landscape bordered on both sides by low-lying, rocky hills. Our path lay between these hills in a flat plain. Had the dust of the road which swirled lazily around us been white, Zos and I could have been mistaken for albinos. My eyelashes were heavy with it.

We both lamented that we could not bathe. An Egyptian was accustomed to bathing every single day, but on the road it was impossible to allow such a luxury, especially when in the middle of the desert. However, each evening, when the caravan stopped, after setting up the tents and before eating the evening meal, we would attend to our simple hygiene using a minimum of water.

Evenings were spent in lessons, writing in my journal and doing scribe business. Word had spread throughout the caravan that there was a scribe with good rates, and I never lacked for customers.

Stretching out flat on the cots inside our tent was the most luxurious moment of the day. Before retiring to bed, we would take the water bladder and rinse our heads of the dust of the road. Though I preferred the flat ground cushioned with carpets and my bed roll, the cot was warmer in these cooler climes and there was less danger of being stung by a stray scorpion. The first days my body felt like it had been flogged after being on the dromedary all day, but I had quickly adjusted. Nevertheless, there was nothing like lying prone after a day of sitting erect. It was as if all the bones settled back into their rightful place. I no longer even noticed the coin belt I wore permanently attached to my waist. Zos and I took turns praying before sleep overtook us.

Movement around our tent usually woke me. I nudged Zos. He moaned. I nudged him again. The dark pre-dawn blue of a sky scrubbed clean, the chill in the air, the smell of wood burning and dew on the tents greeted our weary senses. In silence, Zos unpacked a small sapphire colored bowl and two onyx cups. He filled the two cups with water from the large water skin which hung over the flanks of each of our dromedaries. Into the bowl he shook out a tiny amount of grey powder from the bag I bought in Damascus and then poured just a touch of water mixing a paste that we then rubbed into our respective teeth. It was not unpleasant to the taste, a little salty and minty it left the mouth feeling fresh and clean. Ahhh. I thanked God in his providence for allowing me to live in such a civilized place as Egypt where such simple but wonderful pleasures were commonplace. Zos and I sipped water from our cups and rinsed our mouths, spitting the water onto the dry ground where it vanished into the sandy soil. With the remaining water we washed our faces. We broke our fast with hot flat bread, cheese and olives. By the time we were done and had our dromedaries packed, the blood red sun was creeping sleepily over the unbroken horizon.

CHAPTER TWENTY-SIX

Startled, I opened my eyes to pitch dark. We had set up camp later than usual last night, and according to the crier, we were two days from Palmyra. I had slept as soon as my body lay prone. What had woken me from that profound sleep? Something in the air felt odd. The tie on the door had come loose and was flapping in the wind, an unseasonably balmy breeze invading the interior of the tent. I shivered, wrapped myself more tightly in my cloak and got up to retie the flap. The only sounds outside were the snoring of the dromedaries and a curious whistling, eerie and persistent. I stepped outside of the tent in an attempt to identify the strange sound. A gust of wind blew my cloak open. As I attempted to gather it back round me, a thunderbolt split the night sky and crashed to land opposite the hills to the north, illuminating the entire camp for a hair-raising instant. A loud crash followed almost immediately and continued for some time to rumble off into the distance. The eerie whistling picked up and now began to metamorphose into a howl. Another flash lit up the sky behind me followed by another loud crash and thunder roll. Before the thunder subsided, Zos had attached himself to my waist.

"What's happening!"

"A storm Zos." I said excitedly. "A storm." Overhead, the sky was broken into pieces as bolts of lightning like veins of molten silver spread out illuminating the roiling clouds and the camp now being assaulted by the wind. Fortunately, our tent was on the lee side of our dromedaries that were not in the least disturbed by the weather. They continued sleeping placidly through the lightning blasts and crashing thunder, unknowingly protecting our tent from the increasingly violent wind. I smelled it before it began. "Back in the tent Zos! Quickly!" I felt the first drops on my head as I tumbled in behind him. Then the deluge. "We have to pull everything that might get wet off the ground," I said as I began wrapping up the rugs, putting everything on a low table that sat in a corner. Streams of water were already making their way across the floor of the tent. From Tarsus, this tent was impervious to the rain, not letting even a drop through its oiled cloth, but the floor was another story. Zos and I sat on short stools in the doorway of the tent, our feet propped on the writing table watching the storm tear across the camp. Zos had never seen anything like it and winced every time lightning struck, but I sat transfixed. Watching a good storm was one of my greatest pleasures in life. Lightning struck indiscriminately all around us. Above the din of the rain and the thunder, I could hear the occasional scream of one of the less brave souls in the caravan, probably hiding their head in a blanket. There was nothing to do but to ride it out.

The storm passed more quickly than I would have liked, but the rain persisted for the whole day. Zos and I, after putting out beaten brass basins to collect rainwater to refill our skins, stripped to our loincloths and stood in the rain for a long overdue bath. Shivering in the cold rain, we passed the bar of soap back and forth scrubbing and washing till we could feel our skin again under the grime of the past several weeks. Once again inside, the floor of the tent was a running pool of water. We dried ourselves and put on fairly clean clothes, and as long as we stayed on the stools, we stayed dry. Zos rummaged through our supplies and dug out some stale bread and cheese that we nibbled on throughout the day. We spent the rest of the day between sleeping on our cots, just out of reach of the shallow rivers of water running across the floor of the tent and sitting on the stools watching the rain, practicing Aramaic and inventing palindromes. I read aloud from a recently written series, the first part of which I had picked up in Tyre. The entire collection was called *The Incredible Wonders Beyond Thule*. The story followed an adventurer named Dinias and his son. So far, their travels mirrored our own, beginning in Egypt. Zos and I compared our adventures thus far to the ones unfolding in the novel.

The storm returned in force towards evening before completely departing, leaving behind a sodden city of tents and an exhausted population. Our tent had fared well, but many were not so fortunate, having lost their tents which had blown away in the wind or collapsed under the rain. It was a soggy, enervated crowd that the sun revealed the following morning. The temperature had dropped considerably and the air was crisp and clean. Somehow the food vendors had salvaged their supplies and prepared more than normal to sell the wet, disgruntled assembly. I purchased for Zos and me a generous, steaming portion of hot soup and bread. A crier walked along the road announcing that departure would be delayed till midday to give everyone time to dry out. By the time we were packed and back on board our humped steeds, we were very happy to be warm, wrapped in our wool cloaks, dry, full and ready for the final leg of the journey.

PART FIVE

PALMYRA

Gregorian Calendar – March 6th, 162
Alexandrian Calendar – Meshir 28th, Second Proyet
The Season of the Emergence
1st year of Marcus Aurelius

"When [Solomon] had therefore built this city, and encompassed it with very
strong walls, he gave it the name Tadmor; and that is the name it is called by at
this day by the Syrians; but the Greek name is Palmyra."
(Flavius Josephus, *Antiquities of the Jews, Book VIII*, ca 94)

CHAPTER TWENTY-SEVEN

The sun was low on the horizon when the graceful columns of
the avenues of Palmyra rose like a mirage from the desert floor. At
long last we had arrived. We were barely one-third of the way to our
final destination, but I felt like we had been traveling for months. A
brief respite in civilization was much needed. Palm trees now lining
the road cast long graceful shadows across the sandy plains leading to
the city. This oasis in the middle of the Syrian desert was a welcome
sight. Famous as a caravan crossroads, this is where our guard was
from that we had picked up in Damascus, the guard that would
continue with us to Dura. An immense palm grove on the
northeastern extreme of the city was designated as the caravan depot.
A small city of tents nestled in the shade of the palms. The noise of
dromedaries, camels, donkeys and every other kind of animal,
vendors hawking their wares and people in transit was deafening. I
sent Zos in search of a place to secure our dromedaries and
belongings, so we could spend a night in the city. Sikarbaal had given
me a name and directions to a house where we would be received.
While Zos was gone, I set about organizing our things, and selecting
what we would need. I stuffed our most essential items into two
bags that we would sling over our shoulders to take with us. If I had

been thinking straight this morning, I would have already done this when we broke camp, but I honestly did not believe we would make it this far today. I took down a stool and sat beside the dromedaries to observe the goings on of the depot while waiting for Zos. Night was falling fast. Out here in the desert, darkness fell suddenly, unlike in Alexandria where dusk was long and luxuriant. Zos appeared at my side. He had located a holding stable that still had room. I stowed the stool with the other furniture, gave Zos his bag and we set off leading the dromedaries to their temporary home, two thoughts on my mind, a bath and a bed.

CHAPTER TWENTY-EIGHT

Lamps hung from immense columns lining the main avenue that ran northwest to southeast bisecting the entire length of the city. The pavement was warm on my bare feet. People were out, Romans in tunics, Greeks in togas, Parthians in their baggy trousers and billowy shirts, elegantly dressed and veiled Roman and Greek women, veiled women from further east, people of all classes and races. Zos and I, however, were a rarer breed, two black Ethiopians in white tunics with long dark woolen cloaks and high white turbans. We got quite a lot of stares as we made our way towards the Tetrapylon, the central axis of the city, my landmark to the home of the Roman scribe named Vibius Caedisius Laterensis. A fire was burning in the center of the Tetrapylon, illuminating the streets that converged there to quite a distance. Foot traffic ceased once I turned left onto a narrow street, Zos close behind me. I began counting the doors after the third street. One, two, three, and there it was, a knocker in the shape of a hand holding a pen with a sign above the door reading LEGAL SCRIBE in five languages. I looked at Zos and raised the knocker. The sound echoed up and down the deserted street.

A small window cut into the door opened, and a resonant, gravelly voice inquired, "Who calls?"

"Scribe Kaleb of Adulis and his servant Zoskalis, and you must be Vibius Caedisius Laterensis. I was given your name by Scribe Sikarbaal of Tyre." I could hear a latch being drawn back and the door swung open.

"Please, come in. We have been expecting you."

CHAPTER TWENTY-NINE

A fire blazed at the far end of the oblong table. A steaming soup of goat and lentils and cups of wine sat before us. Zoskalis sat on a stool quietly focused on his soup, taking in the room hung with skins of various animals and stuffed trophy heads of local fauna. Laterensis joined us in the meal though I could tell that it was more out of hospitality than hunger. He had obviously already eaten. We ate in a silence only broken by the sound of supping soup and sipping wine. The rest of the household was sleeping but for the maid-servant that had brought our dinner and Laterensis himself.

"We will do the catching up tomorrow. You must be very tired after the long journey. You will have about a week before the caravan leaves for Dura on the Euphrates. I am anxious to hear how old Ptolemaios is getting along and get caught up on the latest news from Alexandria. And there are quite a few novel developments in these parts as well." Once we were finished eating, he led us to our quarters. The Spartan décor of the home extended to the bedroom. There were two cots, one against each earthen wall, a simple, waist high table between them. High in the wall above the table there was a small window made of glass, a recent introduction in these parts though in Alexandria becoming more and more common. "We are generally up early around here, but you sleep as long as you like. Until tomorrow then," he said as he disappeared behind the curtain separating the room from the hallway. I had not asked about a bath. That could be handled tomorrow at the public Roman baths of which the city boasted. In short order, Zos and I were in bed and sound asleep.

CHAPTER THIRTY

"And King Vologases IV insists that Armenia is part of his ancestral kingdom and that the Romans have no right to it." Laterensis had brought me, after a simple meal of oats and hot goat's milk, to his neighborhood tea shop.

Walking single file behind Laterensis, I could press my palms flat against the walls on both sides of the narrow passageway that snaked among the crowded low stone and adobe homes. The path opened, however, into a spacious courtyard, bordered on every side by a pillared portico. Several lemon and orange trees cast shade on the tables scattered pell-mell across the patio. We sat at a table vaguely shaded by a bushy lemon tree. I purposefully chose a seat in the full sun. After the cold night, I was still trying to thaw my feet and hands.

"Armenia was never part of Parthia." The four men at the table were all about the same age as Laterensis, a decade or so older than me. The one speaking now wore a leather patch over his left eye which he had lost in a skirmish with Bactrian bandits when a mercenary guard in the employ of a caravan bound for Tashkent. "Though that has not stopped them from interfering in Armenian politics from as far back as Tigranes the Great, son-in-law of Mithridates of Pontus. Sitting between Rome and Parthia has never been to their advantage. First allied to Rome by marriage, then to Parthia by marriage, who can tell anymore which line holds more claim."

"Thus are ties between countries established, through the marriage of the children of their rulers" interjected the distinguished one with the high forehead and clear grey eyes.

"Nevertheless, to claim it is an ancestral part of the kingdom is ridiculous. Parthia only came into being after Alexander the Great. If King Vologases wants to get technical, his kingdom is part of the ancestral Seleucid Empire. Ridiculous. This area of the world is one constant battlefield. How it has been able to prosper with the constant conflict is in fact miraculous," retorted the mercenary.

"Whatever the reasons behind it, he is readying for conflict and has already sent his troops into Armenia, and Rome has commissioned the new co-emperor Lucius Verus to confront Parthia militarily. Of course at this rate, he may never make it. I hear he is quite a reveler and will be lucky if he ever makes it out of Italy. He was commissioned months ago, and Vologases has had ample time to solidify his position from Armenia down to Babylon," said Laterensis. "What have you heard in Alexandria about this affair?" he asked me. All eyes turned to me.

"We are suffering under such a tax burden from Rome that we can focus on little else. And my work in the Library has little to do with politics. I am afraid to say I was quite unaware of these affairs." I could tell everyone was quite disappointed by my non-answer.

Laterensis continued, "Once Lucius Verus does make it here, the conflict may impede your return home."

"Is this conflict serious? Might this prove an obstacle to crossing into Parthia?" I asked, now a bit apprehensive that after all the trouble of making it this far, I would be forced to turn around and retrace my steps to Alexandria empty-handed.

"Bah, the movement between Parthia and this province is liquid. There are no impediments. But once the Roman legions arrive, that could all change. Rome likes to handle its conflicts as far away from home as possible. And we in the outlying provinces pay the consequences," said the mercenary.

The fourth spoke for the first time, his ibis nose reminding me of the birds around my home on Lake Mareotis. "Palmyra is well-situated however. I am confident the merchants here will be only too happy to handle any needs Lucius Verus and his legions have… for a price. And you can bet on your right eye" he looked at the mercenary, "that they will pass directly through Palmyra."

"Ever the merchant, finding the silver lining, literally," quipped the mercenary. That brought a laugh from everyone at the table.

The merchant replied, "Not only a silver lining. Maybe the income generated will make up for the reduction of import taxes on agricultural imports from outside the province."

"With Palmyra's population growing, food has gotten more expensive. Thankfully the government lowered the taxes to make it more affordable."

"It sounds like you are blessed with a benevolent government here that looks after its people, not like the bloodsuckers in Alexandria." I paused, shocked that such a thing had even come out of my mouth. "Sorry," I stammered, "I should not have disparaged our leaders. That goes against the teachings of my sacred book. Where do you think the majority of the conflict will take place?" I asked to no one in particular.

"The southern border of Armenia around the capital Tigranakert most likely. If Vologases succeeds in absorbing Armenia, western Mesopotamia is next. Verus may even take the battle to the Parthian capital Seleucia on the Tigris to distract him and draw his forces down out of Armenia." The mercenary knew his geography, and military strategy. "The conflict would most likely not go any further into Parthia. There is a lot of desert between Babylon and Ecbatana and nothing to be gained by making incursions further into the kingdom. The conflict really is over Armenia and the territory between the Pontic and Caspian Seas."

That eased my mind a bit. The thought of being trapped in Parthia as it battled the invincible Roman legions was not a comforting idea. I would not want to be a Roman caught in a city besieged by Romans.

CHAPTER THIRTY-ONE

Zos was in love. While I had been catching up on the politics of the region, Zos had been helping our previous evening's maid servant's daughter with house chores. She was a lovely dark-skinned girl with almond eyes and long brown wavy hair, only one year his junior Zos told me. I found him on his hands and knees scrubbing the tiled floor of the entryway to the house. "Zos, you do not have to do this you know." He looked up at me with his big eyes and then at the young girl who was polishing the table at the end of the foyer and smiled. I laughed, patted his head and made my way to the room for a parchment I wanted to study. I needed to refamiliarize myself with the map of the area, to situate myself now that I had this new information.

Laterensis was spending the day transcribing the proceedings of the city council meeting. He was the official city council scribe, in addition to translating and transcribing legal documents out of his home. He had a thriving business in the city, although his prosperity was administered in the traditional Roman way, devoid of ostentation, austere and disciplined. I now understood Sikarbaal's slightly ironic praise of Laterensis' stoicism. Sikarbaal was anything but austere.

Nevertheless, Laterensis did entertain one vice, theater. I discovered this on the way to the baths the evening of our first full day in Palmyra. Vibius, his eldest son Marius, Zos and I set out for Hadrian's Baths, built by and dedicated to him after his famous visit thirty years ago. We were followed by four servants with baskets filled with soaps, lotions, towels, strigils and fresh tunics. The sun, yet to fall behind the golden dunes beyond the agora, bathed the narrow street in the shadows of the elegant, unfluted columns of the tetrapylon, last night's landmark. Immediately upon turning left, to our left and directly across from the agora was the nymphaeum, a semicircular stone wall with niches filled with huge ornamental vases overflowing with vines and flowers. In the center of the wall, a cascade had been designed that carried water from the top of the wall to a pool at the base. Palm trees graced each side of the fountain, and the sound of the splashing water immediately transported me home. We had no such fountains in Alexandria, surrounded as we were by water, but the sound of water was practically ubiquitous. Immediately on our right was the graceful entrance façade of the amphitheater. "It seats about 1,000 spectators," Marius said as we walked past. "I attend theater once a week. Speaking of which, the family is going to see a play by Terence before you leave. Would you and your young friend care to join us?"

Zos had never seen a play before in his life, and I had seen very few. Attending theater was frowned upon in the Christian community due to the homage paid to false gods, the lewd humor and the excesses of the patrons. But perhaps there was more moderation here. It was worth investigating. "What is the name of the play?"

"*The Brothers,*" he said. "It's supposedly the last and the greatest of his plays. There is a troupe here from Pergamum who will be performing."

"I have read of it." Terence was a slave turned playwright who had achieved quite some fame a little over three hundred years ago. His plays were still quite popular, and I had read *The Brothers*, so there would be no unwelcome surprises if I brought Zos. "Yes, we would be delighted to accept. Thank you for the invitation."

"Do you have good theater in Alexandria?" he asked as we neared an imposing colonnaded façade to our left.

"Yes, but I must admit, I have rarely attended."

I could tell from the look on his face he was quite surprised. "And why is that? Does Ptolemaios keep you so busy?"

"I cannot blame it entirely on Ptolemaios."

"On what then? I can't imagine being deprived of my weekly dose of theater."

"We are Christians," Zos interjected.

"Yes," I said, pleased that Zos had evidently made a decision as to his beliefs and guilty that I had been reticent to admit the true reason behind our avoidance of the theater. "The nature of many of the plays, the low moral quality of the themes, the implicit belief in gods which we do not worship, these are the reasons. But I am willing to try it here. Perhaps the theater here has more redemptive qualities than the one in Alexandria."

"I see." I could see in both Vibius' and Marius' expressions that they were shocked. "We have arrived at the baths," Vibius said. "Enough talk of theater. Now is the time to relax body and mind," he said as we climbed the granite steps leading to the porch and entrance. Vibius passed two *as* to the doorman. I belatedly reached for my purse. "No, Kaleb. You are my guest." I hesitated with my hand in my purse. "Honestly, you will offend me if you try to pay." Zos and I both thanked him.

Inside the apodyterium there was a lot of activity, men in various stages of dress, those who were just leaving the baths, retrieving their things from the niches where their capsaria stood guard while fewer like us were just arriving as it was late in the evening. We made our way to an unoccupied corner with free niches and began to undress. Vibius left two servants to watch our belongings while the other two followed us with the baskets, and we made our way, covered only by a subligaculum or loincloth and each carrying thick-soled sandals to protect our feet from the heated floors of the bathing rooms into the large open palaestra, the exercise ground that was now practically empty.

Before leaving Vibius' house, I had been in a panic wondering where to hide the girdle of coins, knowing there would be no discreet way to handle them at the baths. The thought of leaving it out of my sight terrified me, but I had no choice. In the Spartan bedroom, there was no place to hide anything, and I feared leaving it in either of our bags. In the end, I wrapped it in a soiled kilt and left it in Zos' bag, assuming if someone were going to steal something, they would be more likely to look in my bag than in Zos'.

Now, standing in the courtyard in nothing but a loincloth, I was relieved I had left it in the house. Marius had an inflated ball that he kicked to his father. I was not entirely unfamiliar with this game, but was definitely not very adept at it, as was obvious when Vibius kicked it towards me. It went flying off to my right. I ran to retrieve it, turned and kicked it towards Zos. By this time we had spread out into a large circle. Zos caught the ball between his feet and shot it towards Marius who stopped it with his bare chest. The smack echoed off the courtyard walls. Zos put his hand over his mouth in panic, but Marius just laughed and gave Zos a thumbs up. "Nice kick," he shouted as he returned it to Zos in the air. Zos positioned himself and rebounded the ball off his head to Vibius who backed up to let the ball fall to the ground before sending it toward me with a stiff kick. This time I managed to make contact before the ball sailed off to my left. I was feeling pretty pleased with myself until I realized that I had sent the ball hurtling towards nobody. Zos took off towards it, and once catching it, sent it sailing back to Marius. We kept this up till we were all out of breath. By this time, even with the slight chill I had felt on first coming outside with nothing but a loincloth, I was sweating. Although Alexandria had a public bath, since I lived right on Lake Mareotis, I rarely went. And I never exerted myself like this. Marius collapsed to the ground laughing. You Alexandrians certainly know how to play ball. "What was that head move Zos? I have never seen that before."

"My friends and I do it all the time," Zos said proudly.

"You'll have to show me. Come on, throw the ball towards me," he said as he stood. Zos threw him the ball and he butted it with his head. "Ouch," he said, rubbing his forehead. "Your head must be hard as a rock."

"It gets easier with practice," Zos said. I laughed. They practiced for a bit longer while Vibius and I jogged around the courtyard.

"I try to run ten laps every evening," Vibius said between breaths.

"I must admit. I am not much at exercising. I do swim every morning though." I thought back to the lake and my early morning swims.

Sweating and tired, we walked to the portico where the servants with the baskets had been watching us. The portico led to a series of rooms, the first of which had stools scattered about. There were several servants waiting to attend us. We were among the last clients it seemed. We removed our loincloths and sat on stools. The attendants took our strigils and began to scrape it along our skin cleaning off the sweat, dirt and oil. Once we had been thoroughly cleaned, we slipped on our sandals and went into the tepidarium, a room with heated walls and floor. Our servants spread out towels on the stone benches that lined the walls, and we sat for a moment, adjusting to the warmth. Next, we entered the caldarium, a round domed room with a hot pool in the center that sent steam into the warm air and a waist high fountain at the far end with a jet of cold water shooting from an eye in a circular basin. We were the only ones in the room, most at this late hour having already left the bath house. Vibius sat at the edge of the pool easing his legs into the

75

steaming water. Marius, Zos and I followed. The heat of the water on my skin was almost painful. Zos slid off the edge slowly into the water. The rest of us followed suit. I felt that I was going to boil alive. Vibius and Marius seemed perfectly comfortable. Zos had already gotten out and was splashing himself with cold water from the fountain, his black body a stark contrast against the pale white and turquoise tiled wall behind the fountain. I could not endure the heat any longer. I followed Zos' example and splashed myself from the cold fountain. I held my head under the falling water until my skin stopped tingling.

"Can't take the heat, eh?" Marius said laughing. He and his father continued to lounge in the water.

"I do not know how you can stay in there so long," I said, easing myself back down on the edge of the pool, slowly letting my legs, toes first, descend into the cauldron. It was quiet in this room except for the splashing of the fountain. I slowly slid back into the water, closing my eyes. I had hardly counted to ten when I could take it no more. I got out again, holding my head back under the cold splashing fountain.

"There is a cold water pool in the next room if you want to try that instead," Vibius commented, his eyes only half open. Zos and I went into the next room. It was another large domed room with a myriad of basin-like pools throughout. We were the only ones in there, and it was silent as a tomb. Zos ran up to one of the pools and cautiously dipped in one foot.

"Very cold!" he exclaimed. "I'll get in if you do," he said, looking at me mischievously.

"On the count of three… one, two, three!"

"I'll bet I can stand it longer than you Teacher," he said, eyes wide and teeth chattering.

"We will see," I said, shivering from toe to crown. I stayed perfectly still, hoping my body warmth would warm the water touching my skin, but my shivering foiled my plan. When I could take it no more, I asked Zos, "shall we call it a tie?"

"Yes, please Teacher. I've never been so cold in all my life!"

"At the count of three. One, two, three!" We both jumped out of the pool and skidded back into the caldarium.

"Whoa," said Vibius, "slow down. You should visit the tepidarium first to warm up before jumping directly into this pool. It would be too much of a shock to your system." Zos ran ahead, but I followed, stiff and frozen, trying to maintain a bit of dignity.

Back in the hot pool, Vibius said, "It is a marvel the invention of the baths. Would that all people were as industrious as the Romans."

"It is a gift from God, this search to improve the quality of our lives."

"Most would say it is a curse, a continual struggle against the discomfort of life," Marius said.

"In the beginning, the first man was cursed, cursed to eke out his living by the sweat of his brow. But God ever brings good out of evil. And the good he brought was to give man the creative ability to think, to conceive in his mind, to bring forth ideas like fruit from an ever producing tree."

"How do you mean?" asked Vibius. Zos was watching me intently from the edge of the pool.

"An ancient book says, 'naked came I out of the womb, naked also shall I depart hither.'"

"Wisely said," commented Vibius.

"That very nakedness," I continued, "and the fact that we bring nothing with us, produces thought, and that thought may bring out dexterity, expel sloth, introduce the arts for the supply of our needs, and generate a variety of contrivances. Because he arrives naked, man is full of inventions, being prodded by his necessity, as by a spur, how to escape rain, how to elude cold, how to fence off blows, how to till the earth, how to terrify wild beasts and how to subdue the more powerful of them. Wet with rain, he designed a roof; having suffered from cold, he invented clothing; being struck, he constructed a breastplate; bleeding from his thorn-pricked hands from tilling the ground, he availed himself of the help of tools; in his naked state liable to become a prey to wild beasts, he discovered from his fear an art which frightened what frightened him. Nakedness bore one accomplishment after another, so that even his nakedness was a gift and a master-favor."

Marius clapped. "Bravo!" he said. "That is the noblest homage to a man's intellect that has ever been uttered in my presence." Zos too clapped, caught up in the moment.

Vibius looked at me curiously. "You are very young to be so wise. I see that you are not only a scribe but a philosopher as well."

"I am not wise in my own right," I said. "We all are born endowed with the capacity for reason and understanding. I have chosen to ally myself with the giver of that wisdom, and he makes me wise."

Before leaving the baths, Vibius and Marius had taken us into both the dry and the wet sauna, and we made several more trips back and forth between the hot and cold pools before finally making our way back to the apodyterium. Zos and I rubbed scented oil over our skin before dressing. "That's curious," said Marius, observing us. "We only oil ourselves before exercise, not after a bath."

"Black skin can get very dry, especially in the winter and away from the sea," I said. "We brought this lotion from Alexandria." Scrubbed and steamed clean and dressed in a fresh tunic, I felt like a new man. "Vibius, words fail me in my attempt to thank you. That is the most extravagant bath I have had since leaving my home, and even there this would be a rare delight. I feel clean down to my bones for the first time in over a month." Zos enthusiastically nodded agreement.

"You are most certainly welcome. It pleases me greatly that you have enjoyed our humble baths. You can use them as often as you like as long as you are here. Marius and I come every day, usually much earlier than today. It is much livelier earlier. Perhaps tomorrow you would like to join us again," he said as we made our way down the stairs of the baths to the street.

"I am already looking forward to it," I said rubbing Zos' head. "What about you Zos?"

"Like you Teacher, I'm already anticipating it."

"Impressive Zos. I am happy to see you are employing the vocabulary we are studying. Zos is my star pupil," I said to Vibius. He already speaks three languages and is well on his way to a fourth, and I no sooner teach him one thing but he has mastered it and is ready for the next." Zos beamed at my praise.

"It is extremely rewarding to instruct a bright and industrious pupil, that is certain," said Vibius. "Yet obviously, not everyone is cut out for the rigors of academia."

"That was meant for me," laughed Marius. "I will happily admit that in my case, there is a limit to how much academia one man can take."

"At least you accept it without shame, son," Vibius said, putting his arm around Marius' neck. "Marius' proclivities lie more in the arena of business than philosophy, rhetoric and languages. I must admit though that he is quite skilled in accounting."

"A necessary skill in business," I said.

"Indeed." We continued for some time in silence, the streets now lit with lanterns suspended from the columns lining the avenue, the tetrapylon blazing up ahead.

"How would you and your young student like to see the business end of the Laterensis family?" Marius asked. "I could send someone to fetch you tomorrow after you are up and about. You could join me for tea, and I will show you around."

"Of course. We would like nothing better."

"And later in the palaestra, Zos can help me some more with that head butt move."

Zos smiled, looking up at me expectantly. "He would love to," I said, patting Zos again on the head.

CHAPTER THIRTY-TWO

The week passed quickly. I spent most of my time between working with Zos on his studies of Greek writing, Aramaic and mathematics, studying my maps and reading all I could lay my hands on regarding the histories of the regions through which we would be traveling. Laterensis had an impressive library that he opened up to me. In exchange, I gave him access to the scrolls I had brought along to pass the time, some Greek plays, the letters of Polycarp and Ignatius and a recent writer from Alexandria, Dionysius Periegetes and his increasingly popular *The Habitable World*.

Zos spent every free moment helping his "Palmyran Rose" as he called the young girl he had fallen head over heels for. If nothing else, it was wonderful practice for his Aramaic as that was her native language. Laterensis commented on Zos' industry. I just laughed and explained that Zos did not like to be idle. He had quickly become a favorite in the household, trusted and treated well by Laterensis' family as well as the servants and slaves. We had become regulars at the baths, and Marius' head had stiffened up. He could butt the ball now with as much dexterity as Zos.

Before I knew it, the time for our departure had arrived. It was the final evening, and this was the night Vibius had invited us to attend the theater with him and his family. Zos was very excited as this was his first play. "Just remember Zos, not a word to your mother that I actually took you to the theater. She would never forgive me." Vibius treated us to a royal banquet as it was our final meal with the family. Marius and his wife and all of the other children were present, as were some scribe friends of Vibius' who had befriended me.

Zos and I were in our room packing the few things we had brought from the caravan depot. All of our clothes were freshly laundered. I was wearing my best tunic, covered with a wool cape Marius had given me fastened on my right shoulder and a turquoise turban. I put the finishing touches on Zos' white turban just as Marius came to the door. "Stupendous!" Marius exclaimed. "Where is your cape Zos?" he asked. Zos pointed to the bed where he had very carefully laid the cape out so as not to wrinkle it. Marius had given him one as well, both woven in Armenia from lamb's wool. He had never had such a rich piece of clothing. "Let's get moving then. Father is ready. We are gathering at the entrance." Zos and I followed Marius. Vibius was already walking out the front door when we caught up with him. Everyone was dressed in their finest.

We were all in high spirits, chatting animatedly as we made our way along the streets choked with people going to and fro. The main colonnaded avenue was awash in activity and traffic, but in little time, we were standing before the impressive façade of the Palmyran theater. We were a bit early, so there was not a crush at the entrance. Before I could even reach Vibius, he had paid for everyone. Zos and I thanked him again once inside. Stairs to the right led from the entrance to the beautifully symmetrical rows of seats facing us. Vibius' servants ran ahead of us with cushions and claimed the seats from the servants he had sent ahead to guard the spot that his family generally occupied, midway up the twelve rows of stone seats in the row just to the right of center. The stands began to fill quite quickly. The walls to the back of us had already cast us into shadow, but the stage remained bathed in sunlight. "Don't worry, there is rarely mime here, so it shouldn't scandalize Zos, or you," he added. "This far from Rome, we still retain a taste for more refined theater. You're familiar with Terence you say?"

"I have read some of his plays."

"I suppose you have access to all kinds of literature at your library."

"Yes, I am quite fortunate. The drama archives are quite extensive. And I must say I am partial to writers from my side of the

Great Sea. This play we are going to see now opens a dialogue into several intriguing avenues of investigation. Are we who we are because of who raised us or because of who we were when we were born?"

"Okay, don't spoil it for me. I've not seen this particular play."

"My lips are sealed, but I will be interested in your observations once you have seen the play."

Drums began to beat and a flutist came out onto the stage, piping a tune that contrasted quite nicely with the drums. The audience in the stands grew quiet. The walls behind the stage protected the spectators from the clamber of the avenue on the other side. When it had grown completely quiet, the flutist left the stage and the first act began. Zos was on the edge of his seat. Despite my interest, I felt my eyes growing heavy. The large meal just before, the excitement of packing and all of the activity leading up to this moment, the warmth of the soft wool cloak, all conspired like Achelous' daughters, to lull me away from the play and into the arms of sleep. I could not let myself be overcome. How rude would that be? I looked around to make sure nobody had noticed my eyes struggling to stay open. Marius was looking at me and winked, folding his hands to the side of his head. He had caught me! I smiled, but the mere fact I had been discovered entirely roused me. I was fine till intermission. I stood. Marius bid his parents' leave to take me and Zos to bring refreshments.

"What a relief," I said once out of earshot of Vibius and the rest.

"I was afraid you would lose the battle," Marius said.

"What battle?" asked Zos.

"Never mind Zos. So what do you think of the play?"

"I've never seen anything like it! Is it a true story?"

"Who knows?" I said. "It could very likely just be the invention of the artist's imagination."

"What an imagination!" Zos said. "I could never put together such a tale."

"And who do you think is the better man?" I asked Marius. "The farmer or the city brother?"

"I'm partial to the city-brother myself," Marius said. "But I see a bit of the farmer in my father."

"So strict?"

"Not to the extent of Demea. I never went wild once I had a bit of freedom. But he did instill in our family strong character, solid virtues. We were never given the freedoms Micio allows Aeschinus. I do see how the question emerges about blood or upbringing."

"Well, defer your judgment till the end. You may be surprised yet. And you Zos? Is there anything so far that disturbs you?"

"Syrus is quite sneaky. He doesn't seem to be bothered by being deceitful. And Micio has very low morals, as do the women he knows."

This gave Marius a huge laugh. "You are quite a pair," he said. "I don't think I've ever met a boy with such high moral character." Zos looked at Marius curiously, not knowing whether to take what he said as a compliment or not.

"Pay no attention to Marius, Zos. He has evidently not ever met any young Christians."

"You're right," Marius said. "I'm very intrigued. One doesn't hear very flattering things about Christians. It's too bad you're leaving tomorrow. I am beginning to have many questions come to mind."

"Perhaps I can leave you some things to read."

"Ah, reading. That is not my strong suit. Remember the conversation about academia? Well, in that I am not my father's son."

"On my return then," I said. "You prepare the questions, and I will do my best to answer them."

The rest of the play passed without incident. Zos was rapt again for the entire time. I had never seen him sit still for so long. The themes of the play provided much conversation on the way home. We played ball for the last time in the palaestra and washed enough to last us to the Euphrates. We would not see another Roman bathhouse for months. Vibius had sent ahead to confirm that everything was ready at the caravan depot for the departure the next morning. Zos was already in bed, his travel clothes laid out on the table. I joined Vibius and Marius in the plain room hung with hunting trophies where we had eaten that first night. There were three cups and a carafe of wine on the oblong table.

"I feel that I have known you for years," Vibius said as he poured wine for each of us.

"Likewise," I said. "This parting will be the most difficult so far. I feel that I am leaving behind family. You are a generous man

Vibius, and you have an exceptional family, a tribute to you and your wife."

"That's something I can toast to," said Marius as he raised his cup, looking at his father. We raised our cups as well. "From here, where are you headed?"

"Ptolemaios has tasked me with finding the Avesta and bringing a copy back to Alexandria. I imagine the most likely place to acquire it will be in either Ecbatana or Rhagae."

"I fear you may find it difficult to return this way." Vibius said. "Word is that Lucius Verus and his legions have left Italy. As I mentioned before, by the time you have achieved your goal, you may find this route blocked to you. I advise you to prepare for alternate ways of returning home if that happens."

"I carry on quite a bit of trade with India and have contacts all along the Pars down to the Erythraean Sea. If you find yourself looking for passage in that area of the world, I have written here who to find in the port city of Barbaricum and drawn maps of where you can find them," Marius said handing me a folded piece of parchment.

"Someday, you must come to Alexandria. It would honor me to be able to repay just a fraction of the hospitality you have shown to me and Zos."

"Who we are requires no repayment. Just as Ptolemaios is family, anyone he considers family is family to us as well. And it has been our pleasure to host you in our home. My entire family down to the servants and slaves have fallen in love with Zos. If only all of our guests were like the two of you." Vibius said as he refilled our cups.

"And you have certainly changed my mind about Christians," said Marius. "I've never really known one, and one hears so many foul things about them."

"Marius!" his father said.

"No, please," I said. "It is true. Marius is just being honest. And from what I hear, the new emperor Marcus Aurelius is no friend to Christians. He has already begun a new persecution. One of the manuscripts I loaned you Vibius, was written by a man who was just recently martyred in Rome for being a Christian. So to have found a friend among Romans is a good thing. Is that not at the root of what we do Vibius? We are not only magicians to some who can make the spoken word appear on parchment, but we harbor the belief that knowledge is worth preserving and passing on because knowledge is freedom. Even Christ said, 'you will know the truth and the truth will set you free.' Ignorance is what we fear most." Vibius looked at me for a moment. I reached into the bag I had brought into the room with me and extracted a package I had wrapped that afternoon. "I have a gift for you. And this is the perfect time to leave it considering our conversation at this moment." I passed it to Vibius.

"You did not have to do this," he said, obviously pleased. He held it for a moment.

"Well, open it," said Marius.

Vibius slowly untied the string and let the cloth fall away from the book. "Ta Byblia, The Book" he whispered.

"I copied it myself," I said. "It is the Septuagint which was translated into Greek over 400 years ago, one of the first books commissioned for the newly constructed Library. I have combined it with the more recent Christian Gospels along with the letters of some of the Apostles and Paul, a contemporary of Jesus who we believe to be the Messiah. I brought other books as gifts, but this one I have reserved for people who I believed would honor it."

"Well," said Marius, "I've not heard of these apostles, Paul, Jesus or the Messiah, but I may have to force myself to do some reading after all. Especially a book that you have copied yourself."

"It is beautifully bound," said Vibius. "I have not seen this technique of writing on both sides of the page before."

"It is a technique developed by the Christian community in Alexandria," I said, "because it makes for a more compact package, and because of the writing on both sides of the page, it is very easily transported and easier to protect from the elements."

"A gift I will treasure Scribe Kaleb of Adulis."

"I am honored that you accept my gift Vibius Laterensis," I said bowing my head.

"Enough formality, please," said Marius, raising his glass again. "To the amazing adventures which lie ahead, to new friendship and to Kaleb's god... what is his name?" he asked me with the glass in midair.

"Just God" I said.

"To God," Marius finished, clinking cups with us.

PART SIX

DURA-EUROPOS

Gregorian Calendar – March 13th, 162
Alexandrian Calendar – Paremhat 3rd, Third Proyet
The Season of the Emergence
2nd year of Marcus Aurelius

"Were I a nightingale, I would sing like a nightingale; were I a swan, like a swan. But as it is, I am a rational being, therefore I must sing hymns of praise to God."
(Epictetus, *Discourses*, I, 16, ca 90)

"Everyone ought to worship God according to his own inclinations, and not to be constrained by force."
(Flavius Josephus, *Life*, ch. 23, ca 80)

CHAPTER THIRTY-THREE

The sun brought no warmth. I pulled my wool cloak tighter around me, the hood already covering my closely shaved head. I could see Zos shivering under his dark wool cape. The familiar cacophony of caravan smells assaulted my nostrils. By the end of the first day we had left behind any vestige of greenery and nothing but the wide, flat expanse of the yellow desert lay before us. By noon, I had shed my wool cloak. Zos and I both now had a cloth tied around our faces to protect us from the dust that swirled in the air from every direction, our parasols swaying precariously over our heads. On this leg of the journey, Zos and I kept mostly to ourselves, riding in silence, lost in our own thoughts. We had seen much and met many new people, and I had collected a few scrolls to read along the way.

Zos was overcoming his first heartbreak. The young servant girl he had fallen for had slipped him a note just as we were leaving. He thought no-one had noticed as he sequestered it quickly into his travel pack. Now it was his constant companion. He had looked at it at least a dozen times before the caravan stopped the first evening. Most likely it was written in Aramaic leaving Zos in the dark as to what it said. I was curious as to when he would ask me to start teaching him to read and write Aramaic. Hopefully this potential for inspiration would not fade too quickly. He had already made great strides in Greek and a new challenge would add spice to our lessons.

We quickly fell back into the routine of caravan life, the setting up and breaking down of the tent, meager meals of bread, lentils, cheese and olives. Thank God for olives. They were the only thing that tasted of something other than dust. With a ripe, tangy olive in my mouth, I could rescue the memory of flavor amid the smell, taste and feel of desert. Even my eyes began to feel assaulted by the drab monotony of the landscape.

During the day, I divided my time between reading and dozing in the saddle of my dromedary, its swaying hypnotic in the cold glaring sun. In the evenings Zos and I would run around the periphery of the camp to shake off the soreness of sitting on a camel all day. I employed the services of a slave from the family that camped next to us to guard our things, not forgetting Zos' encounter before Damascus. Providentially, there had been no new scares. Initially on our runs we drew stares... surely we were an odd sight, two half naked Ethiopians, our sweat creating irregular black stripes in the yellow dust of the desert that had covered us during the day. But by the third evening, no one gave us a passing glance. We washed after that, pouring precious water over our dusty bodies before oiling our dry skin and uncoiling onto our cots with a sigh of relief at being supine. The nights were excruciatingly cold in the desert. Although the Pleiades were rising, harbingers of the Persian spring, our travel cloaks were barely enough to keep the chill at bay before the welcome yet perpetually disappointing sun in the morning, never quite fulfilling its promise of warmth till well into the day.

The ten wearisome days passed slowly, and it required some effort to pull myself from the stupor of the tedium to realize we were approaching Dura Europos, birthplace of Seleucus I, cliffside fortress city on the banks of the Euphrates. After the paucity of civilization for ten days, Dura rose like a teeming metropolis from the wasteland though truly it was inferior in size to Palmyra. Our contact here would secure river passage down the Euphrates to Sippar. The caravan halted before reaching the town. Ahead was what appeared to be a temple surrounded by construction. A community of two-tiered town houses filled the space between the temple and an entrance in the long wall enclosing the town. The activity of dismantling and setting up temporary camp ensued with the fervor that accompanied the arrival at civilization after a long trip through deserted territories.

It took some time to locate a reputable stable cum storehouse, but finally I had paid for two nights for our three dromedaries and meager baggage, and with our bags slung over our shoulders, Zos and I made our way to the Palmyran Gate. The wall of the city was punctuated by evenly spaced towers. It ended on the right at a wadi that the rising waters of the Euphrates had yet to flood. Far to the left, the walls rose a bit higher where the Roman camp was located before also ending at another dry wadi. Zos and I fell into place behind a group in Parthian dress talking animatedly. I could make out most of what they were saying, a fact that encouraged me greatly since I had not been able to practice Pahlavi as much as I had hoped on the journey thus far. Most of my studies had been from reading rather than speaking, though its similarities to Aramaic made it much easier to understand than I had imagined. At this point the road was paved. As if we were walking along the banks of a river, we stayed to the right of the pavement just as those emerging from the city stayed to the left to allow for the horses and carriages carrying cargo to occupy the center. The traffic stalled once we neared the gate. It would be a long wait before we were finally inside the city. To the right, I spotted another gate, much smaller than the one towards which we were headed. There was very little foot traffic there. I nudged Zos and we moved towards it as unobtrusively as possible. I did not want to alert the rest of the swarm of people to my discovery or again we would be caught in the jam of humanity.

We were stopped at the small gate by a guard in Roman dress. "You cannot pass through this gate," he said dismissively.

"But I was told I could pay the entry tax here as well," I said offering two sestertii in my open palm. I ignored Zos' puzzled look.

"Oh, well, in that case, proceed," he said, scooping the coins neatly out of my palm and waving us through.

I winked at Zos as we hurried to the first corner where we turned left to get out of sight of the guard before he changed his mind. "As our wise father Solomon once said, 'A feast is made for laughter, and wine makes life merry, but money is the answer for everything.' I could not bear the thought of waiting half the day to pass into the city. That was a small price to pay for half a day of my life." We both laughed, and I noticed a spring in Zos' step for the first time since we had left Palmyra.

Immediately on our left I knocked on a door that bore a fish painted above a rectangular peephole. A Palmyran Christian I had met told me about this house built right on the wall by the smaller gate where the local ekklesia met. Almost immediately, the cover of the peephole was slid back and two large black eyes peered through the opening. "Who is calling?" asked a female voice.

"Scribe Kaleb of Adulis and his servant Zos, traveling Christians from Africa," I said, wincing at the truth I had held back. I was told of this place in Palmyra." I heard the bolts being drawn inside and the door swung open.

"Please come in," the young woman smiled, her right hand to her heart, the clear black eyes now framed by an evenly proportioned face and thick auburn hair. "Follow me. You have arrived in time for the celebration of the Eucharist." Zos and I followed her through the interior of the house and out into a hall-like room where a large group of people stood around a table set with fish, bread and wine. I recognized the Psalm they were singing in Greek as one we often sang in Alexandria at our house church, though the rhythm was different. Zos and I were welcomed into the circle. When the Psalm was completed, a man at the head of the table introduced himself and invited me to introduce myself and Zos. All eyes now on the two of us, I introduced ourselves and asked for permission to pray. Some bowed their heads and some raised them and lifted their hands. I prayed, "Father, thank you for allowing Zos and me to arrive here in Dura safely, to arrive during the days just prior to your victory over death and the gift of forgiveness that you offer to each of us freely. Thank you for these citizens of your kingdom in this lovely city, for their hospitality and for the ability to gather together in your honor, to share with and encourage each other. I pray these things in the name of Jesus, Amen."

A chorus of amen followed as everyone's attention returned to the man at the head of the table, Gaius, as he had introduced himself. "We look forward to hearing more from you Scribe Kaleb," he said, and then after a brief pause, he lifted his hands palms up and began to recite the Lord's Prayer. Everyone in the room joined in the recitation. Gaius then lifted a loaf of bread and gave thanks for it, reciting Jesus' words at the last supper, "This is my body…" He proceeded to take the wine and give thanks reciting, "This is my blood…" After blessing the food, we all sat down and began to eat. I hardly was able to take one bite of food as I was bombarded with questions. Where had I hailed from? Where was I headed? What brought me through Dura? Did I bring news from Rome, from Jerusalem, from Damascus, from Alexandria, from Ctesiphon? Several children at the end of the table had not ceased to stare at Zos and me. "They have never seen anyone with black skin," said Gaius from behind me. "You should be ashamed of yourselves. Let these gentlemen eat in peace. After the meal we can hear all about them, if Kaleb would be willing to share a word with us from the Christian community in Axum," he said looking at me.

"Of course," I said. "I actually have something written recently that came into my hands before leaving home that is of great beauty and will be of great encouragement to the ekklesia here in Dura."

After the meal, thanks were again given to God, and Gaius invited me to share a word with them. I walked to the head of the table, noticing for the first time the walls around the baptistery. Frescoes in rich ochre, blue and yellow of Christ as the Good Shepherd, the healing of the paralytic and Christ and Peter walking on the water decorated the walls behind the baptismal fountain.

"Thank you again," I said surveying the faces looking at me around the table. You have been very kind to receive a stranger. This is a very welcome respite after days of travel from Palmyra and weeks of travel from our home. I am on my way to visit friends in Ecbatana in Parthia. I am a scribe and Zos there has come along with me as my companion and student. His family and mine go back a long way. I am a collector of writings, and before embarking on this journey, I came across a particular letter, written to the tutor of our new emperor Marcus Aurelius. It is an apology, defending the manner of Christians. Although we enjoyed a time of peace under Antoninus Pius, it seems that nowadays, as you know, the closer one gets to Rome, the greater the risk for a Christian. I am sure you heard of the recent martyrdom of Polycarp. Thanks to writers like Justin of Flavia Neapolis, we are beginning to develop a body of apologetics defending Christianity against the calumnies and vicious rumors spread about us. This particular letter is a beautiful testimony of who we are, and I hope it will encourage each of you as you work out your salvation here in this city on the edge of the Euphrates." I took the parchment book out of my bag. I had anticipated just such an occasion when we packed this morning and wanted to be prepared.

I began to read.

"For the Christians are distinguished from other men neither by country, nor language, nor the customs which they observe. For they neither inhabit cities of their own, nor employ a peculiar form of speech, nor lead a life which is marked out by any singularity. The course of conduct which they follow has not been devised by any speculation or deliberation of inquisitive men; nor do they, like some, proclaim themselves the advocates of any merely human doctrines. But, inhabiting Greek as well as barbarian cities, according as the lot of each of them has determined, and following the customs of the natives in respect to clothing, food, and the rest of their ordinary conduct, they display to us their wonderful and confessedly striking method of life. They dwell in their own countries, but simply as sojourners. As citizens, they share in all things with others, and yet endure all things as if foreigners. Every foreign land is to them as their native country, and every land of their birth as a land of strangers. They marry, as do all others; they beget children; but they do not destroy their offspring. They have a common table, but not a common bed. They are in the flesh, but they do not live after the flesh. They pass their days on earth, but they are citizens of heaven. They obey the prescribed laws, and at the same time surpass the laws by their lives. They love all men, and are persecuted by all. They are unknown and condemned; they are put to death, and restored to life. They are poor, yet make many rich; they are in lack of all things, and yet abound in all; they are dishonored, and yet in their very dishonor are glorified. They are evil spoken of, and yet are justified; they are reviled, and bless; they are insulted, and repay the insult with honor; they do good, yet are punished as evil-doers. When punished, they rejoice as if quickened into life; they are assailed by the Jews as foreigners, and are persecuted by the Greeks; yet those who hate them are unable to assign any reason for their hatred."

My heart was beating rapidly after having read this most beautiful description of who we were, of who I was. I offered up a silent prayer as the men and women seated around the table, some with tears in their eyes, began to whisper amen. Gaius stood and thanked me for the reading. He took my place, and using the text I had read, began an exposition on the scripture that supported the tenets put forth.

After the meeting and visiting, which lasted well into the evening, Zos and I were invited to spend the night in Gaius' home. The lovely young woman that had greeted us at the door was Gaius' daughter. When asked if we needed anything, I told Gaius that what I wanted most was a bath. "This is not my natural color. I am actually much blacker," I said. Gaius and his daughter both laughed as they led me to a room in the back of the house, against the city wall apparently since this was the only stone wall in the house.

"I am sure this is not what you may be used to, but it is the best we have to offer until the baths open tomorrow. It is far too late now to go. Give Gaia some time and she will provide you with warm water with which to wash. Meanwhile, you can organize your things in the room we have prepared for you." He led us to a small interior room with two narrow beds and a small table in the middle. It was pitch dark until he lit the lamp on the table which shot tall wavering shadows onto the walls. "I will call you when the water has been heated," he said as he left the room.

CHAPTER THIRTY-FOUR

Appearances to the mind are of four kinds. Things either are what they appear to be; or they neither are, nor appear to be; or they are, and do not appear to be; or they are not, and yet appear to be. Rightly to aim in all these cases is the wise man's task.
(Epictetus - *Discourses. Chap. XXVII,* ca 90)

Barefoot, he entered into the holy chamber. Candles blazed illuminating the geometric and astral designs covering the walls. At the far end, a veil surrounded a raised dais where the mathematicus was seated, faintly visible through the sacred veil. A robed acolyte approached the Carpathian with the cup of libation. He took it and poured out a portion, carefully ensuring that it ran over the handle of the cup before taking a sip himself and passing it back to the acolyte who handed him in turn a box of colored chalk.

Taking the orange chalk from amongst the other colors offered, he bent down and began to trace out two conjoined squares. When he was finished he stood and waited.

"The eight," the deep voice behind the veil spoke. "However, before we can process the experiences you are so anxious to reflect on, I am currently more interested in the seven, the culmination of the progression from the numbers four – manifestation, five – motion, and six – consciousness. How can one jump to the eight before understanding the consequences of consciousness through space and time that form the experience, the manifestation of the seven. It is true what is said of you. You are rash, impetuous. Rather than progressing with equanimity from the balance of the two, you have leapt directly to the eight. Begin at the beginning, and let me decide the direction we will take from here."

CHAPTER THIRTY-FIVE

I opened my eyes to darkness. The sun must not be up over the Mareotis yet. Strange since I was awake. I felt upside down, and my bed felt too small. I experienced a bought of dizziness, disorientation. "Where am I?" I thought for a panicked moment. Then the events of the previous day came flooding back to me in the dark of the room. I cannot see the sun because I am not in my room in Alexandria. I am in the back room of a dark house with no windows. I began to discern noise in the periphery of the house. I slowly stood, careful not to hit my head on or knock over anything. I could not see my hand in front of my face. My arms out in front of me, I began to inch my way forward in the direction in which I remembered the door to be. A flickering light made its way along the hall wall in my direction. My eyes traced the outline of the door to my room. The light finally reached my door where I saw Zos, his face lit, his shadow huge on the wall behind him. He gasped and almost dropped the lamp when he saw me standing there.

"Careful Zos. I was trying to extricate myself from this room. Is everyone up?" I asked, perturbed that Zos had beat me out of bed.

"Only me and Gaia."

"Is the sun up?"

"Not yet, but from the front of the house, there is a bit of light in the sky. It won't be long now."

"Bring that lamp in here and get us some light," I said, taking the lamp from him and lighting the one on our table. "I pray I never am locked up in a place like this. I believe I might lose my mind." I thought of our home in Alexandria with a pang of nostalgia. There was not a completely dark corner in the house when there was light in the sky. I pulled my tunic over my bare shoulders and shivered in the morning chill. Now that I was fully awake, I was beginning to feel the cold in the air.

"Come to the kitchen Teacher; Gaia has made hot tea."

"I need to brush my teeth."

"Come have tea first. It will warm you up. And I'll tell Gaia to not get too close to you."

I popped him on the back of the head, and we both laughed.

CHAPTER THIRTY-SIX

Gaius generously offered to let us stay one more night at his house. If possible, I wanted to secure our passage today on a kalak downriver to Sippar. I had the contact information of one Teofilo who lived in the center of the city. Once outside, I took a deep breath of the crisp morning air and bathed in the light from a cloudless sky. Zos and I continued in the same direction we had begun yesterday, and almost immediately our quiet narrow street was intersected by the main road, only one block from the Palmyran Gate, the avenue that bisected the city from the Palmyran Gate to the Eastern Wall overlooking the Euphrates. Like the Nile in June, the currents of people flowing on the main road were difficult to maneuver, even at this hour of the morning, but Zos and I eventually landed unscathed on the opposite shore. We continued straight to get away from the main thoroughfare and then turned right. The streets here were paved, clean and straight, a well-planned city. Every thirty paces or so, there was an intersection. Three streets east we turned left again, where, at the corner, I knocked on a door that bore a giant painted scriber's pen.

The door opened and a gargantuan hulk of a man moved to occupy the entire space the door once filled. "Teofilo?" I asked, unconsciously taking a step back and getting smacked in the back of the head by one end of a pole from which hung two buckets, carried by a not unwarrantedly indignant matron whose precarious balance I had upset.

The man in the door let out a booming guffaw and said, between sputters, "You must be Kaleb. Wait there. I'll be right back." The door slammed into its rightful place, as if it had ousted the usurper once and for all. I looked at Zos. Zos looked at me. The door opened again, and Teofilo, now wearing a dark cape over his knee short tunic, marched out of the door, turning to lock it with an enormous key which he proceeded to hang from the leather belt of his tunic. "Breakfast?" I pursed my lips and nodded in agreement. "I'm famished... haven't eaten since yesterday morning. I've been working on a blasted translation from Pahlavi that looks like it was written by a three-year-old. 'Have it ready by tomorrow!' he says. Right!"

"Maybe I could help," I offered. Teofilo looked me up and down as we tried to keep up with his pace.

"Right. Do you even speak Pahlavi?"

"I would not have offered if I could not," I said, returning his stare but being careful nonetheless to not run into anything again.

"Hmph."

I looked at Zos and smiled. It was going to be a long morning.

CHAPTER THIRTY-SEVEN

We were seated at one of several tables in a small room with a huge open window facing the street. Our table was spread with roasted goat, fried eggs, toasted barley, fresh bread and warm milk. I was practically drooling I was so hungry, assaulted by the pangs within twenty paces of this place. That is when the smell engulfed me. We had to wait just long enough for my stomach to start rumbling. Zos was laughing at me, but I could tell the smell was affecting him as well. Teofilo had hardly strung together two words since his last grunt at my offer of help. The three of us laid into the food as if it were our last meal on earth. In short order, there was nothing left. Teofilo shouted to the boy waiting the tables to bring a beer. When it arrived, I asked for tea for me and Zos. "Very refined tastes I see," Teofilo said. "So, welcome to the portal of the world," he said. "You couldn't have planned your timing better. You're just going to make it into Parthia before the borders close it seems. Rumor has it that Verus will be here in a matter of weeks. By then though, you should be well into Parthian territory, if you don't dilly-dally here or in Seleucia or Ctesiphon that is."

"I have no intention of prolonging my stay anywhere till I reach Ecbatana," I said. "In fact, I was hoping you could help me book a kalak for Sippar. Ptolemaios gave me your name."

"Is that a fact? Good ole' Ptolemaios. How is that old bastard? I've not seen him since Athens... how many years ago was that?" he said, looking up at the ceiling, as if the answer might be written there.

"He is in excellent health and is running the entire Library now," I said, noticing for the first time a thin man at the adjoining table leaning curiously close to our table. He looked vaguely familiar though I could not be sure since his back was to us.

"I'll bet he's a regular slave driver, that one," he laughed so hard he kicked the table and almost sent the plates flying. The serving boy appeared instantly to clear away anything breakable.

I handed him a coin, "For the meal," I said, looking back over to the now empty seat where the thin man had just been. How could I have missed his leaving? ₊I wanted to see his face.

Teofilo eyed me with new appreciation. "Alexandria's treating you all right then."

"Life is good."

"Yeah, well, life is good here too. We're just growing and prospering like never before. Did you see all the construction on your way in? I swear on Zeus, I think the Palmyrans are taking over. They've almost taken over the western side of the city outside the wall, and now they're expanding their temple. They're even inside the city now."

"You talk like that is a bad thing."

"Palmyra, Dura, they're both Macedonian, so who cares who moves in where right? What do I care as long as business is good? I'm Greek, so these Macedonians can all go hang themselves as far as I'm concerned." I was worried what the people at the other tables might be thinking, but I realized no one was listening. Teofilo must go on rants like this often.

"Can you help us book passage on a kalak then?" I asked, ready to end our morning conversation, pleasant as it was.

"Let's do it," he said, punctuating it by banging his fist on the table. At that moment, I was very glad I had been given the address of the house church in Dura. Otherwise, Zos and I would have been subjected to Teofilo's questionable hospitality until we were on the kalak. I was beginning to regret not having asked Gaius if *he* could help us. But all things happen for a purpose. There was a reason we were with Teofilo this morning, whether I ever understood it or not.

CHAPTER THIRTY-EIGHT

A fool and water will go the way they are diverted.
(Ancient Egyptian proverb)

Sippar. He had been wise not to draw any more attention to himself since the last episode at Kaleb's tent. It seemed Kaleb had written it off as a failed attempt at robbery and nothing more. And his discretion had finally paid off. They were headed to Sippar by kalak. And it seemed Kaleb was going to book passage soon. He had to act fast. After the instructions he had been given last night, he had no time to lose. Between his midnight meeting in the House of the Hypotenuse and keeping an eye on the door of the home Kaleb had spent the night in, he had hardly slept. It was a minor miracle that he had seen Kaleb leave this morning. He had fallen completely asleep on the roof of the house where Kaleb was staying and had only woken up when he heard them exit.

Although he had insisted that the mission might be compromised if Kaleb recognized him, he had been instructed to follow him to Sippar. The mathematicus promised that he would be replaced there, commending him for all he had done so far, even the risks taken. "Hesitate not at the threshold," the mathematicus said, "but part your hair in the middle," meaning that he needed to strive for balance in his thinking, weighing all the possibilities mathematically. After all, the essence of all events was to be discovered in numbers, ratios. There was no such thing as chance. Fate was knowing how to read the signs in the universe, the juxtaposition of the stars, the equations inherent in all things. With these thoughts swimming in his mind, he determined that to take the same kalak as Kaleb was out of the question. It would be impossible to remain incognito on board with so few people. He would follow Kaleb and find a kalak leaving the same day.

CHAPTER THIRTY-NINE

The Via Babylonia took us out of the city to the port, a bustling mixed pot of humanity. Wagons loaded with goods from Palmyra were being unloaded and carted to waiting kalaks, bearing seemingly impossible loads. The timber rafts supported on inflated goatskins rode low in the murky waters of the Euphrates. We continued a bit further downriver, where kalaks were being assembled. Men in all manner of dress from all corners of both empires shouted instructions in a myriad of languages as slaves scurried to and fro. Already I wished I had worn boots instead of sandals, my feet caked in mud and dung.

I stayed close behind Teofilo as we wove amid the traffic. I could only hope Zos was keeping apace. I could not afford to turn and see if he was still behind me intent as I was on keeping Teofilo in my sight. Teofilo approached a man in Parthian dress who was barking orders in Pahlavi to a group of sweating slaves inflating goat skins with a giant bellows. "Sa'lam."

"Sa'lam," the Parthian said during a brief pause between shouted instructions.

"Are you preparing to sail?"

"Tomorrow morning if these malingerers ever finish blowing up the skins!"

"How far are you going? I need to book passage for two men and two donkeys."

And the haggling began in earnest. I confirmed that Zos was still with us and tried to follow the conversation. Teofilo's Pahlavi was quite good, fluent in fact. I was impressed. And his bargaining skills were at least up to Egyptian standards. A deal was struck and the time set. We were to be here ready to load before sunrise tomorrow.

"Fortune smiled on you this morning," Teofilo said as we made our way back to the city. "I have used Urud's services many times in the past. He is an honest man. It was fortuitous that we met up with him. Sometimes, when there is no one available that I know, it's a roll of the dice with whom you find yourself."

"God's providence," I said.

"Right. Is there anything else you're going to need from me?"

PART SEVEN

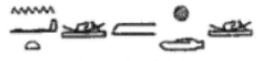

THE EUPHRATES

Gregorian Calendar – March 25th, 162
Alexandrian Calendar – Paremhat 5th, Third Proyet
The Season of the Emergence
2nd year of Marcus Aurelius

"Time is a sort of river of passing events, and strong is its current; no sooner is a thing brought to sight than it is swept by and another takes its place, and this too will be swept away."
(Marcus Aurelius Antoninus, *Meditations, IV, 43,* ca 90)

CHAPTER FORTY

Gaius, Gaia and a few members of their ekklesia saw us off at the dock. Gaius prayed for a safe journey and that Zos and I be salt in the places we found ourselves. A loud argument from a kalak next to ours interrupted our goodbye. Gaius was giving me advice about foods to avoid at the stops along the journey, but my eyes kept straying to the man yelling at the neighboring kalak pilot. Something about him looked disturbingly familiar. His hat hid his features, but the way his tunic hung on his thin frame, and the manner in which he gestured and moved looked familiar. The argument was in Pahlavi, but I caught the hint of an Alexandrian accent in the Greek epithets the man with the hat let escape.

"All aboard!" the pilot yelled, wrenching me from my reverie.

Zos and I waved from the edge of the huge raft as it was pushed away from the shore into the center of the river. The current in the slowly rising river caught us and hurled us forward, the waving hands disappearing completely as we rounded a bend in the river. The cargo of dried apricots had been neatly stacked an arms length from the edge of the raft in a rectangle which formed a frame around the open area in the center. Half of this area was dedicated to the mules and donkeys and the other half was covered and provided shelter for the men and women traveling like me and Zos. We claimed a back corner. The bags of apricots created a tangy smelling wall on two sides. We unfolded our cots and small table, effectively setting up our lodgings for the next several days. One of the passengers had a slave boy who he had left with instructions to not leave his things unattended. I asked if he would keep watch over our things as well, slipping him half an *as* and promising the same every day as long as our things were kept safe. I left Zos to roam the raft, and I climbed up onto the wall of apricot bags to sit and watch the land pass. The river here was wide and the land flat on both sides. The kalak glided along slowly turning in circles, providing me a complete panorama without having to move a muscle. From somewhere on the raft, a flute began to play. Several travelers had taken posts along the edges of the apricot walls. The melancholy tune filled the stillness of the morning air. Alone in this lonely land, striped vista of blue sky, green fields, brown desert and blue river, I was filled with an unaccountable sense of heartbreaking joy. I said a prayer of thanksgiving to God for his providence, for this brief glimpse of pure beauty he had created and allowed me to participate in, for the adventure awaiting me, for wisdom and guidance. Overwhelmed with a compulsion to write, I took out my journal that I carried on me. I wrote of the silence of the journey to Dura, of Zos' companionship and unfailing obedience, of Gaius and Gaia of the auburn hair, of the muddy port of Dura, of the great river and the melody of the flute in the quiet of the morning.

The day passed lazily. The wall became a classroom as I made up for the days we had spent in Dura by giving Zos double lessons. After eating, Zos and I lay down on the wall and I read *The Shipwrecked Sailor* aloud. Zos and I both loved this story. We had also read it on the ship from Alexandria to Tyre, not knowing at the time that we would find ourselves enacting this tale on that stormy night at sea. Zos fell asleep as I read. "'Become a wise man, and you shall come to honor,' young Zos" I said, repeating the last line of the story.

While Zos slept, I read from a collection of Ethiopian stories written in Ge'ez I had brought with me to pass the time. When Zos woke from his nap, he spent the rest of the afternoon writing his lessons, and I continued reading. Before the light completely faded, the pilot deftly guided our kalak to shore at a docking station. After a full day of nothing but empty wasteland, I was surprised to see this small town on the Mesopotamian shore. It was just a collection of small mud brick dwellings with thatch roofs shaded by a smattering of palm trees. Along the banks, water wheels brought water up from the river into irrigation canals that had been cut into the earth around the town allowing the inhabitants to precariously coax some fresh vegetables out of the dusty ground. Before we were even tied up to the dock, entrepreneurs from the town had set up mobile kitchens from which the smell of grilled fish, leeks, onions and cumin wafted. We could have been in Alexandria surrounded as we were by the aroma of the food, the smell of the river, the lapping of the water against the bank and dock. I climbed down from the wall and checked our things. The young slave boy, lounging against the apricot wall obviously fatigued from the tiresome task of spending much of the day in this confined space alone, was still guarding his area. I promised to bring him back something to eat, and Zos and I made our way off the kalak in search of dinner. By now, the sun had set. The Mesopotamian sky was ablaze while its Syrian sister on the opposing side of the river was already black. Torches had been planted all along the dock illuminating the food stands and throwing shadows across the river.

Zos and I pulled up stools against one of the less crowded stands that had been set up a bit to the left of the dock. We ordered beer and the plate of the day. My mouth was already watering. A young man, a soldier from the looks of him, pulled up a stool next to me. "Tanotalkinoi at your service," he said in heavily accented Greek, holding out his hand, "but you can call me Tano." He had a leather band around his wrist and a heavy silver ring on his middle finger with a curious design. Blond hair and shocking blue eyes contrasted sharply with a tanned complexion.

"I saw you reading on the boat. So, you must be educated."

"Somewhat," I said. "Kaleb is my name. It is a pleasure to meet you."

"Likewise. Are you having a pleasant trip?"

"Much more so than traveling by land. Honestly, this is pure luxury. I have been able to spend the whole day reading, writing and daydreaming. And you?"

The cook pushed plates in front of the three of us. I was glad it was Tano's turn to speak because the food so close in front of me was irresistible. Evidently, it was irresistible to Tano as well, as he dove into it with gusto. I looked over at Zos, who was not paying attention to anything but his plate of fish. Conversation did not resume till all our plates were empty. Tano took a sloshy drink of his beer and belched. "Delicious. So, what were we saying? Oh right, yes I am enjoying the trip, but my heart is heavy."

"Why so?"

"My wife and son are in Edessa, so far away."

"You miss them."

"Desperately. I saw you reading today and thought perhaps you could write a letter for me."

"Of course. But why are they not with you?"

"I am in the employ of the Parthian army. I've been sent to Babylon from Armenia to join forces with my regiment there."

"But I do not detect an Armenian accent in your Greek."

"I am originally from Galatia, but I have been in Edessa now for the past year, since King Vologases took Edessa from the Romans."

"Well, I would be more than happy to write a letter for you."

"I'd pay you of course. We can work it out tomorrow when it's light. There's plenty of time. I can post it tomorrow evening at our next stop."

"This here is Zos. We come from Axum, via Alexandria."

"Alexandria," Tano said, his beautiful blue eyes impossibly wide. "They say it is one of the loveliest cities in the world."

"*The* loveliest," said Zos.

"And what makes it so lovely," Tano asked.

"The buildings are all white. The Library, palace and important buildings are white marble. The streets are paved with white marble. The main avenue is lined with columns taller than these palms. The temperature is always perfect. We are surrounded by water, the Great Sea on one side and Lake Mareotis on the other. The air is clean and clear. It is never completely dark because even on the darkest nights, the beam of the great Pharos flashes across the sky. We are surrounded by learning and the most educated people of the empire. There are..."

"Stop!" Tano said, holding up his hand. "I am convinced young Zos. I must one day visit this jewel on the sea."

"And Zos has only just begun," I laughed, rubbing Zos' head. "Although every spot on God's earth is beautiful in its way, I do sometimes long for Alexandria."

We paid for our dinner and made our way back to the kalak. "Until tomorrow then," Tano said as we parted company.

After giving our young guard the meal I had promised him, I hung the mosquito nets I had bought on a whim this morning on the way to the dock. Gaia had mentioned that on the river, the mosquitoes were cannibalistic.

"Good night Teacher. Thank you for the lessons today."

"Good night Zos. Thank you for being such an attentive student. May you dream with angels tonight."

"Most assuredly, Teacher, and you as well."

I lay on my back for some time, listening to whispered conversations around me, to the occasional buzzing of a mosquito safely outside the net, to the water breaking against the boat, to Zos' measured breathing next to me, and filled with a sense of well-being I slowly, slowly drifted to sleep.

CHAPTER FORTY-ONE

It is a bad plan that admits of no modification.
(Titus Livius, *Maxim 469*, ca 35 BC)

What a disaster! Kaleb had a day's lead. The kalak the Carpathian had booked ended up being delayed, and the argument at the pier was counterproductive since all it did was call attention to himself. He was sure he caught Kaleb looking in his direction. Not only would the pilot not give him a full refund but he could not find another kalak that was leaving that same day. In the end, he had hired a four passenger sailboat at three times the price to take him downriver to Sippar. He dared not take the risk of letting Kaleb arrive in Sippar before him, or he may never find him again, granting that he find him anyway. He could not fail. Success could very well propel him from his position as a mere acusmaticus to mathematicus. However, his failure could spell a proportional calamity. He knew what happened to those who failed after being commissioned by the high council. For a lesser offense, he would be counted as dead to the society. For a blunder of this proportion, he would be dead indeed.

CHAPTER FORTY-TWO

The sun was not yet up when I rose from the cot. I pulled back the mosquito net and amidst snoring and odd scurrying noises among the bags that I preferred not to dwell on, I made my way out of the covered area to the open deck. Climbing onto the apricot wall, I could tell sunrise was not long in coming. Already the sky had made the imperceptible change from black to deep blue, presage of morning. A sentinel sat at each of the four corners of the wall. The one nearest me nodded in my direction as I sat down to watch as we pushed off from the shore. The pilot of the kalak was already up and giving hushed orders to his crew. Long poles were employed to push off from the bank, and within minutes we were oscillating in the center of the river where the current was swiftest. I noticed a split in the river ahead. We were aiming for the narrower side to the left of what must have been an island. By the time we reached the split, the sun was peeking his glorious head above the flat green Syrian horizon sending the pointy tips of his golden crown shooting across the heavens. Zos and I spent another lazy day reading, writing and on lessons. The midday meal on the craft was meager, and again we were famished by the time we reached our stop for the night. I had seen Tano once that day, but he had not approached me to write the letter he spoke of the previous evening. Again he joined us for dinner, but this time there was very little conversation. He seemed distracted. I refrained from asking him about the letter. He would ask me about it when he was ready.

Day blended into day, each passing much in the same manner, but the landscape began to change. Whereas the banks on each side had till now been green cultivated fields or groves of trees or palms, the Mesopotamian desert began to make brief appearances. The river twisted to the right and left; one time as we sailed south, we were able to see the northbound portion of the river across an expanse of cotton fields. The desert crept inexorably closer to the banks on both sides. Judging from the position of the sun, we had been sailing due east for the past two days. The goal today, according to the pilot, was to reach Anah, at which point the river would again start to head southwest towards our destination of Sippar from where we would head via canals and overland through Seleucia to Ctesiphon.

Anah was a welcome sight. It was more than the customary collection of hovels we had seen along the way. Though not large, it had simple but attractive mud brick homes with flat roofs separated by small gardens of fragrant fruit trees. There was an inn with tables set up inside, in the outdoor garden and on the roof where our fellow travelers gathered for the evening meal. Zos and I chose the garden in order to feel the earth under our feet after so many days on the water. The tables were separated by date and olive trees. The garden was bordered on all sides by stately palms that rustled in the evening breeze. An elderly man set a carafe of the famous Anah wine on our table with two cups just as Tano joined us along with a young couple.

"Do you mind if we join you?" Tano asked.

"Of course not, please," I motioned to the other chairs around the table. "Sir," I arrested the attention of the waiter as he had turned to leave, "bring three more cups please."

He tilted his head and peered at me with creased eyebrows and an expression of incomprehension. The young woman said something in a language I failed to recognize though it seemed related to Aramaic. The couple joined Tano at the table.

"What were you speaking? It was not Aramaic," I said.

"Assyrian," the young Babylonian woman replied. "And my name is Anata, and this is my husband Acacio."

"Pardon my barbarian manners," said Tano. "I should have introduced you before I sat down."

"No harm done," I said laughing.

"Judging by your accent, you are Egyptian," said Anata, speaking Greek, the common language of the table.

"But by your skin color, I would judge you to be Ethiopian," said Acacio.

"Wrong and right," I laughed. Zos and I are from Adulis, a city in…"

"The Kingdom of Axum," finished Anata.

"Bravo! Your knowledge of geography is impressive. Have you read Strabo's *Geographika*?" I asked, having a flashback memory of the day I was commissioned. Zos and I looked at each other.

"Not Strabo's, Ptolemaios'," she said. "Acacio and I are inveterate geographers. We read everything we can get our hands on concerning the places in this wide world."

"The walls of our small home are painted not with scenes of gods and goddesses but with maps," Acacio said.

"A couple after my own heart," I said as I poured wine in the cups the waiter had just set on the table.

"Anata," I said, "I cannot help but notice your earrings. Is that Nefertem?"

"God of perfume," she said smiling. "Did the blue flowers around his head give him away?"

"How could anyone who has studied in Egypt miss the iconography?" I said. Zos smiled. "Tell me, how do your ears come to be adorned with the image of the Egyptian god of perfume?"

Anata looked at Acacio and the latter responded. "We are traders. We deal with merchants from Sina in Ctesiphon that buy Egyptian perfume and Roman merchants in Dura that buy bronze mirrors from Sina. It works out quite well except for the excessive travel. Anata and I feel that we know this river better than our own home in Ctesiphon."

"How do you know them Tano?" Zos asked Tano as he sipped his wine and feigned interest in the conversation.

"They hired me in Dura to work as their bodyguard to Ctesiphon."

"Well done, Tano," I said. "That is the mark of a true entrepreneur… to take advantage of any opportunity to make a little extra money."

Tano did not know whether I had complimented or offended him.

"Entrepreneur?" he asked Zos.

"Basically a businessman," Zos told him matter-of-factly. Tano smiled broadly and raised his glass.

"One thing we all share in common. I might be a barbarian mercenary soldier, Acacio and Anata Babylonian merchants and Kaleb an Ethiopian scribe, but we all know how to make an *as* here and an *as* there. To business!" he declared as we raised our glasses in salute to Tano's toast.

"What about me?" Zos asked, looking at Tano. "What do I have in common with all of you?"

"You… you speak Greek!" Tano said. "To Greek!" he again shouted and we again toasted. Zos smiled, very pleased that he too had something in common with the table. Tano reached out and rubbed Zos' head.

As we made our way back to the kalak, we agreed that we would meet in the morning for a game of Senet. Tano had never heard of it, but we promised to teach him. I was very happy about our newfound friends and the possibility of breaking the monotony of our days.

CHAPTER FORTY-THREE

Not lost, but gone before.
(Lucius Annaeus Seneca, *Epistles, 63, l. 16*, ca 30)

The Carpathian had narrowed his search down to three possible kalaks. He couldn't be sure since they were unable to get too close without drawing undue attention, but he had decided on a plan of action to eliminate them one by one. He began by following the one that was furthest ahead, determined to put in overnight where it stopped. If Kaleb were not on board, he would work his way backwards till he had located Kaleb's kalak. It was not a perfect plan, but it was the best he could do under the circumstances. Traffic was not bad on the river so far, and this was by far the best chance he was going to get at catching Kaleb before Sippar.

CHAPTER FORTY-FOUR

With one third of our journey down the Euphrates behind us, we now had friends with whom we passed the time playing Senet, Hounds and Jackals and Roman checkers as well as improvising other games that we made up along the way. The evenings were spent in conversations touching on every possible subject. I still took time out during the day to give Zos his lessons. Tano had also joined in. The weather had warmed considerably during the day but was still cool at night due to the extremes in desert temperatures. I had long since crafted together something to block the sun as we sat on our perch on the apricot wall. I positioned long poles that I had obtained one evening on land, and every day I tied a sheet to the four corners, creating a kind of canopy overhead. Others had imitated my example and before long almost the entire length of the wall was fluttering in rainbow colors during the day as the kalak lazily spun its way down the ever narrowing river between endless stretches of either desert wasteland as far as the horizon or dry rocky outcroppings that would block all view of the land beyond.

Three days past Anah, eight into the journey and two from Hit, the air began to smell faintly of rotten eggs. Anata explained that it was sulfur in the bitumen deposits in this area. Laughing, she and Acacio suggested that we accustom ourselves to it. We would smell nothing else for the next five or six days.

The traffic picked up on the river. The pilot could no longer let the kalak drift aimlessly with the current. The crew was busy keeping the craft closer to the edge of the river where the current was slower to avoid the fishing boats and ferries carrying passengers from one side to the other. Towns had become more numerous until finally one could not tell where one town ended and the next began. Thanks to water wheels that brought water from the river to the intricate canal system, there were extensive orchards of date palms but little else in the way of greenery. The smell of sulfur was heavy in the air. Progress was slower until we were past Hit. The river narrowed and the land on both the Mesopotamian and the Syrian sides alternated between date groves and desert. The smell of sulfur faded thankfully at the same time that our friendship with Acacio, Anata and Tano blossomed. We had become fast friends, and Acacio and Anata had already invited us all to stay with them at their house in Ctesiphon for the duration of our time there. Tano had become especially fond of Zos who, as it turned out, was the same age as Tano's son. Tano was increasingly amazed at Zos' command of language and knowledge of the world.

"When I return home, I am going to buy the best tutors for my son. I want him to be as educated as Zos," he confided to me one day as we sat gazing out at the endless plain of desert against a flawless blue sky. "But even if the gods smile on me, I'll not be home for at least two years. So much time will have passed."

"It is never too late to learn," I said.

"It's too late for me," Tano said. "I see how you switch easily from one tongue to another, the things you say when you're teaching Zos. I'll never master all you know. My fate has been sealed. I have lived all my life as a mercenary and will die one, but I don't want that for my son."

Acacio joined us under our canopy. "What do you not want for your son Tano?"

"I don't want him to earn his living by fighting. A mercenary's life is a precarious one."

"What would you have for him then?" Acacio asked.

"Learning. And a life that is stable and happy. I would like for him to be able to enjoy his family, to spend his life with them, not like me, spending most of it in some god-forsaken place fighting for my life, and for enough money to keep the family under a roof with food and clothes. There are very few options outside of fighting where I live unfortunately."

"So why not bring them south? Bring them to Ctesiphon. Your son could be our apprentice if he is apt." Acacio surprised me. Did he know what he was saying? He was offering to be a patron to Tano's son, and by default, his wife as well. What if he turned out to be inept at the business Acacio and Anata ran? What would he do then?

"If you mean smart, yes, he's smart. And he's a hard worker. I've hired him out as a kitchen servant to a wealthy family in our town. He is not involved in the cooking, but he has a keen eye and has learned how to cook any number of dishes. On the occasions when he is home, he cooks us meals fit for a king."

"If you are half a mind to take me up on my offer, I will talk it over with Anata. I know she would agree."

"It would be hard to pull my wife away from her family. She doesn't speak Greek either. She would have a hard time of it."

"If I am not mistaken, Armenian is similar in many ways to Greek. Perhaps she would not have such a hard time learning it once she is here," I said.

"Let me think about it," he said, looking us each in the eyes. "Perhaps you could draft me a letter later to see what she thinks of it. Of course, I don't know that coming south now would be the best thing to do considering the war that's getting ready to start. Ctesiphon might end up being in the thick of it depending on how things go."

"Armenia is quite in the thick of things as well. As long as we exist on this earth, we are going to be in the thick of it. It is hard to find even one stone that does not bear the stains of someone's blood." Acacio stared off into the horizon. Our eyes followed his. "The world has been at war since the beginning of time, especially this area of it. I would not let that stand in the way of making a decision. Nevertheless, you think about it. The offer stands." We sat there in silence, each lost in his own thoughts, me, amazed at the generosity of my new Babylonian friend, Tano no doubt weighing the merits and possibility of living in Ctesiphon and Acacio probably replaying the wars of the past.

Anata peeked her head over the edge of the wall, balancing herself on the penultimate rung of the ladder we had secured in Hit. It made climbing up and down the wall much easier. "What have we here? The three silent sages. Are you contemplating the meaning of life?"

"Something like that," I said.

"May I join you? I find myself stuck on a question on that score, and maybe a bit of meditating will do me good as well."

"Perhaps we have already discovered the answer," I laughed.

"Now that really would be something," Anata smiled. Acacio kissed her on the forehead as she snuggled up against him. Tano continued staring at the Mesopotamian desert.

"Has anyone seen Zos lately?" I asked no one in particular.

"He was playing, what did you call it, Tombs and Temples, with the boy that guards your things," Anata said. After a moment of silence, Anata said something quietly in her ancient language.

"What was that Anata?" I asked.

"Something I read recently, by an Assyrian writer, Tatian. 'Why do you divide time, saying that one part is past, and another present, and another future? For how can the future be passing when the present exists? As those who are sailing imagine in their ignorance, as the ship is borne along, that the hills are in motion, so you do not know that it is you who are passing along, but that time remains present as long as the Creator wills it to exist.'" The last words lingered lightly in the air, and in serene silence we watched the shore pass slowly by.

PART EIGHT

CTESIPHON ON THE TIGRIS

Gregorian Calendar – April 11th, 162
Alexandrian Calendar – Paremoude 2nd, Fourth Proyet
The Season of the Emergence
2nd year of Marcus Aurelius

"Now the whole world had one language and a common speech. As people moved
eastward, they found a plain in Shinar and settled there."
(Moses, *Genesis 11: 1-9,* ca 1,500 BC)

CHAPTER FORTY-FIVE

Sippar was already behind us. We had disembarked for the last time yesterday afternoon, spending the remainder of the day unloading the kalak and finding lodging. Disconcertingly, a sailboat with only two aboard put in at the same dock, the same sailboat that I was sure I had seen on numerous occasions over the past several days. I could not remember seeing it before Hit, but I knew for a fact I had seen it several times since. I paid special attention to the two men who seemed to be in no hurry to disembark. I mentioned it to Tano. "I've noticed it as well," he said. "I'll be especially alert until I'm sure we're not being followed."

None of us slept very well without the rocking motion of the river. Hopefully one night would prove sufficient to adjust to dry land since I could already feel the effects of the sleepless night. Acacio provided space for us in a wagon for the journey to Seleucia from the several that were waiting for him and Anata to load their precious Egyptian merchandise. Our donkeys loaded with our things trotted obediently behind us. Tano shared our wagon, and the three of us were now bouncing along riding atop crates of perfume through the most verdant fields I had seen since Lebanon. This entire area was well irrigated with wide canals and a myriad of irrigation channels. Sippar lay nestled in the center of this Garden of Eden.

"I only know two things about Sippar," I said once we were seated at a table for our afternoon meal.

"Please do tell," said Anata with a smile, pouring us each a cup of date wine.

"In Jewish sacred writings, in a book called *Kings*, written a millennium ago, this place was called Sepharvaim, and when Sargon, then ruler of the kingdom of Assyria conquered Israel, he relocated these people to Samaria, the capital of Israel. And even further back, according to Berossus in his *History of Babylonia*, it is said that Noah buried the records of the world before the flood here, thus giving the place its name which meant *writing*.

"Impressive!" exclaimed Acacio. But I thought Jerusalem was the capital of Israel."

"It was originally, but when the kingdom split into Israel and Judea, Israel made its capital in Samaria. Jerusalem belonged to Judea. Have you been there?"

"No, since the 130s, Jews have been prohibited from entering the city on pain of death. Even the name has changed. Hadrian, after rebuilding it named it Aelia Capitolina."

"I had heard about the name change, but I am certain the name will not stick, not to a city with as much history as Jerusalem."

"You know there is also a university here," Anata said. They say the library that it grew from was founded by Sargon I, almost two thousand years ago."

"Maybe this Noah you spoke of started the university," said Tano. "He did name it *Writing* didn't he?"

"You may be right," Acacio laughed. "If that is the case, we are the oldest city in the world, founded by one of the eight survivors of the flood."

"Now that's impressive!" exclaimed Zos. Plates of food began to arrive. Anata had ordered in Assyrian, so none of us knew what was coming. My mouth began to water.

Once the table was full to overflowing with exotic dishes, I said, "I would like to pray to my God to thank him for our safe passage and this wonderful food."

"Of course," Acacio said. Tano and Anata both registered a bit of surprise. Zos and I both raised our hands palms up, and bowing our heads, I prayed.

"Father of us all, words alone cannot express how thankful I am that you have brought us this far safely. Thank you for the friendships you have given us. Father, watch over Tano's wife and son so far away. Grant him peace in his heart regarding their welfare. Thank you for Acacio and Anata's generosity in offering us a place to stay in their home. Thank you especially right now for the food we are about to eat. Bless it to the nourishment of our bodies and us to your most holy service. In Jesus' name I pray, amen."

"Amen," Zos repeated.

I looked up and saw that Tano and Anata had tears in their eyes. "That was beautiful," Anata said.

"You talked to your god as if he were your friend," Tano said. "I've memorized a few chants, but I've never heard a prayer like that." He rested his hand on Zos' head. "I wish my son were here right now. The two of you would be such good friends."

Zos smiled shyly at Tano. "If he is like his father, I'm sure we would be."

"Let us eat," announced Acacio. Several minutes passed before the conversation resumed.

"Who is Jesus," Tano asked. "Why did you pray in Jesus' name?"

"Jesus is who Christians believe to be the Messiah promised by the prophets in *The Tanakh*, the Jewish holy writings. We believe he is God in the flesh, come to offer himself as the perfect sacrifice to pay for our disobedience to his law, to offer us forgiveness and eternal life."

"What is his law?" Tano asked, now very curious.

Acacio said, "His law is in the *Torah*, the first books of the Holy Writings. There are ten instructions." My face must have registered surprise because Acacio then said, "I am Jewish. So I know what you are talking about, although I do not agree that Jesus was the Messiah."

"I understand," I said. "There is a large Jewish community in Alexandria, and I have had many a conversation with Jewish friends on this subject. Many are Christians, but many are not." I made a mental note to give Acacio a copy of the *Dialogue of Justin with Trypho*. I had a copy with me, so I could make him a copy from mine before I left.

"So what is this law you're talking about? It sounds quite easy... only ten rules?" Tano said.

Acacio and I looked at each other. "You go ahead Acacio. I am sure you have studied them."

"They begin with God saying, 'I am the Lord your God who brought you out of Egypt.' He is identifying himself so those listening would not confuse him with any of the other gods people worshipped at the time. He then says that we are to have no other gods besides him, nor are we to make idols to worship nor bow down to any other god nor misuse his name. We are to keep the Sabbath day holy, the seventh day of the week. We work six days, but the seventh we are to rest and remember God."

"That is basically the first half," I said.

"Hmm, only one god and no idols… strange," said Tano, now dubious. "And?"

"That is the part concerning God. The next six are concerning people. He says we are to honor our parents, not murder, not commit adultery, not steal, not tell lies against our neighbors, and finally not desire anything that does not belong to us."

"Those are all very good laws."

"In the Christian gospel, Jesus narrows it down to only two," I said looking at Zos.

"Love God with all of your heart, mind, soul and strength and your neighbor as yourself," Zos recited proudly. "Jesus said that encompassed all of the commandments."

"It doesn't sound so hard," Tano said. "I've kept most of those. Of course I guess I've already broken the first one since I have not known your god. How could I have loved him if I didn't know who he was? And besides, I thought the gods were beings you feared, not loved."

"James the brother of Jesus said if you break even one of his laws, you are accountable for all of them. And according to God, the penalty for breaking his law is spiritual and physical death. That is why it took Jesus, who was perfect in every way, to pay the penalty for us. Jesus said that if we believed in him, we would have eternal life."

"So what do you say in Tano's case Kaleb? Is he accountable even though he did not know about the laws?" Anata asked.

"Only God knows the answer to that question Anata. Jesus says to judge not lest you be judged yourself by the same measure. But I do know that now Tano does know, so he will be accountable from this moment."

"Whoa, slow down Kaleb. Maybe I shouldn't have started this conversation."

"It's not a scary thing Tano," Zos said. "It's a good thing that you know now. Knowing Jesus is a beautiful thing. He promises life, wisdom, comfort and eternal life in heaven. And all you have to do is believe him. After all, who knows us better than the one who created us? Isn't it a smart thing to follow the rules of the one who made us? It's no different from following the rules of Senet. The better you know the rules, the better you're able to play the game. The better we know God's rules, the better players we'll be in life."

Zos must have been paying close attention to the conversations we had had since the one over Amun's dog. I was dumbfounded that he said it with such ease and confidence.

"You are quite articulate on the subject Zos," said Anata. "You almost convince me."

"It is not for us to convince, only to present the good news and attempt to remove the obstacles to belief," I said. "Only God can move the heart and open the mind." At that moment, the head driver of the wagons came in.

"We're ready," he said. "The men have all eaten and are ready when you are."

"Let us proceed then. If we are lucky, we will find ourselves in Ctesiphon by evening," Acacio said. "It is about fifteen Roman leagues, and we have already traveled about ten."

"Well, I have plenty to think about on the rest of the trip," Tano said. "I may come up with more questions, so be ready."

CHAPTER FORTY-SIX

Seleucia on the Tigris receded from view. We had loaded the cargo, wagons and all, onto a pontoon boat that was ferrying us across the Tigris to the royal city of Ctesiphon. Tano and I had both given up looking for the men from the sailboat. Neither of us had noticed anyone following us. Seleucia was more dingy than I had expected, and although it was officially part of Parthia, it still felt very Greek. In fact, I heard more Greek being spoken than Assyrian or Pahlavi. We were on the line between the two greatest empires in the world. We had for the most part skirted the city where we may have been detained. Anata and Acacio were in a hurry to get home, and I was just as happy to only need to change beds once on this particular part of the journey.

"It will be close, but I anticipate we may make it before nightfall," Acacio said.

"This is the winter residence of the kings of Parthia, Zos. It is one of the largest and most important cities in the world."

"Fortunately the emperor Trajan did not destroy it like he did Seleucia. Seleucia really has never recovered although they say it looks more Parthian now. All new construction is more Parthian in appearance than Greek," said Acacio. We were already almost to the opposite shore, the river being much narrower here.

"The buildings are not very tall," Zos said.

"No, at most a building will be four stories. But have you noticed the arches?" replied Acacio.

"Yes, most of the homes seem to have a giant arch running down their middles, like a raised spine."

"That is very typical of Parthian homes. Instead of the columns used in Greek homes, we have a high arched ceiling called an ayvan that serves as a kind of reception hall."

"Do you have an ayvan in your home?" Zos asked.

"A very modest one," Anata smiled. I was sure Anata was the one being modest. The pontoon ferry came alongside the dock where we could begin unloading. Ctesiphon. I took a deep breath, identifying the smell of this city. At this point I was probably further from the Sea than I had ever been before. According to Ptolemaios' map, the Caspian Sea was over 500 leagues to our northeast, the Hospitable Sea 500 to the northwest, the Pars Sea several hundred directly south at the mouth of the Tigris and Euphrates and of course the Great Sea where we had come from weeks ago seemed thousands of leagues away. I felt a bit claustrophobic suddenly at the thought, as if I were somehow being swallowed by the land, crushed under the weight of so great a waterless expanse between me and the sea, any sea. Fortunately I was rescued from my increasing panic by Zos pulling at my hand.

"We have to get in the wagon again." We climbed on board and sat with Tano who seemed less impressed with any of this than me and Zos. Before the sun had dipped below the horizon in the direction of my beloved Alexandria, we arrived at Acacio and Anata's home. They lived somewhat outside the city center. We had driven down a wide avenue lined with stately date palms. Dates spread in every direction, but straight ahead was a high brick wall graced with a tall arch towards which our wagons were aiming. At each side of the arch stood a man in Parthian dress. They had opened an iron gate that protected the entrance to Acacio and Anata's demesne. Once inside the gate the wagons stopped; we dismounted, and Anata bid us follow her to the house. She indicated that our things would be brought to us shortly. Acacio went with the wagons towards some warehouses that occupied the right side of the walled compound.

Inside the walls and surrounding the house were beautiful gardens of fruit trees of every variety. Climbing flowering vines made their way up the smooth walls of the two storied home. Anata led us through a high arched door built into the smooth facing of the home. We immediately found ourselves in an enormous room with an impossibly high ceiling. The far end of the hall opened onto more gardens. A servant at the door took our shoes and offered us soft sandals. The floor was tiled in white and aqua blue that ran the length of the room like a wide stream of clear water. The walls of the hall all the way up to the arched ceiling were painted. The lower portion, from the floor up to the height of the arched exits that led off the room was solid ochre, but above that point, it seemed no color had been left out of the intricate geometric designs surrounding maps carved into the plaster. "It is stunning," I whispered.

"I am always so grateful to be back," Anata said. "It is startling how delicious it is to enter into my own home. Let me show you your rooms," she said, leading us towards one of the smaller arches. We followed her a few steps down a dimly lit narrow corridor. She turned and faced us, holding out her hands. "This room here," she said indicating her left, "is for Tano. And Kaleb, this is your room," she indicated the room directly across from Tano. Zos looked up at me. "Not to worry Zos, I have not forgotten you."

"I'm nervous about sleeping in my own room," he said.

"Do not be," she smiled. "Your room is right next to Kaleb's, and there is even a door between them." Zos looked relieved. "You can either enter your room through that door there," she said, pointing a bit further down the hall, "or through Kaleb's room here."

"I'll go in with you Teacher if it's all the same to you."

"Of course Zos."

"Scaredy cat," Tano laughed rubbing Zos' head. "If you see any monsters, call me. I'm trained for combat with monsters."

"One last thing," Anata said. "At the end of the hall here are the baths. That is one luxury Acacio and I adopted from the Romans. We were spoiled once we visited a home in Palmyra that had its own baths. The first thing we did when we came home from that trip was put baths on each end of the house, one for guests and one for ourselves."

"This is a palace," Zos whispered under his breath in Ge'ez. Anata gave Zos a curious look.

"He says your home is like a palace," Anata. "We are so grateful to you for sharing it with us."

"I will have some food sent to you, so you can eat before going to bed. Certainly you are at least as tired as I am and can think of little more than retiring as soon as possible. I am going to have a bath and call it a day. We break our fast in the gardens at the end of the hall where we entered. I will have a servant call you when it is about to be served. Now have a bath yourselves, and we will see you all tomorrow." With that, Anata disappeared through the arch back into the great hall, and Tano, Zos and I were left standing looking at each other, incredulous at our good fortune. Before we could speak, several servants approached with our bags.

"The furniture and larger items are in storage until you leave," a young girl told me in Pahlavi. "If you need anything else, please call. Mahsa will be staying here outside your room to assist you if you need anything." A little boy of about Zos' age smiled.

"Take those things in there and these in there," I told the girl in Pahlavi. The servants deposited mine and Zos' things in my room and Tano's in his room.

"Thanks," Tano said. "Good thing you're so good with languages. I have no idea what they're saying."

"That makes two of us," said Zos.

"Come on, let us go," I said. "We will see you in the baths Tano?"

"That's my next stop," he said.

"That will be all," I told the young girl. She bowed and they all left except Mahsa. He was still standing and smiling at us as I went in my room followed by Zos.

CHAPTER FORTY-SEVEN

"Something to drink?" Mahsa said as he set a steaming cup of orange blossom tea on a small acacia table next to the desk where I was working. I had insisted that no drinks were to be placed on my writing surface. Anata had arranged for a desk to be positioned for me in the great hall facing the gardens in a shady spot where direct sun never ventured. Tano was gone into the city to make preparations for moving onto the military base and to post his latest letter home. Zos and Mahsa were playing at Romans and Parthians in the garden when Mahsa was not bringing me tea. Anata and Acacio were in the warehouse inventorying their latest cargo of perfume and preparing it for the Sinese merchants that had been coming and going for the past two days. My story was that I was recording the past days of our voyage down the Euphrates in my journal, but in truth, I was copying the *Dialogue of Justin with Trypho* for Acacio. I was completely caught up with my journal and even with maps of the places we had been. The long days aboard the kalak from Dura to Sippar had allowed me more than enough time to write. I had even made extra copies of John's Gospel to give as gifts along the way.

"I will never surrender! Charge!" I heard Zos yell in the garden.

"What are you saying?" yelled Mahsa in Pahlavi.

"Arrrggghhh," yelled Zos.

"Eeeeyyyyaaahh," yelled back Mahsa, followed by the sound of clashing sticks. They had found their common language. I took a sip of the tea Mahsa had brought me and leaned back against the cool surface of the smooth wall. My mind wandered to the events of the past few days. Acacio and Anata had insisted that we stay here to regain our strength and make preparations at a leisurely pace for our next trek across the desert to Ecbatana. This would be the longest leg of the journey thus far, perhaps as many as three weeks. It may also prove the most hazardous. Acacio told me that the terrain between here and Ecbatana was quite difficult. There were mountains to cross, rivers to ford and bandits to avoid. A traveler could spend as many as four days without seeing any signs of civilization. What Herodotus had described over 600 years ago as excellent roads through continuously populated and safe regions had become a broken system, fallen into disrepair after centuries of war. We had come to the end of the Roman road system, the envy of the rest of the world, and from here on out, the roads were in ill repair, many times no more than trails through the desert.

Sitting here drinking orange blossom tea, watching the boys playing war in the sun-drenched garden, fragile petals like snow floating to the ground at the slightest hint of a breeze, feeling the smooth, cool tile under my bare feet, clean and refreshed, it was hard to imagine the difficulties that lay ahead. At this moment in time I was almost anxious to get started, anticipating the adventure waiting for me, the curious and intriguing characters I was yet to meet, the places I was yet to see, the languages I was yet to master.

Yesterday, Tano had me write his wife a letter requesting that she pack their things and move with their son here to Ctesiphon. He explained Acacio's offer. Acacio had offered Tano a place to live on their compound which covered an area of fifty acnua. Most of the land was covered in date palm groves, but there were some small houses scattered throughout for the workers. Tano's wife could work in the date wine production or in any number of other jobs there were to do while Tano's son could study at the nearby university in Sippar if he wanted. Meanwhile, Tano would be able to visit more often since the plan right now was for his regiment to maintain base on the eastern side of the city near the river.

I should finish this copy of the *Dialogue* today, and then Zos and I would begin to make preparations to leave. I had changed one aureus into Parthian coin with Anata since arriving. I had been able to earn my keep since leaving Alexandria with small scribe jobs on the caravan and kalak, but I did not want to come up short between here and Ecbatana. And Silara? I had not thought of her since the kalak. I needed to write her a letter, to send her something. Perhaps Anata could help.

CHAPTER FORTY-EIGHT

Dinner was served in the open air of the garden in the cool of the evening. Servants kept our cups full with the special date wine from Acacio and Anata's press. Exquisitely prepared lamb with a spicy rice and lentil dish reminding me of home brought accolades from everyone at the table. "What news is there from the front?" Acacio asked Tano.

"Well, I'm sure you are aware that Pacorus, Vologases' vassal king, is now fully in control in Armenia, and our forces now control most of northern Syria and even over the border into Cappadocia. The governor of Cappadocia, Severanius, tried recently to repel the Parthian troops north of the headwaters of the Euphrates and was gloriously defeated. He committed suicide and most of his legion was killed.

"Terrible. Nothing good can come of war. Think of all the wives and children left destitute. And this has all happened since we have been on our way south from Dura?" sighed Anata. "Here we are enjoying a leisurely trip down the Euphrates in the company of new friends while hundreds of men are dying needlessly on the same river."

"Well, actually, they were north of the headwaters, not literally on the river," Tano said.

"It is all the same."

"Supposedly the co-Emperor Verus of Rome is on his way to Asia, but there is no sign of him yet," I said.

"Three Roman legions have been dispatched to form a line of defense along the Cappadocian border. I however am to remain in Ctesiphon as part of the guard Vologases is putting together for the capital in case the Romans decide to come here again like they did fifty years ago."

"The gods deliver us," Anata said.

"This is the way of the world Anata," Acacio said. "The last fifty years have actually been unprecedented. Fifty years of peace. It is unheard of. The return to war is actually more normal than the peace we have enjoyed."

"I actually was beginning to believe that I could live the rest of my life without thinking about war," Anata said.

"Yes, this area of the world does seem more prone to conflict," I said. "Alexandria has enjoyed peace since the passing of Antony and Cleopatra. Peace does not always mean prosperity, but at least we need not worry about our homes, crops and even lives being destroyed. Rome may suck us dry through taxes, but at least we live in peace."

"Who cares what king is on the throne in Armenia? Really, who cares? Parthia and Rome cannot leave it alone," Anata said exasperated. "And they drag all of the rest of us into their quarrel."

"Whoever controls Armenia controls the gate between the East and the West," Acacio said. "It is used as a buffer state. The empires that surround it would rather it were invaded and ravaged than their own territory. No one wants to see it independent. Then it could make its own decisions about with whom it wanted to become an ally. Armenia is truly in an unenviable spot."

"And what about us?" Anata said. "Here we are right on the border, in a capital city nonetheless. We are grapes ripe for the picking. There is no buffer zone between us and Rome."

"That has its advantages and disadvantages," said Acacio.

"So where is it really safe to live?" asked Zos.

"Heaven," I said. Everyone laughed. "I agree that there are degrees of safety, but there is no place that is truly and purely safe. If we are looking for a place that is fairly high on the degree of safety chart, I would say Alexandria ranks well."

"Yes, far away from the conflicts of empire, protected by the Sea on one side, the Nile on another and best of all, by the desert. And most importantly, it is not *between* anything," Acacio observed.

"But even Alexandria is not exempt," said Zos. "Julius Cesar and Antony proved that."

"No place is safe from the ambition of man," I said. "If someone wants to possess what belongs to another, violence soon ensues. Why do you think that is one of God's commandments, to not covet what does not belong to you?"

"Truly said," said Tano.

Earlier I had explained to Mahsa that I wanted him to bring a package I had wrapped when I called him. The next time a servant appeared, as they poured more wine for me, I quietly asked him to send Mahsa. Almost immediately, Mahsa appeared at Acacio's side with the package in hand as I had instructed him.

"What is this?" Acacio asked surprised. Mahsa was holding out the gift with head bowed.

"I asked Mahsa to bring it after we had finished eating," I said. "It is a small token of our appreciation," I looked at both Tano and Zos, "for how wonderfully you have treated us and of the friendship you have offered us."

Anata's eyes sparkled as she said, "Open it Acacio!"

"You open it my flower," he said passing it to her.

"Flatterer!" she said, carefully untying the silk ribbon I had used to secure it. I had bound it in fine embroidered Egyptian linen. She set it on the table, Tano moving things out of her way. She carefully unwound the wrapping revealing two codices bound in book form, a curiosity still in these parts, and a scroll. She lifted the first one gingerly, as if it might crumble.

"Open it then," I said, impatient to see what they thought of it. She slowly and carefully opened it to the middle revealing my careful scribble. She was looking at the *Dialogue*. "That is a copy of one of my favorite pieces by Justin, a Christian of Samaria. This was written about thirty years ago and made its way to Alexandria via Jewish Christians who had gone to Rome to study. This is what I have been working on for the past couple of days. It is a conversation between a Christian and a Jew. Our conversation the other day outside of Sippar brought it to my mind, and I thought you would enjoy it."

"I will treasure it, Kaleb. This is a very special gift, written in your own hand." Meanwhile Anata was turning the pages of the second, thinner codex.

"Zos is a much better artist than I," I said, "so he agreed to illustrate the stories I have recounted. These are some of the more popular tales from Egypt."

"My favorite is *The Shipwrecked Sailor!*" said Zos excitedly. Anata smiled, her eyes wet. Acacio picked up the final piece. It was in scroll form. He unrolled it slowly.

"What have we here?" he asked whistling softly. "What is this a map of? Aha! It is Egypt and Ethiopia!" he exclaimed.

"I apologize that it is only in black ink. I lack the proper tools to color it in."

"I will provide you with the tools, but you must promise to finish it!" Anata said, craning her neck to look at it in the ever dimming light of the evening. "Bring lights!" she called out in Pahlavi to no one in particular, and almost instantly torches were posted around the table and lit, casting immediate light and dancing shadows on the table. "It is so beautiful Kaleb."

"It is actually from Tano and Zos as well. Zos was the artist and Tano secured the materials I needed to bind the books."

"Your thoughtfulness overwhelms me," Anata said. "Thank you, all of you. We will never forget you, and you must know, we treasure your friendship. You are always welcome here in our home." As she said this, she and Acacio took each other's hands.

"A toast, before this becomes any more sentimental," Tano announced standing. "May Anata and Acacio live for a thousand years! Keep them long happy, long healthy, long just! Keep them thus, keep them caring for the deserving! Keep them living and abiding for many years and countless hours! A hundred thousand thousand blessings upon them! May the year be auspicious, the day fortunate, the month propitious in all these years and days and months! For many years keep them worthy to perform worship and utter prayers, to give charity and offerings, being just. May they have health to fulfill all their duties! May they be liberal, kind and good!"

"Bravo!" I said, joining my cup to the others in the center of the table.

"Here, here," said Zos, getting into the spirit of the evening. A servant appeared and Anata gave instructions for the table to be cleared. Another servant brought a Senet set.

"Who is up for a game of Senet?" said Anata taking the game from the servant and coyly displaying it.

"Count me in," said Tano.

"And me," Zos and I answered in chorus.

Acacio had not spoken. Anata looked at him. "Need you even ask?" he asked, his eyebrows raised incredulously. "Roll to see who goes first," he said, sending the dice tumbling across the table.

CHAPTER FORTY-NINE

"A caravan is leaving for Ecbatana in three days" Acacio announced the next morning at breakfast. "We are in no rush to see you leave Kaleb, but it may be weeks before another one leaves, and we know you are anxious to continue on your way."

I was glad to hear the news although it would prove difficult to leave such good friends behind. "We will need to secure camels and make sure we have what we need for the journey," I said.

"Already being taken care of," said Acacio. "My groom, in charge of the camels we use on our trips to Dura has chosen two prime Bactrian camels which are already here tied up behind the warehouse with our other camels."

"I insist on paying for them," I said, feeling uneasy at the thought that Acacio might refuse.

"You can insist away, but Anata and I have already determined that this will be our parting gift to you and Zos."

"That is too kind, but still, I must insist. I could not rest easy having abused your generosity. You have already exceeded all the rules of hospitality by allowing us to stay in your home and feed us. I have the money from the sale of our dromedaries in Dura."

"Keep it. You will need it. You have a long way to go."

"Please let me give you something," I persisted.

"If you continue to insist, you will offend me," Acacio said. "It would please Anata and me immensely to do this for you."

I acquiesced. I did not want to offend them. But at the same time, my mind was racing to think of how I could repay them. I would send them something special from Ecbatana. "Your wish is my command. Jesus says it is more blessed to give than receive. Who am I to deprive you of this blessing? Thank you from the bottom of my heart. You are both consummate hosts and friends."

CHAPTER FIFTY

The following morning, I was determined to write a letter to Silara. I had spoken with Anata, and she had helped me select a spectacular bronze mirror from Sina for which I had insisted on paying full price. Tano would post it for me with the letter when he left for town in two days. On a scrap of papyrus, I made innumerable false starts, searching for the right words, the right tone. A romantic letter was inappropriate. Our engagement was anything but romantic. But then... I pulled the pendant from beneath my tunic and stared at Silara's likeness. Perhaps I should have Anata help me with the letter as well. No, that would be ridiculous. Silara was not interested in someone else's words. I would not be. I decided to describe to Silara a day on the kalak and the beauty of the nights playing Senet by the light of the moon. On a whim, I went into the garden and plucked a pink blossom from one of the climbing vines, pressing it between two squares of papyrus.

Wrapping the mirror and completed letter with flower into a package, I recorded last night's lunar eclipse in my journal. Last night was also the Jewish celebration of the Feast of Unleavened Bread, Acacio had told me, though he did not celebrate the Jewish holidays. We had stayed up late into the night to watch the total eclipse, the orange glow radiating around the blackened moon. Acacio was disconcerted by the celestial event which he believed was a presage of a terrestrial cataclysm, most likely involving the advancing Romans.

The next days were spent in preparation for the journey during the day and late nights talking and playing Senet under the stars by the light of torches. All too soon, departure day arrived.

"It's very hard to keep making friends and then leaving them," Zos lamented our last morning before breakfast.

"Is it not better though to have met them although you must temporarily experience the pain of saying goodbye?" I said.

"I'm not sure. I hate saying goodbye."

"By the time this trip is over, you will be an expert at saying goodbye Zos. It is a sign of great maturity to know how to say goodbye."

"I would rather just sneak out and not have to say anything."

"That is the coward's way out Zos. Remember, it is hard for the one you are saying goodbye to as well. Would you deprive them of one last chance to see you and speak to you?"

"Since you put it that way," he said, staring at the floor. "Do you have another piece of cloth I can wrap something in?" he asked.

"Zos!" I said surprised. "I venture you have a gift for Mahsa? You are truly learning the art of being a guest." I looked through my bag for my collection of linen cloths I used for gifts for my hosts. "Here," I said, handing him a small white linen cloth and some string. "Is this big enough?"

"Yes, Teacher. Thank you," and with that he disappeared again into his room.

This was also Tano's last day. He was moving permanently to the base on the other side of the city. Breakfast was a bittersweet time of remembering our time on the kalak and well-wishes for the future. There was talk of trying to meet each other again at some point, but at such great distances, this may be the last time we ever saw each other. Zos was right. It was very hard to say goodbye. We had to be at the caravanserai by mid-day, so after breakfast we had little time for talk before it was time to go. Acacio, Anata, Tano and Mahsa stood side by side facing us as we prepared to mount our camels. Zos reached into his bag and pulled out his gift for Mahsa. Mahsa's eyes grew wide when he realized Zos was handing it to him.

"For me?" he said in Pahlavi.

"Yes, for you," Zos replied in Pahlavi. I raised my eyebrows. I had not heard Zos speak Pahlavi before. His friendship with Mahsa had benefited him in more ways than he knew. Mahsa unwrapped the object swathed in white linen. Zos had done an admirable job wrapping it. Finally, Mahsa held out a carved figure of the Sphinx. "It's a famous statue at the pyramids in Egypt. I've never seen it, but I've seen many images of it."

"You made this?" Mahsa asked.

"For you," Zos replied.

Mahsa held it to his heart and bowed deeply. "I have nothing for you Zos," Mahsa said, still looking at the ground.

"Your friendship is my gift."

"And you have given Zos the gift of your language Mahsa. Without knowing it, you have taught Zos the beginnings of Pahlavi, a very precious gift indeed," I said. I held my hand to my heart and bowed to the group standing before us. "I would like to pray for you before we leave," I said. Zos and I lifted our hands and bowed our heads. "Father, creator of us all, grand weaver of our destinies, bless this family for their kindness and friendship. Prosper them in the work of their hands. Grant them favor in the eyes of their neighbors and guard them and keep them safe from harm in these troubled times. I ask that you also grant Zos and me mercy in our travels and a peace that transcends the sadness we feel at leaving these dear friends you have brought so very briefly into our lives. In Jesus' precious name I pray, amen."

"Amen," came the response from everyone present.

"May your God go with you," Anata said.

"And with you," I replied looking them each in the eyes. "And now, we are off!" I said, swinging my leg between the humps of my camel. "Zos, are you ready?"

"Ready Teacher!" he said as he leapt onto his camel. Acacio's groom appeared on a mule to guide us to the caravanserai. As our camels rose, Zos and I again said goodbye. Before disappearing out the arched entrance to the compound I turned around one last time. Acacio had his arm around Anata's shoulders. They were all waving goodbye.

"I will write from Ecbatana," I shouted as I ducked under the arch.

CHAPTER FIFTY-ONE

"The least initial deviation from the truth is multiplied later a thousandfold."
(Aristotle, *On the Heavens, Book l., Ch. 5,* ca 360)

Word had been sent ahead for a replacement to be waiting in Sippar. The Carpathian had remained in the sailboat till Kaleb and his party were on their way to the town. Then he snapped into action. He quickly paid a slave lounging on the pier to follow the group and return with news of where they were lodging. He could ill afford to be seen following them again. He was sure he had been spotted, and Kaleb was already suspicious. Kaleb had been quite the socialite on the little kalak. It appeared that he had made quite a lot of friends on board. Or maybe these were accomplices in his nefarious mission. Regardless, it would all be out of his hands shortly. And he would be only too happy to turn the reigns over to someone else. He was not designed for traveling. He was in pitiful shape. He had had continuous bouts of diarrhea on the boat and had lost a considerable amount of weight. He was nothing but skin and bones, not that he had much meat on them before. He had been eaten alive by mosquitoes on the boat. There was not a spot on his entire body free from the scars of his scratching.

The slave finally returned with the name of the inn where Kaleb was lodging. The hooded Carpathian paid off the skipper of the sailboat, purchased a donkey and made his way immediately into Sippar to meet his contact. His mission was almost at an end. Praise Pythagoras. He knew not how much more he could take.

CHAPTER FIFTY-TWO

Innocuous to the curious eye except for a Greek symbol for number meticulously carved into the adobe above a rough-hewn wooden door, the Pythagorean temple nestled anonymously on a narrow street in the center of Sippar. After reciting the universal password, a secret formula known to initiates all over the empire, and raising his sleeve to show the tattooed geometric design on the inside of his wrist, the Carpathian was swallowed into the smoky darkness of the interior. He was led through a series of doors past rooms veiled in shadow to a door sheathed in intricately hammered copper. At the center of the door, in the center of an elaborate pentagram was the symbol for Venus. Radiating from each point of the pentagram were shapes representing each number from one to ten along with esoteric formulas understood fully only perhaps by the mathematicus of this temple. Above the door was the motto, "Speak not in the face of the sun." The Carpathian took this to heart before shedding his shoes and entering with head bowed into the presence of the mathematicus of Sippar.

"Your assignment is complete," the mathematicus spoke from behind the curtain after an interminable wait. His image, cast quivering onto the opaque veil by the torches behind him, was seated. The spy held back a sob of relief. "It appears the pot has left an imprint on the ashes."

"I am not constructed to eat in a vehicle," the Carpathian murmured.

"Granted, it is ordained that we seek pleasure in deep communion with the Aumen, not in travel and adventures."

"Travel does not agree with me."

"Yet you have managed with much success. Your successor is better equipped for this next stage."

"I follow the dictum to 'quit not thy post without the overseer's order.'"

"You have done well."

"You are not only wise but compassionate."

"Cease to spill oil on the seat. Flattery is noxious to me. Give me your report. What do you know of the plans of this Ethiopian?"

"He is on his way to Ecbatana. He is posing as a scribe traveling to visit family. I have been unable to ascertain his plans beyond there. He writes in a journal, but in the interests of remaining anonymous and not alerting him to anything amiss, I have refrained from attempting to get at it."

"So he suspects nothing."

"Nothing," the spy said, glad that there was a curtain hiding his lying face from this holy man who would surely recognize his fraudulent answer instantly.

"Spend the night here, and in the morning, preparations will be made for your return home. Your services are no longer required for this matter." With that, the interview was over. He turned and was led out of the inner sanctum to a cold, dark room where he would spend this last night of his misadventure. Relieved, he lay back on the hard cot and closed his eyes.

PART NINE

BOUND FOR ECBATANA

Gregorian Calendar – April 20th, 162
Alexandrian Calendar – Paremoude 11th, Fourth Proyet
The Season of the Emergence
2nd year of Marcus Aurelius

"The moon has set, and the Pleiades; it is midnight, and time passes, and I sleep alone."
(Sappho, *Fragment 94,* ca 612 BC)

"… geographers, Sosius, crowd into the edges of their maps parts of the world which they do not know about, adding notes in the margin to the effect that beyond this lies nothing but sandy deserts full of wild beasts, and unapproachable bogs."
(Plutarch, *Lives, Aemilius Paulus, sec. 5,* ca 100)

CHAPTER FIFTY-THREE

Drifting in the weightless serenity that ensues upon the consummation of a series of difficult yet not displeasing events, I allowed my mind to float in a thousand different directions. Zos' camel was tied behind mine, and he was soundly asleep, exhausted from the events of the day. The bells tied to his saddle filled the ghostly air with their melancholy chimes. But for the thousand other camels and fellow travelers surrounding me in the dark, I would have been terrified rather than exhilarated at the enormity of the emptiness threatening to annihilate me, endless plains of cultivated fields and grazing land in every direction as far as my night eyes could discern, as I clung, precariously attached to my camel under the immense black void of the sky that I feared might swallow me up when I least expected it.

Zos and I fell easily back into the routine of breaking down and setting up camp, taking time in the cool of the morning for exercise, since now we traveled by night rather than by day as summer was approaching and day travel was becoming unbearable. Three days into the journey, the caravan came upon a small enclave in the middle of the wilderness designed specifically for entertaining passing caravans. Though we had the option of staying in a small dwelling for the night, we opted to save the money and stay in our tent. We did however give our camels a hearty meal and plenty of water although they literally could have gone several more days without water and weeks with no food. It never hurt to fill them up when the opportunity arose.

Through word of mouth, I steadily established a pretty consistent business as a scribe, earning not a little money that I hid away with my closely guarded golden girdle and the denarii I had changed out an aureus for with Anata. My goal of arriving home with the girdle virtually intact, earning my keep as I traveled seemed achievable so far.

Over the next two days, the terrain began to subtly change from flat to rolling to low mountains. Travel became slower and more tedious. Ahead were the Zagros Mountains separating us from our destination. Somewhere in the middle of the range lay the city of Ilam where we planned to stop again for refreshment. Six days into our journey the mountains now rose directly in front of us. We picked up and followed a river formed from the melting snows to the north, keeping it to our left between increasingly tall mountain faces on each side of us. Nevertheless, there was still room in this narrow green valley for several rows of camels to ride abreast. As the river was always to our left, we had no shortage of water. The air was cooler here and more humid causing the chill to pass through our two-layered capes, the thinner ones we had brought from Alexandria and the heavier, soft woolen ones Marius had gifted us in Palmyra. During the night we passed over the now very shallow river on our left into an open valley, the water wearing its stones like gems in a garment, sparkling in the moonlight. The ground was rocky, and dark hills rose on every side. The night was brisk, and this morning, we could see our breath as we set up camp. Like ice in the hot sun however, the cold melted rapidly once the sun invaded the valley. The landscape was quite spectacular. Another larger, more turbulent river lay directly in front of us, the river we would follow to Ilam we were told. It descended from the north and turned sharply east where we had set up camp. Beyond the rocky path we were following, verdant green grass like a sea of emeralds set in gold, lost itself in the rolling hills and high peaks toward the east, the direction we were headed. We were informed that we would pass the night in this same place and set out before sunrise the next morning. The trek tomorrow was the most difficult before reaching Ilam in the evening, and it was better to travel by daylight. I hired a guard to keep watch over our campsite, and Zos and I set out to explore the area. Amun, Zos' friend and servant to Mihret's entourage who had surprisingly ended up in the same caravan with us, joined us as did Omanand, an Indian man my age who had been camping next to mine and Zos' tent.

We decided to tackle the more imposing cliff to the east since that was the direction we were heading anyway. Perhaps we could espy what lay in store for us the next day. Our ascent was pleasant at first, a gentle rise to the spine of a ridge. We passed through a grove of pistachio trees where we sat and caught our breath. Further on, there were no more trees, and the higher we got, the rockier and steeper the climb became. Finally we reached the peak from where we had an uninterrupted view of the caravan far below. To the east, the mountains seemed to go on forever, peak after peak, some still capped in snow.

"That's going to be rough going tomorrow," Omanand said. Zos and Amun set off to explore.

"Stay close Zos," I shouted. "And stay away from the edge. So are you headed home?" I asked, turning my attention to Omanand.

"Home... that's an exotic word," he said. "I no longer am sure where home is. I have been on the move for so long, I feel at home really only when I am moving."

"Curious," I said. "Is that a good thing?"

"Only if I never want to settle," he replied, a hint of nostalgia in his voice.

"And do you?" I asked.

"I don't know anymore. I began this life intending to save my money, get a wife, settle down and have a family. But I've been unable to stop. Every time I tell myself this is my last trip, within a month or two I can't stand it anymore and find myself on the road again."

Looking down at the caravan, I paused, wondering what that would feel like, being incapable of staying in one place. "I have yet to come to that," I said, sounding more confident than I felt. "It is not that I miss home terribly. I am too fascinated with the journey I am on, too busy assimilating the changes that come with each day to give it much thought, but that does not mean I would not relish being back."

"I believe you have identified the allure of the road. Every day brings unexpected novelties. The mind and body are occupied with constant changes, new things, new places, new people. When I find myself in the same place after two or three months, the tedium begins to wear on me, and a fever begins to burn in my heart, calling me back to the uncertainty of the journey, the impossibility of routine."

"You make it sound so appealing. I must admit, I have enjoyed it so far, but I do miss routine, waking up in the same place every morning, eating at the same time every day, traveling the same path in the morning and the evening." I was struck by a fear that I had lost the capability of quotidian life. That, like Omanand, I would be overtaken by a fever for travel.

"Yes, appealing. It is appealing. The question is, which life is the more beneficial in the end? What will I have to show for my life when it is at its end?"

"There are many possible paths in one lifetime. It is impossible to know where our decisions will lead us or which decisions will take us to the most propitious end."

"So what then, we just take it a day at a time?"

"That is the only way. Who can plan with certainty for tomorrow? Plans are important. One must have direction, purpose, objectives, but our existence is as ephemeral and tenuous as a vapor. We travel as best we can the path we find before us."

"Speaking of the path before us, I think the time has come to begin the trek back before nightfall. Darkness falls swiftly in the valley." Zos and Amun were sitting involved in an apparently serious conversation further along the peak, swinging their legs heedlessly over a precipice.

"We are going Zos!" I called. He and Amun rose and joined us as we made our descent. We walked in silence, chewing on our thoughts.

CHAPTER FIFTY-FOUR

Normally I could lie awake for some time and mull over the events of my day before drifting into unconsciousness, but this night sleep caught me unawares. The last thing I remembered was the sound of the river nearby and the low snoring of our camels. The blast of the horn announcing the imminent departure of the caravan wrenched me out of a dream, the details of which vanished as soon as my eyes were open. All that remained was a vague sense of something pending which I could not shake even after dismantling the tent and loading our camels. Zos and I were mounted and ready to go when the second salvo echoed throughout the valley. The sky was still dark and dusted with a million stars. Only the absence of their delicate glow defined the silhouette of the surrounding mountains. How we were to see where we were going was anybody's guess. I could hardly see my hand in front of my face, and vainly hoped, as we sat waiting to move, that we had left nothing behind in the pitch dark.

By the time the middle of the caravan, where we were stationed, even began to move forward, however, the sky had lightened imperceptibly. I could now make out faint shadows and the vague shapes of other people and camels close by me. I pulled my cape more closely around me and turned to make sure Zos' camel was still tied to mine. I did not see him on his camel.

"Zos!" I called. He sprang up in his saddle.

"Yes Teacher?"

"What are you doing?" I asked laughing.

"Star gazing Teacher. Mahsa taught me the names of some of the constellations. I was seeing if I could remember their names."

"Carry on Zos. When I failed to see you, I thought you had fallen off your camel."

Before the sun rose above the eastern peaks, the river had made a sharp turn due east and into a narrow valley. The path had narrowed considerably, and forced us to line up single-file to keep from pushing each other into the rushing river which boiled threateningly on our left. The deafening reverberations drowned all other sound as they climbed to the summits of the soaring peaks on each side of us which at times completely blocked all light, plunging the caravan into a foamy, humid dusk. The magnificence of the setting soon began to wear thin, winding left and right, continually dismounting the camels to lead them along the precarious pathless edge of the raging river. Progress was gradual, deliberate and infuriatingly slow, measured in digits rather than feet. When the sun was almost directly overhead I told Zos to break out from his bag what he had prepared for us. Stopping for a mid-day meal was not part of the equation. The goal was to reach Ilam before dark. These mountains were too inhospitable and dangerous a place to pass the night. Besides, Omanand told me that we would remain in this single-file formation till the mountains opened up at the entrance to the city, so there was nowhere to even set up camp.

We had turned so many times that I no longer knew which direction we were going, and the position of the sun directly overhead belied judgment. Void now of vegetation, the mountains on both sides were stark white. These were the salt domes I had been told about, immense chalky peaks. Once these were behind us, the path widened enough to allow for two camels to ride abreast. Omanand appeared alongside me. The mountains still rose majestically on both sides of us but sloping rather than sheer-sided like earlier in the day.

"We're not far now," Omanand said.

"I would hope not," I said, noticing that the sun was already close to disappearing behind the peaks we had just crossed through. "Tell me about India. I have read some accounts of travelers there, but really know very little. Many of the stories are quite fantastic and hard to believe."

"Such as…"

And until the mountains opened into the broad valley of Ilam, I learned enough about India to make me want to travel there someday.

CHAPTER FIFTY-FIVE

Exhausted from a full day of travel, the caravan was given a reprieve of two days in the city of Ilam before continuing. As soon as I heard the crier announce the pause in the city, I secured a guard for our camels with their loads, and Zos and I proceeded into the center of town with our overnight bags slung across our shoulders. Omanand gave me directions to the most exclusive inn in the city, and we made our way directly to it. I would break a gold coin if need be. I was ready for solid walls around me and a good bath. Turning a corner and spotting the inn, I stopped in my tracks. Mihret and her party were just ahead of us, causing quite a commotion between the servants, slaves, donkeys and Mihret's small entourage. Fortune or providence. Since I did not believe in luck, it must be providence. I told Zos to run ahead and greet his friend Amun and find out if Mihret's party was spending the night there. Zos winked at me before running to join the bustle of the Egyptian party.

CHAPTER FIFTY-SIX

"And we played our last game of Senet the night before our departure," I said in closing, completing the story of our journey down the Euphrates and our meeting of the couple from Ctesiphon. "Forgive me; I am sure I bore you with the details of my journey. Tell me, how did you manage to end up on the same caravan as I? You must not have stayed very long in Damascus."

"I completed my business there more quickly than I had anticipated," Mihret said, her voice paradoxically clear through the veil entirely covering her face. She wore a wide-brimmed hat, from the entire circumference of which hung a thin silky gauze. This time I was prevented from admiring her eyes, leaving only her voice which made our common language of Ge'ez turn to pure poetry. I thought of Silara. Did her voice sound like music? I had never thought of her in that regard. Now I wished I could hear her, that she was here talking to me instead of Mihret.

"Truly, scribe Kaleb, what are you doing so far from home?" I sat still as a stone, unwilling to lie to her, but knowing I could not divulge the truth, even to her. She lifted the goblet of wine with delicate grace. I watched as she raised the veil to drink and for an instant saw her lips, full and red from the wine. "Don't tell me then if it's such an arch secret. I respect your silence."

"I am sorry Madam. I have no desire to lie to you, so I am left silent, but I suspect I am not the only one with secrets."

Her laughter bound me even more deeply under her spell. "Don't call me Madam. I am Mihret, fellow Ethiopian, fellow traveler, alone in the world like you." The final phrase she said in a whisper, as if reiterating a secret we held in common.

"I am not entirely alone," I said naively. "I have Zos, and you are constantly surrounded by members of your party."

"Lonely then," she sighed, her sudden weariness almost tangible. "There are times, since my husband died, that I feel desperately alone. It is a new feeling, a depth of loneliness I did not know before marriage."

"Have you discovered a cure for this loneliness?" I asked, feeling a bit out of my depth, surprised at the intimate turn the conversation had taken, inexplicably afraid of her answer.

I could feel her eyes on mine, penetrating the filmy veil. A moment passed in silence. "Your eyes are honest, Kaleb of Adulis. They almost sparkle with transparency."

"You enjoy an unfair advantage. I only retain the memory of your eyes from our meeting before Damascus." She brought her hands to her veil, but before she could lift it, Sekhet appeared at the table, immaculate in her white robe and turban. I became aware once again of the dinginess of my cloak and the dusty pallor of my skin. "Forgive me for my appearance," I said. "The journey has not been as kind to me as to your party."

"So it's the journey's fault is it?" Sekhet looked me over dismissively before glancing disinterestedly towards where Amun and Zos sat talking.

"Sekhet, be kind," Mihret chided. "Kaleb, I see Sekhet has taken a liking to you."

"Please, Mistress, forgive me for saying so, but perhaps you need to rest." Sekhet was visibly put off by Mihret's comment.

I laughed. "Well, I must admit, I find many admirable qualities in our friend Sekhet as well."

"Please don't assume a mutuality of sentiment," Sekhet replied offhandedly.

"Sekhet, Kaleb will think you inconsiderate," Mihret said.

"You would be surprised Mistress by how considerate I am actually being. More tea?" she said as she stood.

"None for me Sekhet, but thank you for asking," I replied. She rolled her eyes and left the table.

"Please forgive her. She is quite protective of me and sometimes oversteps her bounds, but she has been looking after me since I was a child."

"I admire that she takes her responsibility so seriously," I said. "And I believe she is right. We should all take some rest. It has been a very long day."

"Very long indeed," Mihret said, rising to leave. "I pray we meet again soon Kaleb." Her entire party rose to see her go as Sekhet led her out of the dining room. Zos came over to join me.

"Tired Zos?"

"I can hardly keep my eyes open Teacher."

"Let us call it a day," I said rising to leave as well, simultaneously disappointed and relieved that Mihret's eyes had remained hidden behind her veil.

CHAPTER FIFTY-SEVEN

We grew quite accustomed to following treacherous, narrow paths alongside rivers between mountains since that is about all we did for the next two weeks, apart from stopping occasionally, every few days, in a mountain enclave to refresh the camels, restock our supplies of food and move on. Travel again took place in the daytime, and Omanand was delighted with our parasols, bemoaning the fact that he had not considered a similar solution since he was Indian after all. We occasionally crossed paths with shepherds grazing their flocks or small parties of merchants traveling the way we had come. When these small caravans passed, there was no shortage of business for me as many would want to compose quick letters home or record the details of our progress forward. After twenty days on the road, we ran into a group of merchants who said we were less than two day's journey from Ecbatana. I could feel the ripple of expectation vibrate through the entire caravan. A rumor began to circulate that we would stop and rest for dinner and then continue through the night in order to arrive in Ecbatana in the morning. At this point, I could sleep standing up if need be, so I did not care one way or the other. I could see Zos was excited. This is what we had been aiming at for the past two and a half months. We had finally made it; well, almost...

PART TEN

ECBATANA

Gregorian Calendar – May 11th, 162
Alexandrian Calendar – Pashons 2nd, First Shomu
The Season of Harvesting
2nd year of Marcus Aurelius

"We who of old left the booming surge of the Aegean lie here in the mid-plain of Ecbatana: farewell, renowned Eretria once our country; farewell, Athens nigh to Euboea; farewell, dear sea."
(Plato, *The Greek Anthology*, III, 10, ca 400 BC)

CHAPTER FIFTY-EIGHT

I jerked awake. Zos was on his camel behind me, asleep, his little head bobbing from side to side. In the cerulean glow of the moon, the dark silhouettes of turbaned men and veiled women on camels extended forever on every side against the black, star-studded sky freed from the claustrophobic mountains that had engulfed us for the past three weeks. The air smelled of sweat, dust and camel dung. A ghostly pilgrimage to the gates of Hades. Only it was not Hades straight ahead that rose above the horizon of undulating turbaned heads. It was the snowy peaks and cliffs of Ecbatana. We were fewer than twenty stadion away. I began to lay out in my mind plans for our arrival, but the swaying of the camel drugged me, not unwillingly, back to oblivion.

Suddenly aware, I opened my eyes. The crescent moon hung low on the western horizon behind the caravan. Ahead, in the east, the turquoise sky silhouetted the low mountains far in the distance. Already along the front lines of the caravan, hundreds of tents had begun to rise off the barren ground, shelter against the coming heat. As effective as a knock on the head was the stopping of the swaying motion of the camel on which I was seated. We were always guaranteed to awaken as soon as our camels stopped. We had been on our camels almost non-stop for a full day and night. I could hardly move my legs.

Tents, enormous and tiny and every size between were being set up from the point where the caravan had stopped, like a chain reaction of epic proportion. Fires like stars were popping up all across the plain from the outer rim inward. Morning smells of food cooking, bread baking and camel dung hung heavy in the air. The night breezes were gone. From a particularly large tent on the right I got a whiff of frankincense, probably to keep away the mosquitoes, swarms of which had been attacking early in the morning and at dusk, most likely the fault of the nearness of the Caspian Sea. But Zos and I did not stop to set up camp this morning. We were here, finally here. I wanted to gain entry to the city and settle in immediately. I had no desire to spend another night in a tent if I could help it. We continued weaving our way forward to the outskirts of the city, still some distance from the walled enclosure, to an area which was reserved for caravans, specially set up to receive, house and dispatch of large groups like the one with whom we were arriving.

I made sure the camels were well quartered and would be taken care of until we were ready to go. We rented a mule and piled the belongings we would need on it before heading towards the massive gates of the imposing walled city. The rolling hills of Ecbatana. The fields were full of workers plowing, digging and planting. At last, civilization after the small towns and villages of the mountains. The noise was deafening, like nothing else in the world. The cacophony of a caravan depot. The crush of people scurrying here and there and everywhere. It was almost impossible to make headway while at the same time making sure Zos was not carried away by an opposing current. I had tied him to me, our waists connected by Fang's lead rope. Our robes were drenched in sweat by the time we put some space between ourselves and the controlled chaos of the caravanserai. The sun was well overhead, and there were few trees to shade the way this distance from the gates of the city. The only thing on my mind was a clean room and a bath. I found it difficult to even engage in conversation with Zos, who was staring wide-eyed and open-mouthed at the ever more towering walls ahead. So far in our travels, we had not come across anything as spectacular. The rise of the plain combined with the steepness of the walls lent them an even more imposing appearance. With the snow-capped mountain peaks forming a backdrop to the south, there were few sights more awe-inspiring. "Do you see the white peaks there in the distance Zos?"

No response. I looked down to make sure he was still tied securely to me. He was so engrossed in taking everything in that he had not even heard me. I decided to leave him to his reverie for now.

As we approached the huge arched gate, I thought briefly of the enigmatic Mihret. We had spoken only twice now since that first meeting, though Zos had continued his friendship with Amun. She had invited me to look her up once we were installed in the city. Her contacts here could prove an invaluable resource for me. The crowds had thinned considerably, so I moved closer to the side of the now paved highway leading into the gate, pulling Zos with me. He held tightly to the mule as I untied the rope and detached ourselves from each other. "Stay close now. And keep an eye on the mule. See that no one helps themselves to anything hanging on his back."

The temperature dropped markedly just inside the massive arched gateway. It was almost two paces deep and wide enough for Zos and I to enter with a donkey by our side while a high-turbaned man with a beard to his knees and two camels exited and several guards milled around, checking the comers and goers. I was approached by a smartly dressed guard who demanded my business in the city. Speaking Pahlavi, the language he had addressed me in, I replied, "I am Kaleb, a scribe from Adulis, citizen of Rome, here to visit relatives in the city. And this is my servant, Zoskalis, also of Adulis." The guard, noticeably impressed that I spoke his language, directed us to the scribe at the other side of the entrance where we had to register. The scribe took an undue interest in my name and insisted on knowing where I planned to lodge. His curiosity in who I was and where I was staying alerted my suspicions, so I named a different lodging house that I knew was not too far from where I truly intended to go.

"I could direct one of these lads," he waved his hand at the cluster of brown-skinned boys with close shaven heads lounging by the wall, "to guide you there." My face must have registered surprise at this unexpected and incongruous generosity. "A small kindness to a fellow scribe. I seldom register someone with your obvious education." Avoiding explanations of how I already knew my way around this city I had never visited, I accepted his offer. "Excellent," he said as he waved one of the boys over telling him where to deposit us. Once registered I was directed to the next post where I had to pay the entrance tax. Surprisingly, there were no lines. It was all handled quite efficaciously. Ecbatana was a teeming city, full of people from everywhere in the world. Standing in the gate, I could hear languages of the far East that I could not identify, Greek, Latin, Punic, Aramaic and of course Pahlavi. There were men in robes of every cut and color, women veiled and unveiled, with long braided hair or hair piled on their heads or heads hidden in turbans. Even Alexandria could not boast such a cosmopolitan atmosphere. The ancient capital of the Median Empire, it now was a favorite summer resort for Volgases IV, King of Parthia who was currently on the western edge of his domain, preparing for the coming conflict with Rome. Perhaps he thought he could repeat the victories of his ancestor Mithridates, who gave the Romans quite a run for their money and not meet the same fate.

Zos and I moved on, out of the shaded gate and back into the blazing sun with our guide leading us to our faux destination. It was the time of day that the sun threw no shadows. We walked between buildings two and three stories tall on paved streets swept clean, but the buildings provided no shade. The sweat that had dried my robe to a rough salty sheet proceeded to dampen it again. The streets were wide enough for pedestrians as well as horses, palanquins and of course, our mule. Before leaving Alexandria, I had familiarized myself with a map of the city, drawn by pilgrims who had visited before me. Even inns had been marked and rated. I had chosen four or five since one never knew if what had been would still be. With all the turmoil and transience in these parts, businesses often came and went. I paid close attention to our route, careful to note where we might need to backtrack to the place I actually wanted to stay.

In short order we were deposited in front of a humble two-storied dwelling facing a rather heavily trafficked street. "This is it!" our young guide exclaimed.

"Thank you. You can go now," I said as I slipped a coin into his hand. He hesitated. "What are you waiting for?"

"You don't need any help unloading your things?"

"No, thank you. You have been more than enough help." I waited for him to leave.

"Why are we waiting for him to leave?" Zos asked me in Ge'ez.

"This is not where I want to stay," I responded, "but I did not want the guard at the gate to know our address."

"Why not?" Zos asked.

"The fewer people that know how to find us, the better." I said. The young boy stood meanwhile watching Zos and me talk. "What are you waiting for?" I asked him beginning to get annoyed.

"My master, the scribe at the gate, instructed me to make sure you were settled comfortably before leaving."

"Tell your master that we were settled in very nicely," I said, passing him another coin. "Now off with you." He took the coin and raced back the way he had come. Zos and I stood for a moment longer to make sure we were no longer being observed. I continued in the direction we had been going after a short wait. Zos knew, after all these months, that when it came to finding the spot I wanted in a strange city, I somehow understood where I was going, although my sense of direction on other occasions was pitiful. He had stopped questioning me in Palmyra. Now he followed me with a quiet confidence.

According to the map in my head, we were to stay close to the wall as it wound to the left. The streets were circuitous, and so many branched off of what seemed to be the main thoroughfare that I felt a growing sense of bewilderment, especially as the side streets were narrower and prevented a view of the wall, my landmark. At an intersection, a row of lower buildings to the left, tucked against the wall allowed me a sigh of relief although I allowed Zos no sign that I had ever doubted, not that he would have noticed. He was still entranced with the architecture of the place, the tall buildings, the sloping roofs, the colored brick. And the never-ending procession of colorful people. At once I recognized where I was. There was a rectangular sign above a three storied brick building with balconies on each floor. Seres Inn. This was one of the most highly rated inns of Ecbatana, not extravagantly expensive, but luxurious all the same. Besides, between my frugality on the trip and how soundly my business as a scribe had prospered, I had saved quite enough to afford this place and perhaps have no need to dip into the still practically intact auriferous girdle or the denarii I had exchanged for in Ctesiphon.

At the door to the inn, a young boy took Zos and led him with the mule around the side of the building to help Zos unload the mule and bring our things to our room. I stepped inside, out of the relentless sun, into a portico surrounding a courtyard shaded with cedar trees in the center of which whispered a blue-brick tiled fountain. The floor of the courtyard was inlaid with a red and blue mosaic of oriental design. A fine-featured woman in her fifties, dressed in a black silk caftan approached me; her thick straight black hair hanging almost to her feet was pulled together at the neckline by a scarlet cord. "Peace," I said in Pahlavi.

"Peace," the woman replied in Greek. "I'm sorry, I don't speak Pahlavi," she apologized, surprised at the native language coming from a black man.

"Not to worry," I responded in Greek. "I am just trying it out to see how it suits me. After all, what better place to practice than in the heart of the country. I am looking for a room, for two, me and my young servant. And I will most assuredly avail myself of your baths. Your reputation reaches to the ends of the earth, literally."

"You are too kind. And the gods smile on you as we are currently only at half capacity. The spring festival has just ended and the city is practically empty. I will give you our best room."

After all the polite courtesies had been exchanged and the price for the room was agreed upon, she led me up a narrow flight of stairs to the top floor. The staircase was lit by tiny windows along the way. Even so, it was disconcertingly dim after the blinding light outside. Smells of recently scrubbed wet tile and dry plaster, not unpleasant, hung in the still air. The stairs ended at a long hall, dimmer than the stairs, with a rippling, slightly uneven floor of earthen tile. I followed to the end of the hall to a high arched door. The woman inserted a giant key and smoothly turned it to reveal a spacious room with large windows on two sides, one looking out towards the city gate and the other towards the city center. Light gauzy curtains rustled languidly in the slight breeze that fortunately reached higher than street level where the air was as stagnant as inside a closed room. A huge bed dominated the center of the room, four stately posts hung with a transparent blue curtain which I assumed was to keep out the mosquitoes.

"The baths are located on the first floor where we met, on the opposite side of the courtyard," she smiled. "I'll make sure your things are promptly brought up. I'm sure you'll be comfortable here."

"I could not agree with you more. It has been many nights since I slept in an actual bed. Please leave the door open. I will wait here for my servant boy and my things."

"As you wish," she said as she exited the room. I turned again to admire how tastefully yet comfortably the room was appointed.

The views were fantastic, and I relished the thought of watching the city by night from the privacy of my balcony. I looked around for where Zos could most comfortably install himself. There was a long bench built into an alcove on the wall without a window. That would suit him perfectly. It was covered in cushions fit for a king. He would love it. As I stood looking out over the city, Zos and the stable boy arrived panting, lugging the luggage on their backs. Another two boys had been recruited to bring it all up the steep flight of stairs.

"Just lay it all over there in the corner," I pointed. "We will organize later." I put a one *as* coin in each of the boys' hands, including Zos', a generous tip that would guarantee future favors if need be. I put an extra *as* in the stable boy's hand, asking that he return the mule to the caravanserai giving him instructions as to whom it belonged. The stable boy and the two helpers left with huge smiles on their faces.

"Thank you Teacher. You are very generous."

"Especially to the well-deserving Zos. Now let us organize ourselves before hitting the baths." I pointed out to him where he would sleep. He was ecstatic with the room and his bed. He kept running from window to window, exclaiming at the views, at the people on the street, at the huge bed where I would be sleeping, at the furniture, basically, at everything. "Calm down Zos. We need to unpack."

With everything in its place and a clean set of clothes laid out on the bed for after the bath, we descended with a basket containing everything necessary to scrub off the dust, sweat and grime of seventeen days. The bath was a paradise. Gleaming pools of cold and hot water, a steam room with hot coals ready to be primed, showers with running water to rinse between baths, soap to scrub off every last speck of dirt. And finally, before drying off, we rubbed oil into our dry Ethiopian skin and close cropped hair. Heaven. We returned to the rooms with a new layer of skin just trying itself out, tender, smooth and brilliantly black. Once dressed, I piled everything that could be washed into a heap by the door of the room. I had Zos do the same. "I am going to ask that everything be cleaned, even what we have not used. It is all covered in the dust and dirt of the trip, and it smells like camel dung. Now, let us pay a visit to an old friend of mine."

CHAPTER FIFTY-NINE

"Kaleb! Praise God! When did you arrive?" I was wrapped in a hug that nearly broke my ribs. Yonas was a huge man, also Ethiopian and Christian like me. We had met when my family emigrated from Ethiopia. In fact, it was my father who secured Yonas' father a job at the Library of Alexandria, and Yonas and I were among my father's first students at the Library. They were a family of translators. Yonas' father was in charge of the translation of Ethiopian literature into Greek at the library. And they loved books. I allowed my eyes to roam. Two walls were floor to ceiling books, one wall exclusively dedicated to scrolls. The floor was spotless, but dust and cobwebs had overtaken the nether regions around the top shelves of books and the ceiling. The brilliant sun shone into the shop which fronted a large plaza in the center of the city. Directly across, on the other side of the plaza, stood the magnificent royal palace, nearly seven stadia in circumference, built of precious woods sheathed in plates of gold and silver. To the right of it was a huge slant-roofed structure, four stories tall with lapis covered columns forming a porch that ran the entire length of the building. The columns against the green brick and the blue sky were spectacular. "What a view Yonas. I see you have done well for yourself. I just arrived this morning."

"You look no worse for the wear. Traveling seems to suit you well." He grabbed my hands, lifted them up with his and said, "Let us give thanks to the beneficent and merciful God, the Father of our Lord, God and Savior, Jesus Christ, for He has covered us, helped us, guarded us, accepted us unto Him, spared us, supported us, and brought us to this place. Let us also ask Him, the Lord our God, the Almighty, to guard us in all peace this holy day and all the days of our lives."

"Amen! What suits me is a clean room and a long bath. I feel like a new person." I stepped back to take in this huge old friend. His frame rivaled the columns across the plaza. And his blue black skin shone like onyx. As he smiled, his brilliant white teeth contrasted with the bloodshot eyes. "You spend too much time in your books Yonas."

"Not as much as I would like Kaleb. With a wife and three children now, I have less time than I did in the past. Sit down, sit down. You have probably been on your feet all day." Yonas motioned me to take a seat on one of the low cushioned stools by the door. Zos stood behind me, watching this interaction. From his stool Yonas called behind him. A young boy, about the same age as Zos, burst through the door in the back. "Go fetch some tea for our guest, and take this young boy with you and get him something to drink."

"Zos," I said, "his name is Zos. He is the son of the servants of my parents, and has come to help me on my trip."

"Zos then; take Zos with you." The young boy eyed Zos up and down as Zos did the same. Then he took his hand and led him through the narrow door at the back of the shop. Once the boys had gone, Yonas addressed me in a quieter voice, "so what brings you here, so far away from the comforts of home?"

"I have a new commission," I said quietly. "Purportedly, I am a scribe from Adulis visiting family here in Ecbatana. See if you can guess what my latest quest is."

"Ah, the life of a spy, undercover, traveling the world. How exciting. What a life! So, a new quest, eh? Well, let me see. I have a bit of an advantage you see, since I know which department you work for in the Library." Yonas' son brought out a tray of tea and deposited it on the table between us. I looked at the entrance and saw Zos. He hurriedly waved the other boy back and both disappeared behind the curtain. "And I know your specialty. And here you are in Ecbatana, seat of the Avesta. Hmmm. Let me see…" He mockingly put a finger to his lips.

"Alright, alright. I see that was too easy a riddle. So what can you tell me? You are of course my number one contact here in the city. And your maps of the city proved invaluable for finding the perfect place to install myself while here."

"So you are at the Seres Inn? You know, you are more than welcome to stay here. We have plenty of room, and you would be spared the vexation of roaming around looking for places to eat."

"You know me. If possible, I prefer to have my own place. You are too kind to offer though. Zos might find it more pleasant to stay here where he has someone his age though. It seems he has already made a friend in your son. I really will have no need of him while I am here. In fact, he might get in the way."

"Your wish is my command."

"I have been teaching him to read and write Greek, to speak Aramaic, and we have covered the rudiments of mathematics."

146

"Leave it to me. I will tell my son to only speak to him in Aramaic, and he can sit in on the lessons with my son. I employ a teacher who is working with Alem on Greek as well."

"It is settled then. How wonderful to have friends that are as generous as you Yonas."

"You only need ask. Besides, I know you would do the same for me. So, back to being your contact. What do you need?"

"Well, what can you tell me?" I took a sip of tea. It was stuffed with mint leaves and had a faint hint of cinnamon. "Are the manuscripts I am looking for accessible? And if so, with whom should I speak?"

"You are actually in luck. Serendipitously, King Vologases IV is currently on the same quest as you. He has issued an edict for any and all copies of the Avesta to be taken to Rhagae to be collated and organized into one codified work. There are any number of loose manuscripts claiming to be writings of the Avesta floating around. And the Zarathustrans are none too pleased with the idea of their manuscripts being read, studied, critiqued and possibly even translated for all eyes to see. There are many secret texts that they will go to great lengths to keep from being vulgarly popularized."

"And where is King Vologases now?"

Yonas raised his eyebrows at this question. "You are not seriously considering talking directly to him are you? He is not known for his benevolence."

"Perhaps I could get assigned to be one of the collators, legitimize my search. I could help with the collection and make a copy to take to Alexandria." My thoughts began to swirl with the possibilities, of taking a legitimate copy of the entire Avesta back with me. It would be the greatest achievement since the translation of the Septuagint into Greek. And to think that my name would be attached to that.

"Slow down Kaleb. Exactly how do you propose to gain an introduction to the king? You cannot just show up at his palace and say 'Hey, I don't have an appointment, but I need to talk to His Majesty Vologases.'"

The image of Mihret popped into my head. "I have it! I met a woman on the caravan"

"Of course you did. I would have expected nothing less. Yet one more point on which to envy you."

"Her name is Mihret, and she is the widow of the late secretary to the governor of the Province of Egypt. She has invited me to look her up while I am here. I am sure that God in his providence put her in my path."

"Or you in hers," Yonas murmured. "Did she give you any indication of where to find her?"

"Are you joking? Her maid, or perhaps I should say, her bodyguard, had lips sealed as tight as the Caspian Gates. But it should not be hard to find her. How big is Ecbatana anyway?"

"Seriously? This is one of the biggest cities in the world. It is 250 stadia in circumference with a population of almost half a million. And you think to find her just like that?" He snapped his fingers. The sun on my feet and face soothed the excitement building inside me.

"I am sure she is inside the walls. That is less ground to cover. And she is fabulously wealthy and beautiful, and Ethiopian. She cannot be that hard to find. I am certain you know who to ask. Your resources know no bounds."

"You place quite a lot of faith in my abilities Kaleb. I know you have heard it many times before, but I will repeat it for all those who care about you back home. Use caution. I will see what I can dig up." My third cup of tea was now tepid, and I was getting hungry.

"Zos!" I called out. Zos and his new friend, Yonas' son, came running out breathless. "Zos, come here; we need to talk." Zos came over, eyes downcast, sure that I was getting ready to reprimand him for something. I walked out into the street with him while Yonas busied himself with straightening books on their shelves, and his son cleared away the tea. I explained Yonas' proposal and left it up to Zos to decide. "You know where I am, and you are always welcome to come back there anytime. I assume however that you will be more comfortable and have more fun here with Yonas and his family. What do you say?"

The look on Zos' face was pure relief. "I will obey Yonas as if he were you Teacher."

"You had best. I gave him a very high account of your character. Do not disappoint me. So, off with you. I will have your things sent round as soon as I am back at the inn." We walked back in, Zos bowing in front of Yonas and thanking him before disappearing behind the curtain. "It is settled then. And do not hesitate to send Zos back if there is any trouble."

"Go on and find your mystery lady," Yonas laughed. "Come back tomorrow and let us see what I have been able to discover. Whoever finds her first wins."

"And what is the prize?"

"Let us say, a night in the inn at the top of the Zagros, for the whole family."

"You come off the winner no matter how that turns out," I laughed. "But you are on anyway."

"I almost forgot. I have a stack of correspondence for you from Alexandria. Give me a moment, and I will bring it out to you."

I waited, keeping the mounting excitement at bay. News from home. This was not entirely unexpected, but a *stack*? "Here it is," Yonas handed me a bundle of letters bound with a cord. "There are several that smell of perfume. Is there something you have not told me?"

"We still have much catching up to do. I will save that story for next time." I took the bundle under my arm, resisting the urge to tear into the letters immediately.

From Yonas' shop, I walked back to my inn, ate in the lovely dining area and retired to my room for a nap. I was exhausted from the exertions of the day. Although I wanted nothing more than to begin reading the letters, I needed to sleep. Almost three weeks of caravan travel had made me lazy, and today I had not stopped moving since I got off my camel. As I lay down on the bed, a light breeze played on the gauzy curtains covering the open windows and caressed my face. I thanked God again for His goodness and providence and good friends like Yonas.

CHAPTER SIXTY

The boy stood transfixed by the scar-faced man staring at him from the partially opened door. "Speak!" he barked, making the boy jump.

"The Alvand Inn," he managed to stammer. The door slammed shut, and he stood frozen for another instant before turning to run down the stairs and into the safety of daylight.

CHAPTER SIXTY-ONE

The king was not due in Ecbatana for another two months. Although spring was well under way, the air was still quite chilly, especially in the evenings. There was still a thick cap of snow on the mountains to the south reflecting the moonlight. I pondered these facts as I sat in front of my balcony at a low desk, looking out over the city center. I had pulled the curtains back for an unobstructed view. Lights glittered as far as the eye could see in every direction. This was in fact an enormous city. The streets were lively with movement. And somewhere amongst all those twinkling lights was a beautiful star named Mihret. And I would find her. I knew I would. I closed the windows, shutting out the lights and sounds of the city and the cold chill of the night, started a fire in the small chimney, lit the candle on the desk and unrolled my journal. It took more time than normal to document the events of this long day. I took perverse pleasure in exerting the willpower necessary to not rip open a letter from the still-bound package by my bed, to handle business before pleasure, an act which made the pleasure, once enjoyed, more acute. Once done, however, I rose quickly, cut the cord with my knife and spread the letters out on my bed. Which one should I read first? The majority I deduced were from Silara, the ones that smelled of perfume. I could not imagine who else would sprinkle perfume on a letter to me. There was one from my father and two from Ptolemaios. Several of the letters were from friends. I could not decide where to start. I did not want to read them all at once. I would prolong the pleasure of the news, reading no more than a couple a day. Business first. I took the two from Ptolemaios and went back to my desk. I broke the seal on the first letter and unrolled it. It began in simple hieroglyphics. He must have chosen that to foil any attempt to read it in the event it fell into the wrong hands. True to form, he wasted no time on formalities but cut directly to the chase.

Sikarbaal informed me that you made it safely to Tyre. I imagine by this time you are nearing Damascus. I had expected some type of communication from you before now, but since I have received none, I must stress that I expect a thorough accounting once you return of all you have seen and done. You are missed here at the Library.

I am concerned about word of war against Parthia. News has arrived that Rome is gathering an army in Asia in preparation to move against the Parthian capital on the Euphrates. You must take care to avoid this conflict. Stay informed of events, and if need be, come home by another route.

The letter continued in Greek, recounting recent events at the library and the recent literary conquests, the new additions to the vast collection that daily grew larger. The second letter was much the same, written when I was still in Ctesiphon. I thought with regret that I did not send him a letter from there, but as I had nothing to report, I had not. I would definitely have to write him now, a detailed account of all that had any bearing on the Avesta, and the good news about the Parthian king's edict.

Silara was next. Yonas had dated them, so I took the first one she had written. It must have been written soon after my departure, as Yonas had received it three weeks ago. Her perfume clung tenaciously to the paper, even after all this time. As I unrolled it, a thin bracelet woven from colorful thread fell to the desk. She had sent me another gift. Now I definitely felt guilty. Not only had I not given her something on my departure, I had not sent my gift till much, much later. She had most likely still not received it. My eyes were drawn to her flowery script, graceful and feminine. I was impressed that she could write. Already I was learning something new about her. She was educated.

Kaleb, perhaps you think it presumptuous of me to write you while you are away. However, I find it easier to be frank knowing that you are thousands of leagues distant. I feel I must tell you that this betrothal was not my idea. Perhaps you think I had some hand in orchestrating it. I did not. There is no one else that competes with you for my affections however. Truth be told, I was proceeding quite happily with my life when I was informed of our impending engagement.

As are all occurrences in this life, your departure was providential. Coward that I am, I can now voice my fears knowing that I am safe from recrimination, from the guilt I might otherwise feel upon seeing your disappointment.

Perhaps my education has spoiled me, has led me to expect something more from marriage. My parents certainly think so, bemoaning my learning since the day they realized I had an opinion of my own concerning who I married.

I have nothing against you. At issue is the fact that I hardly know you. I am however, making every attempt to become acquainted with your family, a more marvelous group of people I could not hope to associate with. The signs are encouraging, but I need to know who you are, how you think, what moves you, what drives you. The mere act of a response, or lack thereof, will provide much of an answer. Please do not allow yourself to be carried away by the perfume. It was necessary to inhibit my parents from reading this letter before it was sent. I have given them the impression that it is in some regards romantic, and they are thus too embarrassed to read it, thankfully respecting my privacy in this one matter.

I hope you like the bracelet. It is inspired by Joseph's coat of many colors. For some reason, the story reminds me of you, a son who is sent into a faraway land.

Your reluctant fiancé
Silara

I sat for some time staring at the shuttered windows. Paradoxically, Silara's education, honesty and reluctance combined to make me think more highly of her. She had probably arrived at the opinion that I was worthless, bothering neither to initiate nor respond to a letter from her. So she wanted to *know* me. Was that even possible? I was not sure I knew *myself* that well. I would have to give some thought before I responded.

I took out the maps I had brought. Rhagae looked to be about a fifteen day journey from Ecbatana. It was within a day's journey of the Caspian Sea. I could feel the familiar tingling sensation at the back of my neck and the quivering deep in my chest. I knew at that moment that I would know Rhagae, as surely as I was sitting here in Ecbatana. It was providence.

With two months to spare, I could acquaint myself with anyone and everyone who might exert some influence for me with the king. I could also perfect my Pahlavi and Avestan in order to be ready for the big moment. How could the king refuse? I would be speaking on behalf of the greatest library of the world, offering my services as translator. But wait, I could not give that away. What if he did not want the Avesta in the hands of the Library? What then could be my motive? Why would I be offering my services? What excuse would sound plausible enough that it would convince the king that I would be valuable on the team he was sure to put together? Something to ponder.

CHAPTER SIXTY-TWO

"Every science and every inquiry, and similarly every activity and pursuit, is thought to aim at some good."
(Aristotle, *Nicomachean Ethics, bk. I, ch. 1,* ca 360 BC)

"The edict has been out for over a month your majesty, but the number of manuscripts that have made their way to Rhagae are meager relative to what we had expected. Without having the king's men go from temple to temple gathering the documents themselves, we may find ourselves compelled to wait five years to assemble all of the documents in one place."

The king and his two counselors sat clad in cloaks with fur lining on a porch of the palace overlooking the blue waters of the Euphrates, in the center of Babylon at the western extreme of the Parthian empire. "We must provide some assurances and incentives it seems," offered another of the counselors.

"Speak on," encouraged King Vologases. "I am listening."

"As for assurances, we must guarantee that the manuscripts will not fall into any hands except the hands of the faithful. As for incentives, would not the offer of receiving a copy of the full Avesta be incentive enough. Once the compilation is accomplished, every temple in Parthia could possess its own full copy of the sacred scriptures. It appears the priests have not fully comprehended the magnitude and benefits of what we are attempting to accomplish."

"Well spoken," the king said. "How do you propose these assurances and incentives be communicated to the various temples?"

"A letter to the individual priests, sealed by the king himself."

"How soon can this be accomplished?" the king asked.

"Once the letters are signed and sealed, one fortnight. And within another fortnight, all existing manuscripts should be in Rhagae, awaiting the team we are putting together."

"Tell me more about this team," the king said.

CHAPTER SIXTY-THREE

Knocking at the door startled me out of my thoughts. I stood and opened the door of my room, wondering who could be calling on me this late, wondering if Zos had suddenly decided to come back for the first night in a strange city.

A servant boy said a woman in white was waiting for me in the courtyard. I followed him down the stairs, now ink black but for the light thrown by the lone candle in the boy's hand. When we emerged onto the courtyard, I exclaimed, "Do my eyes deceive me? Sekhet, I am honored. How did you find me?"

"It seems your boy found our boy and the rest is history. And against my better judgment and in spite of my protests, Madame Mihret insisted I come to see if you were being properly treated and to invite you to dinner tomorrow evening."

"I am stunned at the kindness and generosity of your mistress," I said, genuinely shocked.

Sekhet held out a card with a name painted in gold ink. "Madame Mihret and her hosts will be expecting you at the beginning of the first watch, the Hour of Going Below the Horizon." She reluctantly let go of the card as I took it. Scowling, she asked if I had spent a pleasant day.

"Of course, thank you for asking, and you?" She humphed and turned away to leave.

"At dusk tomorrow evening."

"Until then."

CHAPTER SIXTY-FOUR

A faint dawn light filtered into my room just as I was beginning to get restless in my too-comfortable bed. The fire had died in the chimney. The room smelled of crisp air, polished wood and a hint of something I could not quite identify. I threw off the covers, stood and stretched in front of the window. I opened it to observe the city waking up and braced myself against the chill air that invaded the room. The light coming from over the mountains in the distance had yet to touch the streets of the city. As I watched the city wake up, the card Mihret's maid gave me the night before caught my eye. I had laid it on the low desk in front of the windows. I picked it up and rubbed the gold lettering under my thumb. Very fancy. I decided that instant to indulge myself in another long, luxuriant bath. Maybe there were some clean clothes waiting for me. I was tired of the smell of camel.

CHAPTER SIXTY-FIVE

I found myself at a low table drinking a cup of hot tea. Yonas had not opened his shop yet, so I decided to take in the view and hear some of the local gossip. It was good practice for my Pahlavi. There were several old men sitting around low tables, discussing the latest news. Evidently, the caravan I had come in with also boasted of a Roman envoy. How had I missed that? Or maybe I misunderstood what was being said. From the sounds of it, the envoy was on its way to Sina to set up trade relations. In addition, Vologases had arrived in Babylon from Armenia. Tired of waiting for Verus, he had left Armenia well fortified to enjoy the late spring from his southern palace. Not very pleasant things were being said about the Romans, who were obviously as disliked here as they were in Egypt where they were ruining the economy, and literally killing the population with taxes; sometimes it felt as if they were taxing the taxes themselves. And the resulting devaluation of Egyptian coin made it even worse. Of course it was great for the Romans. It made Egyptian exports, primarily wheat, very cheap for the capital. With Egypt on my mind, I admired again the façade of the palace across the plaza. It mimicked the Egyptian style in many ways. It was fascinating how commerce and movement of people had homogenized so many things in our world. Even in the construction of the palace, one could see Egyptian as well as Asian influence. The thick, solid columns. The stylized designs along the wooden porticos forming the roof of the porch. Unique, however, to the style here was the use of glazed brick on the first floor and from that point up, tooled wood. It was quite stunning.

The enormous wooden doors on the front of Yonas' shop swung open. Swirls of dust glittered in the morning sun at the front of his shop. One of his children threw a bucket of water on the area in front of his shop and began to sweep. The air had warmed considerably since I woke this morning. I sipped my tea and watched as Yonas got his shop ready for another day's work. I spied Zos bringing out a tray of tea. As he set it on the low table at the entrance to the shop, he looked up and caught my eye. Zos, he was very observant. I would never be able to pull anything on him. I winked at him. He smiled, turned and disappeared again into the bowels of the shop where the sun could not reach. An early, brisk morning, foreign smells and sounds, a hot drink in a stunning setting, wonderful prospects for the coming day. Evanescent yet delicious. If I were a cat, I would purr. If I believed in the cat goddess Bast, this would be the time to offer up an oblation to her. The prayer of Moses came to mind, "Satisfy us in the morning with your unfailing love, that we may sing for joy and be glad all our days."

When I lifted my head from the recitation, Zos was standing by me. "Good morning Teacher."

"Good morning Zos. Did you sleep well?"

"Like a rock, Teacher. And you?"

"Unbelievably well Zos. My bed was like a prelude to paradise."

"Master Yonas wants you to join him for tea Teacher. I've got to go prepare for lessons."

"Study hard Zos, this is a great opportunity for you to learn in the company of a friend. Speaking of friends, how did you run into your friend from the caravan, Omar, Ahmed...."

"Amun," Zos countered. A palanquin passed through the plaza soon after you left yesterday, and Amun was following it with a group of people. I got his attention to let him know where to find me later. And he did. He came by before dark to tell me where they were staying so we could meet if I had free time."

"Well done, Zos. You saved me what could have been days of searching. And you won me my bet with Yonas." Zos smiled from ear to ear. "Run along now. I am on my way."

CHAPTER SIXTY-SIX

Some days are meant for working, others for resting, and then there are the days that neither is accomplished. Those days a body can sit down at the end of the day and wonder where the time went. But as King Solomon said, there is a time for everything, and today was a time for preparing, for organizing, for setting up, for orchestrating. And that I did very well. I did it every time I arrived in a city, ready to begin the search, to plot my course. These are the days I love. I could spend my whole life plotting the course. The harder piece is to stay the course, to abide by the plan, to hold to the routine, to commit to the path that has been charted.

I had arranged a reasonable rate for a two month stay at the Seres Inn. Yonas had found me a Pahlavi and Avestan teacher; we had met and established a daily schedule. Yonas was going to take me to the Christian fellowship that met outside the city on the Lord's

Day. Zos was situated, and I had insisted on paying Yonas for his room, board and education for the duration of our stay. All of my belongings had been cleaned and smelled as fresh as mountain snow. And lastly, Yonas had agreed to let me set up a scribe's table outside his shop to earn some extra money. Zos had agreed to take me to Mihret's house at dusk. So here I sat, ready to go, dressed in a freshly laundered green linen robe with a high white turban, Ethiopian style. I went down to the courtyard and there met Zos who had just arrived. Zos had cleaned up as well, wearing spotless white linen and his scribe's cap cocked slightly to the side. "You are looking very elegant this evening young sir," I laughed.

"Yonas told me I had to dress well to accompany you. It's important to make a good impression he said."

"Well, he is right. First impressions are very important, and I have no idea who I am going to meet this evening. So off we go."

The coolness was back in the air. Zos and I must have been quite a sight for the people we passed. There were few black Africans in this city, and especially none dressed as extravagantly as Zos and I. I had to admit; we did look good. The road wound and climbed until I was thoroughly disoriented. But I let Zos take the lead. He had a sixth sense for direction. He never got lost in our caravan tent cities. He seemed to know instinctively where the tavern was, where his friends were, where virtually anything we needed was. I may be a good map reader and interpreter, but Zos had a gift, and once he knew the lay of the land, his sense of direction was flawless.

"Here it is Teacher." We ducked through a narrow tunnel that led down a short path, bordered on both sides by high mud brick walls. There was a small door at the end of the path with a large iron knocker. I took it, and looking at Zos, rapped twice.

A peephole at neck level opened. When the eye had taken in my color and my dress, the door immediately opened. A maid, Persian by the looks of her, apologized profusely and ushered us inside. The doorway led into an opening almost as narrow as the door and immediately up a flight of stairs. At the top of the stairs, there was another door that opened from within as we reached it. Now we were in a hallway that ran perpendicular to the door we had just exited. The maid turned right and we followed. "I will never find my way out of here," I whispered to Zos in Ge'ez. He smiled.

"Just stick with me Teacher. I've already been here twice. I know my way around this whole place."

At the end of the hall, another door opened, and we were ushered into a huge colonnaded hall. Carpets covered the floor and walls. A fireplace the size of my room burned at one end. Candles hung from the columns and from the impossibly high ceiling in silver tiered disks. Between two prodigious columns a table had been set up dripping with every possible delicacy from East to West. At the far end, a group of musicians played some lively, exotic Persian tune and professional dancers were gliding back and forth entertaining the small group of guests seated watching. Other guests were scattered in small groups, some reclining, some seated on floor cushions around small tables, talking in low voices, eating and sipping what was surely the choicest of wine.

"Wow," I heard Zos gasp. The feeling was mutual. I stood quietly, taking it all in when the hostess, Mihret, glided towards us from the center of the hall. Her robe glittered as she walked, red, shot with gold and silver thread. Her head was topped with a vertiginously high turban of red and white with a ruby the size of an egg holding it in the front. She no longer wore a veil, and now the other features of her face held competition with her sparkling, almond eyes. She was indeed, extraordinarily beautiful. I took a deep bow.

"Please, no formalities fellow Ethiopian cum Egyptian. I am delighted you came. I apologize for the late notice. I see you brought a companion. Thanks to this young man, we meet again." I was pleased that a lady of her dignity and status deigned to know the goings on of someone as low on the strata as Zos. He was beside himself at having been complimented by what he considered royalty; however, he stared resolutely at the floor. I'll see if I can locate his friend, and perhaps he would prefer to spend the evening in his company rather than with a bunch of boring, formal adults." Zos nodded his head while continuing to stare at the floor.

"You are so kind," I said sincerely, looking her full in the eyes.

"Not at all, I just remember what it was to be a child in these settings. Abominable." She smiled while raising her hand. A young woman was instantly at her side. "Find this young man's friend," she commanded gently without turning her head. Zos disappeared with the young woman, and it was the last I saw of him till I was ready to go. The stories he would have to tell when we got back. "There are many people you must meet. But I don't want to tire you. You must be hungry. See what you would like to eat and follow me. I will seat you with someone who will not bore you too much and have food brought to you."

"I trust no one knows my true occupation here."

"Heaven forbid. Your secret is safe with me. My only intention is for you to pass an enjoyable evening while meeting some of the luminaries of the city where we will be spending some time."

"And why might I ask are you being so kind to me?" I asked, chiding myself at the same time for being so direct.

"You are a fellow countryman, educated, successful and may I add at the risk of damaging my virtuous reputation, handsome. Why would I not want to have you around me? I need a friend here, someone who understands where I come from."

"Again, sincere to a fault." We worked our way to a gathering near the center of the hall, with a good view of the dancers, but not too close to the music. I could tell as we approached that two of the gentlemen were Roman by their dress. The other man and woman appeared to be Greek from their dress and manner. And lastly, an Indian woman in a stunning garment, even more shimmery than the one Mihret wore.

"May I introduce your sixth companion? We just arrived in yesterday's caravan. We met briefly there. Kaleb from Adulis, a fellow Ethiopian."

All eyes were on me as I settled onto my cushion. Introductions were made. "According to the Ayurveda," the Indian woman said, "there are six tastes necessary to balance a healthy diet, sweet, sour, salty, bitter, pungent, and astringent. Which, Kaleb, do you bring to the table?"

"Which is lacking, and I will make every effort to provide the flavor required?"

"Well said" Prochorus, the young Greek man laughed. "That is an excellent question, and one I would like to explore further."

"Stop it," said Gaiane, the Greek's female companion. "Of course Rajni and I are the sweet and salty. What do you say Rajni? But I would venture to add that we are a little of each. Sweet to the taste, salty in conversation."

"I fear to name who is pungent, especially after having just been liberated from a month long camel caravan," Septimus interjected as he clicked goblets with me. And the conversation from that point continued for most of the evening, never losing the momentum Rajni so deftly set in motion upon my arrival. As it turned out, Septimus and Tatius were the envoys sent as an embassy to Sina. As the evening progressed, it became apparent that I spoke several languages. Rajni, although she spoke Greek well, spoke Pahlavi better since she had spent a large part of her life in the eastern part of Parthia, and occasionally she would search for the right word in Greek. I was able to supply it more times than not, although I admitted I was still studying to perfect it. I also could converse equally well in Greek or Latin, and at one point they overheard a brief exchange between me and Mihret in a language none of them recognized.

"So just how many languages do you speak, Sir Polyglot?" Tatius asked.

"I am fluent in six, competent in two and can converse simply in several others," I said as humbly as I could muster. I never enjoyed when the conversation turned in my direction, preferring to keep as quiet about myself as possible. "I am a scribe after all. Language is the currency of my livelihood."

"Good scribes are hard to come by," Tatius said, looking at Septimus as he spoke. "We'll remember your name Kaleb. Now it's getting late, and the morning comes early tomorrow. We have much to do before the journey continues."

CHAPTER SIXTY-SEVEN

The following morning, I found myself sitting at the same table in the open plaza, sipping tea, waiting for Yonas to open his shop. I had only been in the city two days now, but I had a job, a place to stay, Zos was taken care of, I was going to be taking classes, and I now had some friends who were actually quite influential in Ecbatana society. I had a ways to go before I became a friend of the king's, but I was not doing too badly for myself.

My journal grew daily with each new entry. Mihret had been a wonderful hostess. I thoroughly enjoyed the evening and the conversation. It was a true pleasure to engage in stimulating conversation with intelligent, well-traveled people. There was not a droll moment. Who knew, something might even come of the Roman envoys. They did say they would remember my name after all.

My thoughts turned to Silara's second letter that I had read this morning. She sounded as if she repented of the first letter, assuring me that she was not against the betrothal, just concerned. Again, there was a gift rolled into the scroll, a purple hibiscus, reminding me of the flowers that grew at the door of my home on the lake.

Yonas pushed back the doors to his shop. His son began to sweep again. There was no sun today though. The sky was completely overcast and the air was frigid. I had worn a warm coat, sheepskin on the outside, wool on the inside. My Ethiopian skin was thin, unaccustomed to the cold climes in the north. If I were lucky, it would rain. I looked forward to a good storm. The storms here were legendary, crashing thunder, violent wind, lightning bolts the size of tree trunks. I would like to see at least one true north Parthian storm, this time from the comfort of a warm, dry place that would not blow away with the wind.

I made my way to Yonas' shop and greeted my old friend. I already felt that I had lived here my whole life. I set up a low table beside his shop and propped up a sign I had made. *Scribe*, it read, in huge letters written in every script I knew. Zos had made me a new price list written in Latin, Greek and Pahlavi. That should do it. I settled in to see what results the lot I had cast would bring. My Pahlavi lessons were later in the day and would transpire right here on the spot. I was not required to move a muscle all day long. Of course, I was doubtful whether that was a good thing or not. I might go crazy sitting here all day long. Only time would tell.

CHAPTER SIXTY-EIGHT

"We know how to speak many falsehoods which resemble real things, but we know, when we will, how to speak true things."
(Hesiod, *Theogony*, *l. 27*, ca 700 BC)

It had taken almost two weeks to locate Kaleb once he realized that the information about where he was staying was wrong. The Alvand Inn had had no Ethiopian visitors. No one had even seen an Ethiopian on that street. Either the recorder at the gate was incompetent or Kaleb was craftier than he had anticipated. And why would Kaleb feel he had to lie about his lodging unless he were suspicious. Suspicious of what? Had the Carpathian lied about not arousing Kaleb's suspicions? He would certainly include that in his report. The more important order of business was to locate the Ethiopian, a task which he was confident he would accomplish. His first act was to offer up a sacrifice and pray, as he had been taught to never start on a task before imploring the blessings of the deities. And they had favor on him. There Kaleb sat, in the main plaza of the city, waiting for a customer. But he needed to assure himself that this was really Kaleb. From his seat, shaded by the overhang of the portico, as he sipped his tea, he watched as the scribe spoke at length to a young Ethiopian boy. A plan formed in his mind as he watched them talk. He called over the boy attending the tables. "I require someone to run an errand," he pronounced. The young waiter returned after a brief pause with an errand boy, probably a friend of his who was waiting around to earn some money. Putting down his tea, he showed the youth a coin and proceeded to give the boy instructions. "If you're fast, you'll get two of these," he said tossing two coins up and catching them in the palm of his calloused hand. The boy's eyes followed the rise and fall of the coins before speeding across the plaza.

Within the space of time it took him to finish his second tea, a middle-aged woman in Parthian dress appeared at his table beside the youth who had retrieved her, his palm extended. Reaching into his purse, he extracted two coins and waved the boy away. The woman joined him at the table. "I need you to go over to that scribe," he directed her gaze with his eyes, "and have him write a letter for you. Anything will do. Gather as much personal information about him as you can, and then meet me at the Arvand Inn."

"Done," she said rising.

CHAPTER SIXTY-NINE

It had been a busy week. We were in the middle of the month of Pashons, the interval between Christ's resurrection and ascension, and I was celebrating my first Lord's Day since Dura in the company of a local ekklesia. I was amazed at how many Ethiopians lived in the city, most of whom were Christian. The day was generally celebrated in the home of a friend of Yonas' who had a large villa outside the city walls in the countryside. They were all-day events since it took most of the day just to arrive at the villa. There was even a Bishop of Ecbatana which was news to me. I did not expect the ekklesia to be so organized this far away from home, especially in light of the recent persecutions closer to Rome. I thought again of Polycarp. Parthia, however, appeared to be more tolerant towards different religions, perhaps due to the cosmopolitan nature of its cities, being centers on the Silk Road where people of many nationalities and religions mixed freely.

The festival began with singing, mainly Psalms set to Ethiopian and Egyptian tunes and a few choruses that I did not recognize. This unity in diversity was truly supernatural. My heart was warm with a sense of family, the same sense I had felt in Dura. As Paul had emphasized in his letter to the Ephesians, our temples were not built of lifeless brick and mortar but of living and breathing stones, each playing his or her part in the kingdom of God on earth. There were not only Egyptian and Ethiopian Christians present but converts from as far away as Sina and as close to home as Damascus. There were a multitude of languages represented although the common language of worship at this assembly was Greek since that was the language common to the majority. There was a small group at the back of the gathering however where a woman was interpreting from Greek to Pahlavi for the locals. A homily on the resurrection was given, focusing on the account from the Gospel of Luke. Prayers were offered for peace among the peoples of Parthia and Rome where conflict had already begun in Western Armenia. More music and then a feast at which the holy sacraments were first given and then a meal that lasted till the evening. We all returned to the city singing and praising God for his beneficence in the midst of our displacement. Zos and I conversed in Aramaic. He had made marked improvement in just over a week of study.

"You are an amazing student Zos."

"I study under a great teacher and Yonas' son, my friend Alem refuses to speak to me in any language other than Aramaic." Zos said, returning to Greek.

"And in what language does Yonas speak to you?"

"Pahlavi. I must confess that sometimes I get very confused. Greek, Aramaic, Pahlavi; where does it end?"

"It never ends Zos," I said, ruffling his thickening black hair. He had let it grow since we had arrived. "The tower where God mixed the languages is very near here, and the effects keep spreading. One could spend one's entire life learning languages and still only touch the surface. You are learning the most common, the ones that will most benefit you in your life. So keep on studying and practice continually. You may never have such a great opportunity again. Besides, we only have about thirty more days before we leave."

"Thirty more days," Zos whispered. "Thirty more days."

CHAPTER SEVENTY

There were no more letters to read. My father's was brief and recounted anecdotes from home. He had included a list of names and addresses for me in the event that I passed through Adulis and Berenice. Ptolemaios had told him of his advice for me to return by an alternate route if the war continued. His subordinate must have written out the list since it was in a different hand. I scanned the list. There were many names that I had never heard mentioned, and curiously, of all the names on the list, there was only one woman. Her name too was unfamiliar. Thinking nothing more of it, I tucked it into my copy of Egyptian tales. I had read Silara's final letter last night. She had surely despaired of hearing from me. She probably sent it about the same time I was setting out from Ctesiphon which meant that by now she would have received the letter and gift from me. Her last few letters no longer mentioned the engagement. They were vignettes of her life, descriptions of my family, of hers, attention paid to the smallest details. Each letter contained a small gift, something to connote my life in Alexandria. I found myself thinking of her often, pulling out the pendant that hung always around my neck to gaze at her likeness. Was it possible that I was falling in love with her?

I was at the end of my second week in Ecbatana and business was booming, not least of all, the enormous undertaking that Mihret had hired me for. She wanted me to compose a biography of her husband's life. I told her that one month was not sufficient to complete a work of that scope. She had convinced me though, with her supplicating eyes and beautiful pouting lips. She would tell me everything, she said. I could take notes and write it over the ensuing months, to be delivered to her when we met again in Alexandria. In the end, she convinced me, and I spent a quarter of every day in a room dangerously close to her, smelling her perfume, watching her lips as she formed the words that I translated into notes on my parchment. And each day Silara's pendant grew heavier against my chest until yesterday.

I was no expert at reading women, but I was beginning to feel uneasy with Mihret. It seemed she wanted something, but I was evidently too obtuse to decipher what it was. The day was hot, and I was shirtless, Egyptian style, with only my linen kilt and scribe's cap. Mihret wore a semi-transparent robe that clung to her like skin. I had seen women in similar style in Alexandria, but never at these close quarters. As an Egyptian, nakedness did not fluster me, so why was I flustered now? Why did I feel that events were spiraling out of control? Wine was brought. It was not my custom to drink wine in the middle of the day, so I let my cup remain on the table between us. Mihret was petulant. "Try it Kaleb. I had it brought just for you. It is from Alexandria, sweet and light, perfect for today's weather, and I had it chilled."

"Just a taste then," I said, barely wetting my lips. Mihret moved closer, and took my hand in hers, pushing the cup back to my lips. Incongruously I realized that Sekhet had not made an appearance today. In fact, no one had come into the room since I arrived except the slave that had just brought the wine. Mihret's face was dangerously close to mine. Her hand moved to my bare chest. As if shocked by lightening, I stood, almost throwing Mihret to the floor. "What's wrong Kaleb?"

"Mihret, I have not mentioned it before, but I am engaged."

"And?"

"I belong to someone else," I said weakly, my resolution wavering.

"Not yet," she said, moving closer.

"I should go. Thank you for the wine," I said as I walked towards the door.

"Wait!" she reached for me, grabbing my forearm, her hand closing on the brass bracelet.

Not trusting myself to be alone with her, knowing that if I did not leave now, my entire course would be altered, I pulled away from her, leaving her holding my bracelet as I rushed to the door and the freedom of the street beyond. Never had I been tempted to that point. I had been protected in the community I lived in. I could never have found myself in the situation I had just extracted myself from with superhuman effort. I had been a hair's breadth away from losing my chastity. In the street, I struggled within myself to leave. This was a chance I would not have again with Mihret. I could go back, apologize and indulge in my wildest fantasies or keep walking and save my integrity, my purity for the woman to whom I was betrothed. I realized now that I had been a fool, deluding myself into thinking I could play this dangerous game. I believed I could spend hours every day in a room alone with her, savoring her attention, reveling in the sexual excitement she elicited, and have it stop there. The further away I got from Mihret's house, the more intensely I became aware of how close I had been to making the biggest mistake of my life.

CHAPTER SEVENTY-ONE

More quickly than I wanted, the time came to leave for Rhagae. The weather had turned warmer, and the air smelled less of cold, wind and clouds and more of the earth, alder wood and barley. This was my kind of weather, when I could not tell where my skin ended and the air began. Mihret had not invited me back to her home, but she had sent Sekhet with a package the day after my Great Temptation, the name I had given that day in my mind. After Sekhet left, I opened the package hoping to find my bracelet but instead found a small box containing a card with four words. "I will not forget." Will not forget what? Will not forget me? Will not forget her humiliation? The letter left me uneasy, but there was nothing I could do. In two days I would be on my way to Rhagae and could put this chapter of my life behind me.

One thing I could not begrudge Mihret is that she had introduced me to many people, and I had made many friends in the city, all of whom were aware of my interest in the edict to compile a complete edition of the Zoroastrian Avesta.

"Why such interest?" Prochorus asked me one day as we meandered along the city streets going nowhere in particular. I had spent a lot of time with him and his wife since settling here.

"There are supposedly many similarities between the Jewish Tanakh, the barbarian Gospels of the followers of Jesus and the Avesta. However, it is practically impossible to see the writings themselves. They are held in such secrecy. It is for this reason that I have been studying Avestan so avidly and working to perfect my Pahlavi. I hope at some point to read the Avesta and see what all the fuss is about."

"I have a surprise for you," Prochorus announced. "But it must wait till tomorrow evening."

"You know I am leaving the day after tomorrow," I countered. "How involved is this surprise?"

"Patience my young friend. All in good time. You must report to my home before the end of the ninth hour and all will be revealed!"

"You know I love a good mystery," I smiled. "I am hooked. I will be there, and hopefully be prepared for your surprise."

CHAPTER SEVENTY-TWO

The evening came all too quickly. I had spent the day closing out accounts at my lodgings, with Yonas, packing my things and making sure Zos was ready; he was spending his final evening with Yonas' family. I had gone to the caravan depot to check on our camels and make sure everything was in order for leaving on the morrow. I had to coordinate our departure with the next caravan heading east. I purchased everything necessary for the first days of the journey and reviewed my finances to see where I stood after a month of work. I only had to dip into my funds I brought from Alexandria once, to pay for my time at the inn. Otherwise, I was able to pay for everything, including Zos' studies, from the money I earned working as a scribe outside Yonas' shop. I had earned quite a reputation and rarely had time to spare all day, not only working at my makeshift stand but being called hither and yon to interpret or translate court documents into the more obscure Punic or Ge'ez, once it was out that I was also proficient in those languages. Having now practically perfected Pahlavi was a huge asset as well. In the end, I even had enough money to pay for the caravan to Rhagae and to get set up once there. My travel expenses I had left Alexandria with were almost entirely intact, a fact which gave me a feeling of security. One never knew when an emergency would arise, when earning was impossible, when one had to fall back on what one had at hand.

As the sun sank to the horizon, the time drew nearer for me to be on my way to Prochorus' house; I was fairly exhausted, but ready for a quiet evening with friends, the last for some time. The sun dropped silently below the horizon, unseen from within the city, just as I found myself at the unassuming door to the gate of Prochorus' home. The door creaked open. I had told him more than once that his door was creepy and that he needed to oil it. He would just laugh and say it kept the superstitious away. I was led into the open courtyard which ended at another door painted blue to keep away the evil eye. Speaking of superstitious, Prochorus was the leader of the pack. He had an idol in every niche, incense burning to every god he could name. He wanted to make sure he was covered. It was difficult to do, living in Ecbatana, where each new visitor brought a new god or two to the table.

The blue "evil eye" door opened and Prochorus walked out, followed by a man I had not previously seen. He wore a scribe's turban in the colors of the royal house of Parthia. "Kaleb, Kaleb!" my friend called out jovially. "You made it."

"Did you ever doubt I would? I must admit; I had to move heaven and earth to accomplish everything that had to be done today. Why do I always wait till there is almost no time left?"

"Because you're Ethiopian?"

"That has nothing to do with it. It is a personal character flaw that in no way reflects on my country of origin."

"I do not know that I would call it a flaw," interjected Prochorus' friend. "One could say the flaw is to forever worry about getting everything done with time to spare. Moderation in everything; that should be the golden mean."

"I think I'll let that serve as an introduction Aschek. And this is my best new friend Kaleb."

"I appreciate the qualification," I said as I bowed to the visitor. "It is an honor to meet a friend of my good friend Prochorus."

"The honor is mine," Aschek said as he returned the bow. "Your reputation precedes you. Your name is mentioned in many circles. It seems you have worked in many and varied venues in the city in your short time here."

"God has been generous," I smiled.

"Indeed," Aschek returned my smile.

"I know you're anxious to find out who Aschek really is," Prochorus said, as a table, chairs and wine were brought to the center of the courtyard. "But first, a toast to our friend Kaleb here and to his last night in Ecbatana." The small clay cups clinked as they met under the now starry sky above us. Although the moon was almost full, it had not risen over the open ceiling of the courtyard. Nevertheless, its light precluded the need of candles. The only light in the courtyard were three small lanterns set in a triangle, equidistant from the center of the table where we now sat.

Prochorus continued, "First, I'd like Kaleb here to tell us everything he has concluded about our friend Aschek. Kaleb is quite the observant one, and can often tell the most amazing things about someone just after meeting them."

"Pure flattery."

"Please, proceed," Aschek said. "My curiosity has been peaked, and one loves nothing more than to hear the surmises of others regarding one's person."

"Vanity," Prochorus said as he took another sip of his wine. "We are all victims of our own vanity."

"Sad but true," I said. "Even our father Solomon declares that all is vanity. But I digress. Hmmm," I paused as I looked at Aschek. "On first glance, I see that you are a scribe of the royal house of Parthia. You are married with children. You own land outside the city which you enjoy working, sometimes wondering if it would not be better to quit the work of a scribe and dedicate yourself entirely to agricultural pleasures. You are honest and sincere, qualities that are rare in the environs of any royal court. You possess a good sense of humor and enjoy a good cup of wine." This last sentence I said as I raised my cup in another toast.

"Here, here," shouted Prochorus. "What did I tell you Aschek. Amazing. Almost as if he could read minds. I'll admit, sometimes it's a little spooky."

"Not minds Prochorus, signs. Your turban, Aschek, gives away the occupation. The ring the marital status and the graying hair around the temples at such a young age the children. Your hands are rough, not the hands of a scribe, so you must be involved in some manual labor, and I guessed the most likely that came to mind, your fields since as a man of means you must have an estate. As for your character, the fact that you are a friend of this man here," I said looking at Prochorus, "speaks volumes. He would not associate with anyone that was not honest, sincere and willing to laugh at his jokes!" At that, everyone laughed.

"Impressive. Now I will fill you in on the details you failed to mention. I am secretary to the head of the team that has been put together for the compiling and editing of the Avesta in Rhagae. Prochorus has informed me that you are interested in reading it, perhaps becoming a follower."

"As for becoming a follower, I would have to read it first. My knowledge of your faith is very rudimentary, but I am extremely curious about it. I have read what I could find, but there is a great dearth of information. It seems it is quite a closed society."

"Zoroastrians do not proselytize. You are either born one or seek it of your own volition. Unfortunately, even initiates often encounter difficulty getting to the core doctrines since there are no complete compilations of the writings in any one place. That is why our great King Vologases IV is intent on making a complete Avesta, one that can be transcribed and used in every center of our spreading faith."

"Yes, I have heard of the edict and must confess that for this very reason, I intend to leave for Rhagae tomorrow. I feel compelled to be present at such an auspicious undertaking."

"I too leave tomorrow. I am grateful to our companion Prochorus for introducing us in time to take advantage of the journey to get better acquainted."

"To the joys of the journey!" Prochorus shouted, raising his cup.

"To the joys of the journey," Aschek and I repeated in unison, raising our cups to meet in the air.

CHAPTER SEVENTY-THREE

"Evil enters like a needle and spreads like an oak tree."
(Ancient Ethiopian proverb)

After watching Kaleb for these few short weeks, he was amazed at how careless the Ethiopian was being at revealing his intentions. His initial concern over Kaleb's suspicions had seemingly proven unfounded. It was general knowledge that Kaleb was interested in learning about the Avesta. He was sure Kaleb intended to somehow obtain a copy. This must be the objective of Kaleb's mission. He had instructed a member of the temple to follow Kaleb to Rhagae and report on where he landed, find someone there who could keep an eye on him and send back reports on his actions.

PART ELEVEN

BOUND FOR RHAGAE

Gregorian Calendar – June 12ᵗʰ, 162
Alexandrian Calendar – Paoni 5ᵗʰ, Second Shomu
The Season of Harvesting
2ⁿᵈ year of Marcus Aurelius

"Rhagae is said to have had its name from the earthquakes which occurred in that country, by which many cities and two thousand villages, as Poseidonius relates, were overthrown."
(Strabo, *Geographika, Volume II*, ca 10 BC)

CHAPTER SEVENTY-FOUR

Fifteen days to Rhagae. That was the projection anyway. The morning had been a flurry of final activity. Zos' tearful farewells. Yonas and his entire family had come out to wish us Godspeed as had much of the Christian community with whom I had become friends. Several pressed gifts on us as we made our way to the depot. It was pure chaos at the caravanserai. Yonas had sent a servant ahead of us to bring out the camels. The boy met us at the entrance of the depot and we transferred our belongings from the mules we had hired to the camels. My stomach was in knots. Yonas pulled us all to one side and prayed for a safe journey and for God's providence in the days to come in Rhagae. The prayer calmed my nerves somewhat.

It was always more difficult to leave than to arrive. My favorite part of the day of departure was when everyone had left me alone and I was seated on my camel with no one but Zos by my side and nothing but my thoughts to keep me company. Then I had time to ponder what had transpired, to calm my thoughts. Zos and I mounted our camels and made our way slowly but surely to the center of the caravan. Once there, we let our camels be seated, and the wait began. I expelled a huge sigh of relief. Zos, beside me, imitated my sigh, exaggerating it immensely. "What are you sighing so loudly about?" I asked in Aramaic.

"I'm relieved!" he said. "My heart was beating so fast this morning when I woke up I thought it would burst. But now we're here, all the commotion is over, and a new adventure is getting ready to begin!"

"Truly said, Zos." I was amazed that he felt exactly as I did. "Are you hungry?"

"Yes!" he exclaimed. "I could hardly eat this morning for all the excitement."

"Well, we have plenty of food," I said as I unwrapped the first parcel that came to my hand from the bucket hanging from Fang's side. It was good to see Fang again. He looked healthier than ever. The rest had done him good. Zos and I ate, seated in the midst of all the noise, dust, flies and the smell of dung. Such familiar smells, almost sweet. It was difficult to remember how sick of them I was when we arrived. If it just were not for the flies. Flies were such a plague.

A loud horn blew in the distance from the head of the caravan. The moans of thousands of camels simultaneously rung throughout the vast plain at the foot of the walls of Ecbatana as they rose from east to west. From the walls of the city, it must have looked as if the sea had turned brown and come to the foot of the city. Horns blew, people shouted, the noise was deafening. Fang and his companion lazily stood, Zos and I munching on our lunch, already feeling that we were on the road again, the road to three thousand year old Rhagae, place of the Assyrian exiled Jews, ancient city of the kings, center of the Zoroastrian leadership, city where I planned to finally lay my hands on a copy of the Avesta, completing my mission. "Do you wish we were heading the opposite direction Zos? Back to Alexandria?"

"Are you joking Teacher? I'm not ready to go back yet. There's still so much to see."

"A man after my own heart!" I said, adjusting my parasol. "So off we go then." We began to slowly make our way forward. The journey had begun.

CHAPTER SEVENTY-FIVE

Once we were a day's journey from the city, it was easier to judge the size of this caravan. It was considerably smaller than the one we had taken from Palmyra. But then, this leg of the journey was much safer than that one. We had crossed vast regions of wasteland, through canyons and mountains, frontier regions that were often involved in conflict, especially with the rising aggression of Parthia against Rome and the build-up of Roman troops heading to Armenia. Now we were securely in Parthia, moving from one of its most important cities to one of the royal cities. Although the spring was not over, word had it that the king would not make an appearance this year as was his wont. He was far to the west, managing the war on Rome, protecting his interests in Armenia from his palace in Babylon. Rumor was, though, that the royal family was in Rhagae for safe keeping.

I had yet to sight Aschek, and unfortunately, since Zos had not met him, it would be fruitless to send him on a search. Zos had eagle eyes and could spot a known target a league away. Therefore, once we had stopped after traveling non-stop for almost a full day and night, I set off on my search. While Zos guarded the camels and tent, I proceeded to zigzag through the camp keeping my eyes open for Aschek's turban. The sun was quite hot, confirming for me the decision to only travel at night from here on out. There was a forest far to the left, but there were few trees along the road, and they were all taken by other members of the caravan. Riding in the center also had its disadvantages. Our only shade was our tent. I felt that my search was a futile attempt. There were hundreds of people, and most had already retired to their tents to sleep. I wondered if that were not the best option for me right now. I could always continue the search in the afternoon when more people would be up and about. Having convinced myself that there was no longer any use in searching, I turned around and began to zigzag back to our tent, taking opposite zigs and opposite zags from what I had taken to this eastern extreme. At least I had covered half the caravan. I could cover the western half after a long nap.

CHAPTER SEVENTY-SIX

I woke up to Zos' voice, "Teacher, Teacher."

"What is it Zos," I replied sleepily, hardly able to open my eyes. It was as if the dust had sealed them shut. I rubbed them and looked up.

"There's a man here to see you. He says his name is Aschek."

Aschek! How did he find me? "Take him some tea Zos. I will be out right away." I hurriedly pulled myself together, washed my face in the tepid water from the bowl in the corner of the tent and donned my turban. I emerged from the tent to a tranquil afternoon. The sun was well past its zenith. The air smelled of grass and sea, although we were quite some distance from the Caspian. There were times that its smell reached this far inland. If only the mosquitoes were as reticent to venture this far as the scent of the sea. "What an honor," I said as I offered my hand to Aschek, who smiling, clasped it in his. "How did you find me? I spent the morning searching for you in the eastern half of this caravan."

"I am only a stone's throw away on the western side of you. Fortunately I decided to search the east as well. Otherwise, we may have totally missed each other."

"Once we are on the move again, you must join us. Are you traveling with anyone?"

"Now I am."

CHAPTER SEVENTY-SEVEN

The days passed quickly in Aschek's company. We had countless extended conversations on the beginnings of things and the essence of good and evil. I learned more fully the foundational tenets of Zoroastrianism, and I hoped that I had adequately expounded on the truth of the holy writings of Moses, the Prophets and the Gospels. Aschek explained that Zoroaster, who had lived some one thousand years after Abraham and some five hundred years after Moses, taught what he believed was a revelation from Ahura Mazda himself. He wrote these things in the form of hymns in what were known as the Gathas. Later writings that expounded on these Gathas, along with the Gathas themselves were what were known as the Avesta.

The cosmic beginnings of things according to Zoroastrian belief was fascinating, and although theologically divergent in most aspects from the teachings of the Old and New Testaments, also coincided in many interesting ways. After all, had not Abraham proceeded from Mesopotamia? Would not the ultimate truths about God have been known to man from the earliest times although corrupted through man's innate desire to be god himself, to supersede the divine plan laid out by God before time began?

Traditional Zoroastrian teaching explained that before time, when only infinity existed, there existed two forces, Ahura Mazda, the supreme God and Angra Mainyu, ultimate evil. They each occupied a space, infinite on one side yet finitely bound to a frontier on the other in the midst of which was a great void. Ahura Mazda knew of Angra Mainyu's existence although he did not occupy the space inhabited by Angra Mainyu. Angra Mainyu, on the other hand, was ignorant of the existence of Ahura Mazda. An event of epic proportion took place, however, in this time before time, the mere idea of which, in my opinion, defied logic – how could an act occur before time began? Would not that itself have been the beginning of time? Nevertheless, it so happened that Angra Mainyu crossed the void and discovered the existence of Ahura Mazda, at which point, he attempted to attack him. Ahura Mazda, infinite in knowledge including foreknowledge, knew that the time had not come when evil would be vanquished, so instead of conquering Angra Mainyu then and there, made a pact with him that would last 9,000 years.

These 9,000 years would be divided into three epochs. The first, Ahura Mazda alone would rule. The second, both would prevail in equal proportion, and the final 3,000 years would be presaged by the advent of Zoroaster, who would expose the workings of Angra Mainyu, teach the right way to live and prepare people for the advent of the Saoshyant, or savior, who would appear 1,000 years after Zoroaster, from his lineage. This Saoshyant would herald the final judgment where the elixir of immortality would be distributed among people and evil would be vanquished.

"You say that this coincides with the beliefs you hold. In what ways?" asked Aschek.

I explained that Christianity also held that there existed one good God and an evil angel called Lucifer. We also held that a savior would be born at around the same time predicted by Zoroaster, not of the house of Zoroaster but of the house of David, king of Israel, of the lineage of Abraham, the father of the Jewish race. The story however diverged in most of the details. For instance, the Christian God, known as 'I am' because he was existent outside of time, in all moments present, never past, never future, had no limits or boundaries in his infinity. He was not embroiled in a cosmic battle with another almost equally powerful evil entity. The evil one, Lucifer, was his creation, created as an angel of light but who, in his quest to stand in the place of God, was expelled from God's presence although allowed to continue to exist. Since the angels are immortal, rather than annihilate him, he was allowed to exist on earth till the final judgment when he would be thrown into hell with the other angels he had brought to his side in the great heavenly rebellion. In that way also, there was a similarity with Zoroastrianism, the final judgment and the casting of the evil one into hell. There was no pact though between God and Lucifer. Man, in male and female form, God's final and greatest creation, was placed in a perfect place free from the taint of evil. Lucifer was allowed to tempt man, who had free will to choose between obeying God or not, as Lucifer was, to set himself in the place of God by eating from the tree of good and evil.

"We are evidence of what happened in the end. Man chose his own way, and here we are, living every day with the consequences of Adam's decision."

"Do you blame Adam for what he did?" Aschek asked.

"No, who is to say that I would not have done the same thing? Adam was perfect, without a speck of pride or evil, living in the presence of God, and yet he allowed Eve to be deceived, put up no argument against what she was doing and then chose to enter into the secret knowledge of good and evil with his wife, fully aware that he was breaking God's explicit command. Eve was deceived. God had spoken to Adam, not to Eve about the tree. Adam knew full well what he was doing. Who can say I would have done any different? Secret knowledge is the most delicious, is it not? Are we not always tempted to discover what no one else knows? And then the greatest temptation of all, to let on that we posses some knowledge that only the very few can handle, the elite, the initiated. We set ourselves in the place of God. I believe that if something is true, it is true for everyone. If it has to be kept secret, then there is a flaw somewhere that the 'select few' are afraid will cause their entire house to come tumbling down if discovered for the farce that it is."

"Harsh words my friend," Aschek said, "but I see your point. The Avesta has become that in many ways. It is a secret that is closely guarded. We are even having trouble getting the various temples to bring their fragmented copies to Rhagae to be compiled. I must admit, I do not understand the immense fear they feel at having the writings brought into the light. Was not Zoroaster's mission to teach man the ways of Ahura Mazda? How can that happen if his writings are held in the utmost secrecy, only available to a select few?"

"What are your feelings regarding that secrecy, Aschek? It sounds as if you are of the opinion that the writings should be made public." I was tempted to tell Aschek at that moment of my true mission, of my intention to take a copy of the Avesta back to Alexandria. I felt that his next words would seal the fate of my mission. I had come so far, had studied so avidly to prepare myself for this. And here was the second in rank on the team that was compiling this sacred work. Only God, in his infinite wisdom could have orchestrated this series of events, the compilation taking place right when I began my journey, my meeting Mihret, my befriending Aschek. I sat watching him as he pondered his answer.

At that very moment, it was as if every camel in the caravan began to moan. The sound was deafening. Fang and Zos' camel stood and began running west, back in the direction we had just come. Shouts rang out at the south end of the camp. The air was filled with a dull roar. I had never heard anything like it. It was as if the air were vibrating with a dull thunder, but how could it when the sky was a flawless blue? The ground began to shake, and I suddenly found it difficult to stand. My first thought was of Zos, who was on an errand to find bread. Tents began to cave in and the ground began to crack between me and Aschek. The split widened. I began to back away on my hands and knees. Aschek, who was still standing seemed unsure as to what to do, jump to my side or back away himself on the opposite side of the rift. "Back up, Aschek!" I shouted, but it was too late, another shift in the earth and Aschek had fallen into the crack which had now widened considerably. "No!" I shouted, as I scrambled to the edge to see where Aschek had gone. There he was, clinging desperately to the edge of the side where he had fallen. I could not see the bottom of the crevice, and I knew it was only a matter of moments before his fate would be sealed. The rumbling stopped as suddenly as it had begun. I stood and ran to a point where the gap was narrow enough to jump over. I darted back to where Aschek had fallen in and grabbed his wrists. He was slipping. "Hold tight, Aschek! I have you." I pulled him up and out of the gaping hole in the ground.

We both lay panting on the ground when the roar began again. We both scrambled away from the crack where Aschek had fallen. The ground moved under us as if we were standing on water. My strength failed me. Was it the end of the world? The gap where Aschek had just fallen suddenly closed with a crash and the ground buckled creating a ridge that ran as far through the camp as I could see. Again, the roaring stopped as suddenly as it began. Aschek and I lay gasping beside each other, in shock, Aschek in the knowledge that he had barely escaped being crushed and me, horrified that I had almost *seen* him be crushed. I pulled myself up on my knees, lifted my hands and gave thanks to God for our near escape, his providence and the strength to help those who had not been so fortunate.

Zos came running towards us. "Teacher!" he shouted. "Are you alright?" I embraced him from my kneeling position.

"Zos, I am so glad you are okay. We are both alright."

"What was that?" I looked at Aschek.

"It was what is known as an earthquake. They are rare, but they do happen. Kaleb, you saved my life. How can I ever repay you?"

"It was God's will, Aschek. It could have just as easily been reversed, and I could have been the one saved by you."

"But it was not, and I will find a way to reward you for what you have done."

CHAPTER SEVENTY-EIGHT

"Truth should not be hidden," Aschek said to me the next morning, as we were setting up our tents. We had spent the whole of the previous day walking around the camp, helping where we could, while Zos stayed and watched our things. It had taken quite a bit of time to locate and bring the camels back, but once that was done, we began our mission of mercy. It seemed, as far as we could tell, that the earthquake had inflicted more fear than damage. Each of us, in his own way, had comforted people and calmed their fears.

"Meaning?"

"Meaning, I agree with you that if an account cannot hold up to the scrutiny of criticism and be reasonably defended, it is not worth believing, and that should include accounts of the essence of God."

"How does this relate to the Avesta?" I asked, hoping that another earthquake did not hit just as Aschek delivered his answer.

"It should be public knowledge, available to whoever wants to study it."

"Take a seat Aschek. I have something to confess."

CHAPTER SEVENTY-NINE

Without going into too much detail, I outlined my trip up to this point to Aschek. I explained my position in Alexandria as head of Religious Acquisitions of the Library. I listed the various other sacred works we housed, the Egyptian religious texts including the Book of the Dead, the Septuagint translated over 400 years ago, the Christian Gospels and letters, the musings of Pythagoras, Plato and Aristotle on religious issues among countless other essays and letters on the innumerable facets of religion gathered from as far away as Gades and my fervent desire to include in that collection the writings of one of the largest religions of the east, the Avesta. I recounted my studies of Pahlavi and Avestan to that end. I expressed how God, in his providence had brought us together.

"It is quite extraordinary how we come to be traveling this road together," Aschek said, "almost as if fate had intended for us to meet."

"I do not believe in fate Aschek," I said.

"So why exactly are you telling me all of this? Do you intend to somehow use my influence to obtain a complete copy of the Avesta? Do you realize that no such thing exists? There are fragments, scattered far and wide. King Vologases, in his wisdom, is attempting to put together a compendium of all the writings, but it is still in its initial stages."

"I am a patient man. In fact, I would even be willing to help in the compilation process. I am very experienced not only in translating and transcribing but in the processes of organizing and cataloguing. I have worked in the Library since I was seven years old, my whole life basically. I would prove an invaluable resource for you and your team. I could work with them to standardize the compilation and transcription process."

"And how am I supposed to introduce you? We have guaranteed the priests that no eyes but those of the initiated will see the scriptures. They would never permit a Christian, much less one who works for the Library of Alexandria to lay a finger on the holy writings."

"Food for thought. I am sure you will think of something. Where better to preserve the writings for posterity, in what more secure spot than in the greatest library in the world where it can be read and studied by some of the most educated and prolific writers of all time. And I could even promise to keep its existence secret for our lifetime in order to protect your good name."

The conversation ended without having come to a conclusion as to how I would be incorporated into the team, but I was confident that my secret was safe with Aschek. After all, I had saved his life. He himself said that he owed me recompense.

PART TWELVE

RHAGAE

Gregorian Calendar – June 24ᵗʰ, 162
Alexandrian Calendar – Paoni 16ᵗʰ, Second Shomu
The Season of Harvesting
2ⁿᵈ year of Marcus Aurelius

"Inquire about everything that you may understand it. Be good tempered and
magnanimous, that your disposition may be attractive."
(Ancient Egyptian proverb)

"A man's homeland is wherever he prospers."
(Aristophanes, *Plutus, l. 1151*, ca 400 BC)

CHAPTER EIGHTY

On the 16ᵗʰ day of Paoni we reached the outskirts of Rhagae.
The caravanserai located outside the city was a flurry of activity.
Aschek had mules brought from the city to aid us in transporting
everything to an inn after I refused as delicately as possible his
invitation to stay at his home. I had insisted on not infringing any
more on his hospitality. After all, that is not how I wanted to spend
the credit I had earned. Besides, I had learned on past excursions
that it was much more pleasant to preserve one's own privacy. The
freedom far outweighed the conveniences of staying in someone's
home.

This city was much smaller than Ecbatana and not as important
for the silk trade. More than anything, it was a sort of replenishing
point between Ecbatana and Hecatompylos. It was however, for my
purposes, more important than both combined. It was the center for
Zoroastrian leadership, and most significantly, was where the
compilation of the Avesta was taking place. Aschek had introduced
us to a well situated inn at the center of the city, perpendicular to the
Grand Temple of Zarathustra and directly opposite the spring palace
of the King of kings Vologases IV, who was still being detained in

the west of the empire due to the impending war with the Romans. The room was simple, two low narrow beds, a table, bare wooden walls and a fireplace. From what I had heard of the winters here, that was probably the most important accoutrement of the room. The only other piece of furniture was what looked like a bookcase though empty of books. It would serve nicely as a place to keep our things. The pièce de résistance, however, was the row of giant open-latticed windows, shutters pushed wide to afford an unobstructed view of the plaza. Zos and I, as was our custom, once unpacked and organized, both took a long bath to wash away the grime of the journey, worse now for the heat. We were in bed early the first night in the city, but I lay awake long after lying down, meditating on the events that would unfold here. How long would I remain here? How long had I been gone already? I had expected the mission to take at most a year, and so far things were looking good. I had accomplished much in only a third of the time I had allotted. But the compilation process was just beginning, and experience told me that it took longer than six months to edit, categorize and consolidate the amount of writing that was expected to arrive from all corners of the empire. I closed my eyes and smiled at the images behind my eyelids, images of the Library, nestled between the Nile and the Sea. From the great porches along the northern wall, there was an unobstructed view of the towering Pharos of Alexandria, the greatest lighthouse in the world. When would I see the lighthouse again, smell the Sea, hear the calls of the churches on festival days. In my imagination I wandered to the edge of the Sea, the sand sticking to the bottom of my feet, caressed by the lapping of the cool water. Sleep came over me unannounced, on the edge of the Sea under a cloudless Egyptian sky.

CHAPTER EIGHTY-ONE

Aschek never told me how he did it, but within five days of being in Rhagae, I was on the team. It was unprecedented; a foreigner, a non-Zoroastrian no less, in charge of the Avesta team or the Z-team, as I had dubbed it. My secret was out, part of it at least. It was now known that I was from the Library of Alexandria, but it was believed that I had been called there for the explicit purpose of training and overseeing the Z-team. I would not be allowed to read any portion of the manuscripts, only organize their compilation. The fact that I could understand Avesta was kept secret, and mention was never made of any interest in obtaining a finished copy of the final document.

Work would take place in the temple, which was conveniently situated less than fifty steps from the door of the inn where I had been installed, a fact I gathered from Zos who had counted it off. An entire wing of the temple had been dedicated to this momentous effort. There was a room for housing the documents that were arriving every day. Some were in scroll form, very few in the more modern codex form. There was a room for the documents to be examined and classified as to date of writing, place of origin and category, Gathic, Datic or Hadha-manthric, and then a room for housing the documents once they had been categorized. There was a large hall dedicated solely to the transcribers, and finally a large room set up in the style of a mini-amphitheater where the training would take place.

I started immediately, assessing what we would need to carry out the project. A long high table and stools were needed for the examination and classification room. Special bookcases needed to be constructed for the room that would house the categorized documents with places for labeling the shelves. But most importantly, we needed parchment. Papyrus was used in such great quantity in Egypt, the sole manufacturer, due to the prolific copies of texts being incorporated in the Library there, that there was little to none left for export. Parchment had grown to be the most popular medium of writing in the East these days. Besides, the Christians in Egypt had developed a revolutionary system for creating codices from parchment, and most Christian literature was bound this way. We also needed copious amounts of ink, primarily black, but also in more spectacular colors for the decorating of the text. Special copying desks were constructed for the transcribers, tilted ever so slightly to facilitate the copying with a surface area sufficiently large to allow for an original and a blank parchment. There were a myriad of smaller items that had to be obtained which I detailed in long lists. I was in my element. This was second nature to me as I had participated in this type of activity on a continual basis in my work in the Library. It was common knowledge that all manuscripts that arrived on any vessel stopping in the Alexandrian port were confiscated and copied, the original staying in the Library, the copy being sent back. It had become a very quick and efficient process, and the accuracy of documents transcribed in the Library was legendary. Fortunately I had the reputation of the Library behind me; otherwise, gaining the respect of the team, made up entirely of Parthian devotees to Zoroaster, would have been impossible. The fame and legacy of the Library I hailed from was the only thing I had going for me, a young, gangly Ethiopian of dubious origin.

"And this is Kaleb of Adulis, scribe and expert in transcription from the Library of Alexandria. He is fluent in many languages including Pahlavi, and has extensive experience in leading teams such as ours. It is an honor to have him here guiding our historic endeavor to create a comprehensive compendium of all literature relating to our cherished Avesta and an ordered compilation of all the sacred writings of our beloved Zoroaster."

Unenthusiastic grunts of acknowledgment greeted me as I took the podium. Aschek had set up this meeting to introduce me and to clarify my role in this venture. More than anything, it was to establish my rank of authority with the Z-team. I was more excited than nervous. I had spoken in front of large groups any number of times, and I was confident of what I was doing. I was elated in fact that I found myself in this spot, at this moment, on the verge of a historic event that would find its culmination, for me at least, in having a copy of the fruits of this team housed in the Department of Religious Archives of the Library. This would be my greatest acquisition to date.

"Thank you Scribe Aschek and all of you on this illustrious team for allowing me to not only take part but to aid in the organization of this process. This is not an easy task we are undertaking. Nevertheless, what we accomplish here, in these next months, will bear fruit for centuries to come. There is no greater task than to pass on to future generations the sacred writings of our forebears, nothing that will live longer than the written word if correctly preserved, and our job is to make every conceivable effort to maintain the integrity of what we are transmitting to our progeny. I would like to begin by outlining the framework under which we will be working." With that, I expounded on the various tasks we would be performing, the order in which things would be accomplished and then left it to Aschek to assign the jobs to the members of the team. As he knew them better, he was better able to determine who would be best for what. My job was to train and oversee. I sat back and watched as Aschek spoke. There were fifty people currently on the Z-team, and it consisted of an equal number of both men and women. A couple of men were still casting surreptitious glances at me, trying to decide how the interloper wiggled his way into this effort. The majority of men however sat with long, dour faces under towering turbans, eyes less eager than mine, disappointingly unenthusiastic. All but one. He sat in the back, face eagerly turned to Aschek, hanging on his every word, eyes sparking, seemingly itching to commence. Unlike the other Z-team members, he was young, perhaps my age, clean shaven with a smooth high forehead and fair skin. At least there was one man on this team with whom it might be fun to work. All but one of the women was older than me, but unlike the men, they looked on excitedly as Aschek spoke. They had also been markedly more interested in what I had to say than the men. All except for Zayba. She wore a compact varicolored turban that sat on her head like flatbread on a stump. Her face bore a scowl that showed signs of being a permanent feature, not an expression reserved just for me. It did not change when I traded places with Aschek. Her nose was long and hooked, and her eyes peered out of deep sockets, *seeking whom they might devour*, the expression came back to me from the apostle Peter's letters. How ironic that her name meant beautiful. The one young woman had a sweet face, hair escaping in all directions from her head scarf, white skin, black eyes and ruby-red lips. Her eyes were glued to Aschek's face, and she sat as still as a marble flower vase.

Looking at Zayba carried my thoughts to Zos and the teacher I had lined up for him. She was old enough to be my mother and reminded me of Mihret's maid Sekhet. But she was sure to keep Zos in line, and I was sure he would achieve fluency in Greek, Aramaic, mathematics and anything else she decided to teach him before we left here. "Is she really my teacher?" Zos asked with a bewildered look on his face, like a bird suddenly caught in a cage. "Is there no family here like Yonas' who I could study with instead?"

"Zos," I said, suppressing a smile, "she comes very highly recommended, and she can teach you everything rather than my having to deal with two or three tutors. Just wait; you will grow to love her." Zos looked at something crawling on the ceiling, the closest he would come to rolling his eyes.

"Your word is my command Teacher," he responded now, as if submitting to a fate he knew had been predetermined long before he was born. "I will be the best student she has ever had," he said unenthusiastically.

"That is more like it! You even have your own spot in the temple where I will be working every day, so I can check up on you to make sure everything is going smoothly and that you are making progress with your new teacher." I could tell Zos was holding his tongue. He was a good boy, Zos, obedient and intelligent. I would make a scribe of him yet. He might not be excited now about the prospects of the coming months, but I knew he would look back on this as the time that prepared him for his future success.

CHAPTER EIGHTY-TWO

Documents had been piling up in the arrivals chamber. We organized them according to their points of origin, from as nearby as Hecatompylos to as far away as Tashkent and Pattala. Thirty people had been chosen for the initial stages of processing in the examination room, the young man and woman among them. As nothing else could be accomplished till all the documents were in order, I put the majority of the team members on this job. I had requested that Aschek place the younger members with me since that is where I would be most often, and I looked forward to perhaps making some friends since I had little idea of how long I might continue here. Each examiner had a runner, young boys and girls about Zos' age. Their job was to obtain one document at a time from the holding chamber, make sure it was labeled with point of origin and carefully bring it to the examining room for their "boss." Zayba was the keeper of the holding chamber, and the runners tried as hard as possible to avoid going to that room alone. Everyone was afraid of Zayba.

"Don't pull on it like that!" she would snap if the document was uncooperative when lifted from the pile. "Careful! You're going to tear it," you could hear her shriek from the examining room. "Where did you learn to handle parchment, while shearing sheep? You damage that document and it's *your* head that will roll!" The runners would cower on the way in and practically crawl out, but they handled each document as if they were carrying a snowflake that might melt.

Once the document was in the hands of the examiner, it would be carefully spread out on a portion of the long table. Each examiner had a section of table that was assigned to him or her, where there was a stack of small rectangular sections of parchment to be used as labeling cards, a pen and ink and strips of soft cloth for tying the documents and attaching the card before they were sent to the library, the name we had given the room where the documents would be filed once labeled.

I had hung a large sign on the wall of the room listing the items that were to be recorded on the card and in what order: the provenance, the Nask category: Gathic, Datic or Hadha-mânthric, whether a compilation or partial piece, the sub-category, the number of pages if it were a codex or length of the scroll if it were parchment or papyrus, and a number from one to three indicating where it would fall in the final compilation. It was a tedious process, but it went fairly quickly. It was unnecessary to read an entire document to determine its placement. Once a document had been processed, it was sent via runner to the library where it was housed in one of three sections according to the number it had been given.

This process was going to take months. There were more than 200 documents so far, and more were arriving. But as I told Aschek and the Z-team at one of the daily morning meetings, there was no time limit, no deadline. The goal was a masterpiece, and masterpieces took time. We would finish when we finished. Every step in this process required time, focus and precision. None of the jobs were easy, but they were all equally important. I tried to send the team to their jobs each morning with something inspirational, mostly a quote that had been gleaned the previous day in the examination process. I encouraged each of the members to be on the lookout for something inspirational that could be used the following morning.

Aschek was struck at the smooth workings of my system. "You are amazing!" he commented one morning. "I had not really given a lot of thought as to how this all needed to be set up, but watching it in action, I am truly dazzled by your ingenuity."

"I am not ingenious. This is a tried and true process that we use daily at the Library." Although I feigned nonchalance, I was secretly proud of the way things had been organized. It really was impressive. "Of course, none of this would be possible without having such an excellent location to carry out this work. We could be working in some dark and moldy hole with two people. Having the tools we need makes all the difference."

"Has the mutual admiration meeting adjourned yet?" Zayba announced as she entered the room, now empty of examiners. Everyone had apparently gone home except her.

"Not yet Zayba," Aschek turned to look at her. "I would like to compliment you as well on your careful handling of the documents under your care."

"Humph," was her only response, but I could see she was pleased. "I came to ask for an aid. I need someone to label the pieces as they arrive. I can't be doing two things at once, watching those imps running in and out while scribbling notes for the incoming documents."

"You are absolutely right," I said. "You will have an assistant tomorrow. My main concern is that this process go smoothly."

"Right," she said dismissively as she turned to leave. Aschek winked at me as she left.

"And who do you propose we punish with that duty?" he asked.

"How about one of those dour faced old men that we have left waiting in the docks. They might even enjoy each other's company."

"Excellent idea. I will assign Zardusht. He will be delighted I am sure."

AUTUMN

"Perseverance is more prevailing than violence; and many things which cannot be overcome when they are together, yield themselves up when taken little by little."
(Plutarch, *Lives, Sertorius, sec. 16*, ca 100)

CHAPTER EIGHTY-THREE

Days turned into weeks, and weeks into months, and one morning I woke up with my cover pulled to my chin, exposing my feet. Parthians were generally quite a bit shorter than I was. It was late in the month of Thout. Through the open window, I noticed that the sky was overcast, the first time in weeks. A faint smell of rain blew in with the wind. I had yet to see a storm here. Maybe today was the day. Zos entered with a steaming bowl of water. "I thought this might warm you up Teacher," he said in Aramaic. "It's freezing this morning." He shivered and proceeded to lose half the water in the bowl, scalding his hands as he did so. But he bore it stoically, and passed me the bowl, wincing at the pain in his hands.

"Dip your hands in the bowl on the table there Zos. It will calm the stinging. I am sure the water is cold this morning." I sipped from the bowl he had handed me. The warm water coursed down my throat, into my belly and warmth spread throughout my body. Amazing. As our custom was to bathe in the evenings, I was ready to go in minutes. Zos and I walked together across the plaza to the temple. Normally the sky was still pink when we covered this short distance, but today it was cloudy and ominously caliginous.

The temple was icy and shrouded in shadow. We made our way to the Z-team transcription room. As usual, we were the first to arrive. We lit the lanterns along the walls, and I built a fire in the stove. It was going to be a frigid day. And this was just the beginning of the cold season. I needed to have Zos and myself fitted for winter clothes. I had not intended to be away for so long. My thoughts traveled back to Alexandria. At this time of year, the floods had begun to recede, a shallow sea of glasslike beauty still covered the land, and canoes instead of camels were the favored mode of transportation. Here the harvest was past, and rather than fertile, flooded earth, the air smelled stale and thirsty. Rain was coming though. A storm was on its way. I was sure of it.

The sorting, examining and categorizing was finished. Now began the even more tedious process of harmonizing duplicate copies. Similar documents were read simultaneously in silence by teams of readers while one copy was read aloud in the hearing of all. It was read very slowly. Faraz and Shirin, the youngest scribes, had been chosen for this job. They had good eyesight and strong, pleasant reading voices. As they slowly read, as many scribes as were necessary to cover all of the identical passages that had been sent in sat silently and read their copies. When a word diverged, the scribe's hand would shoot up and a runner would announce to stop. When discrepancies like this occurred, a team of scholars, not part of the 50-member Z-team, would decide how to handle differences, which would be taken as authoritative and whether or not the pieces at variance would be included as footnotes. Sometimes those discussions could take all day, at which point, all work would cease until consensus had been reached.

The day before, we had just finished the portion of the Gathas comprising seventeen hymns composed purportedly by Zoroaster himself eleven hundred years before. It had been a monumental task, but afterwards, we celebrated with a party. Aschek hired musicians, and at his home, we had a dinner and dancing. Today would commence with the next portion which included the creed, commentary and supplementary material supporting Zoroaster's hymns. Aschek would assign eleven scribes, one of whom was the reader, the new task of making copies of the first seventeen chapters. The goal was to create 500 copies of the complete Avesta which would be distributed all over the empire. I had dealt with a feeling of unease at being party to the distribution of what I believed to be a false representation of God. Was I furthering the ignorance of an entire generation of people? Was I the facilitator in setting in motion the spread of a false religion over an even wider area? I still had my doubts, but my primary goal here was to secure a copy for the Library where it would be exposed for what it was, the misguided writings of an eastern mystic who tried as best he could to record what he understood of the truth of God.

The transcription room was ready. Each desk was set up with a supply of reed pens, a ceramic inkwell ingeniously built into the desk and a fresh sheet of parchment, cut to twice the size of the codex, folded and sewn together, making a page that could contain writing on both sides. Aschek and I had discussed what we believed would be the most convenient size for the codices of the Avesta. Should the entire work be in one single tome? Should each of the three collections of Nasks have their own binding? It was decided to bind each collection of seven Nasks separately to facilitate ease of use, and the size of the codex would be more manageable. A small army of runners were seated along the walls, ready to come to the assistance of the scribes, to refill inkwells, to replace sheets of parchment, to blow on freshly written parchment to insure it did not smear. A reader stood at the front of the room and read the approved copy of the first eight chapters. As he dictated, the scribes would painstakingly copy out in delicate script the words he intoned. When a page had been completed, it was read again, from the bottom up, to insure that every word had been written correctly, that no mistakes had been made. Finally, the number of words and then number of letters on the page were counted and compared to the original.

The majority of my time this particular day was spent observing the process of transcription, to make sure protocol was being followed and to be available in case any questions were raised. The only piece left at this point was the binding. And it would be weeks before we had anything to bind. After all, we were only one Nask into the twenty-one of the complete Avesta.

That evening, I suggested to Aschek that we increase the number of scribes involved in the transcription process to fifty. At that rate, the script would only have to be read ten times to obtain the required 500 copies. At this rate, we would never finish. I had underestimated the amount of time and labor involved.

"That is a good suggestion, but we will be compelled to search high and low for forty more scribes. We have already employed every scribe from here to Babylon to work on this project," he stated in his hyperbolic manner.

"Surely not," I countered. "We could have criers sent out in Ecbatana, Hecatompylos and the other neighboring cities. I guarantee you there are scribes out there that would jump at the chance to be involved in this work."

"You are forgetting, there are very few people who still know Avestan and fewer still who can write it. It is unlike Pahlavi or Latin or Greek for that matter. It is a very ancient language, not in use anymore outside of the temples."

"So why not translate the Avesta into Pahlavi and then send out 500 copies of a Pahlavi Avesta?"

Aschek stared at me as if I had just announced that the world was going to end. "Ahura Mazda forbid that we write his holy word in a common language like Pahlavi. The message was delivered in Avestan, and in Avestan it will continue to be transmitted."

"Right," I said somewhat ironically. "So Ahura Mazda speaks Avestan? What if, just what if it was written in Avestan because that was the language people spoke at that time?"

Aschek and I often had this type of discussion. He seemed to enjoy defending his points against a non-believer, but I immediately discerned that this was not a topic for discussion. "It must be in Avestan, and that is final," he said mirthlessly.

"Who am I to argue, Aschek? I am here at your whim. I will not mention it again. Avestan it is."

CHAPTER EIGHTY-FOUR

Aschek was right. It took another three months to gather as many scribes as we needed. By then, we had finished the entire first set of seven Nasks and were in the middle of the next Datic section. There were already fifty copies of the Gathas which were in the process of being bound. It was only a matter of time before the other 450 were completed now that we had 55 scribes working all day.

The binding process required a new room, or rather rooms, to be set up. It was decided that the covers of the books would be made with thin sheets of polished olivewood to protect the pages from bending. The individual pages of parchment were sewn together. Holes were first made with a wooden awl rather than a metal one to avoid touching the pages with an instrument associated with war. The pages were then sewn together, one by one, to form the codex. Finally, the cover was attached. Leather pouches were also being fabricated to serve as protective covering for the codices. The name of the book would be stitched on the front of each pouch. The final product was going to be quite beautiful.

Meanwhile, I had not only finally sent a fairly detailed account of my travels and current situation in Rhagae to Ptolemaios and my parents, I had written Silara several letters, glimpses of moments in my day, of the snow on the mountains around the city, of the sun over the temple in the evening from the windows of my room. I retrieved my latest letter from her. She had received my gift from Ctesiphon. Sitting in front of the fireplace in my room, I reread her letter for the tenth time, lifting the scroll to my face to inhale the fragile perfume still clinging tenuously to the paper.

Kaleb, how I wish I had your likeness hanging round my neck as you have mine. The days run one into another as I wait for word from you. I have read your letters one million times, hearing your voice, faint, distant, seeing what your eyes see, what your mouth describes.

The mirror is hanging in the family room. I stare sometimes into the mirror, wishing it were a portal to you, wishing I could see your face looking back at me instead of my own sad reflection. My mother has taken to calling me vain, for staring so often into it. I have not told her the true reason for my obsession.

Zos entered carrying several scrolls and dumped them onto his bed. I put away the letter, but not before Zos caught me. "Studying something Teacher?" he smiled mischievously.

"It is none of your concern young Zos," I said. "What do you have there?"

"Homework," he sighed. "There is no end to it. I study all day and work all evening."

"Not every evening. I do not remember ever seeing you bring back so much to read."

"You are right Teacher. I exaggerate. It is rare I am given this amount of work. I hope there is plenty of oil for the lamp because I may not sleep tonight."

"What are you studying?"

"Astronomy. We are to try to explain the cause of the lunar eclipse from last month."

"Do you have any theories?" I asked smiling, thinking of all the resources he would have if we were in the Library."

"None," he said with a despairing look in his eye, his palms upraised.

"Allow me to draw you a diagram." With that I began to draw out Ptolemaios' diagram from his most recent *Almagest*. Zos hung over me rapt.

WINTER

"Not snow, no, nor rain, nor heat, nor night keeps them from accomplishing their appointed courses with all speed."
(Herodotus, *Histories, VIII, 98*, ca 460 BC)

"Antiphanes said merrily that in a certain city the cold was so intense that words were congealed as soon as spoken, but that after some time they thawed and became audible; so that the words spoken in winter were articulated next summer."
(Plutarch, *Morals. On Man's Progress in Virtue*, ca 100)

CHAPTER EIGHTY-FIVE

The fifteenth day of Koiak and all of Rhagae commemorated Zarathust No Diso in memory of the death of Zoroaster. We had been gone almost a year now. Alexandria seemed a distant memory, a previous lifetime. Here the world was a blanket of white. I could not even remember what it felt like to be warm. It was as if I had been born cold. Zos and I stood in front of the latticed windows of our room, the shutters pulled back, observing the roiling gray-black clouds amassing over the snow-capped mountains in the distance. We were dressed Parthian style. I had adopted their dress when the temperature began to drop. The baggy pants, tunic, leather boots and wool cape provided much more comprehensive protection against the cold than the normal Egyptian tunic. Over my scribe's cap, I wore a fur hat that covered my ears. Zos' outfit mirrored mine. We each held a cup of hot tea in front of us, warming our hands, the steam swirling in the air before us, disturbed by the winds invading our room.

Faraz, the young reader of the Z-team, invited us before leaving work yesterday to a small gathering in his home to celebrate the occasion. Zos and I were grateful to escape our frozen cell for any reason. It had snowed during the night, something neither Zos nor I had ever seen. We had both seen snow-capped mountains at a distance, but we had never touched snow with our own hands or seen it covering houses and streets. It was magical. Now here we stood, transfixed in front of the window of our room, covered head to foot in Parthian winter clothes sipping tea, silently absorbing this most spectacular view.

"Ready?" I said, still staring out the window. Zos leaned towards the window and breathed, fogging a portion of the wooden lattice. Then, with the index finger of his right hand, he spelled out "yes" in Aramaic.

"Zos! You have learned Aramaic script!"

He smiled up at me. "You were right Teacher. My teacher has taught me many things. I was wrong to doubt you."

"I am very proud of you Zos," I said as I squatted to be at eye level with him. "You have worked very hard since we arrived in this city. In fact, the times I have heard you speak Pahlavi, you sound almost like a native of these parts. You have picked up the sound of it even better than I. You are going to be an exceptional scribe. Your parents will be so proud of you when you return."

Zos beamed at me. Unexpectedly, he wrapped his arms around me and hugged me. "I would be working the fields with my brothers if not for you Teacher," he said. "I will never forget what you have done for me." I took his shoulders and held him at arm's length looking him squarely in the eyes.

"All I did was provide the opportunity Zos. You are the one that has taken full advantage of it. And look at how tall you are getting. I am sure you have grown the span of three fingers since we left Alexandria. This traveling agrees with you."

"I love it Teacher. Now shall we try another new thing?"

"Such as?" I asked standing.

"Walking in the snow! I'm ready to get out in it."

"Let us go then, before we freeze in this ice-box of a room." The hallway and stairwell were no warmer than our room this morning. I smiled watching Zos exhale slowly to see his breath. He never tired of it, like a game that brought him immense pleasure. "Watch where you are going Zos," I said as he almost missed the final step before reaching ground level. Falling forward, he caught himself just before hurling his body headlong into the front door. Seemingly on cue, the door opened from the outside. As if brought forth from the dark clouds gathering in the distance and the bitter blast of wind blowing through the open entryway, a hooded grey figure stepped into the foyer. Zos' gasp was audible. "Peace," I said bowing slightly. "Can I be of service?" I had automatically spoken in Pahlavi, the language of my daily discourse.

"Peace," came the gravelly voice from the depths of the hood. Rag-wrapped hands rose to the hood to pull it back, revealing a head chiseled from granite. The stranger's hair was close cropped in military style and a deep scar framed the right side of his face. "I am looking for a room," he said, his cold grey eyes reflecting the color of his cloak, his face devoid of emotion.

"I will call the innkeeper," I said as I turned. Zos instantly appeared at my side. The stranger stood motionless, feet firmly planted beside the open door, impervious to the gusts of wintry wind ruffling his heavy cloak. Shortly we were back with the innkeeper, Zos still close by my side. Of no further use, we made our way outside.

Zos paused at the entrance to the inn, before stepping into the snow. "What are you waiting for Zos?" I asked.

"I don't want to spoil it. Look at the footprints the scary man in grey left," he said quietly as if fearing lest the stranger could hear him talking. "It's so perfect, and we're going to spoil it."

"There is no way around that Zos. As Solomon said, 'where there are no oxen, the manger is clean.' Sometimes we have to make a mess in order to get anything done." Zos took a few tentative steps into the snow. "See, it is not so bad." Gaining courage from this brief foray, he ran into the middle of the plaza and jumped up and down turning in circles. He scooped up a handful of snow and threw it into the air watching as it fell around him. "Well, you got over that quickly enough," I said as I approached.

We meandered through the winding streets of the city, stopping occasionally in tea shops to thaw out and drink some hot tea when we were too cold to go any further. We had not spent this much time together since arriving in the city several months before. "Zos, besides the classes, how have you been keeping yourself occupied?"

"I've made friends with some of the other students in my class. Our teacher gives us plenty of work, so there is not a lot of time to spare. Our favorite pastime though is to go to the hill north of our inn where you can see the entire city and the mountains in the distance. There we take turns telling stories, competing to see who can tell the best one. Sometimes, when a story is exceptionally good, I later set it to writing."

"And how many stories have you written?"

Zos sat in thought for a time. I lifted the green porcelain cup to my lips and took another sip of the jasmine tea. "Maybe twenty." "Twenty!" I said. "That is fantastic Zos. You will have your own contribution to make when we return home." Heads had turned in our direction when I shouted twenty.

"When are we returning home Teacher?" Zos asked quietly.

"Lord willing, we will be home this time next year," I said, finishing off my tea. "Shall we continue? Show me where you and your friends meet to tell stories."

Although my feet were dry, thanks to the fresh coat of wax Zos had applied to our boots, they were numb with cold by the time we reached the top of the hill. A very light snow had begun to fall, dusting our fur caps and wool capes with fragile snowflakes. Zos and I both stopped and held out our tongues to taste the snow, fresh from the ever darkening clouds. Zos ran on ahead to a gnarled tree on a rocky ledge at the cusp of the hill. "This is it Teacher. This is where we sit and tell stories." I surveyed the vista before me. I could see the back of the inn where we were staying and the plaza and temple across from it. The city continued on for some distance before disappearing in the foothills of the Alborz Mountains, Mount Tochal towering in the distance. We both sat on the stone ledge and watched the snow fall over the city.

There was little movement on the streets. This festival was primarily celebrated indoors with prayers and study of scripture. A lone figure, almost camouflaged, pale grey against the white floor of the plaza, made its way towards the temple. Could that be the stranger that we had met before leaving? "Let us go Zos; I can no longer feel my posterior. We will make one more tea stop to warm up before going to Faraz' house party."

CHAPTER EIGHTY-SIX

"And then he said, 'I think she likes me.'" Faraz was barely able to finish the last sentence before collapsing into a fit of laughter. I grinned remembering the twinkle in Zarthust's eyes when told he had been assigned to work with Zayba.

"As they say," I said, "beauty is in the eye of the beholder."

Zos and Faraz' younger brother Taj were in the front room by the fire playing a board game while Faraz, Shirin, her brother and I sat around the table in the dining room sipping warm wine. The other guests had gone home leaving just the six of us. "Shirin, why don't you play something for us?" her brother asked.

"Taj, bring my barbat," Faraz called to his brother. "Kaleb, do you play an instrument?"

"I am decent at the Egyptian flute," I said, "but I do not have one on me."

"Not to worry." As Taj handed Shirin the lute-like instrument, Faraz asked him to bring the ney as well. Shirin lifted the barbat to her lap and began to pluck a tune with the quill Taj had handed her. Taj brought me the flute. Although it was a bit different from the flute I was accustomed to playing, I thought I could handle it.

"I will need to try this out," I said, blowing into it and testing the sound of it, trying the combinations as I covered the holes, discovering one for my thumb. Zos had joined us and smiled at the quite inharmonic sounds emanating from the instrument in my hands. "I have not played since I left home," I confessed. I tried again, this time working out a simple scale on the flute. Once I had my bearings with it, I tried a popular Egyptian tune I often played at home. When I finished, Zos clapped his hands.

"I like the sound of it," said Shirin. "Play it again, and I'll accompany you on the barbat." Faraz whispered something to Taj as I repeated the tune, growing more adept with each try. Shirin imitated the tune the first time round, waved for me to repeat it again and improvised harmony the second time. Taj returned with drums which he handed to Faraz. This time, with the three of us playing, Zos began to sing in Ge'ez. All eyes turned to him as he sang the ancient song of the fish king and the princess. Taj began to dance around in pirouettes. The song ended and we all applauded Zos.

"Another, another," Taj insisted.

"You play something this time Shirin, and I will accompany you." Shirin began slowly, the minor key haunting in its beauty. I listened to the entire thing before attempting to play along. Faraz joined in with a slow, steady beat. I mimicked the tune on the flute. Shirin's brother stood and began to dance with Taj and Zos. Faraz picked up the drum beat. As I became more familiar with the tune, I began to play harmony. Shirin picked up the tempo. Taj and Zos began to clap their hands over their heads as they turned in circles around the table. We played innumerable variations before Shirin, looking at me, began to slow the tempo. I played more softly. Faraz ended it with a flourish of the drums.

"Wonderful! Wonderful!" Shirin's brother applauded. For the rest of the evening, we played music, danced and sang. Faraz' parents joined us from their adjoining apartment along with their servants, and by the time we were ready to go, we had quite an audience, dancing, laughing and applauding.

"We must do this again," Faraz said as Shirin, her brother, Zos and I paused in the doorway before leaving.

"Agreed," I said. "But next time Zos and I must be your hosts."

"Nonsense," Shirin said, looking at her brother. "You must come to our home, right brother?"

"Definitely," he said clapping. "We will invite our friends, and it will be a true concert."

"I fear that we are ill prepared for a concert," I said worried. "I will need to start practicing."

"It's agreed then. We will plan for our next musical gathering. I must inform our parents to find the appropriate evening, and we will let you know," Shirin said.

"It's dark out. Can you find your way Kaleb, or shall one of our servants see you home?" Faraz offered.

"Not to worry. Zos and I have become well acquainted with your city by now, right Zos?"

"Right Teacher." I pulled his cap more firmly around his head, and we made to leave. "Thank you for a wonderful evening Scribe Faraz," Zos said as we exited the door of the apartment.

"Yes, Faraz, thank you so much for including us on this special day."

"The pleasure was all ours," his father said. "We look forward to repeating this many times."

Taj appeared with a lantern. "Take this; you'll need it to see your way home."

The street was as dark as the room in Dura. But for the lantern, we would not have been able to see even one step in front of us. Shirin and her brother parted ways with us at the corner, the flickering light of their lantern disappearing beyond the curve of the narrow cobble-stoned road. "This is creepy," Zos said as we made our way slowly forward. After the warmth of Faraz' home, the cold seemed even more intense, biting through my cape and making me shiver.

"We are not far," I said. "The plaza is one street up, and then we are home." The street opened up into the wide expanse of the plaza just as the moon emerged from behind a bank of clouds. Our shadows extended far to the right, ghostly on the white snow. The temple was silhouetted against the night sky. Clouds scurried across the face of the moon now. Light blinked from the windows of our inn. At the threshold, I extracted the key from the chain at my waist, and with fingers half frozen fumbled to open the door.

"Let me Teacher. Your hands are cold from holding the lantern. I've had mine tucked under my cape." I let Zos open the door, locked at sundown, and we made our way as quietly as possible up the stairs to our room. Before doing anything, I lit a fire to take the chill out of the air of our room while Zos lit candles. Slowly, the warmth began to spread to the corners of the room.

"I think we should skip a bath tonight, young Zos," I said as I changed into my bedclothes.

"I agree Teacher. I'm far too cold and tired." We stood in front of the fire waiting to warm ourselves enough so we could transfer a bit of the warmth to our icy beds. "Can you teach me the flute Teacher?" Zos asked as we slowly turned like goats over a fire pit, to warm every side of ourselves, the rug at the edge of the hearth doing little to keep my bare feet warm.

"Certainly Zos. But first we need flutes. I will give you money tomorrow, and you find us a couple of flutes after class." Zos rewarded me with a huge smile. "Now to bed. We have an early day tomorrow."

With the fire popping and crackling, we climbed into our beds after blowing out the candles. Being cold was not all bad. There was certain comfort in the warm blankets, the orange glow of the fire dancing on the bare walls of the room and the smell of wood burning. I began to fret that the fire would go out too soon leaving us to freeze in our beds. I knew I could throw on another log to prolong it, but I did not want to get up and lose the battle I had been waging with my sheets to warm them up a bit. Finally, I jumped out of bed, stepping quickly to the fire and tossed in another log. Sparks flew all directions as I ran back to my bed, pulling the covers tightly up to my chin. I lay for a time watching the flames dancing over the logs. In my head I replayed the music we had made at Faraz' house among the camaraderie of my new friends. I closed my eyes, and somewhere between mentally composing my next letter to Silara and

The Ethiopian

going over what had to be done tomorrow at the temple, I fell fast asleep.

CHAPTER EIGHTY-SEVEN

It was the second morning after Zarathust no Diso. The snow had melted leaving grey piles of icy slush where it had been swept out of the way and half-frozen puddles treacherous to the unsuspecting pedestrian. Zos and I made our way across the plaza to the temple. There was no wind but the icy air stung my face and further dried my cracking lips. We were stopped at the door by the scar-faced man we had met two days before at the door of our building. I had not seen him again and had actually forgotten entirely about the encounter. "Peace," I said as I reached to open the door to the temple.

"Halt," he announced in an unnecessarily hostile voice.

"Excuse me," I said. "I work here. Who exactly are you?" Zos stood behind me evidently expecting that I would be the one doing the defending here.

"I am the new temple guard," he said, his hostility not abating. "Allow me to consult my list of names, names of those permitted to enter."

"Who has given you this task of guarding the door?" I asked, my annoyance growing in proportion to the loss of feeling in my hands and face. "My servant and I are freezing and would like to begin work immediately."

"Aschek, the venerable scribe of the king has hired me," he said proudly. "Hold on, I recognize you. You live in the building across the plaza. I ran into you my first day here in the city."

"Am I that memorable?" I asked sarcastically. As far as I could tell, I was the only black man in the city. "Have you found our names yet, Kaleb and Zos."

"Yes, yes, a thousand pardons," he said, appearing authentically apologetic. At that moment, Aschek opened the door from the inside. He stood for a moment taking in the scene before him before speaking.

"What is going on here, Shash? Are you detaining these two out here in the cold?" he said, his anger rising.

"I was checking that their names were on the list," he said, the hostility replaced by mortification.

"I told you the head of this whole process was an Ethiopian and his boy servant and to be sure not to detain them at the door!" he said, exasperation and bile visible now in his face.

"Calm down Aschek, you are evidently the one who hired him, and he is just doing his job," I said feeling less generous than I sounded. "I just want to get inside before I turn into an ice statue here with Zos."

"Come in, come in," Aschek stood aside allowing us to enter. "I will just have a word with our new doorkeeper."

I closed the door behind us, but it failed to block Aschek's muffled shouting. "I wouldn't want to be that man right now," Zos observed.

"Well if he had not been so obtuse as to forget that the only two Ethiopians in the entire city, who he actually met two days ago, were the only ones Aschek specifically indicated were to be let in, he would not have any problems. That is what happens when you fail to listen to instructions and refuse to use your head."

Fires were already blazing in all of the stoves and the enormous fireplace in the transcribing room. "Aschek certainly got here early."

"Yes, I did," he said from behind me, startling both of us. "I have hired this new caretaker cum door guard, for what it is worth. I am beginning to entertain second thoughts."

"It is his first day on the job, Aschek. Give him a chance."

"You are quite the generous one. And you are the one he kept waiting outside for who knows how long, treating you like a criminal."

"Well, that is probably the treatment everybody who passes that door is going to receive today. Perhaps we should direct Shash to stay inside today and meet the team, so he will know who not to stop tomorrow."

"Good idea Kaleb. I will bring him in."

"You saved a lot of people from a cold wait at the door Teacher." Zos said as he turned to make his way to his classroom. "I'll see you later today," he said in Aramaic, "and you can begin teaching me how to play the flute."

CHAPTER EIGHTY-EIGHT

Despite getting off on entirely the wrong foot, Shash soon redeemed himself. He had the fires blazing and tea prepared every morning, besides braving the cold at the door to greet and hold the door for everyone as they arrived in the morning. Aschek explained to me that Shash, a native of Tashkent, had heard about the project from a scribe friend of his, and as an ex-mercenary out of work and an avid Zoroastrian, he thought he could serve in some capacity on this historic project. Shash was so enthusiastic about his job, he even beat me and Zos to work, and we were usually the first ones to arrive. I would see him from the window of our rooms standing at the door, stamping his feet to ward away the cold. And sometimes, I was certain I would catch him staring at our window. "That man is creepy," Zos said. "I don't trust him."

"What is not to trust, Zos? He is just a doorkeeper."

"I have a bad feeling about him. He may act polite when he opens the door for us, but his eyes deny his kindness. When he thinks we're not looking, I've seen him stare daggers at you."

"You are just imagining things Zos. He has been nothing but kind since that first morning." I said that to Zos, but I took his words to heart. He had no reason to hold a grudge, and he had good instincts about people, a fact I had grown to appreciate over this past year.

SPRING

"Now spring brings back balmy warmth."
(Gaius Valerius Catullus, *Carmina*, *WLVI*, *l. 1*, ca 50 BC)

"Even as in wintertime you cannot tell the healthy trees apart from the withered trees but in beautiful springtime you can tell the difference…"
(From the walls of the temple of Luxor)

CHAPTER EIGHTY-NINE

"I look forward to hearing that tune accompanied by Shirin's barbat," I said as I finished packing the list I made last night in my waterproof oiled bag. "Now let us go." Zos put away the flute he had been diligently practicing through the long, cold winter months. Shirin, Faraz and I had taken turns hosting dinners since Zarathust no Diso, and Zos grew steadily more proficient with each passing week, but not only on the flute. His language skills were improving by leaps and bounds. Besides the languages he left Alexandria with, Greek, Ge'ez and Egyptian, he now was fluent in Pahlavi and Aramaic. He could also read and write in all but Egyptian which I had not had the time to teach him, occupied as I was with the Z-team. I stood distractedly gazing out the window as Zos donned his cape against the torrential downpour. I could barely discern the temple through the curtain of rain. It had been coming down non-stop for three days, sometimes just a drizzle, sometimes hard like now, as if God had decided once again to drown the world in water.

Pulling our hoods over our heads and our capes tightly around us, we hurled ourselves out the door into the watery onslaught. In the span of two heartbeats, rain was matting my eyelashes and dripping from my nose, pernicious streams making their way past the collar clutched tightly in my right hand and down between my tunic and my bare skin causing me to shiver involuntarily, but not enough to slow down our voyage across the plaza. The roar of rain on my hood and the pavement was deafening. We pushed on, heads down crossing paving stones like frothy waves in a vast sea. More quickly than usual we found ourselves passing through the open door of the temple, Shash, looking like a water-logged statue, holding it open for us. He closed the door behind us leaving my hearing momentarily supremely acute with a dull ringing in the sudden silence. Zos and I stood for a moment, our capes creating puddles at our feet. Having caught our breath, we walked purposefully towards the blazing fire at the opposite end of the great entry hall. Zos hung our capes to dry and we stood before the fire doing slow motion pirouettes, our arms outstretched to allow for maximum coverage of warmth from the blaze. I rubbed my shirt against my skin, absorbing the stray drops of water that continued dripping down my chest tickling me with their icy tendrils.

By the time we were dry, the others had begun to arrive, taking our place at the fire. Zos and I parted ways as we did every morning, he to his classes and I to organize for the coming day. Reports were already coming from all over the empire of how pleased the priests were with the first set of Nasks that had reached them. The Gathas had been bound and sent out to temples far and wide as soon as the ground thawed from the last snow in early March. We were now in the process of packing for shipment the second set of Nasks, the legislative portion of the Avesta. The team here had produced one thousand books, five hundred of each set of Nasks, a monumental task worthy of the best teams of the Library in Alexandria. I felt quite proud of our achievement. We were now in the process of collating and transcribing the final seven Nasks, the Hadha-mânthra. This was the largest and most tedious portion as it was a miscellaneous collection of musings on everything from religion to hygiene to astronomy. But I could finally see a light at the end of the tunnel. We would surely be finished by fall if all continued smoothly, and by year's end Zos and I would be in Alexandria, Lord willing. I imagined our homecoming, my mother presiding over a feast at which the neighbors and my friends and colleagues at the Library were in attendance, tables spread with food all over the roof of our home, my head still damp from a swim in the lake, cooled by a salty breeze brought from the direction of the Pharos whose light flashed across the city colored pink by the setting sun.

"Tea?" I became aware of Shirin holding a small tray with a steaming cup out to me. I took it, reeling my thoughts back from Alexandria, disoriented, my attention refocused on the cup of tea scalding my hands.

"Ha, this is hot," I said trying to hold the cup by the top edge. Shirin quickly took the tea from me.

"Are you okay?" Shirin asked concerned.

"Yes, I am fine. I was just thinking of home," I said, gathering my wits. "Thank you for the tea. I should be able to hold it now." I took the cup from Shirin.

"We should get started I suppose," Shirin said as she turned towards the transcribing room. Aschek suddenly appeared at my side.

"It is a landmark day!" he remarked, in obviously high spirits. "The second of three books completed and ready to distribute. Truly an achievement worthy of celebration."

"Are you proposing a party? That is not a bad idea. The team could use a break, and this is a perfectly legitimate reason to take one," I said, pulling myself back to earth.

"Free your mind of worries," he said. "I will put it all together. How does tomorrow sound? The second set of Nasks goes out today. We can take tomorrow off and in the evening have a dinner party."

"It could not be in more capable hands," I said, mock bowing. "I will leave you to make the announcement. After you," I said holding my hand out for Aschek to lead the way into the next room.

"…and Aschek wants to say something that I am sure will please all of you," I said in closing before taking my seat at the front of the room.

PART THIRTEEN

BOUND FOR BAKTRA

Gregorian Calendar – April 15th, 163
Alexandrian Calendar – Paremoude 6th, Fourth Proyet
The Season of Emergence
3rd year of Marcus Aurelius

"Hateful to me as are the gates of hell, is he who, hiding one thing in his heart,
utters another."
(Homer *The Iliad Bk. IX, l,* ca 800 BC)

CHAPTER NINETY

Sunlight streamed through the open windows of our room overlooking the plaza. A cacophony of sound from the weekly market rose with the smell of drying goat and camel manure, cooking fish fresh from the Caspian, and dust from the open bags of ochre, red, brown, yellow and black spices from unpronounceable cities so far east one who ventured there would be in danger of falling off the edge of the world, if the world were flat that is. Although it was almost a year to the day since Zos and I passed under the arch of Anata and Acacio's courtyard on our way to Ecbatana, I felt that I had spent several years of my life in this city on the eastern fringe of the Parthian Empire. Ptolemaios' *Geographia* gave few details on anything further east apart from cities Alexander passed through or founded on his way to India. Nevertheless, this was the direction we were now headed.

The Avesta was complete and copies had been sent to centers of worship from Rhagae to the far reaches of the empire. Save one that is. Every copy had to be accounted for before being sent by courier to its intended destination. A strict count was made before the 500 copies left the Rhagaen temple. Rather than permit me to make my own copy, which he strongly opposed, Aschek agreed to mail me a copy. We had agreed that it was no longer feasible for me to travel back the way I had come. The war between Rome and Parthia was currently raging all along the western frontier. My only hope of making it back to Alexandria in one piece was to take the route towards Purushapura and south down the Indus to the Erythraean Sea. There was scanty information on the maps and journals I had with me on those regions, but I was comforted with the knowledge that I had contacts Marius had given me of traders he dealt with in the port city of Barbaricum. I had informed everyone in Alexandria to send any future letters there giving one named Inas as the receiver. I had also written him letting him know I would appreciate his keeping my correspondence till I arrived there since that was the only city through which I was sure to pass before sailing for Africa.

My copy of the Avesta was already on its way to Baktra, over 650 Roman leagues and more than two months of hard travel away. There it would remain in its package with a trusted though apparently exceedingly eccentric friend of Aschek's, waiting to be retrieved by me. Only Aschek and I would ever know what he had done to provide me with a copy of the sacred Zoroastrian scriptures.

"I'll be an old man by the time we arrive home," Zos despaired. "According to this map, this new route is at least four times further than that by which we arrived here." My copy of Ptolemaios' map lay spread out on my bed.

"I can see your mathematical studies have served you well my young Zos."

"I'm not joking Teacher. If it took us almost half a year to reach Ecbatana from Alexandria, we will not be home for," he paused as he did the calculation in his head, "another year and a half!"

"You forget something my budding mathematician. Over half the return journey is by water, and we will move much faster than by land."

"I suppose that's some consolation," Zos said, adjusting his scribe's cap. "One thing does not console me though, and that's the fact that Shash is accompanying us."

"He will prove a valuable asset, especially once we leave Hecatompylos. It is a dangerous road from there to Merv, and Shash is not only familiar with that area, but he is experienced in battle and can protect us."

"Hmph," Zos rolled the map up and slipped it into its oiled leather tube with the other scrolls. "We're almost ready Teacher. We haven't accumulated much in a year."

"Nothing material anyway."

"You're right. I'm taking away much more in my head than I arrived with. My tongue can handle three more languages now and my hand four, and I can play the flute and the drums besides managing mathematics and some rhetoric."

"Impressive Zos. Solomon said that wisdom is more precious than jewels. I would say you have accumulated quite some amount of treasure so far on this trip."

There was a loud knock on the door to our room. I opened it to the ever stoic Shash. We stood looking at each other. "Yes?" I finally ventured.

"The camels are at the atrium door sir," he said, a glint in his cold grey eyes.

"We are ready, are we not Zos?" I said turning, only to have to move aside as Zos hurried past, a large parcel resting on his head. "I guess that is a yes," I said as Shash moved to let Zos pass. I passed another parcel to Shash and told him I would be down presently. Sitting on the writing table near the window were the last things that would go into the bag that traveled on my person: my journal, my pen and ink, a small canteen of water, a book to read and a piece of flint for starting a fire, good for an emergency. Before putting the journal in the leather pouch to keep it from opening and bending in my bag, I opened it to the place I had marked to read my last entry from two nights ago. The book fell open to the page the ribbon marked, but it was not the last page I had written. I immediately felt a knot begin to form in my stomach. Had Zos tried to read my journal? I had expressly forbidden him from touching my things, and he had always respected that rule. The ribbon was marking a random spot in the journal which would be entirely incomprehensible to anyone trying to read it. I wrote using the ancient Phoenician cuneiform mixed with Egyptian hieroglyphics though the language was my own Ge'ez. My plan was to transcribe it when I reached Alexandria. There was no time to dwell on it now anyway. The camels were already almost loaded. I looked up and started. Shash was standing in the doorway with his eyes on my journal. Neither of us spoke for a moment. He then looked at me, turned and disappeared.

I gathered the rest of my things, did one last check of the room and headed downstairs, the anticipation of the journey now marred by an uneasy feeling that someone was spying on me, again.

CHAPTER NINETY-ONE

Just outside the door of our inn sat three Bactrian camels, blocking pedestrians that were trying to avoid the center of the plaza, now taken up with stalls selling everything from vegetables to knives to clothing. A woman in a colorful tunic straight in front of me saw us getting on our camels and yelled in Parthian, "Fresh fish, fresh fish, the best in all Rhagae! She held the fish out in hands bloodied from gutting them all morning. I kicked my camel bringing it up, and letting Zos fall behind Shash, I brought up the rear as we wound our way out of the city single file. Zos and I had both said all of our goodbyes the evening before. I lifted up my hands and offered a prayer of thanksgiving to God for his bounty and providence, for my family, for Zos, for Aschek and even for Shash. The noise and business of the city center grew fainter until we had reached the city's edge. The snows had melted. Ahead of us lay an endless rippling wasteland of stone and sand sprinkled here and there with flowers and shrubs that had yet to wither under the beginnings of the summer heat. Zos looked back at me and slowly unwound part of his turban, wrapping it around his face, protection against the dust of the road. I reluctantly did the same, resigning myself to the claustrophobic mask, asking myself for the millionth time how some women could stand to wear veils all the time.

Our caravan was small, only twenty or so camels. No one was on foot. Shash was the only familiar face. He was now in the rear, guarding the tail of the small train. At the head was the camel puller, in charge of keeping us on course and keeping the camels on track, followed by two boys on a single camel who would act as the caravan's camel herders when the camels were left to graze. Each camel had a ring in its nose through which a rope ran connecting all the camels in the line. There was no danger of anyone straying away. With that in mind, I was soon fast asleep, lulled by the familiar rocking back and forth of my camel.

The cessation of movement woke me. The train had been halted for a break while the travelers had a bite to eat. I had prepared a meal for the two of us which we ate with much pleasure though I was a bit too groggy to fully appreciate it. "Did you happen to open my journal by accident Zos?" I asked, careful not to sound accusatory.

"Absolutely not Teacher. I would never touch your journal unless you asked me to. Why do you ask?"

"The ribbon marker was in the wrong place. But that could have just been an oversight on my part."

"No Teacher. It is no oversight. You have never done that before, and there is no reason you would start now. I didn't mention it, but I felt that someone had been in our room when I got up this morning."

"Why?" I asked, the knot in my stomach returning.

"There was nothing very obvious, just clothes out of place, things out of their normal order on the writing table. I checked the door, but it was locked. I don't know how anybody could have gotten in, especially with both of us sleeping right there."

"I think both of us are pretty hard sleepers Zos, especially after the exhausting goodbyes all day yesterday."

"Truly said. Do you think someone is spying on you?"

"I do not know Zos. I doubt it. Perhaps we are just being a bit paranoid." I smiled, but it was only on the surface. In the pit of my stomach, I knew it was more than paranoia. That was the second time on this trip that someone had tried to go through our things. I would have to be very watchful from now on.

The sun was turning the horizon pink over the sandy brown mountains. The ground took on a yellowish tinge and our shadows stretched off into the distance. The puller rang a bell, and everyone mounted his camel. We were off again. At this rate we would make good time, much better than with the enormous caravans we had traveled with up to now.

CHAPTER NINETY-TWO

I reflexively slapped a mosquito on my face waking myself. My skin prickled in the brisk night air. The moon illuminated Mount Damavand in the distance, still covered in snow. I recalled the Zoroastrian myth of the three-headed dragon Azi Dahaka who was chained within the mountain where he would remain till the end of the world. His fiery breath could be seen in the tell-tale plumes of smoke that rose eerily along the edges of the mountain, penciled white against the night sky. The camels stopped. We were in the midst of a grassy plain where the camels could graze while we slept. Zos sleepily took our cots and bedrolls from the camels and set them up beside the road. Before the puller's boys had loosed the rope from our camels, we were fast asleep, my blanket pulled close to my chin.

CHAPTER NINETY-THREE

The third day into our trek, we found ourselves crossing through the Caspian Gates, the ancient border of the Parthian and Median Empires and the spot of Darius' last chance against Alexander before he was betrayed by his own courtiers. The day was overcast, and a cool, dry wind blew down from the north, carrying the scent of the melting snow from the Alborz mountain range which had followed us since Ecbatana. To the south was the desert, an endless sea of undulating brown, as if the earth itself had been submerged for too long in the water and left with the same prune-like rippling that too much time in the water produces in the skin. Too soon, we were past it, the place with the magical name that had seemed so distant and impossible to reach as I had traced my fingers along the maps in the Library of Alexandria. I had never dreamed that I would actually find myself on the other side of those gates, following in Alexander's footsteps. I took out my journal and recorded what I was seeing, certain that there were very few accounts in the Library of anything past this point. If I had been as alert to my immediate surroundings as I was to the romance of the moment, I might have noticed a pair of eyes at the rear of the camel train boring into my back as I wrote in my Phoenician scribble.

HECATOMPYLOS

"From the Caspian Gates to Rhagae are 500 stadia according to Apollodorus, and to Hecatompylos, the royal seat of the Parthians, 1260 stadia."
(Strabo, *Geographika, Volume II,* ca 10 BC)

CHAPTER NINETY-FOUR

The fourteen day journey was thankfully completely uneventful. We arrived in Hecatompylos, city of a hundred gates, on the Lord's Day, the twentieth of the month of Paramoude. The caravan was only stopping in the outskirts of the city for a couple of days to restock and join with a larger group before leaving for Merv. Shash said he was going to stay with the caravan, so Zos and I left our things in his care and made our way into the city. I was determined to have a good bath, spend at least one night indoors and eat a couple of decent meals. The past two weeks Zos and I had slept, sometimes in daylight, sometimes at night, completely exposed to the elements, having no time to set up and break down a tent on our short stops. We got quite a lot of stares. Evidently few Africans made it this far north. There were Indians, but none as dark-skinned as we Ethiopians. Once inside the city gates, I asked a vendor where I could find a good inn. He stood staring at me, evidently not sure what to make of a black man speaking Pahlavi. "Speak up man. Can you not understand me?" I looked at Zos, impatient.

"Where are you from?" he asked, looking us up and down. We were dressed in typical Parthian fashion.

"From the other end of the world. Now tell me, where can we find a place to sleep and clean up?" He pointed towards a street that led off to his right.

"Ask for the Hormazd. You can't miss it. Take that road till it ends, go right, and it will be on your left. My cousin runs it. It's the best inn in the city. Tell him Suren sent you."

"Thank you for your help," I said as I guided Zos in the direction of the street towards which he had pointed.

That same evening, freshly oiled after a long, luxurious bath, both Zos and I had dinner in the finest restaurant in the city, or so Eran, Suren's cousin and patron of the inn told us. Much of the talk around us centered on what was going on hundreds of leagues away on the frontier. It seemed that the hottest battles had moved from Armenia and that the army under Marcus Aurelius was now moving towards Seleucia. I lifted up a prayer for our friends along the Euphrates and in Ctesiphon.

The following morning, after restocking some basic items and preparing a meal for the road, Zos and I rejoined the caravan. It had grown to about a hundred and fifty strong, and now there were eight pullers who had hired a small guard for the long journey across what was reputedly often dangerous terrain. Eight lines were formed, one behind each of the pullers, rope connecting the camels. I had secured a spot right in the center of the caravan. It had cost extra, but after much bickering and haggling and rearranging, Zos and I had a safe spot.

CHAPTER NINETY-FIVE

Zos and I were both getting bored. These caravans neither stopped at night like the ones we took from Tyre nor for the day like we did from Ctesiphon. We stopped whenever the pullers decided the camels needed to rest. The routine Zos and I had established on earlier caravans became a fond memory. On our first stop out of Hecatompylos, we transferred everything to one camel except our bedding which we used as a cushion where we could both sit comfortably. Now we could at least keep each other company, talk and practice Zos' language skills. On the infrequent stops, we started running. Our joints were cramped after so much sitting, and a good run around the caravan was enough to shake out the soreness. The downside was that we could only wash on the occasions the caravan passed an artesian well or a stream since the caravan would always stop for water.

Fourteen days into our journey, we crossed into rough terrain, low hills on each side of us. The sky had been overcast since dawn, but by midday it had grown dark and ominous. A Pallas' fish-eagle that had been following us since Hecatompylos circled high above us. A storm was definitely on the way, but there was nowhere to seek shelter. A bolt of lightning shot out of the low hanging black clouds and struck just beyond the hills to our left. The head puller called out that there was an abandoned village not far ahead. We continued forward at an infuriatingly slow pace, the lightning growing more frequent and, at least to me it seemed, closer. Just as the first huge drops of rain started falling, I spotted the ruined houses ahead. By the time we had dismounted and pulled our camels into a ruined mud brick hovel, we were drenched. The roof of the hut was entirely gone, but we were able to stretch our tent over us and our things, and the protection of the walls kept the wind from carrying our tent away. Outside the thunder roared across the barren rocky wastes. Zos set up the cots as I fastened the tent posts to the walls of the hut. At least we could get off the ground that was now puddling all around us. Once everything was set, we stripped, stood in the pouring rain and washed ourselves and our clothes. Back inside the tent, we dried as best we could and after wringing out our clothes, dressed and proceeded to shiver till we fell asleep.

CHAPTER NINETY-SIX

I woke, the hair on my arms standing on end, with the distinct feeling that somebody was watching me. It was still dark, but I could make out a silhouette that was black against the side of the tent glowing softly in the moonlight. The storm was past but another of a different sort was about to break loose.

"I'm going to make an end of you and your mission Scribe Kaleb of Alexandria."

I involuntarily sucked in my breath. The voice was Shash's. "Mission?" I said, feigning confusion while stifling the beginning of fear.

"Don't pretend ignorance. I know lying comes as naturally as breathing to you, but don't even try it on me. I know who you are and what you have done."

"What have I done?" I asked, authentically baffled. I could hear Zos' regular breathing which assured me he was still asleep.

"I have been directed to take what you have stolen from the Avestan Temple of Rhagae and then take your life."

I experienced a wave of relief. At least my life came second, and the Avesta was already on its way to Baktra. "I do not possess that of which you speak."

"Don't play games. We know you have a copy. Otherwise you would not be leaving. We know that is the only reason you made this journey, to steal from the Zoroastrians the same way you stole from us."

"What are you talking about Shash?" I said, a faint light beginning to blossom in my head matching the barely discernable change in the way Shash's silhouette stood out against the tent. Dawn was on the way. Zos was awake. I could tell by the almost imperceptible change in the rhythm of his breathing.

"Don't play stupid," he said, taking a step forward. Until now I had been lying prone. I raised myself up on one arm.

"Just tell me what you think I have done Shash. I have never stolen anything from you. And who is this 'we' to whom you keep referring?"

"Does the name Delphi bring anything to mind?"

"Are you a Pythagorean?" I asked, stunned that their vengeance could reach so far. Now I knew I was in trouble. He could very easily justify murdering me, the one supposed to have revealed their sacred literature to the eyes of the uninitiated.

"Don't even say the name," he spat. "You defile it with your barbarian tongue."

"What do you want from me?"

"Give me the Avesta."

"I do not have it. It has been sent on ahead of me. Only I can retrieve it from the one who holds it."

"I'm certain I could do that for you," he said moving closer. "I just need a name and a place. Perhaps I could cut it out of you." Now I began to really worry. I could feel the cold sweat breaking out on my forehead. I sent up a desperate prayer. How could I ever extricate myself from this situation? By now dawn was in full bloom. The tent was entirely lit. There were shouts from outside the hut, then a scream that was cut short. "This doesn't end here scribe," he said jabbing at me with his knife as he turned and left.

I immediately jumped up as did Zos. "Teacher, I thought we were both dead! I told you I didn't trust him. He has always stared strangely at you, and he is so... so evil looking."

"We must get out of here Zos. Something is very wrong outside." The shouts had increased and I could hear fighting and yelling in a language I did not recognize. "Leave everything and come out the back with me." Zos took up his pouch that he always carried around his waist, and I grabbed my bag with my journal. We lifted the back side of the tent so as not to be seen from the door of the hut. There was a small room to the back that was missing part of its wall. I stuck my head out and looked around to see if I spotted anyone. There was another ruined house just behind ours. Zos and I darted out of our hut and into its gaping side. The screams and shouts continued even louder than before. We hurried to the opposite side of this house and into the next one, making our way as quickly as possible to the back edge of the ruined town. There was nowhere to hide. If anyone came into any of these houses, we would be clear targets, and neither of us had a weapon. I determined in that instant to learn to use a knife for defense and to teach Zos as well. This traveling was a dangerous business. The last house we came to was two storied and a portion of the roof on the second floor was still intact. If we could lie flat on the roof, perhaps we would pass undetected. I boosted Zos up and then scrambled up after him.

It was impossible to see what was happening, but we could hear it all too clearly. I was afraid that if I lifted my head to look, someone would spot us and we would be discovered, so we both lay flat and tried to control our breathing. The fighting had been going on for a long time when we heard a horn call in the distance. There was a momentary pause in the conflict and then calling back and forth in the foreign language. It definitely had Aramaic roots, but was too unlike Pahlavi to make any sense of it. I could hear horses approaching at a gallop.

"Halt!" I heard in Greek. I decided to take a peek and see what was happening. About fifty Romans in military dress were chasing a band of scythe and club wielding barbarians across the plain. The muddy ground around the ruined village was covered with the bodies of mutilated corpses.

"Let us get down," I said. I prayed as we ran back the way we had come, giving thanks to God for saving us twice this morning. We ducked into the hut where our tent was. Everything was intact. Nothing had been touched. Outside was another story. Close by the entrance lay Shash, his right arm missing and his head crushed, a violent denouement, timely yet tragic. The man next to him, one of the camel pullers, moaned. I told Zos to go for water. I knelt over Shash and ripped the border of his tunic to use for a bandage. His severed right arm lay beside him, palm up. Before instinctively averting my eyes, I noticed a tattoo on the inside of his wrist, geometric with a number in the center. It was hard to make out, smeared as it was in blood. I wanted take a closer look, but first, I took the cloth I had torn from his tunic and wrapped the man's head where he had taken a blow from a club. He was mumbling incoherently. Zos returned with a water skin and tried to wash away the blood from the man's face. The Romans had ceased the chase and were returning. As they neared, I recognized the two in front. It was Septimus and Tatius, the envoys I had met in Ecbatana at Mihret's dinner party.

"God be praised," I said rising. "You could not have arrived at a better time." I did not realize it, but I was trembling. Septimus dismounted and approached us as Zos continued tending to the injured puller.

"What in the name of Zeus are you doing here?" he said. "How did you escape this massacre?"

"Zos and I hid on the roof of one of the houses on the edge of the village." Other men began to emerge from the ruins. "We need to identify and help the ones that are still alive," I said, slapping Septimus on the shoulder. "Then we can sit and talk." At least half the men from our caravan were dead or injured. Many had managed to hide, but if Septimus and Tatius' party had not arrived when they did, there may have been no one left. I spotted one of the pullers. "How far is the nearest village?" I asked. "We need to take these injured men someplace where they can be tended to."

"Sabzevar is half a day's journey from here."

I called to one of the Romans in Greek. "Did you happen to pass through a village about half a day's camel-ride from here?"

"Yes, we stayed there last night."

"Do you think you could convince someone there to send a cart out here to help ferry back the injured?" Before I had even finished speaking, he had gathered another four of their party and was galloping in the direction of the town. Some of the men were already dragging the dead to the edge of the village. Zos and I began helping the injured into one of the larger ruined buildings out of the sun. By the time we were done, we were covered in blood. I had read very little about medical practice, only in the scant medical books I had brought with me, but I knew that clean hands were important to keep away infection. Zos and I washed each other's hands and began washing and bandaging wounds.

"Are you a doctor as well?" Tatius asked, appearing at my side as I dressed a leg wound.

"I have many talents," I replied smiling. "We need more water Zos. It is going to be a very long day," I said, wiping the back of my hand across my forehead.

Outside, the Romans had begun to dig a large open pit to serve as a common grave for the bodies. "Scythians," Tatius said. "They've surely been following you for days waiting for the right moment. This morning was perfectly timed, catching you at your most vulnerable after the storm last night. Everyone was scattered throughout the ruins, disorganized, easy to pick off. Your guards should have been more vigilant."

"It looks like they paid for their mistake with their lives. I do not think a single guard survived. How many were there?"

"About fifty. We dispatched with all of them. None will tell the tale of today's disaster." He looked in the direction where they had chased and killed them. Vultures were already circling incongruously in a crystal blue sky. The crisp, clear air was poisoned by the acrid smell of blood.

"I am ready to quit this place," I said looking up at him.

Too late I remembered the tattoo on Shash's wrist. There would be no chance now to investigate it further. The last shovels full of dirt were being piled on the newly covered grave when three empty carts appeared. We carried the injured men to the carts and once they were on their way began to gather the camels together. Only three of the pullers had escaped unscathed. The camels were formed into five long lines, two directed by volunteer pullers, more than half empty of their riders. As we began the slow, mournful journey to the town of Sabzevar, I looked back at the ruins we were leaving behind and spotted the fish-eagle that had been following us since Hecatompylos. It rose from its perch on a high crumbling wall, circled the village once and headed back towards the Caspian. I felt a shiver run up my spine.

Septimus and Tatius rode alongside me. I had installed Zos on his camel so he could sleep. He was exhausted.

"So tell us, how did you come to be in this caravan?" Septimus asked.

"It is a long story. I have spent many months in Rhagae and am now on my way to Merv. The war between Rome and Parthia has made it impossible to return the way I came. I have chosen to make my way to the Indus and then to the coast and return to Alexandria via the Erythraean Sea. Tell me; are you already on your way back from your expedition to Sina?"

"That is another long story, but I will give you the short of it. We made it to the court of the Emperor Huan where we spent several months. We are now on our way back to Rome to report on what we have seen."

"And you have very fortuitously run into me. I would like to propose a slight change to your plans. How would you feel about joining me on my route? I have contacts in Barbaricum that can facilitate our voyage to Ethiopia and from there up the Nile to Alexandria. From there you can easily sail home after enjoying some Egyptian hospitality."

"We must discuss it with the rest of our party, but it is a tempting prospect."

"Think on it. Of course I would reap the benefit of having a Roman escort all the way home, and you and your party would get to see a completely new part of the world. It is so dull to return the way one has come. Do you not agree?" They both laughed.

"You are very convincing. So come; tell us the long version of your story. Start from the beginning. The whole day is ahead of us, and we have nothing new to say to each other, right Septimus?"

"I have heard all of your stories so many times, I am beginning to confuse my stories with yours."

"If you insist," I laughed. And the rest of the day, I recounted the adventures from Alexandria to this most sad and desolate spot where we currently found ourselves, leaving out any reference to my mission, the copy of the Avesta awaiting me in Baktra and the most recent attempt on my life.

The sun was relentless. There was no shade. The desert stretched out endless before us. Zos and I had reinstalled our parasols to protect head and face from the sun; nonetheless, I had to frequently wring out the cloth I had tied around the crown of my head. To our left, low hills broke the monotony of the horizon. There was great relief all around when we finally sighted the domed roofs of the village of Sabzevar. The Romans that had stayed in the town came out to meet us and guide us to a building that had been set up as a temporary hospital. The wounded were left there while the rest of the caravan set up a bivouac for the night.

CHAPTER NINETY-SEVEN

The following morning, before the pre-light of dawn had penetrated the walls of our tent, Tatius called me from outside the door of the tent. "Come in Tatius," I called from my prone position on my cot.

Lifting the flap of the door, Tatius poked his head into the tent. "Have I woken you Scribe?" he asked with a smile in his voice. I hope you were serious about our accompanying you on your route back to Alexandria. Septimus and I discussed your idea with the rest of the company, and there was unanimous agreement to take you up on it."

"Praise God!" I said sitting up on my cot. "I believe we will both benefit from this alliance."

"Now get moving sleepy head. We're breaking camp and plan to set out before the sun rises."

"What of the wounded?"

"We have no choice but to leave them here. They'll have to be tended before they can proceed." Once Tatius was back outside, I immediately rose and removed my golden girdle. The puller I had tended was an honest man. I would leave money with him to cover the care of the wounded and get them on the road again, a thank offering to God for saving me and Zos. Zos had risen and was preparing the paste to clean our teeth, watching me out of the corner of his eye. I explained what I was doing and why.

"We have not really had a chance to talk about what happened yesterday Zos." Zos silently passed me the small dish of paste. "We will talk later," I said as I began to rub the paste into my teeth and gums. Zos handed me the water skin. I took it, poured a portion of water into my mouth, rinsed, stuck my head outside the tent and spat. Zos had already broken down the cots and was packing our belongings.

As Tatius had desired, the caravan was on the move just as the sun made its first dazzling appearance. It would blind us till the third hour, forcing us to look anywhere except straight ahead. Our caravan had shrunk to fewer than a hundred camels, and with only three pullers left, we were divided into three lines of about thirty camels. The guard hired in Hecatompylos had been all but decimated in the attack, but by the grace of God they had been replaced by the Roman centuria led by one called Gnaeus. He answered to Tatius and Septimus, the ambassadors, but he was the Centurion in charge of the ten contubernium or tent groups. We were actually better protected now than we had been when we were attacked.

The next six days I got to hear about the ambassadorial journey to the heart of Sina, the court of Emperor Huan, the overtures of the Emperor and his desire to send his own embassy to the heart of the western empire of Rome and the many adventures Tatius and Septimus had there and back. Of particular interest to me was mention of a curiosity they had come across, a writing material that resembled papyrus but was supposedly made from tree bark or rags.

The road began to twist through red hills partially covered in green scrub grass. We used a narrow wooden bridge to cross a river bordered on both sides by fields of yellow flowers, a welcome sight after the barren waste through which we had just come. Tucked into a crevice in the rolling rocky mountains we came upon the village of Sanabad, a collection of domed homes that seemed to have grown straight out of the rocks from which they sprang. The villagers were happy to host us, thanks to the goodwill the Romans had left behind on their recent pass through in the opposite direction on their way towards Hecatompylos. Before the sun topped the low peaks along the horizon the following morning, we had left the village far behind, heading into the final days of the journey to Merv.

Zos and I were sharing a single camel again. Too many days had passed since we had spent any time together, in lessons or general discussion. He had been unusually quiet since the episode with Shash.

"So exactly at what point did you wake up Zos?"

"I heard Shash say something about the Avesta." I did not respond. I was racking my brain trying to remember exactly what was said. The last thing I wanted was for Zos to be involved with this in the event that he was questioned. "And I heard you say you did not have it on you, that it had been sent ahead. What did you mean Teacher?"

"You need not worry about it anymore Zos," I said trying not to sound dismissive. "Now recite the Pahlavi poem your teacher taught you before we left Rhagae. We were interrupted the last time you began."

I was unable to see the expression on Zos' face, but I could guess he was rolling his eyes at my feeble attempt to change the subject and distract him. However, I knew that he understood from my change of subject that this was a topic I was not prepared to continue discussing.

We soon left the hills behind us and were once again confronted with an endless plain, flat in every direction. Though the ground was dry and brown, one morning, after a night of rain, the land transformed into a garden. A profusion of yellow, red, white and blue flowers amidst short green grass where yesterday there was only rock and dust infused the entire company with a sense of elation and hope.

MERV

"The eastern extremity of the known earth is limited by the meridian drawn through the metropolis of the Sinae, at a distance from Alexandria of 119.5 degrees, reckoned upon the equator, or about eight equinoctial hours..."
(Ptolemaios, *Geographia*, Book *VII, ch. 5,* ca 150)

CHAPTER NINETY-EIGHT

The ancient city of Merv, crossroads of empires. The Kushan kingdom and further on the fabled land of India lay to the southeast, Sina due east. Directly north lay the wilds of Scythia and to the west Parthia. Its size belied its importance. This was undoubtedly the most cosmopolitan city we had passed through; people of every size, shape and color in a dizzying variety of dress mingled in the market where we were attempting to restock. An amazing display of wares from Sina to Spain cluttered the stalls packed into the cramped main square. Earlier in the day, I had taken the third coin from my girdle, the first of which I had changed with Anata. At a money changer, I had traded the gold coin for its worth in copper and silver coins, enough at least to get the two of us to Baktra. I had run through all of the money I had accumulated here and there working as a scribe, particularly in Ecbatana. In Rhagae I had been too busy to make any money on the side, though the work in the temple paid for our food and shelter. I had refused any other payment from Aschek since, as I told him, a copy of the Avesta was payment enough. The only thing

I had spent out of pocket there was for Zos' studies, money very well invested. Though I regretted having to use any of the money from the girdle, I consoled myself with the knowledge that I had only spent three of the coins and that we were more than halfway through our round-trip journey. Perhaps I could recover some of it before reaching Alexandria.

Talk in the market centered around the war happening thousands of leagues away on the westernmost border of Parthia. Rumor was that the Parthian front was weakening. Many were seeking alternate routes to the Great Sea and the markets of the Roman Empire. It looked as if the route I had chosen to Barbaricum was gaining in popularity.

Our next stop, Baktra, took another twenty days. Our small party joined a larger group of traders, some heading home, some leaving home behind to trade further west. On the one hand, there was safety in numbers. On the other, we were a more attractive target due to all the wealth that such a large group represented. I was confident though that God was watching over us since he had already saved us more than once. Besides, we had a full Roman centuria watching over us.

PART FOURTEEN

BAKTRA

Gregorian Calendar – June 20th, 163
Alexandrian Calendar – Paoni 12th, Second Shomu
The Season of Harvesting
3rd year of Marcus Aurelius

"It is possible to fail in many ways... while to succeed is possible only in one way
(for which reason also one is easy and the other difficult – to miss the mark easy,
to hit it difficult)."
(Aristotle, *Nicomachean Ethics, II, 6,* ca 350 BC)

CHAPTER NINETY-NINE

The road to Baktra was more of the same dusty, rocky, flat terrain, the monotony of which was wearing on my senses. From what I had seen so far of Parthia, most of the country was dry and empty, a simultaneously exotic and depressing prospect for one brought up on the water amidst gardens, greenery and trees aplenty. Baktra was no more than a continuation of the same gray thirsty scenery. We set up camp outside the town, supposedly one of the most ancient in the world, burial place of Zoroaster and birthplace of Roxana, the wife of Alexander the Great. It was fitting that the copy of the Avesta that I was to carry to the premier learning center of the known world was hiding in this dusty town at the end of the universe where the author of that document lay buried.

We had settled into the town for a couple of weeks at least. Zos and I had been traveling practically non-stop for two months, and we needed a break. Tatius and Septimus had been traveling from the opposite direction but for about the same amount of time. They were in agreement that we could spend time here resting and restocking for the next leg of the journey over the Khyber Pass toward Purushapura near the head of the Indus. That would prove a very tiring journey, and we needed to be well rested and prepared before tackling it.

Besides, this gave me time to retrieve my copy of the Avesta. The first thing I did after establishing us in a comfortable inn was locate the contact Aschek had given me. Not wanting to involve Zos, I went alone after leaving him in charge of buying supplies in the market. I had traded by now the Parthian dress for a simple white Egyptian tunic. I wore my scribe's cap on my freshly shaved head and the sandals I had left Alexandria with that were going to need repairing soon.

The instructions that Aschek had given me were fairly clear. Due south of the Temple of Anaitis, on the outskirts of town I would come upon a sharp rock face with a narrow path leading up its sheer side. Along the path there were caves, some inhabited, some not. Near the top, at a point where the path widened, I would find a semicircular stone hut built up against the rock face. That was where I would find Bagabigna, Zoroastrian ascetic. He held the package that Aschek had sent ahead of me.

I stopped at the temple in the center of town dedicated to the Lady of the Water, Anaitis, a goddess of the Avesta often mixed with the Mesopotamian Ishtar and the Roman Venus. Engraved on the lintel above the two pillars framing the entrance to the temple was a verse I remembered from the fifth Yasht of the Avesta. "She makes ritually pure the semen of all the males, of all females. She makes ritually pure the wombs for giving birth. She gives easy delivery to all females, and brings down milk to all females in conformity with the established rules and the models." The thought occurred to me that she must not be much of a goddess if she could only make semen and wombs ritually pure and not pure indeed. Of what good was ritual purification if the heart of the matter was not pure? I recalled the words of the Jewish prophet Jeremiah, nicknamed the weeping prophet, "Circumcise yourselves to the Lord, and take away the foreskins of your heart." That was more than ritual purification. Ruminating on what it meant to be pure, I made my way to the edge of town, to the rock face Aschek had described. Here it was quiet except for the call of the huge black carrion hunters floating high above the cliff face. It took me some time to locate the beginning of the narrow path that climbed precariously to the top of the precipice. After removing my sandals, I began the treacherous ascent, often having to press myself completely against the rock wall progressing with finger and toe holds, not daring to look down, not allowing myself to consider that I had to repeat this same terrifying route back to the foot of this cliff. Each time I passed the opening to a cave, I prayed that no one would emerge just as I passed. The slightest push would send me hurtling to the pile of rocks at the base.

Slowly but surely I neared the semicircle of stone, the only thing I permitted myself to focus on at this point. When I finally reached it, I was drenched in sweat. I wiped my sleeve across my face and called out hello. No answer. I looked back the way I had come, amazed that I had been able to make it this far. The ground seemed much further away from here than this rock outcropping did from down below. I turned back around only to find myself staring down into the wild eyes of Bagabigna. Involuntarily I stepped back, almost losing my balance. If the path here had not been a bit wider, I would surely have plummeted to an untimely death. Bagabigna just stood there watching my discomfiture. Shading the black pools of his eyes was a pair of white and gray bushy eyebrows. His thick white hair was long and stuck out in every direction, and he had a beard that almost touched his knees. He held a tall staff in his right hand and stood staring at me. As abruptly as he had appeared, he turned and disappeared into the stone hut. I followed, reluctant to let him out of my sight now that I had found him. I was momentarily blind in the dark, cool interior until my eyes adjusted to the dim light put out by a single candle in the back of the room. Bagabigna was sitting on a small rug on the dirt floor, his back against the far wall near the candle which illuminated the cave end of the room. To the right of Bagabigna was a black hole, a door into the recesses of the cliff. I looked back at the little white-haired man seated on the floor. I quietly approached him and sat on the ground facing him. From the bag I had slung over my head and across my shoulder before making the ascent, I took two small bowls and a knife, fruit and a skin of milk that I had bought in the market. I slowly began to peel the fruit and place it in the bowl. When I was done, I poured milk from the skin into the second bowl and set them both near Bagabigna. He continued to stare at me without speaking. I focused on the ground just in front of me, waiting now for him to make the next move.

"You also as waters and you as milk-giving cows and you as mother cows, not to be harmed, nourishers of the poor, giving everybody to drink, we call hither, O best ones, O most beautiful ones! I, with long arms, shall offer you my help."

"Aschek sends his greetings," I whispered. I could hear him eating the fruit. My eyes adjusted further to the light of the candle. I continued to wait.

"What are you called?"

"Kaleb," I replied looking up at him. He had pieces of fruit in his beard and the milk had dribbled down it onto the dirt floor creating a dirty puddle at the base of his beard.

"I have something for you Kaleb."

"Yes, Aschek told me you were his most trusted friend."

"You will wait for me here," he said rising and vanishing into the black hole that led further into the cave. After a bit, I readjusted myself, attempting but failing to find a more comfortable position. I continued to wait. The candle sputtered. I stood and began to look for another candle. The room was entirely empty except for the small rug Bagabigna sat on and a low table near the door. On the table there was a single fresh candle. I took it to where the other candle was just about to go out and lit it with the struggling flame. I pushed the new candle into the soft wax of the now extinguished one. Still he did not emerge. Aschek had warned me that he was eccentric, but assured me that he was completely trustworthy and would give me the package when I came for it. I began to worry about Zos and what he might do if I tarried much longer. Eventually I sat down again. The flickering of the candle and absolute silence mesmerized me, and I found my eyes getting heavy. Before I realized it, I was asleep. I know not for how long I had been sleeping in this upright position when Bagabigna reappeared.

"Where have you been?" I wanted to shout, but I kept silent. He had a package in his hands. That package represented an investment of over a year. I could wait a bit longer. I was actually more worried about getting down the cliff in the dark than that Bagabigna would refuse to give me the package.

He held out the package towards me. "The wished-for things are in the wish for him, to whomever Mazdâ Ahura, commanding at will, shall give them," I said, quoting from the seventy-first Yasna. Aschek had instructed me that this was the appropriate thing to say upon receiving a gift.

For the first time, Bagabigna smiled. I took the gift and bowed deeply. He put his hand on my head and mumbled something. I stood and turned towards the door. I could not resist asking though before I left, "Where did you go just now?"

"I took a nap. The fruit and milk made me very sleepy."

"Indeed." I could not help but smile as I made my way out into the dusk. The fires of the many caravan camps encircling the city sparkled like grounded stars. The city itself was swiftly descending into darkness. I felt a moment of panic. "God, help me reach the bottom safely," I prayed as I began to feel my way along the wall, the package securely tucked in my bag.

CHAPTER ONE HUNDRED

"Where have you been Teacher?" Zos asked when I entered our room at the inn, his voice betraying his anxiety.

"I had errands to run, and it took much longer than I had anticipated. Have you eaten?"

"Not yet, I was waiting for you."

I fought the urge to tear immediately into the package Bagabigna had given me. I put my bag on my bed and turned back to face Zos. "Well, I am back now. Thank you for waiting here for me. Go on down and claim a table. I will be down in a moment, as soon as I take care of something."

"Yes, Teacher."

As soon as Zos was out of the room, I took the package from the bag and unwrapped it to confirm that Bagabigna had indeed given me the copies I had come for. There were four leather bound packets. There should only have been three. I slipped the books gingerly out of their protective covering, the olive-wood facing of the books smooth and aromatic. I opened each one. The fourth leather case was smaller than the three housing the volumes of the Avesta. I slid a narrow box out of the pouch, thinking that Aschek had perhaps sent me a copy of something from his personal library as a parting gift. I opened the intricately carved box inlaid with mother-of-pearl. Inside was a letter and another, smaller box. I took the letter and read it.

Scribe, if you are reading this letter now, Ahura Mazda be praised. This means you have not only arrived safely in the city but have retrieved the copies you were so instrumental in making become a reality. You will forgive me for sending this small token payment for your services, since you insistently refused it when I offered it as recompense for your invaluable work. I could not, however, in good conscience, send you away with no material remuneration. Perhaps these coins,

*symbolic more than compensatory, will be of some assistance on the remainder of
your long journey home. Remember us with fondness as I can assure you, you will
be ever remembered among your friends here.*

Coins? He had not signed it, most likely as a precaution against
its discovery since only I could trace this back to him. I took the
small box and lifted the lid, turning it upside down as ten gold coins
tumbled into the palm of my hand.

CHAPTER ONE HUNDRED AND ONE

"What do you think of the gods of this city?" I asked the two
Romans seated with me at the table. Tatius swirled his wine and
watched the tears as they made their way back down the glass. He
fancied himself a sommerlier, and as this was wine country, he was
availing himself of every possible opportunity to test it.

"I really have not given it much thought," Septimus said,
watching Tatius study his wine.

"I wondered if you were impressed that we are in the city where
Zoroaster himself purportedly lies buried."

"Zoroaster?" Tatius finally spoke. "And who might he be?"

Authentically surprised, I remained silent for a moment.

"I think you have stumped our scribe," Septimus laughed.

"As ambassadors to this region, it surprises me that you do not
know the name of the founder of a religion whose influence spreads
across the Parthian and into the Kushan Empires." I could tell I now
had the attention of them both.

"Is it related to the Cult of Mithras?" Septimus asked.

"There are some similarities," I said, "but I am not familiar
enough with Mithraism to say confidently."

"Yes, now that does sound very familiar," Tatius said, his eyes
roaming the wall to the left as if the answer might be scribbled there
somewhere.

"And you say the founder is buried here?"

"So they say," I said, having another drink of tea. The various
plates, empty now of the grilled goat, salads of cracked wheat, mint,
garlic, lemon, tomatoes and green onions, three varieties of bread,
sauces and pastes, fried croquettes and various cheeses were being
cleared.

"I'm an Epicurean myself," said Tatius. "All these gods and goddesses, too many to number… what are they but manifestations of man's need to explain the unexplainable. Happiness is the ultimate virtue, and leading a temperate life; abstaining from all excesses is the highest goal."

Septimus had not taken his eyes off Tatius from the word Epicurean. "You are a Hedonist Tatius. Do not try to dress it up in virtue. Temperance serves its purpose, but I would not say you lean in that direction very often. As for me, I fancy myself more a Stoic. I attempt to face everything this life throws at me with equanimity and a will of steel."

"Indeed. You certainly had a will of steel with that courtesan the Sinese Emperor gifted you," Tatius said rolling his eyes exaggeratedly.

I laughed. "Have either of you heard of the Pythagorean Cult?"

They both laughed. "Kaleb, by the gods where do you come up with these questions? Does Pythagoras not have something to do with mathematics?" Septimus asked.

"Indeed!" I said, laughing with them, inordinately relieved to see that I had nothing to fear from either of them. After my brush with Shash, I felt it prudent to make certain of the sympathies of my protectors assuring myself that they were not involved in any nefarious plots against my person. I had considered telling them about the Avesta I was carrying, but decided against it at the last minute.

PART FIFTEEN

𓏏𓏭𓂋𓎡𓏠𓂝

BOUND FOR THE INDUS

Gregorian Calendar – July 20th, 163
Alexandrian Calendar – Epip 12th, Third Shomu
The Season of Harvesting
3rd year of Marcus Aurelius

"Give me neither poverty nor riches;
feed me with the food that is needful for me,
lest I be full and deny you
and say "Who is the Lord?"
or lest I be poor and steal
and profane the name of my God.."
(Sayings of Agur, *Proverbs*, ch. 30: 8-9, ca 800 BC)

CHAPTER ONE HUNDRED AND TWO

Although happy to make any move that brought us closer to home, I was a bit sorry to be leaving Baktra behind. I had begun to establish a routine, and surprisingly, in this city of foreigners, I had discovered a small group of Egyptian Christians with whom I had been able to worship. The contact with the local ecclesia had also secured me some work as a scribe by which I had earned no small amount of money as the work had kept me extremely busy. Zos meanwhile had worked as my secretary, doing the easier jobs and earning some money of his own. Traffic in the city had picked up since it was being used more and more as an alternative route for anyone returning to the West, trapped as we all were by the military forces tying up the Euphrates.

Two days out of the city the plains ended. We followed a road that wound up the side of a mountain and then led us to an ancient bridge precariously spanning the narrowest point of a deep canyon, the tattered remains of a spider's web between two towers. As the caravan we were traveling with was enormous, it took several hours for everyone to cross since no one wanted to risk more than a single file line. We had dismounted from the camels to disperse the weight, and I could feel Zos holding his breath as we crossed.

"I fear you may not make it all the way across," I whispered in his ear. His face began to turn a darker shade of mahogany and his eyes were bulging. Suddenly he gasped, blowing out the air he had been holding in. At that very moment, one of the few remaining stone posts that must have previously lined the border of the bridge toppled over and fell crashing against the walls of the canyon, shattering and echoing up the length of the chasm. Zos sucked in another lungful of air and resumed his breath holding. This time he made it to the end.

As soon as our camel was safely on the opposite side of the canyon, Zos turned to me excitedly, eyes wide, "Did you see what happened when I couldn't hold my breath any longer? Imagine if I hadn't held it as long as I did!"

"You saved us all Zos," I laughed. "But for your prowess at holding your breath, the bridge would have collapsed entirely."

"Do you really think so?" he asked, his voice incredulous. I was unable to restrain myself from laughing, remounted and kicked the goads of the camel in tune with the puller catching up with the line in front of me. For once I was at the head of a row, the camel directly behind the puller. Instead of dust blowing constantly in our faces, we were able to enjoy the scenery. Ahead of us, hills covered with little more than scrub brush rolled into the distance to a horizon dominated by another tall range of mountains colored dark purple and green.

Shaded from the overpowering sun by our umbrella, Zos read from a journal I had copied on the Kushan Empire. Ptolemaios had written about Kaboura, but I had compiled more information on the history of this region while in Rhagae. I had also written a rudimentary Sanskrit grammar, sure that a knowledge of this language would prove useful while traveling along the Indus River. Zos and I drilled each other on the pronunciation of the letters of their alphabet and practiced simple phrases with each other from my personal dictionary where I kept words I learned from different languages. I had begun this alphabet and collection of Sanskrit phrases with my Indian friend Omanand as we traveled to Ecbatana.

Mountains that looked as if their tops had been shaved off gave way to rice fields bounded on all sides by craggy cliffs. Towns thrived in the verdant valleys and atop the mountains, dusty white in the day, purple in the evening. Stone temples perched precariously on the edges of precipices. Bare-chested men rode about in patrols wearing nothing but a short flared skirt, a simple lapis colored turban of twisted cloth and a quiver full of arrows at the ready, the Kushan Guard of the Imperial Highway, distinguishable by the tightly tied flat turban. Into our second week the road converged with a river. Zos and I, at our first opportunity, bathed, washing the dust of the past week from our dry skin. Other members of the caravan watched with curiosity as the two naked black men splashed and laughed in the cool mountain water.

Mountains devoid of growth rose wraithlike from green valleys. Our guides maneuvered us through winding paths and mysterious passes, always bounded on both sides by denuded mountains. Sometimes the path was so rocky the camels had difficulty walking, slowing our progress to a snail's pace. The Kushan Imperial Highway was discernable but in no way compared to the highways I was accustomed to within the borders of the Roman Empire. At the end of two weeks, we finally began our descent into Kaboura from the north side of the city. The city was bounded on all sides by forests of evergreens, a welcome sight after so much desert. By the ninth hour, having left our camels outside the city in a caravanserai, we had installed ourselves at an inn in the center of the city, beside a Buddhist temple. Tatius and Septimus were in their own room, and Zos and I, exhausted from the exertions of the day, lay down to sleep the sleep of the dead.

KABOURA

Gregorian Calendar – August 4th, 163
Alexandrian Calendar – Epip 26th, Third Shomu
The Season of Harvesting
3rd year of Marcus Aurelius

"He was a wealthy man, and kindly to his fellow men; for dwelling in a house by
the side of the road, he used to entertain all comers."
(Homer, *Iliad, VI, l. 14,* ca 800 BC)

CHAPTER ONE HUNDRED AND THREE

Before the sun was up, I was awake, my toes wiggling involuntarily, anxious to be up and moving. I got up quietly, slipped on my tunic and made my way to the roof of the inn to watch the sunrise as I did my daily devotions. I stared out at the dark mountains to the east as I meditated on the goodness of God and his providence in bringing us this far safely. Slowly, the contrast grew between the darkness of the eastern peaks and the cobalt blue sky. As yet, the valley lay in darkness. Only the flawless sky changed colors. I turned to see if the mountains to the west were visible yet. As I turned back, I saw Zos' head peak above the floor of the roof. The sight was vaguely unsettling, as if his head had been left on the roof to dry. Before I could call out, he had disappeared again. By the time I finished my meditations and prayers, sunlight illuminated the top fringe of the mountains to my back.

"There is someone I think you would enjoy meeting," Septimus said enthusiastically over breakfast. "He is a Kushan but has lived most of his life in the court of the Sinese Emperor Huan. We met him while we were there, but I have been told that he is here visiting family."

"Where in the world could you have heard that?" I asked, amazed that Septimus had this information, and we had barely arrived in the city.

"Yesterday evening after you had retired, I visited the city Ksatrap to announce our arrival and inform him that we are ambassadors from Rome. We are invited to a state dinner this evening, and Lokaksema will be in attendance."

I looked at Zos. "We must wash our clothes Zos; there is no time to waste," I said as I rose.

"Sit down Kaleb," Septimus laughed. "You have all day. At least break your fast calmly."

I smiled. "You are right Septimus. I need to take things more stoically, right?"

"Hah, you are absolutely right. And here comes the antithesis of stoicism, our very own Tatius, avoiding all excess, even of sleep." Tatius joined us at the table rubbing his eyes and yawning.

"And a good morning to you too Septimus," he said as he winked at Zos who had been eating in silence listening to Septimus' and my conversation without comment. "How do you put up with it Zos? You need someone your own age to chat with first thing in the morning."

"I'm perfectly happy to eat with my teacher ambassador," Zos said calmly.

"So perfectly polite. You are a tribute to your teacher's training Zos. Would that my own son exhibit an ounce of your virtue." Zos looked down at his plate.

"Pride goes before a fall," he said quietly. "I am only what I am by the grace of God and thanks to my teacher."

"Stop, Zos, stop," Tatius said. Such good manners so early is throwing me off balance." We all laughed. Zos smiled.

CHAPTER ONE HUNDRED AND FOUR

Scrubbed clean and dressed in our Egyptian best, Zos and I met Septimus and Tatius in the dining hall of our inn to have tea before leaving for the dinner. "Spectacular!" Tatius exclaimed upon seeing our high turbans, Zos' sky blue and mine green. We both wore white linen Egyptian tunics with long coats matching our turbans. We wore simple leather sandals. Tatius himself was dressed in a full Roman ambassadorial toga, off-white with a broad purple border and leather boots. Septimus stood by his side similarly dressed. Gnaeus was the most impressive, in full military dress, a highly polished and heavily decorated silvered cuirass over a leather vest. The lower edge of the cuirass was curved and had rows of long tongue-shaped lappets which formed a skirt. On the front of his legs he wore ornate greaves from the ankle to above the knee which were attached by straps and buckles. He had an ornate sword on the left and dagger on the right. Over it all, he wore a cloak pinned to the right shoulder with a silver fibula. His dark leather boots laced up to his lower calves. Zos could not take his eyes off him. "We are going to cut quite a fine figure tonight. I believe Kaleb and Zos will steal the show though."

"Not true," Zos protested. "Centurion Gnaeus is by far the most impressive!" Gnaeus gave Zos a quick wink before Septimus feigned offense.

"Do you mean we do not look fine in our togas Zos?"

"No, of course I didn't mean that," Zos stammered.

We laughed. "They are just playing Zos. Centurion Gnaeus is truly impressive in his uniform," I said. Finishing off my tea, I stood. "Shall we?"

CHAPTER ONE HUNDRED AND FIVE

The dining hall in the palace of the Ksatrap of Kaboura was ornately hung with Sinese silk and Indian woolen tapestries. Immense candelabras hovered impossibly low over serving tables spread with delicacies from East and West, indicative of the incredible mix of cultures represented at this gathering. Small tables for guests were scattered throughout the cavernous hall, each graced with a lantern suspended on a gracefully curved floor post. Gnaeus had been quickly cornered by his Kushan counterpart. He was currently involved in an anecdote that had all eyes at his table on him. Zos was the youngest person here, and although the company was quite cosmopolitan, Zos and I were an oddity. After initial introductions by Tatius to the Ksatrap who invited us to his table, we were approached by a young Kushan in Sinese costume. He introduced himself as Lokaksema. His eyes and demeanor were honest, pure, and his manner was confident despite his obvious youth. The Ksatrap explained that Lokaksema, although born here, had spent ten years in Luoyang, capital of the Han Empire. He had been an acolyte in the Kabouran school of Buddhism for the past two years and was destined for great things. I was curious as to why the most important man in Kaboura would know a young Buddhist acolyte. I could tell Zos was intrigued.

Septimus exchanged greetings with him in the language of the Han, but Lokaksema immediately switched to Greek, the common, though second language of us all. "Your name is Sanskrit, is it not?" I asked once we were seated.

"You know Sanskrit?" Lokaksema asked quietly.

"I have only begun to study it," I said, "but it is fascinating. I am beginning to discern similarities between it and Pahlavi and even Greek and Latin."

"A fellow lover of languages," he said as he took a sip of his tea. His plate was practically empty. He had only taken a few simply prepared vegetables and fruit.

"I am more expert in the languages of the West," I said. "Zos here however is becoming quite expert at the languages of the areas we are traveling through. He speaks Pahlavi like a native."

Zos smiled at my unexpected praise, and I am sure was embarrassed that all eyes now turned on him. He focused on taking a bite of lamb from his full plate.

"What do your duties as an acolyte at the temple entail," I asked.

"I am studying the Mahayana sutras. My goal is to translate them into Sinese, to carry the practice of the path to the Sinese people."

"Lokaksema is a prodigy. He has already begun the translation of some of our most ancient texts."

"Buddhism," I said quietly. "I know very little of your religion. I would like to know more."

"It would please me greatly to teach you," Lokaksema smiled.

"How would you define the central belief of your religion, in just a few words?" I asked.

"Attaining pure enlightenment by following the path."

"And who laid out the path?" I asked.

"Buddha."

"What is pure enlightenment?"

"Perfection."

"How does perfection manifest itself?"

"Absence of suffering."

"How is that achieved?"

"By following the middle path and understanding that nothing is permanent, even our concept of self, of who we are. We are nothing more than an emanation, an illusion."

"What then is real?"

"Nirvana."

"What is Nirvana?"

"The state of final release."

"When does one reach this state?"

"When one achieves enlightenment."

"And there you have it. Back to the beginning, a beautiful circle, the circle of existence, the wheel that never stops spinning, we end where we started and start where we ended." The Ksatrap raised his cup. "Lokaksema here is going to achieve great things in this life," he said. My mind was whirling. I began to wonder if I had discovered my next mission. I needed to get hold of some of the literature of this Buddha.

"There are definitely circular phenomena such as the course of day from morning to night, the seasons, from spring to winter, but the wheel spins along a road that is linear. There is a beginning and an end."

"Fodder for much debate," said Lokaksema. "I can only hope that time permit more conversation on the matter. I can see that you too think deeply on these matters."

Septimus and Tatius had been quiet for the duration of our exchange, but now Tatius piped in. "All this talk of wheels and roads is making me anxious to continue our journey. Ksatrap, what is your recommendation regarding the road ahead. We are bound for the Indus."

"Past the Khyber Pass lies the capital of our empire. You must stop there and greet the King of kings, the Son of Heaven, Huvishka. All roads in the empire lead to Purushapura. No one of any importance traveling through our lands can pass by it without stopping."

"How many days' journey is Purushapura?"

"With the guides I will send with you, it should only take three weeks. You will stay in the royal inns along the road. They are spaced at day journey intervals."

"You are too generous," intercepted Septimus. "We could not possibly intrude on your hospitality. We have traveled long distances and are quite happy to sleep in tents or under the open sky."

"A tribute to your Roman hardiness and the virtue you place in disdain for comfort, but in this I will not accept no for an answer. Until you cross out of our land, you will be treated in the manner of any state visitor." Septimus and Tatius both rose and placed their hands over their hearts.

"We thank you on behalf of the Roman Emperor Marcus Aurelius. Your generosity will not go unnoticed."

"Please, please, be seated. You draw excessive attention to our table. The other guests will think I have offended you," he laughed.

The night passed leisurely with stimulating conversation, delicious wine and pleasant company. The next few days were spent preparing for the journey ahead of us through the range of mountains separating us from Purushapura and beyond that the Indus. The Ksatrap had already assigned us a party of five guides that would lead us safely through the Khyber Pass and to the capital. Gnaeus, eternally suspicious, was sure they were spies whose job was to monitor our every move and conversation.

Zos and I were both excited that we would be staying in royal quarters every night for the next three weeks. No more living with the dirt and dust of the road for weeks on end. We could take a bath every night and sleep in real beds. I could not believe how wonderfully things were working out for us on this return trip after the hardships of the outbound journey.

KHYBER PASS

Gregorian Calendar – August 12ᵗʰ, 163
Alexandrian Calendar – Mesori 4ᵗʰ, Fourth Shomu
The Season of Harvesting
3ʳᵈ year of Marcus Aurelius

"The dawn speeds a man on his journey, and speeds him too in his work. "
(Hesiod, *Works and Days*, I. *579,* ca 700 BC)

CHAPTER ONE HUNDRED AND SIX

The grass glittered from the drizzle that had fallen all through the night. The soggy trees hung limp under a grey sky. At the caravanserai, Zos and I were surprised when two horses were brought out for us, bronze pectorals over the shoulders and a silver frontlet with an intricate beaten geometric design. I was told that our things would be sent to Purushapura with the next caravan as all we would need would be supplied at the inns along the way. Zos and I retrieved what we considered necessary for the trip from among our things we had stored at the caravanserai, excited to be traveling by horse rather than camel. The Ksatrap's guides, dressed in simple flared skirts, close fitting shirts open at the neck and lapis colored turbans belying their royal status were already present when we arrived. As we mounted our horses, they and the Roman centurion guard that had been quartered at the caravanserai with the camels mounted as well. Four of the guides led the contingent with half the centurion guard in front of us and half to our rear. Gnaeus, the ambassadors, the lead guide Yuezhi and Zos and I rode in the middle. Shortly after passing through a forest of low evergreens we were confronted with the first of an endless range of mountains that rose like stony Goliaths from the flat plain. The imperial road wound between these monoliths like a serpent in a maze. I was soon spattered head to toe with mud from the kick-back of the horses at both sides. I looked over at Zos just as a splotch of mud hit him square between the eyes. I erupted in laughter at the look of disgust on his face. As I turned around, I was caught by a splatter on my cheek. Though I did not turn to look again at Zos, I was sure he was laughing back at me.

CHAPTER ONE HUNDRED AND SEVEN

The sky was still overcast and growing quite dark by the time we reached the first royal inn. It stood several passus from a sand-colored mountain whose base was littered with broken stones of all sizes. We were greeted by the keeper of the inn and several servants who, ignoring the soldiers and guides, came directly to our small group and began fussing about us, offering to carry our things, to see to our horses, to lead us to our quarters. I felt like royalty. Though simple on the outside, the interior of the inn was positively lavish. We were led down a hallway to a room with tubs of steaming water. Our clothes were taken from us, and we proceeded to wash the mud from our filthy bodies. Zos' hair was matted with it. I began to splash water on myself from the tub, intending to wash before getting in to soak. Septimus looked at me like I was crazy. "Just get in. There is a clean pool of hot water waiting for us in the next room."

"How do you know that," I asked incredulously.

"I just told him," said Yuezhi.

"Good enough for me. Go on and get in," I said to Zos who had been following my lead.

Fresh tunics had been laid out in our extravagant rooms. Zos and I had been put together per my request. Amongst so many strangers, Zos did not feel comfortable having his own room. Our room had two beds, both sumptuously covered with silk sheets and soft blankets and pillows. The floors were covered with carpets and a large latticed window looked out on the mountain behind us; the full moon hidden behind the clouds threw its outline into sharp relief against the glowing blue-black sky.

A servant at our door informed us that dinner was being served. Zos and I looked at each other. I shrugged, and Zos held out upraised hands to his side tilting his head to the right as if to say, "What can we do then but eat?" I had not expected to eat at this point. It was already late, and I was tired, but we followed the servant. We were led up stairs to the roof of the inn. A table had been set up in the center of four columns. The roof of the un-walled portico had been taken down to allow for an unobstructed view of the glowing sky. Lanterns hung from the four columns, illuminating the table without obscuring the occasional brief appearance of the moon. Plate after plate of Kushan cuisine was set on the table. The Romans set in with gusto. Zos and I were more sparing.

The next morning we were up before daybreak. Our horses were saddled and waiting for us as we stepped out of the inn after a sumptuous breakfast. I was having difficulty walking after spending the previous day on a horse. It would definitely take some adjusting. It had taken time for my body to accustom itself to the rigors of riding a camel, and it seemed a horse worked different parts of my anatomy. I would definitely have to do more stretching this evening with a run or at least a walk to work out some of the kinks forming in my posterior.

The terrain throughout the day was much the same as the latter part of yesterday, sparse greenery, scrubby trees and crumbling mountains rising out of eons of rubble washed down from the tops of the hills though the imperial road was in fairly good repair. Everyone was in high spirits after a good night's rest and a hearty breakfast. The sky continued grey, threatening rain, but the air was dry and crackly.

By the ninth hour, storm clouds were gathering up ahead. Yuezhi informed us that we were not far from our next stop. We were in an open plateau surrounded on all sides by mountains. Nestled above the pass between the mountains just ahead the darkest clouds were settling in the way a wool blanket wraps itself around me as I toss and turn in my sleep. A soft wind began to blow from the direction we were heading. The nearer we drew to the pass, the stronger the wind became, bringing with it the smell of rain. Without warning, a huge bolt of lightning shore the sky between the two mountains, illuminating a small structure that had been camouflaged by the surrounding bland, sandy landscape. "Pick up the speed," Yuezhi yelled in Greek. Immediately, we goaded our horses and were galloping at full tilt towards the inn. The single precocious bolt of lightning seemed to have set off a chain reaction. Bolt after bolt began to rain down all around us. The wind picked up and blew dust in our faces as we raced to the opening of the pass. The smell of rain grew stronger. As if running into a wall of water, we passed into the deluge at breakneck speed. I was immediately drenched, the raindrops like wet pebbles stinging my face. I stole a sideways glance at Zos who was struggling to keep up, his eyes wild but focused. The thunder of hooves was drowned out by the rumbling thunder echoing off the mountains ahead and the torrential downpour. Sooner than I had expected, we reached the inn, dismounted in disarray and ran for shelter as a bevy of servants ran out to take our horses. The soldiers made for the stables and their quarters. Reaching the door of the inn, I wiped my face and stood barefoot on the wet paving stones of the front portico till the pounding of my heart calmed. The rain continued beating down as lightening flashed in the now black sky, illuminating the ghostly shapes of gnarled trees and the mountain beyond. "Come in Kaleb before you are struck yourself." Septimus took my arm and led me inside, out of the cacophony of thunder and rain. My ears rang with the sudden silence. "There is a hot bath for us in the back," he said. I followed him back and found the others, including Zos, already soaking in steaming tubs.

"What a fantastic storm," I said as I shed my dripping tunic.

"Fantastic he says," laughed Tatius. "We're lucky we didn't get fried out on that plain when the lightning began."

"The hour of our end is already written," said Septimus. "Why worry? There is nothing we can do to change it."

"Well, there's no need to rush it. There is such a thing as common sense."

"It is in God's hands," I said as I slid into my tub. "If it is his will that a bolt of lightning finish me off, then I submit to his plan, which is perfect by the way. We could be done in by a tiny insect as easily as by a bolt of lightning."

"Comforting words Kaleb, comforting words." Everyone laughed. Zos was the first out of the bath.

"I'm going to explore a bit," he told me as he wrapped a towel around his waist.

"Explore away," I said. "Just keep the explorations inside."

"Not to worry," he said as he walked out the door.

"Your son is very bright," Yuezhi said.

"He is not my son, though with each passing day I feel more like he is. His parents are very good friends of my family. I brought him along as an apprentice scribe. Before the outset of this journey, my intention was to travel alone, but my family, and his, convinced me that he would prove an invaluable asset to me."

"And?"

"And they were right. I cannot imagine having made this trip without his companionship and his help."

"I have two children of my own waiting for me in Rome," said Septimus. "I miss them terribly. They will have changed so much in the time we have been away."

"Why did you not bring them with you?"

"It is just not done. I did not even consider it an option. The road is dangerous, and besides, their mother would never have allowed it."

"Nor I," interjected Tatius. "Besides, your children are just babies. Zos is a young man. He can fend for himself."

"My skin is beginning to wrinkle," said Yuezhi. "I'll see you lot at dinner."

Before going to my room to dress, I stood again in the door of the inn, barefoot and wrapped in a towel, and watched the storm that had not abated since we arrived. A servant appeared at my side with a cup of steaming tea. I took it without taking my eyes off the magnificent scene before me. Lightning continued to crash setting off thunderous rumbling that went on forever, the sound bouncing off the mountains around us. The rain roared, the wind so fierce at times it sent sheets of water flying horizontally. The stone inn stood like a fortress in the midst of the apocalypse. I was full of a feeling of well-being, warm, dry, safe, looking forward to a delicious meal and a comfortable bed, surrounded by friends and my adopted son Zos who at this moment was exploring the inn hopefully not getting into any trouble.

CHAPTER ONE HUNDRED AND EIGHT

Dinner was served indoors this evening. Candles lit the table which had been laid with vegetarian dishes according to Buddhist dictates. Yuezhi had requested that no meat be served at this meal, to demonstrate how well one could eat without harming another living thing.

"Interesting," Tatius commented.

"Hmph," grunted Gnaeus.

Zos appeared excited, anxiously looking up every time someone came in with another dish. A plate was set in front of me; I gasped. "Ethiopian flatbread! How did they know how to prepare this?" I looked up at Zos, his eyes flashing, smiling from ear to ear. "Zos, did your exploring take you into the kitchen by chance?"

"It wasn't difficult Teacher. I wanted to surprise you. Did I surprise you?" he asked expectantly.

"Of course! And what a wonderful surprise it is. A bit of home here in this forgotten corner of the world. What splendid memories this brings to my mind. May I say a word of thanks to my God before you all?"

"But of course," said Septimus. Zos and I bowed our heads and held out our hands palms up. The others watched expectantly.

"Father in heaven, you have carried us safely so many leagues from our home, and yet you can surprise me with a piece of home even in this foreign place. Thank you for reminding me that you, like the beautiful memories you are bringing to my mind right now, are ever present, no matter where I find myself. Thank you for Zos' kind and generous heart, for Yuezhi's skill and patience in bringing us to this safe spot in a sea of storm, for Gnaeus' diligence in protecting us and for Septimus and Tatius and their willingness to accompany us on this journey. Watch over and protect Septimus' family back in Rome and soothe his heart as he misses them. Now bless this food to the nourishment of our bodies. It is in Jesus' precious name I pray, Amen."

"Amen," everyone at the table responded. No one spoke for a moment.

"Zos, you should have the first taste," I said.

"No Teacher, I made it for you," he said still smiling. I tore a piece off and scooped up a portion of lentils that were steaming from a plate nearby.

"Mmm, so many delicious memories accompany this bite, Zos. You have made my heart soar."

"Well, we must try some too," said Tatius, helping himself to a piece of the flatbread.

"Thank you for that beautiful prayer Kaleb," Septimus said. "You pray to your God as if he were your friend."

"He is," said Zos. "He is not only our Lord but our friend."

"Present in the storm, in the quiet, in solitude and in the midst of a multitude," I added.

"In my religion," Yuezhi said, "there is no god to whom one may speak."

"But I've seen you sitting with your eyes closed," said Tatius. "What are you doing if you're not praying?"

"We practice bhavana and jhana, a type of meditation."

"What are you meditating on?" asked Zos.

"Different things. It is an exercise to gain total consciousness of oneself and at the same time free oneself from the constraints of suffering and desire, to achieve a sense of unification with infinity, with nothingness."

"Interesting," said Tatius. "I'm not sure what that means, but it sounds very interesting."

"But is that not sad, that to achieve perfection, one must relinquish everything that makes one unique?" I said.

"It is who we are that makes us sad."

"Only if we fail to understand the purpose that God had for us when he created us. Jesus teaches that we are a beautiful creation, created in the likeness of God with the purpose of glorifying God through our existence."

"And what does it mean to glorify God."

"To allow Jesus to live out his purpose through our lives. That usually manifests itself through a love for others. Rather than looking inwards for perfection, we look towards God."

"Yet only through introspection can one fully know oneself."

"I would say that even with extensive introspection, one can never fully know oneself. One will only find disillusionment because at our core there is only imperfection. Our failure to achieve the perfection towards which we aim will constantly disappoint us."

"I have achieved great peace through my meditations."

"Meditation does quiet the soul. One of the prophets in our holy book says that God's voice is not found in the violent wind, in the earthquake or in fire but in the soft whisper. We too believe that one can more easily hear God's voice in quietness and peace, but we also believe that God is present in the midst of the violent wind, the earthquake and fire because he is God. We need not depend upon a special place or adopt a special posture to be in his presence. But to hear him, we often need to find that quiet place."

The servants cleared the table and brought tea. The conversation turned to the more pressing and mundane business of what to do on the morrow if the rain failed to cease.

Once back in our room, we prepared for bed. "See the conversation that your wonderful act of kindness sparked Zos? You not only blessed me but everyone at the table."

"By the grace of God, Teacher," Zos said, but I could tell he was pleased with my praise.

CHAPTER ONE HUNDRED AND NINE

The days passed quickly once a routine had been established, but the ease and comfort worried me. "Kaleb is bothered by all this ease and comfort," Tatius mocked me in friendly banter with Septimus. "He's afraid he'll get used to all this luxury and not be able to readjust to living a deprived existence like a common mortal."

"He has a point," said Septimus, ever the stoic. "Too much luxury makes a man soft, and then when a trial comes, he is unprepared."

"You're both insane! You take what you get and enjoy it while it lasts."

"Sometimes however, that can open appetites that otherwise would have lain dormant. And then, on top of all the other ways that we must deprive ourselves, we are encumbered with yet another lust to hold in check."

"What are you, a Spartan? What a negative way to look at life, as a series of lusts that must be restrained. Why not just enjoy what comes your way instead of fearing that you are too happy or comfortable and then wishing things were different while missing what's right in front of you?"

"In a way, you are right," I said. "We need to enjoy what is right in front of us. Solomon said that there is nothing better for a man than to eat, drink and enjoy his work. I guess I worry too much. I should not be afraid that I will be unable to adjust to the life of a mere mortal after this is all over. You are right Tatius; I should stop worrying that I am opening a Pandora's box of new expectations that cannot be closed later when those expectations cannot be met."

And so the discussions went over dinner, from the meaning of life to politics to religion to the weather. Zos and I had begun to run in the evenings, a couple of Kushan guards always near us on horseback. The mornings, once on the road, were reserved for lessons with Zos, conversations in the languages that he was mastering. Reading and writing were impracticable on horseback.

He tried it, but each time it made him nauseous, the light, the jostling of the horse, the dust. We gave it up after a couple of days. Days turned into weeks, farmland carved out of dust and mountains to our south, a river and more verdant plain spread towards the foot of barren mountains to our north, until finally we arrived at the base of the Khyber Pass, a towering range of mountains, the final barrier between us and the Kushan capital.

We spent the night in an inn that also served as a guard post over the entry of the Pass. Both sides of the road were bordered by barracks for the Kushan military outpost, guards of the imperial road. Any attempt to attack or invade the capital from this direction would prove nearly impossible and would definitely never be a surprise. The king would know well in advance that something was afoot.

A hazy blue-gray dawn swallowed us into is womb as we emerged from the inn. The barracks on each side of the road were almost invisible in a suffocating fog. Once on the road, I felt that our small party was alone since the entire contingent fore and aft were smothered in the mist, only the ones closest to us barely visible; the sole confirmation that we were not alone was the muffled clip-clop of the hooves of our horses on the stone pavement, without the outline of which we would have been unable to proceed, having no point of reference. The fog not only handicapped our vision but seemed to stifle conversation. We were as lost in our own thoughts as we were in this ubiquitous ground-level cloud. Though the rhythmic music of horseshoe on stone was vaguely hypnotic, my mind felt as if it were shooting sparks, brilliantly lucid in the miasma. Memories more vivid than this present reality flashed before my mind's eye, as if I were behind the screen of a shadow play. I allowed the images to play in my imagination, not even attempting to organize them, to categorize them, to explore them further, this exercise in abandon contrary to my nature. It was a rigorous yet exhilarating exercise to allow my mind to race from one memory to the next with wild abandon, the vibrancy stunning against the backdrop of this dull vapor. Lake Mareotis in the moonlight. I could feel the warm water lapping at my chin, the cool currents swirling between my feet, blood red hibiscus against the white front and sky blue door of my home. The touch of Silara's hand on mine as she gave me the pendant, gulls calling me seaward. My chest pressed against the rough stone balustrade of the columned balcony watching the business of the Tyrian harbor while making sure Zos did not fall

over the edge. Losing at Senet on a starlit evening, Anata's laugh like
a music score read from the stars overhead, Zos' eyes reflecting the
candlelight from the lantern by the table, Acacio and Tano toasting
to Anata's win. Running the perimeter of the caravan, sweating
stripes like an African zebra, too out of breath to laugh. Tasting
snow for the first time in the temple plaza of Rhagae, standing
beneath the gnarled tree on the hill above the city as if Zos and I
were the last humans on earth. Beautiful Mihret calling me to her
table and my feeble attempt to appear nonchalant. Holding my
breath on the roof of the ruined building while Scythian bandits
hacked up half our caravan. Seeing Shash's knife as I lay on my cot.
Calling out to the man that was staring at us on the voyage from
Alexandria. Who was that man? Someone tried to steal something
from our tent. Someone was listening to our conversation in Dura.
What about that sailboat that was never out of sight on our trip down
the Euphrates? Was Shash just a continuation of something that had
started from the very inception of our journey? I began to trace
every suspicious thing that had happened since we had left. We must
have been watched and followed this entire time. Could there be a
Pythagorean spy among us right now? How could they possibly have
followed us once Shash was dead, unless Shash had an accomplice?
What if someone else was in that caravan that had continued on with
us? Impossible. We were no longer in the company of anyone that
was on that caravan. I shook my head emphatically, my body
attempting to convince my mind while my mind raced to imagine
other ways that we could be tracked. It would not be difficult for
someone trying to discover where we were headed.

For the first time I noticed the fog had lifted and Zos was
looking at me curiously. "Why are you shaking your head?"

"Thinking."

"What are you thinking about?"

"Remember our morning baths in Lake Mareotis?"

Zos sighed. "I haven't thought of home in ages," he said, an
expression between surprise and guilt on his face.

"There is nothing wrong with that Zos. There are so many
other new things to ponder. I guess the fog made me introspective."

"Were you able to free your mind from present worries?"
Yuezhi asked.

"On the contrary. I find myself as firmly attached to what makes me who I am as ever." I kept my newfound suspicious to myself. There was no need to worry Zos.

The mountains surrounding us reminded me of the range we passed through on our way to Ecbatana, although here the towering cliffs did not press claustrophobically in upon us. Here, the vistas were wide and open, the path relatively easy. We would pass the night near the eastern end of the Pass and by the end of the next day be in the capital. There were many leagues to go before reaching Alexandria, but it seemed far closer now that this last great barrier was almost crossed. The lead guide blew the horn announcing our stop for the midday meal. Before we dismounted, a table was already being set for us. Tatius, as if reading my mind, said, "It's definitely going to be painful getting used to not having this kind of treatment. Maybe you could keep up this tradition Septimus. You could be in charge of table settings and I'll handle the food."

"Keep dreaming Tatius. Was it not you who said to appreciate what you have while you have it and not wish that things were other than they are? Well, here is your chance to put your words into action. Rather than trying to figure out how to maintain this level of luxury, you should just be accepting it for what it is right now."

"Alright Sir Philosopher, enough talk. Let's eat."

"Spoken like a true Epicurean," I said.

PART SIXTEEN

PURUSHAPURA

Gregorian Calendar – September 4th, 163
Alexandrian Calendar – Mesori 26th, Fourth Shomu
The Season of Harvesting
3rd year of Marcus Aurelius

"– A fire – that's what the earth is, Gautama. Its firewood is the year; its smoke is space; its flame is the night; its embers are the quarters; and its sparks are the intermediate quarters. In that very fire gods offer rain, and from that offering springs food."
(Chandogya Upanisad 5.6, ca 500 BC)

CHAPTER ONE HUNDRED AND TEN

The Ghandaran vale spread out before us, fallow green fields dotted with yellow wildflowers lay checkered amidst recently harvested fields and pastures as far as the eye could see. The winding descent from the Khyber Pass took most of the morning, but by midday we were in the plains, the massive walls of the capital and an impossibly tall tower visible even from this distance.

As we drew nearer, I grew increasingly amazed at the sheer size of the smooth undulating walls, like nothing I had ever seen. They rose like vertical dunes, as if Moses, rather than parting the sea, had parted a sandstorm and then frozen it in place.

Mammoth metal plated doors stood partially open to allow our entry into the city. I watched Zos as he craned his neck to see the tops of the ornately carved doors rising several stories above our heads. I imagined this is what an ant felt upon entering a house. Immediately our gaze fixed on a structure taller than any I had seen in my life, taller I was sure than even the Pharos in Alexandria. "Magnificent," I heard Tatius whisper.

The base of the Kanishka Stupa as Yuezhi called it was hidden behind the canopied roofs of the giant bazaar that pushed up against the gate through which we had entered, but its shadow fell across us as we made our way through the mass of humanity concentrated in this market. I was too caught up in observing my surroundings to wonder why the guard would have brought us in what must be the busiest gate in the city at this time of day. Past the market, we turned right onto a street of ornate façades and balconies, the multi-storied buildings hovering over us. I felt a rising sense of claustrophobia, of being swallowed, when without warning, the street opened into a wide plaza dominated by the impossibly tall Stupa.

The enormous base was painted in brilliant detail. Above the towering base rose layer upon layer, gold and silver plated, studded with statues of Buddha in various poses, pointed towers at different intervals culminating in a sharp spire so high up that it touched the sky. Yuezhi explained that Kanishka, the father of the current King of kings, built this Stupa to honor Buddha and to house his relics.

We entered another narrow street off the grand plaza, leaving the Stupa behind. I was beginning to get an idea of the size of this city, perhaps the largest I had seen since leaving Alexandria. Ahead I could now see the walls of what could only be the palace. We were led to the right of the main gate and into a walled courtyard where Yuezhi bid us dismount. Our things were carried into the various rooms that gave onto the courtyard. A wooden portico gave shelter to all of the rooms surrounding us. The courtyard was alternately paved and grassy, flowering bushes strategically placed, a fountain splashing in the center, an arbor to the side of the fountain. "This is where you will stay during your sojourn in the capital. We are in the right wing of the palace, in the ambassadorial quarters. If you require anything, please do not hesitate to ask. All of your needs will be taken care of as long as you are guests of the imperial palace. I will return before nightfall to make sure you have everything you need."

Tatius, Septimus, Gnaeus and I were too overwhelmed to do anything but nod. "Where do we go to eat?" Zos asked. I smiled.

"Food will be brought shortly," Yuezhi grinned. "When I return, I will let you know if an audience has been planned with his highness the Son of Heaven, Huvishka." With that, Yuezhi withdrew, leaving us standing in the center of the courtyard staring at each other.

"I guess we should get squared away in our quarters," Septimus said, moving towards the room where he had seen his things being carried.

Walking towards the room where our things had been taken, I noted Zos standing in the grass looking up at lettering above the portico in front of our room. I could hear him sounding out the Greek letters. "Strange," he said. "What language is this? It's written in Greek but doesn't sound like Greek at all."

"It is Sanskrit." Zos jumped. "Were you talking to yourself? I thought you were directing those questions at me."

"I don't have eyes in the back of my head Teacher. I didn't know you were standing there. So if it's Sanskrit, why is it written in Greek?"

"The Kushans have adopted the Greek alphabet among other things Greek though they still speak Sanskrit. This is as far east as Alexander made it in his campaign to conquer the world. Though it has been 500 years since he passed through this land, his legacy remains in the letters you see written above the portico."

"Have you ever been in Alexander's tomb Teacher?"

"Yes, Zos. Have you not?"

"Not yet Teacher, not yet. I can't believe I live in the city where he lies, and I have never seen him."

"We possess a proud heritage Zos, not only because we live in the greatest city outside of Rome but because we are Ethiopian. But for all of that, we should never harbor the idea that we are better than anyone else. It is only by the grace of God that we were born where we were and live where we do."

At that moment, a bell sounded from the far end of the courtyard. A servant girl ran towards us and made an announcement. Zos and I must have had the same expression of confusion on our faces because the girl repeated herself, this time in Greek. "Dinner."

"Right," I said. "Dinner. Say it again in Sanskrit?" And thus began my intense lessons in Sanskrit which I would learn passably well before leaving this Kushan capital.

CHAPTER ONE HUNDRED AND ELEVEN

Once again, we found ourselves dressed in our finest, on our way to an audience with the King of kings, the Son of Heaven, Huvishka, ruler of the Kushan Kingdom, last bastion of Greek culture before reaching India and the unknown lands of the east. Gnaeus had almost been prohibited from accompanying us after refusing to leave his arms behind. Tatius finally convinced him that we were safe and that if the king wanted us dead, we would have been dead long before this evening. We entered the Royal Chamber of Interviews surrounded by a bevy of escorts, courtiers and guards. We had been prompted prior to this visit on proper etiquette. Standing behind our designated seats which were arranged in a semicircle facing a raised platform on which sat an ivory throne, we waited for the entrance of King Huvishka. A trumpet blew and everyone in the room prostrated themselves, forehead to the ground. Our small party bowed our heads, the most a Roman would do in the presence of a foreign ruler. We had been instructed not to look at the king until he was seated on his dais and had given everyone permission to rise. I resisted the urge to rub the back of my head.

After an interminable period of waiting while the king was adjusted on his throne, the trumpet sounded a second time and the crier at the king's side called out something in Sanskrit. The hall softly rustled as the prostrated audience began to rise. As I lifted my head, the crier called out in Greek, "The ambassadorial party from Rome may be seated before the Son of Heaven."

We took our seats and waited to be addressed. "Welcome to Ghandara gentlemen. We are pleased to host such an auspicious party."

I nodded my head in acknowledgment of the compliment when Tatius responded, "And thank you King Huvishka for your most generous reception and the honor of an audience." I could sense the tension exuding from Septimus as we had been instructed to remain silent unless directly asked a question. The king was evidently nonplussed as he smiled and accepted the compliment. Then the questions began. What part of the Roman Empire did we hail from; what were we doing in this part of the world; how did Huvishka's kingdom strike us; what did we think of the Stupa his father had constructed; where were we headed, and on and on. I could see Zos battling to keep his eyes open.

"Zos!" I whispered as quietly as possible. His head snapped up so quickly he cracked it against the back of the hard acacia chair and let out an involuntary yelp. The king smiled.

"Your son looks tired."

"He has been studying all day your highness."

"What have you learned today in your studies?" the king addressed Zos directly. Zos was wide awake now, and mortified that everyone in the room was looking at him.

"Speak to the king in Sanskrit Zos," I whispered.

"Today is the second day of the week." Zos stated confidently in Sanskrit. The king let out a roar of laughter.

"Superb! I would have this young linguist study with my own son for the duration of your time here," the king declared. Zos' eyes bulged, as did mine most probably. "Now l must retire. This has been a most fascinating exchange. We will see each other again soon," he announced as he stood. There was an audible whoosh as everyone in the room instantly went to the ground. We stood and looked at the floor.

CHAPTER ONE HUNDRED AND TWELVE

Zos was beside himself, thrilled and frightened at the same time. His schooling with the Prince came with a room in the royal compartments. The meager belongings in his possession had already been moved to his new quarters. "Not to worry Zos. I am going nowhere. If you need anything, you can send for me or come see me yourself."

The courtier that had been assigned to Zos appeared in the doorway of our room. "If everything has been moved, I will now take you to your rooms my lord," he said, bowing his head.

Zos turned and looked up at me with raised eyebrows mouthing silently, "My lord?"

"Comport yourself with dignity Zos. This is a rare opportunity. You are an ambassador of the Roman Empire, of Alexandria and Ethiopia. You are very likely the only taste the prince will ever get of our home, so represent us well."

"I will Teacher," he said, fingering his necklace. "Thank you Teacher," he said in Ge'ez, impulsively hugging me before turning to follow the young courtier to this newest on his growing list of novel experiences. As he walked out the door, I felt a wave of loneliness sweep over me. I had not been separated from Zos since Ecbatana. Though not my son, he had become like one to me, two chords knotted together more and more tightly since setting sail from Alexandria what seemed like years ago. Before my thoughts grew too maudlin, Septimus knocked on the lintel announcing his presence. Though looking straight at him I had not noticed him standing there.

"Missing Zos already?"

"Am I that transparent?"

"May I propose something that will serve as a needed distraction to tide you over this momentary despondency?"

"Propose away."

"Yuezhi has offered to take us on a tour of the city."

"Splendid. When?"

"Right now."

"After you my liege," I mock bowed, waving Septimus ahead of me as I slipped on my sandals on the way out the door.

CHAPTER ONE HUNDRED AND THIRTEEN

To orient us, Yuezhi began the tour by leading us atop the city walls which I judged to reach about twice as high as the platform of the Pharos, my standard for comparing all tall structures. Wide enough to ride two chariots side by side, the flat paved area felt more like a highway than the top of a wall. On one side, the flat semi-arid plain extended as far as the eye could see in the direction of the great Indus where we would begin our southward journey to the Erythraean Sea. Inside the walls however was a different story. Though the many two and three-story-tall buildings were dwarfed by the magnificent palace, that royal edifice was in turn dwarfed by the towering Stupa which cast its long morning shadow over half the city. I could not take my eyes off it. As Yuezhi explained about the history of the city and the many landmarks we could see from this vantage point, I was only half listening, caught up as I was in imagining the incredible artistry and time that must have gone in to the construction of the Stupa. It was easily taller than the Pharos of Alexandria, the tallest thing I had ever seen apart from the pyramids which I had seen only twice, once as a child on our way from Adulis to Alexandria and once, briefly, on my mission down the Nile.

"Perhaps you would like to begin by seeing the Great Stupa up close?" Yuezhi put his hand on my shoulder.

I nodded agreement and started back down the steep stairway to the base of the wall. Yuezhi took the lead at the foot of the stairs, directing us past foot traffic along a fairly open thoroughfare that led directly to the Stupa. Monks in saffron robes stood guard in pairs at each entrance. Yuezhi brought his hands together as if in prayer and bowed his head to each of the monks at our entrance before leading us into the cavernous interior. We found ourselves in a forest of pillars, the shortest over twice my height. As we neared the center, even taller pillars rose like sentinels protecting a giant golden statue of Buddha. Yuezhi motioned for Septimus and me to wait while he continued forward to join the group of monks seated on the floor chanting in front of the giant statue. Again, Yuezhi did the praying motion with his hands, this time performing an elaborate genuflection before bowing and touching his forehead to the ground, then rising and repeating the entire routine three times before coming back to where he had left us standing observing the whole scene. Meanwhile, I took in golden Buddha. He was dressed in a monastic robe. High on his head, he had an abundant topknot wound round the crown of his head like a flower garland. A faint mustache outlined his upper lip, and in the center of his forehead was a gigantic ruby. In the palm of his upraised right hand was a mark that looked like a wheel while his left hand hung at his side.

When Yuezhi had again joined us, I asked him to explain the meaning of the many symbols evident in the statue. "And what was the motion you did with your hands?" I asked after he finished answering my first questions.

"Enough with the questions, Kaleb. I want to climb to the top of this tower," interrupted Tatius. Yuezhi smiled and bid us follow him. Behind the Buddha was a narrow spiral staircase, the stone steps appearing to hang suspended in thin air, disconcerting Septimus who had a not so well-kept secret fear of heights. I watched him cling to the center post as we made our way up attempting to crush his fear under pure Stoic will-power. The stairs opened onto the next level, an airy, open space different in every way from the lower level which was dark and smelled heavily of incense. Here, the air moved freely through ornately carved windows on all four walls. Though much smaller in perimeter from the base, this room was still immense. Intricately carved wooden pillars replaced the stone ones below. The pillars ran in rows, supporting meticulously carved and painted beams that ran the length of the room. At one end of the room, stairs led to the next level. Up and up we went, the ornately decorated and designed rooms getting smaller and smaller until finally we found ourselves on the top level under a high silver domed roof. The room was entirely empty, the blue-green tile floor expanding in ever-widening concentric circles to the windows that Septimus was very cautiously approaching. I felt like a bird, so high above the city. My psyche was filled with a sense of being removed from the mundane concerns of life, above the little people that moved anonymously below in the dirty streets, fulfilling their meaningless destinies. I shook my head to clear it of this false sense of superiority with which the height had filled me. What was wrong with me? Is this why God intervened in the construction of the Tower of Babel? How easily pride swells.

We stood silent for some time. Septimus' stomach growled. "Anybody feel like getting a bite to eat?" he laughed.

"Follow me," Yuezhi said, disappearing down the stairs.

CHAPTER ONE HUNDRED AND FOURTEEN

I sat reading *True History* on the veranda surrounding our courtyard. It was one of the few books Sikarbaal had gifted me on my departure from Tyre. Lucian of Samosata, a new writer from greater Armenia, had concocted a story of travel through space to the outer planets. I was currently engaged in a battle with the inhabitants of the sun when a conversation that until now had blended with the buzz of the dragonflies hovering over the fountain in the center of the garden broke violently into my repose. "What?" shouted Tatius.

"Due to the exceptional rains this past rainy season, the waters of the Indus are far too high and dangerous to travel now. At least two more moons must pass before attempting travel." I closed my book. Had I heard right? I did not recognize the voice of the speaker. Walking in the direction of the voices, I could hear Tatius mumbling something in response to the last announcement.

"Did I hear correctly," I poked my head into Tatius' apartment, lightly rapping on the wall as an afterthought, belatedly announcing my interruption.

A courtier I had not seen before was seated across from Tatius, both on low stools drinking tea and playing dice. Both looked up at me as I invited myself in.

"Meet Dhanu," Tatius volunteered. "Dhanu, this is Kaleb." Dhanu stood and made the prayer gesture. I returned the greeting. "Dhanu here has just announced that we have the honor of enjoying the generous royal hospitality to which we have grown so accustomed an additional three months."

I looked at Dhanu whose expression revealed his ambivalence between taking Tatius' comment as sarcastic or complimentary. "Three more months," I sighed. "I thought we would be on our way in two weeks at most."

"And I," said Tatius standing to join us.

"Are you sure Dhanu?" I asked, unable to conceal the pleading in my voice, my hand massaging the crown of my head.

"The floods are the effects of the rains. The illusion of our lives is tossed by cosmic causes and effects that are beyond our control."

"You are right in a sense Dhanu. God in his infinite wisdom has seen fit to have us wait here a bit longer."

"Not God, Kaleb, the cosmos."

"Curses on them both!" fumed Tatius. "I'm ready to be home, and now I must figure out how to entertain myself for three months, the time it would probably take to make it back to Rome."

"It is your desire to be home that is causing you pain," Dhanu said. "In Buddhism, we learn to empty ourselves of desire to also empty ourselves of pain."

"Right. Thank you Dhanu. I think that's enough philosophy for one day. What one can't change, one must learn to accept. Kaleb, now that you're here, join us for a game of dice. Dhanu was just teaching me the Kushan version of knucklebones."

"Why not," I said. "After this news, I do not think I can concentrate on reading."

CHAPTER ONE HUNDRED AND FIFTEEN

The next morning, after my prayers and daily reading of the sacred scriptures, I made my way back to the Stupa where I hoped to learn more about the religion of this kingdom. The conversations with Yuezhi on the trip had left me intrigued. Buddhism seemed almost more a philosophy of life than a religion, and I hoped to get a better handle on what its tenets were before leaving, especially since we were going to be here for a while. The idea also occurred to me last night as I lay in my bed thinking how to best employ myself while here that I could begin a translation of the Avesta into Greek while my Avestan was still linguistically fresh, and I knew just the place where I wanted to work.

A group of monks in saffron were gathered around the giant Buddha chanting in the dark interior, thick with the smoke of incense. I sat apart watching the scene, contemplating the various ways man attempts to attain the eternal. Lost in my thoughts, I did not notice a monk join me. A bell sounded and the chanting monks rose. Suddenly aware of my surroundings, I looked at the monk beside me. He was quietly observing me. "I did not want to interrupt your meditation," he said quietly in broken Greek.

"I apologize. I was not meditating, just thinking."

"About what?"

"How lost we are."

"Lost?"

"Yes, endlessly trying to find the meaning in our existence."

"And?"

"We invent answers and then cling to them against all logic, proud in our ignorance."

"What answers have *you* invented?"

"None. God has revealed his answers in his book."

"God has a book?"

"Yes, we call it *Ta Biblia*, The Book."

"And where is this book? Do you carry it with you?"

"I carry a copy."

"I would like to see this book. In what language is it?"

"The copy I possess is Greek. Can you read Greek?"

"Yes, though as you can see, my knowledge of it is lacking."

"Jesus says 'Seek and you shall discover.' If you read his book, he will reveal his truth to you."

"Who is Jesus?"

"He is God in the flesh, the redeemer of the world."

"That sounds like Krishna. Where is he now?"

"He is in heaven."

"Where is heaven?"

"It is where we are after we die."

"And meanwhile?"

"Meanwhile, he inhabits us, placing his kingdom in our hearts, giving us a taste of what we will be once perfected."

"So I am an extension of God."

"We are a creation of God, a vessel for God to inhabit to carry out his perfect plan for our lives, but we are not an extension of God. He is a separate entity. And you? What answers have *you* invented?"

"None. I follow the teachings of Buddha."

"And what does he teach?"

"Desire ties us to this earth and is the cause of all suffering."

"What happens if desire is quenched?"

"We end the cycle of rebirth and are absorbed into the essence of all life."

"What is this essence?"

"Nothingness."

"We are absorbed into nothingness?"

"Yes, the end of all desire, of self."

"Your aim is to cease to be an individual?"

"Yes."

"So is my individuality is a bad thing?"

"Yes. We are all part of one whole. Our individuality separates us. When we realize we are all and we are nothing, we have achieved bliss."

"Bliss."

"Yes, bliss."

"Is this written down somewhere?"

"Yes, in the Mahayana Sutras."

"Do you have a copy?"

"There is a copy here in the temple."

"May I read it?"

"Yes, but they are written in Sanskrit."

"Is there no translation into Greek or Pahlavi?"

"Not yet."

"Why not?"

"No one has done it."

"Perhaps I could."

"Perhaps."

"May I ask your name?"

"You may ask."

"What is your name?"

"Jiyu."

"Jiyu, who need I petition to come here and write."

"Me."

"Who are you?"

"I am the teacher."

"I am honored. I am Kaleb."

"I know who you are. You have met Lokaksema."

"How do you know that?"

"He told me."

"Is he here?"

"Yes. He arrived yesterday. He desires to speak with you again."

"Ah, desire."

"Yes, perhaps a misbegotten choice of words."

"There is no way around desire Jiyu. The fact that we get out of bed in the morning is fraught with desire."

"A thought to ponder."

"Speaking of desire, I have one. I wish to use the room at the top of the Stupa to write. I have a work I would like to translate, and I have found no more perfect spot in all of my travels than that room."

"Come back tomorrow, and I will give you an answer."

I rose to take my leave, bowing and giving the praying gesture. "Until tomorrow then. I will bring a copy of the book about which I spoke."

"Tomorrow."

The sunlight blinded me and the heat had become oppressive, but the clear air after the suffocating incense was like ambrosia to my lungs. I took deep breaths as I walked back to the palace.

CHAPTER ONE HUNDRED AND SIXTEEN

"What were you doing in the Stupa today Teacher?" Zos asked me over dinner. I had gotten permission for him to join me and catch me up on what his first two days of study were like. Also, it was the first day of Thout, New Year's Day in Alexandria, so I had instructed the cook as well as I could on some dishes from home for our meal.

"The head monk has allowed me to use the top room at the peak of the Stupa to do some writing and translating."

"That's fantastic. I haven't been up there yet, but Vasudeva has promised to take me."

"Vasudeva?"

"The prince."

"I may see you there then. Tell me about your classes."

"Our teachers are saffron robed monks. We have five teachers. We rise very early in the morning and after ablutions, we break fast and meet the other students on the second floor of the Stupa."

"Your classes are in the Stupa? And there are other students? How many?"

"We are eight in all. The first teacher says our number symbolizes the eight-fold path to enlightenment and has tasked us with reciting one by one each of the steps of the path. I am right action."

"And what does right action entail?"

"The avoidance of wrong action, like murder, stealing, adultery and such."

"Good so far. Then what?"

"The teacher turns a sand dial and we spend the next interminable period in meditation. Fortunately the sounds that come up from the street muffle my growling stomach."

"I thought you said you eat before meditation."

"We do, but it is a very light meal. Vasudeva says if it doesn't grow from dirt, it is forbidden. They are strict vegetarians. I am constantly hungry."

"On what do you meditate?"

"I mostly pray. When I run out of things to pray for, I practice my lessons in my head."

"It sounds like a profitable time then."

"Yes, Teacher. It is boring but profitable."

"And then?"

"Our next class is Sanskrit. Of course everyone except for me speaks it, but the lessons are for reading and writing. The teacher spends a lot of time with me since I can barely understand what's happening. Vasudeva helps me a lot. Next is Greek and then Latin. Since I am ahead of everybody else in those classes, I help Vasudeva. Cosmology is next."

"What do you do in that class?"

"The teacher reads sutras on the creation and destruction of the universe, the placement of the worlds and so on."

"Pay close attention in that class Zos. When we get back to Alexandria, you will read Ptolemaios' Almagest. I would like to see how their understanding of the cosmos differs from what Ptolemaios has discovered."

"I will write down everything I learn Teacher, so I don't forget. The last class before sports is on Buddhist precepts. Again the teacher reads from various sutras and lectures on them. Vasudeva says sometimes we have class discussions."

"Zos, this is a great opportunity for you to learn another belief system. I recommend that you compare everything you hear to what you have learned about God and Jesus Christ. Look for similarities but be sure to understand the differences. Record your questions and thoughts in writing. We will have ample time to discuss all that you are learning on the rest of our trip. Now, what sports do you play?"

"Today I learned to throw a discus. Vasudeva says we also practice archery and the use of a dagger."

"Take care Zos. I do not want you getting hurt. Let me know if the practice becomes dangerous." Zos averted his eyes. "I am serious Zos. I do not want you losing an eye or worse."

"Yes Teacher. After that we eat. Of course, by then I feel I might faint from hunger."

"Your body will adjust."

"That's what the teacher says."

"What do you do after lunch?"

"Vasudeva says the classes change periodically. Right now, the class is learning sculpture. It is very interesting. That is my favorite class."

"It seems that you and Vasudeva have already become fast friends."

"I think so."

"Are you in the Stupa all day?"

"No, Teacher. Only until sports. The midday meal is in the palace, and the sculpture class is in a different wing of the palace. Our art teacher is not a monk."

"Fascinating Zos. I look forward to hearing all that you learn. You can be my teacher once we leave here." Zos' eyes widened. "It is true Zos. You are learning things now that I have never learned. Particularly about this Buddhism. So pay close attention. I expect you to be an expert teacher at the end of these three months."

"Three months!"

"Did I not mention this? The Indus is flooding right now. That is the river we must navigate to reach the coast. We have to wait till the floodwaters subside. God has a plan for us Zos. There is a reason why we are being detained here. I am sure part of his plan is that you learn as much as you can."

"I will Teacher. I feel I have already learned so much, and this is only the second day."

"Are you satisfied with your living quarters?"

"Very. Vasudeva and I share a room. He says he has never seen anyone with skin as black as mine."

"How old is he?"

"We are the same age. He asks me so many questions about Egypt. I am teaching him Senet."

"See Zos, you are already practicing your art as a teacher. Be a good influence for him. He will one day rule this empire. You are in a very special position, and your influence on him now could have very far-reaching consequences."

Dinner over, Zos left with much more on his mind than that with which he came. "When will I see you again Teacher?"

"I will arrange that we spend each Lord's Day together. We can worship together and discuss what you have learned during the week."

"Good night Teacher."

"Good night Zos. Perhaps I will see you on my way to the top of the Stupa."

CHAPTER ONE HUNDRED AND SEVENTEEN

Within a week I had established my routine. Early morning devotions and meditation, breaking fast with the others in my compound and finally the morning walk to the Stupa, stopping for tea at a vendor that I had become familiar with in a spot that afforded a clear view of the grand plaza from where the Stupa rose like a majestic mountain in the center of this sprawling city. From my vantage point, I watched as Zos' group of students made their way into the Stupa for their daily lessons. Soon after I saw them again as I made my way up the endless flight of stairs, 800 in all. Eight for the eight-fold path times ten for the ten precepts. Jiyu had allowed for the setting up of a writing table, ink and a selection of ivory styluses, parchment, blotters and stack of paperweights in the center of the domed room at the peak of the Stupa. I sat on my cushion, prayed that God prosper the work of this day and began the translation. The only item I never left in the room was my original copy of the Avesta and the translation on which I was working. I would work on the Avesta till midday, leaving the pages to dry as I ate the meal that was brought to me by a young monk. After lunch, I would take a short nap until the Greek speaking monk Koju joined me to help in my translation of the Gospel of John into Sanskrit. I would read a sentence; Koju would ponder for a moment and then write it in Sanskrit. After every ten lines, he would orally translate what he had written back into Greek to confirm that he had captured the essence. Our daily goal was two pages. After Koju left, I would take what he had written and make two more copies. I wanted to leave one for Jiyu, one for the King and the original for me for my collection. I intended to add it to the already copious number of translations housed in the Library.

Finally, I would collect the pages of the Greek Avesta that had dried to carry back with me and make sure the pages of John we had worked on that day were ringed by paperweights to dry till morning. Before leaving I would spend some time standing at a window watching the city. I always stopped on my way back to the palace at the same tea shop, the Avesta and my newly copied pages safely tucked away in the bag that always hung over my shoulder.

"You work too much Kaleb. How can you stand to be cooped up in that room all day alone writing?" Tatius lifted another heaping spoon of goat soup to his mouth making a loud slurping sound. Fortunately for him, the cook was Hindu and had no qualms about serving meat, so long as it was not from a cow.

"It is peaceful. There are no distractions, and I am making phenomenal progress. Besides, that is why I run in the evenings, to stretch my legs after sitting most of the day. I am even learning Sanskrit little by little."

"You and your languages," Septimus laughed, undisguised admiration in his eyes. "You will speak half the languages of the world by the time we reach Alexandria."

"Lord willing," I said, slurping on my own spoonful of soup. "This is delicious."

Once back in my lamp lit room, I added the day's translation to the slowly growing stack of papers, rolled them back up to fit into the wooden tube I had purchased and, with the door and windows shut, climbed precariously atop the wardrobe where I could just reach the beams that ran the length of the ceiling hiding the tube where it could not be seen from the floor. Tired in mind and body, I stretched out on my low bed after sliding the leather-bound Pahlavi Avesta under my pillow.

CHAPTER ONE HUNDRED AND EIGHTEEN

I awoke to the sound of rain. It had not rained since our arrival. The consistent patter of raindrops on the tile roof and the slight chill in the air were a recipe for staying in bed. Like a snail in its shell, I sunk further into my pillow and pulled the coverlet up to my chin staring into the dark. I could take the day off, just lie here and read all day... or not. Yesterday was the Lord's Day, and I had spent it worshipping with Zos and relaxing. I could not take off two days in a row. But why not? There were more than two months to go before we left, and I was already ahead of schedule on the translations. My toes began to wiggle, the signal that my body was itching to be out of bed. I groaned and rose up into a sitting position throwing the coverlet off my half-naked body.

Standing, I fumbled with the fastener to open the shutters. Thunder crashed into the room making me jump as a dim grey light slunk stealthily across the floor. I inhaled deeply the pungent odor of wet wood, earth and sky. Shivering, I shuffled to the wardrobe to retrieve a tunic. Halfway across the room I felt something crush under my bare heel. I would investigate that further once I was decently covered and had more light. The boy that generally lit the lamps in the room had evidently succumbed to the soporific effects of the morning. Beginning to feel the blood run through my veins again, I stepped out on the veranda, the floor slick with water under my feet. I took a lantern that still hung lit and brought it into my room to light my lamps. First though, I searched for what I had stepped on. There it was. Though I had smashed it firmly into the floor, the outline was clearly a scorpion the size of my thumb. I quickly inspected my foot to confirm I had not been stung, though I was sure I would have felt it if I had been. Though smaller scorpions were deadlier, one this size would have been debilitating. How it got in did not bear thinking about. God had once again saved me. I offered up a prayer of gratitude and scraped the remains into a tea cup to toss outside under the veranda where no one could inadvertently step on it again barefoot. I rinsed the cup out with water pouring off the roof and hung the lantern back in its place. It looked as if I were the only one alive this morning. There was no movement from any of the other rooms, but wait. Struggling to rise under the pelting rain, smoke above the kitchen on the opposite side of the courtyard signaled that food was being prepared. I grabbed my bag and made my way under shelter of the porch roof to the kitchen, the cool, wet wood under my bare feet refreshing.

Hot tea. The missing factor this morning. It seemed that cook and I were the only ones moving this morning. After a few failed attempts to start a conversation, I refilled my cup and shambled slowly back to my room, for the first time noticing that my bag seemed lighter than usual. I felt it, immediately realizing I had failed to put the Avesta in the bag. My pace quickened. Once in my room, I raced to the pillow under which I hid it every night and retrieved it every morning. The familiar feel of the leather binding sent a wave of relief coursing through me. Morning ablutions and a lonely breakfast behind me, I decided to go ahead to the Stupa and spend the day writing. If this morning was any indication, I would die of boredom if I stayed here all day, rain or no rain.

It seemed the city was taking a holiday. The rain was coming down in sheets, spattering the hem of my tunic with dust turned to dun colored mud. The cook loaned me an umbrella that at least kept my upper body dry. I was going to have to strip once I reached the Stupa and borrow a robe from a monk at this rate. Either that or spend the day steeping in a wet tunic. The tea shop where it had become my custom to stop was shuttered. I made straight for the Stupa. Monks in drooping robes stood guard in the rain trying hard to appear impervious. Before I had even reached the giant Buddha, Jiyu was by my side chiding me for coming out on a day like this.

"What better day to write Jiyu? In this weather, there is nothing to occupy one's time but work or sleep."

"At least I can provide you dry clothes."

"I would appreciate that very much Jiyu. The wet is already beginning to soak into my bones."

"Come with me." He walked ahead of me leading me into an area I had not seen before. It appeared to be the apartments where the monks lived, past the Buddha where the pillars melted into a wall. Jiyu disappeared behind a curtain. I followed him down a long hallway to a door that opened into a large room, empty except for a blazing fire at one end. Jiyu led me to the fire and bade me wait while he found me a dry robe. Shortly he was back carrying a neatly folded pile of saffron material. "Try this on," he said, shaking it out.

"Are you trying to convert me?" I asked, shedding my wet tunic.

"The robe does not make the Buddhist," he said.

"Truly said," I returned, allowing him to help me wrap the material around my waist. A second piece wrapped around my torso and draped over one shoulder. "How do I look?" I asked turning in a circle once he was finished.

"The robe has never looked more beautiful than against your ebony skin."

"You are too kind," I said, spreading my tunic in front of the fire.

"I will take that," he said. "It will be brought to you later when it is dry."

"What is this room?"

"It is where we meet for councils."

"Why is it empty?"

"We believe in simplicity. There is no need for furniture. What a monk carries with him is all he needs."

"There is nothing simple about this Stupa," I said.

"The Stupa is in honor of the Buddha."

"So extravagance can be employed in honoring the Buddha but not to make your life more comfortable."

"I said nothing about comfort. We are very comfortable here."

"I am having a difficult time reconciling the extravagance of the Stupa and the call to simplicity."

"If it were up to us, we would make do with a thatch hut if any shelter at all, but our rulers see fit to build structures like this Stupa to honor the memory of the Buddha. It is not wrong to inhabit this structure, only to depend on it for our happiness. Happiness does not arise from comfort or security but from emptying ourselves of the desire for them."

"That almost sounds Christian," I said. "Everything except the emptying ourselves of desire. Paul, a writer of much of the collected works of the second testament of our book, instructs us that even though we buy, to live as if we possessed nothing, though we have dealings in this world, to live as though we had no dealings with it, for this present world is passing away. Jesus says we are but sojourners in this world, only passing through. The object is not to empty ourselves of desire but to not become tied to anything in this life since it is all temporary though there is no prohibition against enjoying that with which God has blessed us."

"It almost sounds contradictory."

"Not as contradictory as desiring to empty yourself of desire. How can one ever succeed in that kind of conundrum? Solomon says to eat, drink and enjoy the toil of your hands. Job says that naked we come into the world and naked we leave, the Lord gives and the Lord takes away. What comes into our hands and our path during this short passage through life is a means to the eternal, not to be coveted but to be shared and enjoyed, not despaired of once it is taken away."

"Enough to ponder for one day. You must be ready to begin with your work."

"Actually yes. Thank you for the robe. I should fit right in today."

"Except that you are about a head taller and several shades darker."

"Yes, except for that."

CHAPTER ONE HUNDRED AND NINETEEN

As I gathered the slightly damp pages from yesterday's translating session from the floor, I got the distinct impression that someone had been moving things around. Of course, Jiyu could have sent someone up here to clean things, but surely he would have mentioned it. I would have to ask him later when I saw him. My stylus and ink were on the opposite side of the desk from where I usually kept them, and my copy of John's gospel was askew. Once everything was in order and I was ready to begin with the Avesta, I stood at the window and watched the rain continue to fall. A light mist had moved in shrouding the tower in a fine, barely tangible cloud. It almost seemed to reach in and engulf me. I could taste and smell it.

Shaking off the unease that was slowly creeping over me, I sat in front of my desk and began working. Yasna 51. Meticulously I filled my stylus with ink, careful not to spill any on the fresh parchment. I read the line in Avestan, thought for a moment and slowly began to write in Greek, "*And one of you, the greatest, has indeed attained to that wisdom which is thus blessed with a promise, Kavi Vîstâspa has reached it in the Realm of our great cause and moved in his toil by the chants of the Good Mind.*"

I woke to the sound of a tray being set on the bare tile floor. How long had I been sleeping? The two sheets of parchment I had completed this morning lay spread out near the writing table, the original copy of the Avesta safely repacked in my bag. My body ached from lying on the cold floor. The rain had stopped and a dense torpor lay over the city. The monk who brought the food vanished as quickly as he had appeared. Steam rose from a bowl in the center of the tray. I pulled myself into a sitting position and slid the tray beside me. The warm hot soup put life back into my limbs. Just as I was draining the bowl of the last drops of soup, the young monk who had brought my tray appeared with another smaller tray of tea and a neatly folded padded cloth which he spread out beside me, evidently to lie on if I fell asleep again. I smiled and thanked him in Sanskrit. He smiled back, took the tray with the empty bowl and vanished down the stairs again. I stood with my tea and walked to a window. I could barely make out the streets below, the thin fog still blanketing the city.

"I was surprised when master Jiyu told me you had come. Not even the royal classes are being held today," Koju said as he approached me.

"This is the perfect day to write," I said, still looking out over the fog enshrouded city. "Tea?" I asked, returning to my writing table and pouring Koju a cup from the still steaming pot.

We settled down to the business of translating. Neither of us noticed the passage of time until the sky grew so dark and ominous that I was unable to make out the words on the page in front of me. "I will go for lanterns," Koju said, standing and stretching.

"Just send them up." I said. "I will copy what we have done today and then retire."

"As you wish, Kaleb," Koju said. "It looks as if it may rain again. I can smell it in the air."

"Perhaps I should lay out the pages to dry downstairs."

"Allow me to help you," he said. I could feel the sky grow darker and the wind pick up. We gathered the pages scattered around us and carried them to the room below. I arranged them along the windowless wall on the northern side of the room where the stairs were while Koju returned upstairs for the writing table. This room was much darker but less open to the elements. I began setting up an area to write as Koju descended for lanterns and more tea. While waiting, I sat and prayed, thanking God for all I had accomplished today, for Zos, for accuracy in the work I was soon to begin, copying what we had translated today. Though I had told him he need not, Koju returned accompanied by two other monks carrying lanterns and my dry clothes. Once they were all gone, I changed and sat at my table tucking my bare feet under me, ready to start copying.

The rain had resumed, loud, thunderous and windy, but I was protected in my dry corner of the room. My eyes were getting heavy, but I still had one page left to copy. I stretched out on the padded spread I was sitting on, succumbing to the hypnotic rhythm of the storm outside.

A loud crash shocked me out of my sleep. What was that? I sat up disoriented. In the pitch dark the outline of the windows on the far side of the room were faintly discernible. My brain caught up with my eyes, and I remembered that I was on the level below the tower room. The lanterns had evidently gone out while I was sleeping. I stood silently, deciding what to do next. Barefoot, I walked across the room, the cold floor growing wet as I approached the windows. I heard movement on the stairs on the opposite side of the room, but it was too dark to see anything. "Who goes there?" I asked the empty room, my voice surprisingly confident. My heart unexpectedly began to race. How long had I been asleep? Moonlight suddenly filled the room, silhouetting a figure dressed head to foot in black coming directly towards me yet still halfway across the room. Just as suddenly, the room was cast into darkness again as clouds raced across the roof of the Ghandaran plain. With nowhere to hide, I slipped over the threshold of the window closest to me and onto the slick tile of the slanted roof. I was at a corner of the octagonal room where the roof extended out to a spire twice my height. If I could get behind the spire, I could hide from the black figure. My bare toes curled searching for a grip on the slippery tile. I let go of the windowsill just as a sliver of exposed moon flashed its silvery light on the masked face now at the window, leaving me in plain view, exposed and precariously perched high over the city. I watched as if in slow motion as the intruder raised his left fist. Moonlight glinted off a long blade before the moon again disappeared. I instinctively pulled back as I felt the wind of the blade come within inches of my neck. Losing my balance, I reached behind me, praying that I was close enough to the spire to catch it before I slid off the roof. My hand made contact and I threw myself at the spire, hugging it with all my strength, impervious to the pain that shot up my arms from the awkward way I had grabbed it. My eyes had adjusted to the dark allowing me to watch horrified as the figure climbed out onto the roof. I could feel his eyes, invisible in the inky darkness, searching for me. I clung more tightly to the spire, my mind searching for a way out of this impossible situation. He took a step towards me, the dark blade of his knife upraised, searching for its target. Another step. He had let go of the windowsill and with one more step would be on top of me. The clouds raced across the sky, exposing once again the feckless light. A gust of wind shot across the roof knocking the assassin off balance. His feet, clad in cloth shoes slipped on the wet roof. I saw the look of disbelief in his eyes just as the moon again hid behind the clouds, and he slid helplessly and silently off the rooftop, plummeting to the ground below. There was an anticlimactic thud as he made contact with the wet earth far below me. I stood frozen to the spire, as if I were just one more stone carving, a black Buddha with bleeding hands.

How much time passed, I was not aware. The windows that now seemed endlessly far away filled with light, and I could hear Jiyu's voice calling for me. I started to reply, but my voice just crackled, my throat unbelievably dry. I swallowed and called Jiyu's name. The sound of my own voice brought the reality of what had just happened crashing down on me, and I felt my grip slacken on the hard stone. Jiyu raced to the window and held the lantern out, gasping when he caught sight of me gripping the spire with all my might. "Hang on, Kaleb! You are going to be okay. I am coming out for you myself." A rapid conversation in Sanskrit ensued, and Jiyu, tied about the waist with a thick rope, climbed out the window.

Once I was safely back on firm footing inside the now extremely well lit room, I collapsed against the wall and put my face in my hands, gathering my wits before I could talk.

"What happened, Kaleb! Did you know that man?" My bag! I jumped up but before running to the other side of the room, I stopped myself. I needed to proceed carefully. No one needed to know about the Avesta.

"I have no idea who he was," I said, more calmly than I felt. I walked to my writing table where my things were still laid out. "I need to gather my things," I said, picking up my bag, tasting bile in my mouth as I realized the Avesta was not in it. Feeling dizzy, I quickly sat again before my legs gave way under me.

"You need to breathe for a minute," Jiyu said, shooing the other monks away. "Go, go, Kaleb needs some space."

"I need to see his face, to see if I knew him," I said, thinking that if I could see him, perhaps he had it on him. I could grab it before it was discovered.

"Was he after something? Are you missing anything?"

My mind searched for the right answer. "I do not think so," I said, surprised that the lie came so quickly. I needed time to think. I needed to get below and see the face of my attacker, to be sure that he was the one that stole the Avesta. I would not be able to rest till I knew where it was. "Let us go down. I want to see who almost killed me."

The Royal Inspector had already arrived. Guards were holding back the growing group of people that stood surrounding the dead assassin. Foiled by the presence of so many onlookers, I pushed my way to the front only to meet a face ensconced in a helmet with the royal crest emblazoned across the forehead. Jiyu was close on my heels. "Let us through," Jiyu demanded politely, bowing, his hands in a praying gesture. The guard stood to the side as I followed closely behind Jiyu. The inspector, a handsome man dressed in black and silver was bent over the assassin. "What can you tell me Monk Jiyu?" he asked without looking up.

"This is the man he almost killed," Jiyu responded motioning towards me. I studied the dead man. The inspector turned him over and removed his mask. I did not recognize the face, though it was so covered in blood it was difficult to tell.

"Do you know him?" the inspector asked matter-of-factly.

"I do not recognize him."

"We will try to determine where he came from before disposing of the body."

"May I come with you? I would like to see him with the blood washed from his face. Perhaps then I could tell if I had seen him before."

"Very well," the inspector replied, standing, looking me up and down. "You are very fortunate. This man looks to be a professional assassin. How did you elude him?"

"The thunder woke me in the dark of the room, and I had just enough time after seeing him to climb out the window of the turret. He was almost upon me when he slipped and fell. God has saved me once again."

"Once again?" the inspector raised his eyebrows.

"It is a long story," I said.

"One I would like to hear," he replied. "Come with us."

"He must be very tired," Jiyu protested.

"Nonsense Jiyu, my nerves are still on edge. Do not worry about me. Thank you for rescuing me up there."

"Good night, Monk Jiyu."

"Good night Inspector. And take care of our Scribe Kaleb. He is a guest of the King."

"You have my word." At that the inspector turned, leaving his men to bring the body behind him. I jogged to catch up with him. "You have had a very eventful evening Scribe. I am anxious to hear all about it," a hint of irony in his voice.

CHAPTER ONE HUNDRED AND TWENTY

I had not noticed my hands were still bleeding till one of the inspector's servants brought me a wet cloth to clean them. "So let us begin at the beginning, shall we?"

I recounted the events of my day up to the point where I was left clinging to the spire, the assassin in broken pieces on the saturated ground far below.

"You have left out why you think this man was after you in the first place."

"Honestly, I have no idea," I said, immediately feeling guilty at the lie.

"I find it hard to believe that someone would send a professional to do away with you and you have no idea why."

"Perhaps he confused me with someone else." The inspector looked me up and down with half a smile under his carefully manicured moustache.

"Well then, maybe not. But it was very dark. Might he not have mistaken me for someone else in the dark?"

"Who else spends time in the tower room every single day?"

"No one."

"Exactly. Could he have been after something?"

"What do you mean?"

"Are you working on something that might inspire someone else to murder you?"

"What could a scribe be doing that would inspire murder?"

"You tell me. I feel you are hiding something. You keep answering my questions with questions."

"Can I see his face again? Perhaps I will recognize him."

The inspector led me to a subterranean room seemingly carved out of bedrock. A wide stone table stood in the center of the room surrounded by blazing candles. The assassin's naked body lay exposed on the cold granite, his dark body slim and muscled. "I do not recognize him, but he looks Indian."

"I agree. So what would an Indian assassin have to do with you?"

I took his right arm and turned it palm up. There was the mark I had begun to suspect, a small triad tattooed on the inside of his wrist.

"What is that?"

"It looks like a tattoo."

"I can see that. Why were you looking for it?" Was I that transparent? I did not make a good liar or spy. "Scribe, I cannot protect you if you do not tell me what is going on."

"Was anything found on him?"

"It is lying over there." My eyes followed the direction his finger pointed, my feet following in rapid succession.

"Is this everything?" I asked, trying to keep the growing panic out of my voice. I was certain I would find the Avesta among his belongings.

"There is one other thing." My heart raced as the inspector took a key from a chain at his belt and unlocked a drawer. He brought out my book from the drawer, the familiar shine of the leather with the name of the book stitched in Avestan. He was watching my reaction closely. "This is yours, is it not?"

A wave of relief flooded me, and I took hold of the counter to steady myself. "I am a terrible liar," I confessed. "Can we sit somewhere and talk?" I reached out for the book.

"I am afraid I cannot give this to you till I know the whole story." He returned the Avesta to the drawer and locked it.

CHAPTER ONE HUNDRED AND TWENTY-ONE

"So there you have it. Much like Lokaksema is planning to translate your books of Buddhism into Sinese, I am taking a copy of the Avesta to Alexandria, but a group is seeking to take my life before I make it back. I do not understand why, but it is not the first time, as I have said, that this has happened on this trip, although I hope it is the last. I honestly thought I was safe now."

"What group?"

"You saw the tattoo?"

"Yes."

"That is a symbol of the Pythagoreans, a Greek cult that is evidently much more extensive and organized than I imagined."

"And why are they after you?"

"I secured a copy of their sacred writings, and they hold me responsible for profaning their secrets. What I do not understand is why now, after all these years, they are suddenly trying to get revenge. I was a much easier target in Alexandria."

"Perhaps not. There you were well known, and the crime could have been more easily traced to them. Here at the edge of your world, no one would ever know what had happened." I shivered. "We will need to assign you a guard for the remainder of your time here."

"That is not necessary."

"I must allow no harm to come to you while you are within the borders of Kushan."

"It is late. I should return to my quarters. May I have the book now?"

"Of course. Wait here while I find someone to accompany you home."

PART SEVENTEEN

THE INDUS

Gregorian Calendar – November 13th, 163
Alexandrian Calendar – Hathor 4th, Third Akhet
The Season of the Inundation
3rd year of Marcus Aurelius

"Just Libra weighs the hours and makes the nights equal with days; then pays the
winter nights hours which the spring had taken away"
(Lucan I, 8, ca 60)

CHAPTER ONE HUNDRED AND TWENTY-TWO

Black and lovely, the pre-dawn waters of the Indus cooled me as
I swam along the bank, afraid to go out too far. I was told the
current was still quite strong. I had not seen this much water since
the Euphrates, over a year past. This river, a tenuous umbilical cord,
reconnected me to the waters of my homeland, thousands of leagues
away. The Romans were breaking camp. Zos and I were alone,
silent, worshipful, lost in our own thoughts, remembering morning
swims in Lake Mareotis. Back home it was the beginning of Dog
Days, when the Nile receded from its banks following on the heels of
the autumnal equinox. Much had transpired since my near
assassination in Purushapura. Smiling, I remembered how graciously
Jiyu had accepted the Sanskrit copy of John I had presented him at
the epic going away feast the king had thrown for us. Seated at the
king's table, it was only the second time I was in the king's presence,
and this time, rather than sit silently unless spoken to, he encouraged
us to talk, to share our plans. The copy of John I gave him went
directly into the hands of his son, who handled it appreciatively. The
king in turn gave me a silver coin suspended on a gold chain
necklace. He explained that to commemorate our visit, he had
minted a special coin. Serapis, the Greek-Egyptian god invented to
unite the two cultures smiled on one side while the goddess Roma

stared out in profile on the opposite face. Septimus and Tatius also received one.

Over the next few days we made our way across fertile plains, mountains to the south and the promise of the river due east. I could hardly contain my excitement. We were on the road again, closing the gap between us and home where my thoughts seemed to drift more and more often, particularly to Silara. Barring any unforeseen events that could slow us down, we should find ourselves in Alexandria in two months. This morning, after our swim, we would board our river boat for the journey down the Indus, a journey that would claim a month of the return trip home, longer even than the voyage down the Euphrates. The distance we would cover on this river was difficult to fathom.

A subtle change in the color of the night sky brought me back to the present. Still floating on my back, I called out to Zos. "Zos, the sun is on its way. We should return to camp to see if we are needed."

"Absolutely," he called back from somewhere in the distance. Naked, I climbed out of the river and dried myself with my tunic before slipping it over my head. As I tied the sash around my waist, Zos pulled himself out of the water, dripping and smiling.

CHAPTER ONE HUNDRED AND TWENTY-THREE

A small fleet of river boats waited in line along the shore; the pointed bows, appendages that seemed to be tacked onto the stub noses as an afterthought, rode dangerously close to the high flat sterns of the boats in front. A small army of porters, courtesy of the King of Kushan, were loading provisions he had sent along with us for the journey. The soldiers of the centuria led by Gnaeus stood in formation, divided into rows of ten, the rising sun glinting off the daggers tucked into their belts, waiting to board their respective boats.

"Board!"

The shouted command made me jump. Single file, the soldiers waded into the water, climbing without talking into what would be their floating home for the next month. I heard my name called and squinted into the rising sun to see Septimus waving to me from the top of a brightly painted cabin on a vessel a few passus from where Zos and I stood. Tossing my bag over the low slung center, I first hoisted Zos over the side and followed behind him, slinging my bag back over my shoulder once on board. The boat rocked as Tatius followed close behind. The char-woman, wife of the pilot, was grilling fish; her son and daughter, around Zos' age, were warming their hands over the fire in the stone bowl of hot coals where the three-legged pan stood.

"Cast off!" Slowly and effortlessly, the boat slid out into the center of the river, quickly surrounded on all four sides by the convoy of ten other boats. Our travel party was exclusively made up of the Roman centuria. Gnaeus had not allowed any others to join our group after I had filled him, Septimus and Tatius in on my suspicions regarding the assassination attempt. After talking to each of the pilots, he had chosen the one he felt was most trustworthy for us. I noticed then that the cabins of the other boats were thatch. We were obviously on the most luxurious river boat in the convoy.

Before the sun had disengaged from the horizon, we were racing towards a split in the river. Aiming to the right where the river narrowed, we shot into a gorge, moving ever faster as the current picked up. Scrubby mountains rose on both sides of us as the river grew increasingly narrow blocking the morning sun completely and throwing the river into a murky gloom. I threw the cleaned bones of my second fish into the water, watching it disappear quickly in our wake. My arm stretched along the side of the boat, and leaning against a bale of hay, I daydreamed, the tall hills on both sides of us cutting patterns out of the sky. The music of the water and the occasional calls from one pilot to another soothed me. A languor I had not felt in months overtook me, a weariness that went to the marrow of my bones. Laughter echoed off the hills, bouncing from boat to boat, joining with the call of birds and the occasional splash of water onto my bare arm.

I woke to the sound of shouting. We had slowed to almost a stop. The sun was high and the mountains were gone. The eastern bank was bordered by verdant farmland, but dead ahead loomed a rock wall blocking the passage of the river, as if it somehow had come to a sudden, anti-climactic end. A sandbar to our right extended towards the wall. The shouting continued. Zos came over and sat with me. "The pilot says the river turns sharply to the right here."

"Lunch," the young son of the pilot beckoned to us from before the open door of the cabin. Septimus climbed down from the roof, and Tatius emerged from the hut itself rubbing his eyes and yawning. Zos and I joined them and soon were feasting on a spicy rice and vegetable dish.

"Delicious," Tatius burped. "This is the highlight of the day. I don't know how I'm going to endure a month of this mind numbing boredom. There is nothing to occupy my time except sleep. I'll be fat as a cow if all I do is eat and sleep for thirty days."

"Nonsense," Septimus said. "For once, we have time to read, talk and meditate. I for one am excited about having nothing to do."

"An idea occurs to me," I said. "Why do we not take turns choosing a topic for debate, and each day we will spend some time after lunch in discussion?"

"That is a superior idea," said Septimus.

"Bah," Tatius rolled his eyes. "That means once every three days I must actually think hard."

"Four days," said Zos. "I'd like to participate."

"If this trip takes 30 days, that means we will each have about seven turns to lead the discussion."

"Hmm, seven debatable topics. I guess I can rise to the occasion."

"I knew you could," Septimus slapped Tatius on the shoulder.

"Shall we begin today?" I asked.

"I say we take today off." Tatius said. "After all, boring or not, it's our first day on the river, and I'm ready for a rest after the last few days on the road."

"Agreed," said Septimus. "I have been enjoying watching our progress down the river, watching the landscape change."

"And I have been meditating," I said.

"More like sleeping, Teacher," Zos smiled and looked down at his empty bowl.

"What have you done to pass the time Zos?" I laughed.

"I've been talking to the pilot, learning how he navigates the river."

"Of course you have," Tatius patted Zos on the head. "You are an inveterate student. It seems the more you learn, the more you want to learn."

I could tell Zos was pleased with the compliment. He kept his head down, and his right hand played with his necklace. The pilot's daughter collected our bowls and moved to the low edge of the boat to wash them in the river. I stood. "Time for more meditation," I said smiling.

"I think I'll continue meditating as well, scribe. But I'll do it inside. This sun is far too bright." We all laughed.

That night we spent anchored alongside thin rows of salt rock that stretched their bony fingers out into the darkening water. The silence except for the lapping of the water against the boat, a sound that would generally have brought me a sense of security, was eerie in this barren, faintly phosphorescent landscape. Zos and I slept under the stars on the roof of the wooden cabin. Wisps of clouds skittered past the gibbous moon. Dying embers of fires the sentries on land had let burn out glowed red against the grey green glow of the land. I slept fitfully, chased in my dreams by indefinable shadows, phantasms with no voice, no name. I awoke in a sweat, Zos shaking me. "Wake up Teacher. You were talking in your sleep. I think you were having a nightmare."

"I am sorry Zos. Did I wake you?"

"No Teacher, I was already awake. The sun will rise soon." The sky was ablaze with starlight, glorying in the space between moon and sun.

"Pray with me Zos." I bowed my head and lifted my hands to the dark heavens, asking God to bring me peace, to rely on his mercy and wisdom, to clear my mind and spirit of anxiety, to appreciate this next phase in the journey, to be light and salt. Zos too prayed, for his family, for me, for the friends he had met and left behind. When we said amen and looked up, Septimus was watching us, not having climbed all the way to the roof but instead leaning onto it, his chin cupped in his hands.

"There is tea," he said quietly. Zos and I pulled our wool capes more closely around our shoulders and climbed down. Before sitting in front of the fire, I leaned over the edge of the boat and splashed water in my face. Standing back up, I decided that was not going to suffice. I dropped the cape, shed my tunic and dove into the black water, the cold shocking my system fully awake. I swam until I felt the tug of a current, turned and made my way back to our boat. I climbed in as quietly as possible. Zos ran to me with a towel and my tunic and cape. After drying myself and dressing again, I sat on a low stool beside Septimus facing the fire.

"You are crazy," he whispered.

I shrugged. "It is an old habit that I cannot resist now that I am on the water again."

"I still say you are crazy."

I rubbed my head and smiled. Zos left for a moment and reappeared with my skullcap. "Your head must be cold Teacher."

"Thank you Zos," I said as I pulled the cap down to my ears. I saw Zos had also donned his. I took a sip of hot tea. We sat in silence sipping our tea as the sky imperceptibly grew lighter. There was movement on the other boats. The sentries that had kept watch all night were boarding their boats. The pilot pushed off from where we had been docked, and instantly we were in the current. Hundreds of bony fingers reached out from the banks as if attempting to lure us back to shore or worse, to puncture our hull with their claws, like skeletal night specters. I forcibly silenced my morbid musing and addressed Septimus.

"What got you up so early this morning?"

"I could not sleep."

"That makes two of us."

"I guess it is the first night on the boat. After all of this traveling, you would think that it mattered little where I was."

"It sometimes takes the body some time to adjust."

"I guess. I am afraid my age is catching up to me."

"Well I had no trouble sleeping, till now that is," Tatius emerged yawning and stretching out his arms skyward. "Who can sleep with all the chatter going on out here?"

"Meditating again?"

"Not this time Kaleb. I really was sleeping. What did you say about age, old Septimus?"

"Nothing that concerns you Tatius. Tea?" he said, handing him a cup. "Unless you would like to dive into the river first."

"Hah, that isn't likely," he grinned. "Let me guess, Kaleb went for a morning swim."

"Fish that he is," Septimus smiled. "Something about an unbreakable habit." Zos smiled.

CHAPTER ONE HUNDRED AND TWENTY-FOUR

The days passed, indolent, unhurried, the clear blue sky overhead punctuated only by occasional red-beaked gulls swooping down for a meal of fish, skinny yellow legs tucked under them, black helmets like the flinty head on a white feathered arrow. Most of the days were spent continuing the translation of the Avesta. I had explained to Zos what we were doing and why. Though he did not know Avestan, the language in which the document was written, his recently acquired skill at writing Greek was proving extremely helpful as we made our way through the writings I had helped compile in Rhagae. By the time we reached Barbaricum, we should be done.

Beyond the task of translating, we indulged in the after-lunch debates.

"My subject is death," Septimus announced.

"How depressing, and on such a fine day," Tatius countered.

"Not depressing at all," I said. Socrates said that the purpose of philosophy, the love of wisdom, is to prepare for death."

"Well I entirely disagree with Socrates. Death is the end of existence and not to be planned for or desired."

"Feared then?" asked Septimus.

"Only in the sense that one ceases to be. I anticipate no reward and fear no punishment. I only regret my annihilation. We are but a collection of atoms which, upon our death, will be dispersed and reorganized into something else."

"Though not something I think on often, I do believe that death is a beginning rather than an end," said Zos slowly, visibly hesitant to enter into the conversation.

"Interesting, Zos, speak on," said Septimus.

"I sense my own immortality. How can it be that I could cease to exist? My religion teaches that I am immortal, and I feel it to be true."

"Feelings can mislead," said Septimus.

"Indeed," I said.

"They must be examined in light of the common human experience," Septimus continued.

"And what conclusions have you drawn from your investigations?" I asked.

"We are made of matter, and into the anonymity of matter we will return when dead."

"So our individual nature is lost at death."

"Precisely."

"What is the difference then between what Tatius says and what you say?" Zos asked. "You both believe that you will cease to exist."

"Not exactly," Tatius said.

"But ultimately, the effect is the same; you as an individual entity will cease to exist as such," I said.

"Yes," they both said.

"So what is the purpose of life?"

"Ah, that is another question," said Septimus. "You veer from the topic."

I laughed. "Death, as young Zos has said, is the beginning. As you said Septimus, it is a transition. As you said Tatius, we do cease to exist in our current body."

"You cannot agree with all of us," Tatius smiled, "though your intent be to stay in everyone's good graces."

"Our mortal body ceases to exist, though we will be given an immortal one," I continued. "We will transition from mortal to immortal but without the loss of our unique individuality. God has created us all with a purpose, and that purpose is not to be reabsorbed into a cosmologic mass of unthinking matter. It is the beginning of an eternal existence that will culminate in the judgment of all mankind and life in a new heaven and on a new earth."

"And what do you base that fairytale on?" Tatius smiled.

"Pathos, ethos and logos."

"Come again?"

"All three of Aristotle's modes of persuasion. I am completely persuaded that this is true."

"You obviously bear an unfair advantage Kaleb; have you literally read everything in your Library?" Septimus laughed. "You will have to explain yourself."

"In brief, pathos is the appeal to my emotion. As Zos said, I feel it to be true, not because I want it to be true but because deep inside me I know it to be true. I cannot believe that I will only exist for this season and once I am dead that I will cease to be. I cannot believe that the friends I have had who have died have ceased to be."

"And ethos?"

"Based on the belief of the vast majority of people, there is life after death. We cannot dismiss the testimony of countless people, each with their religions, each giving some type of explanation of what happens after death. It is human nature to believe that we will continue to exist in some form after death."

"And finally logos. I am reasonably convinced by logical argument that the faith in which I believe is the true faith, but that is a topic for another day."

"Yes," said Septimus.

"You know what I feel?" asked Tatius, his face serious.

"Tell us," Septimus asked.

"I feel it is time for a game of dice," he said, suddenly whipping the box of dice from behind him.

Our afternoon games often ended in all four of us stretching out for a nap. The evenings were generally spent either playing more dice or Senet. I also resumed lessons with Zos. He had made astounding progress while in Purushapura with the royal tutors. We would often spend long periods in conversation, working our way through the questions and comments Zos had noted while in lessons with the prince.

Halfway into our trip downriver, we stopped in the city of Alor; her sister city lay like a reflection in a mirror on the opposite bank. I had already invited Septimus and Tatius to dine in the town, explaining an announcement that I had for Zos at which I desired their presence. The pilot, familiar with the city from the many times he had been up and down the river, had sent his son to reserve a place for us. The sun was setting, the sky ablaze in orange and purple as we made our way along the dusty streets, past rows of compact, square mud homes to the top of the highest hill in the town where a two-storied building stood, the same dust color as the rest of the town, but graced with palm trees and climbing vines. We were led up stairs to the rooftop where a table had been laid. Wine was brought, and we toasted to being on land just as the sun sank behind the horizon, the sky rapidly descending into darkness. The town spread out below us like so many landed stars, the river a black ribbon winding its way through the center of the randomly sprinkled lights. Servants brought lanterns which they hung on posts surrounding the table. The dinner was simple but sumptuous after the mostly fish, rice and vegetables on the boat. Wiping my mouth, I stood and asked Zos to stand as well. Septimus and Tatius looked on with curiosity.

"Zoskalis of Adulis," I said in Ge'ez.

"Yes, Teacher," he replied.

"You have been in my company now for almost two years, studying daily amongst some of the best tutors and teachers in the world. You have mastered reading, writing and speaking in Greek, Aramaic and Pahlavi. You are proficient in Latin and Sanskrit besides speaking Egyptian and Ge'ez. Your studies in mathematics surpass many of my contemporaries. Though you are still a student and can expect more years of study ahead of you, I wish to honor you tonight for your progress and bestow on you a new title. You are no longer Zos but Scribe Apprentice of the First Order. When we arrive in Alexandria, you will no longer merely be my servant. You will be a scribe in training, my apprentice and protégé." Zos came round the table and knelt in front of me, kissing my feet. "You may rise my young scribe," I said, my voice thick with emotion. Zos rose, took my hand and kissed it. I removed a ring I had fashioned for him in Rhagae that I had worn on my little finger in anticipation of this moment. I slid it onto his middle finger. It was gold with a square of onyx bearing the seal of the Library of Alexandria.

"Teacher, it is beautiful. How many times I have admired it on your finger. You show me too much honor. I am so poor, the youngest son of a poor family. I do not deserve any of this."

"I have been considering this for months Zos. I had planned to wait until we reached Alexandria, but I can wait no longer. You are ready now to know what lies in store for you. And I wanted it to be a solemn occasion, with witnesses." I motioned to Septimus and Tatius.

"It was very short notice young scribe-in-training, but we managed to bring something to the occasion as well," Tatius said, pulling a long rectangular package wrapped in gold cloth out from a bag he had unaccustomedly carried with him this evening. "This is from the two of us."

Zos' eyes were sparkling with excitement and disbelief. He took the gift and went quickly back to his seat. The table had been cleared. He placed the package on the table and stared at it.

"Well, open it!" Tatius insisted. Zos slowly untied the silver cord and unwrapped the cloth revealing a beautifully smooth acacia wood box. "Open it," Septimus said impatiently. Zos slowly lifted the lid revealing a writing kit. There were two depressions where small marble bowls sat snugly fitted where ink, colored or black, would be mixed. Along the side, in another depression carved out of the solid block of wood lay two writing brushes. Below the two bowls for mixing ink another depression held a miniature water flask for moistening the ink and a jade pestle for mixing ink powder.

Zos' eyes filled with tears as he looked up at me pleadingly. "It's too beautiful. I can't accept such an expensive gift."

"Nonsense young Zos. Tatius and I searched all day for this and we are certainly not returning it. We cannot use it, can we Tatius?"

"Well *you* certainly can't, at least not till you learn to write."

Septimus feigned indignation. "I will learn to write when you learn to read," he countered. There was a moment of silence, and then we all burst out laughing. Septimus lifted his glass, "To Zos, may you live long and prosper alongside your illustrious master Kaleb!"

"Here, here," Tatius shouted happily.

Zos raised his glass and looked me full in the face, something he very rarely did, and in Ge'ez whispered, "Thank you, Teacher."

BARBARICUM

Gregorian Calendar – December 14th, 163
Alexandrian Calendar – Koiak 4th, Fourth Akhet
The Season of the Inundation
3rd year of Marcus Aurelius

"The lot is cast into the lap, but its every decision is from the Lord."
(Solomon, *Proverbs 16:33*, ca 900 BC)

CHAPTER ONE HUNDRED AND TWENTY-FIVE

Pattala, at long last, the penultimate port before Barbaricum from where we would transfer to a ship to sail for the coast of Africa and home. The city was in a sad state, boasting of little more than the remnants of the grandeur Alexander had in mind when he built his docks and established the ports that he believed would make this city great. Barbaricum had taken over the trade meant for this now defunct port city and had grown to immense proportions in the succeeding decades. And it was Barbaricum where I would find the contacts of whom Marius of Palmyra had informed me. The lateness of the day and the traffic up and down the river forced us to spend a night docked along the banks of the city. Our Roman guard was on high alert, standing guard all night around our convoy.

The following morning, before the sun was up, we pushed off into the river headed for Barbaricum. The river split into several branches at this point, but we kept to the most traveled, which was the only one truly navigable from the mouth of the sea inland. The land on all sides was a brilliant green; palms and great leafy shade trees lined the banks. Hundreds of boats going up and downstream laden with goods plied the waterway. We spent the day atop the roof of our cabin talking, watching the activity, and discussing what we missed most about home, only descending to eat. Our progress was slow, and in the end, we did not reach Barbaricum till the second evening. Having barely docked before the sun disappeared over the horizon, we decided against venturing into the city until the following morning. Again, the Romans set up a sentry around our boats, the ports being notorious for night banditry.

Early in the morning, after breaking fast and saying our final farewells to the pilot and his family, Gnaeus, Septimus, Tatius, Zos and I ventured into the disorganized chaos that was Barbaricum. Gnaeus had given all but a quaternion of soldiers leave to roam the city for the next four days while we got our bearings and hired passage to Africa. I led us to an inn that Marius had recommended where, for the first time in weeks, we would sleep on land in a real bed in our own rooms. Dropping my things at the inn and taking only Septimus and two of the guards Gnaeus had brought along with us, I began the search for one of our contacts in the city. Marius had given me three.

We found ourselves back at the port, weaving among the hundreds of porters, hawkers and merchants inspecting their cargo. Somewhere in this miasma of humanity, we were supposed to find a man to match the first name on my list. A long two-storied grey stone building ran perpendicular to the docks, fronted by an arched colonnaded porch. Septimus suggested we start there. Traffic thinned as we stepped up onto the paved porch, and Septimus in the lead, we entered the first door into a small office. A portly man with a weathered face and stubble hiding what vaguely passed for a chin sat at a desk. Without looking up from a document he was reading, his finger tracing each line of script, he sighed heavily saying, "Not now, I've already told you, the shipment isn't scheduled to arrive for at least another week."

"Are you Puzur of Cappadocia?" I asked.

He looked up. "And who's asking?" he said, eyeing Septimus and the guard suspiciously.

"Scribe Kaleb of Adulis, friend of Marius of Palmyra."

"I am not he, but perhaps I can help you," he said a bit more enthusiastically, calculating that we were there for business, not harassment.

"Do you know where we might find him?" Septimus asked.

"Have a seat," he waved in the direction of two stools that stood to the side of his desk against the bare wall. "Ka! Tea!" he shouted, making me jump. "When did you arrive in our fair city?" he drooled obsequiously, rubbing his ink-stained hand through his greasy hair.

"I am afraid we must decline the tea, though it is very kind of you to offer. If you do not know this Puzur, we should be on our way."

"Nonsense!" he said, the shout turning into a purr. "I'm sure I can point you in the right direction. Hm, Puzur, of Cappadocia. The only Cappadocian I know of is Meskiagnunna. Quite a mouthful right? I wonder if he wouldn't know this Puzur for whom you're searching." A small darkish boy walked in, staring at the floor, carrying a cup of tea on a tray. As quickly as a cobra, the man reached out and smacked the boy on the back of the head. "How many guests do you see sitting here, eh? What do you mean bringing only one cup of tea?" The boy, barely keeping the cup balanced on the tray, bowed and left the office.

"Thank you for your time," I said and followed the boy Ka out the door.

"Well that was entirely unprofitable," Septimus smiled.

"And unnecessary," I said. "Let us try further down." Four attempts later, we found someone who knew the second name on our list. Inas, the Nubian merchant to whom I had directed my correspondence, was supervising the unloading of cargo from a ship anchored offshore and would return in the evening. "Please give him this," I said, proffering a card where I had written the name of our inn and my name in Greek script. "We are friends of Marius the Palmyran."

"I'll make sure he gets your message," the white-bearded man tucked my card into his voluminous pocket. "It's always a rare pleasure to meet with someone from our parts," he said in Ge'ez.

"Likewise," I said, ducking as I stepped back out into the portico.

"Lunchtime," Septimus said. Bolstered by the quick success, we headed for a delicious smell coming from the far end of the building.

CHAPTER ONE HUNDRED AND TWENTY-SIX

We were finishing dinner, and I had almost given up on seeing Inas tonight when a tall, smooth-skinned man, black-as-night in a white linen ankle-length tunic bordered in indigo walked into the room. Every eye in the room turned to him. I rose, "Inas of Nubia, I presume."

"At your service Scribe Kaleb of Adulis," he said in a deep baritone, bowing slightly and approaching our table. "May I?" he asked as he took a seat next to Zos. I motioned for the kitchen boy to bring us tea. "It has been a long day," he said, sighing as he sat.

"Have you eaten?" Tatius asked, sending the boy back for a plate for Inas.

"Please don't bother," he said.

"Nonsense," Tatius motioned for the boy to bring food.

"So you are friends of Marius'?"

"Kaleb and Zos know him." Septimus said, joining the conversation. "Kaleb is confident that you can arrange for our transportation back to civilization."

"By civilization, Septimus means Alexandria. But if you can just get us to Berenice, I can take it from there. I have family there."

"Of course," he smiled. "How soon would you be ready to travel?"

"Tomorrow!" Tatius interjected. All eyes turned to look at Tatius, his overeager face drawing laughter from all at the table.

"We are all anxious to be home," I said. "We are one hundred and four in all. Septimus and Tatius are ambassadors and are accompanied by Gnaeus," I nodded in his direction, "centurion in charge of protecting the ambassadorial party."

"And how did you come to be a member of such auspicious company, if I may be so bold as to ask."

"You may, but it is a very long story."

"And we are all tired. My friend at the port told me you only arrived today."

"True. And you have been out in the harbor all day."

"So let's reconvene tomorrow for dinner, at my home. I would be honored to host such an illustrious group of gentlemen. I should be able to tell you what options are available for travel at that time." He rose. "I'll send a servant before the first watch who can guide you to my home."

The kitchen boy was just arriving with a steaming plate of food. "Stay and eat something," I insisted.

"I must go. I am weary, and tomorrow I have an early start. I will eat at home. Thank you for your kindness. Until tomorrow then."

CHAPTER ONE HUNDRED AND TWENTY-SEVEN

Though excited to be in a bed on dry land, sleep evaded me. I tossed and turned all night. Was it the absence of the soft slapping of water against the hull of the boat? Rather than the customary hypnotic river rocking, the soft mattress and rock-steady floor conspired to foil my first night's sleep on dry ground. Across the room, on his own bed, Zos' steady breathing only exacerbated my inability to sleep. I sat up on my bed and watched him, moonlight filtering through the latticed window reminding me of home. Home took my mind to Silara. Outside, palm fronds whispered deep secrets to the wind. My heart felt it would burst at the beauty of this moment. I stood and walked to the window, looking out past the garden, past the sleeping city to the horizon, to the vast dark, star-studded sky. I felt a sudden desire to go up on the roof, to feel naked under that immense void of space, to remind myself of how tiny, how insignificant I was in this vast universe. But I was tired. I also wanted to lie down and sleep. The moment was past. I lay back down on my bed and stared at the dark ceiling, listening to Zos' breathing, to the whispering of the palms, to the confused yearnings in my heart.

Morning broke clear and fresh. I opened my eyes, surprised that they had been closed. The sun was already up, and Zos was gone. Why had he let me sleep so long? *How* had I slept so long? I could not remember the last time I had slept past sunrise. I stood and cupped my hands into the bowl Zos must have brought in earlier. Splashing water on my face and over my head, I walked to the window. A crisp breeze blew past the palms into the room, smelling of the sea, of salt, sun and fish. I brushed my teeth and took a cloth and washed my naked body before dressing in a clean tunic and donning my scribe's cap. Just as I neared the door, it opened slowly and silently and Zos peaked in. "Ah, you're awake Teacher! Come have something to eat. Septimus says he and Tatius want to spend the day touring the city, but they want us to come with them."

"How long has everyone been waiting for me?" I asked, following Zos obediently to the cantina. "Not long at all Teacher. Septimus has just eaten, and Tatius is not even out of his room yet." My stomach growled anticipating the fresh bread I could smell.

"Health and good morning to you my friend," Septimus clapped me on the back as I sat next to him at the table. Tatius came in behind me, stumbling, wearing nothing but a loincloth.

"You are indecent, man. We are no longer on the boat. We are in a public place." Septimus feigned indignation.

"The only public I see in here are the four of us. Oh, the five of us," he grinned as a young girl emerged from the kitchen with a steaming tray of bread. She was having trouble averting her eyes while at the same time stealing a glimpse of the disrobed Roman ambassador.

"Zos, go fetch Tatius a tunic." Zos jumped up and was back in an instant, pulling the tunic over Tatius head.

"Can't a man eat in peace?" he complained, pushing his arms into the short sleeves.

"Disgraceful," Septimus mumbled, taking a sip of tea.

"I'll tell you what's disgraceful," Tatius said, stuffing a hot piece of bread into his mouth. We both looked at him.

"Yes?" Septimus said.

"This sunlight. How is a man supposed to sleep with the sun blasting full on into his bedroom? Have these people not heard of curtains… or shutters?"

Septimus almost spat out his tea, the laughter catching him unawares. Zos too was caught by a fit of it.

I sat back and chewed my bread, watching all of them and enjoying the moment, the delicious bread, the smell of the air, the anticipation of sailing home. Today was the perfect day. "So what is on today's agenda?" I asked.

"Souvenirs," Tatius said. "This is our last chance to buy things for gifts. We've got the official gifts and such, but I need some things for my family, my nieces and nephews."

"And your friends?" Septimus asked.

"What about them?"

"Will you not get something for them?"

"Have the cases of Bactrian wine we've been lugging halfway around the world escaped your attention?"

"A man after my own heart," Septimus said. "I did not notice yours because I assumed they were mine."

"I see we think alike in one thing at least," Tatius yawned. "I'll go prepare for a day in the market. Is everyone else ready?"

"We are just waiting for you," I said.

CHAPTER ONE HUNDRED AND TWENTY-EIGHT

"It sets sail in three days," Inas said. "You would need to start loading your things the day after tomorrow once the ship has been thoroughly scoured and its fresh cargo loaded."

"You are amazing, Inas. Our own private ship, and procured after only one day," I said, still clutching the packet of letters Inas had been collecting for me. For my part, I had not sent a letter home since shortly after arriving in Purushapura since it was entirely possible I would arrive home before the letters.

We were seated around a table in the courtyard of Inas' villa. Servants came and went bringing food and refilling our cups of wine. Lamps hung from the arches in the small garden illuminating the table against the ever darkening sky.

"Who wouldn't be willing to transport such a distinguished group, and with its own escort of a centuria?"

"Well, since you put it that way." Septimus said.

"It's precisely the ship I was overseeing yesterday. It has just arrived from Berenice and was scheduled to leave port next week, but they are willing to speed up departure for your sakes. Tomorrow it will be loaded with cargo, the following day with your things, and will set sail first thing the following morning."

"We need to arrange the price."

Bargaining ensued, and in the end Tatius obtained a fair discount for the protection the centuria would guarantee.

PART EIGHTEEN

THE ERYTHRAEAN SEA

Gregorian Calendar – December 19th, 163
Alexandrian Calendar – Koiak 9th, Fourth Akhet
The Season of the Inundation
3rd year of Marcus Aurelius

"Love, unconquerable.
Waster of rich men, keeper
Of warm lights and all-night vigil
In the soft face of a girl:
Sea-wanderer, forest-visitor!
Even the pure immortals cannot escape you,
And mortal man, in his one day's dusk,
Trembles before your glory."
(Sophocles, *Antigone, I. 781, Ode III*, ca 410 BC)

"They that go down to the sea in ships, that do business in great waters; these see
the works of the Lord, and his wonders in the deep."
(King David, *Psalm 107:22-24*, ca 1000 BC)

CHAPTER ONE HUNDRED AND TWENTY-NINE

Twelve days from the celebration of Epiphany. Zos and I
began the day by reading the events of Jesus' life starting with his
birth, to culminate on the morning of the celebration with the actual
reading of his baptism. Saturnalia began yesterday, the soldiers on
board bemoaning the fact that they were stuck on this ship during
what they considered the best festival days of the year. As there were
no women on board, there was no chance of an orgy or naked
singing in the streets. From the stories the soldiers told, the
festivities were much more intense and destructive in Rome proper
than in Alexandria. Nonetheless, Gnaeus kept the men busy with
drills, sword practice and wrestling.

The knife drills reminded me of my resolution to learn the skill of using a blade. I spoke with Gnaeus on the matter, and he agreed to assign a trainer to both me and Zos, who had already had some training in Purushapura. A rectangular palette was set up at the bow of the ship, and the knife trainer, Decimus by name, positioned me in proper throwing pose. "Sinistral or dextral," he asked brusquely.

"We're both right-handed."

"Left foot forward then, thus," he demonstrated. I stepped forward noting that Zos was already in proper stance. I also noted that a crowd was gathering, perhaps expecting to see some fancy Ethiopian knife tricks.

"Shoulders square!"

Nervously, I assumed the position I imagined he was commanding I take, extremely self-conscious with so many eyes on me, terrified that I was going to make a fool of myself. I stole another oblique glance at Zos and proceeded to copy his posture. Decimus stepped behind me and adjusted my shoulders to his liking.

"Now, imagine the stick you hold is a knife. Bring your right forearm towards you." I slowly drew my arm towards me. "Your elbow should stay firmly planted in midair. Only your forearm should be moving!" I jerked my elbow back out, dropping the stick. Decimus muttered something under his breath as Zos bent to retrieve my faux knife. A feeling I had never sensed before began to creep over me. A sense of ineptitude. Well, I would learn. I always learned. I steeled myself to endure Decimus' impatience and my impending humiliation before the entire centuria and determined in that moment to become the best knife thrower he had ever trained. Zos passed me my stick, stealing a quick anxious look at my face. I gave him a wink and smiled. The tension eased, and Decimus began again. "Stance! Shoulders square! Draw back your knife, elbow firm. Now whip your arm forward thus," he demonstrated, "while at the same time leaning forward into the throw. Release your knife towards the target. The boy first."

Zos leaned into his throw and released his stick. It crashed into the right quadrant of the large X chalked into the palette. "Bravo!" Decimus shouted, as generous with his praise as he was with his barking instructions. "Now you scribe." Mimicking perfectly Zos' performance, or so I thought, I leaned forward and threw my stick. It sailed past the palette, over the bulwark and into the sea beyond. A loud guffaw broke the silence. I turned to see Tatius, tears streaming from his eyes in an uncontrollable fit of laughter. Decimus rolled his eyes.

Zos took my hand. "It was your first time Teacher. You'll learn, just like I have. I'll help you practice."

"He'll need more than practice," Decimus commented under his breath.

"Now Decimus. You've trained far worse than Kaleb here. He's a quick study. You'll see. He'll be hitting the center of the X before we reach Adulis."

"Do not raise Decimus' expectations too high Tatius. I feel I have discovered a thing I may have no aptitude for."

"This does not require aptitude Kaleb. It's purely physical. You must learn to feel and control your body, your shoulders, your arm, your hand, and measure with your eye. You will learn. Holding a knife is much like holding a pen. Once you master the basics, it becomes second nature."

"Zos, find me another stick. Decimus, are you willing to give me another chance?"

"That's what a good teacher does Scribe. You will learn." And with that, the lesson continued.

Three days at sea and a light breeze moved us along at a slow and leisurely pace. The weather was perfect, though a stronger wind from the west would have been welcome.

The letters Inas had delivered to me provided a brief respite from the tedium of life on a ship. I only permitted myself one each day, prolonging their enjoyment as long as I could. The majority were from Silara. She had taken to writing me one letter per day, though thriftily sending the whole bundle only once every week. The single letter from my father was perfunctory, principally wishing both me and Zos god speed and assuring me that everyone was anxious to see us safely home. "Daydreaming again scribe?" Tatius took a seat on a spool of rope opposite me.

"Thinking of home," I said, folding the letter from Silara I had just finished and slipping it back into my bag.

"Home," Tatius sighed.

"Though a world of experiences lie between us and our destination."

"Indeed."

"Do you ever tire of the travel, Tatius?"

"Never."

"Nor do I," I smiled, "although my thoughts wander home more frequently the closer we get." I rubbed the back of my scalp, noticing I needed to cut my hair.

"That's completely normal."

"Though I cannot discern which sensation is paramount, regret or excitement that the trip is near its end. I seem to vacillate between one and the other; generally the two cancel each other out, and I just feel content that I am where I am right now."

"A true mark of a man of the moment. You live in the day, not the past or the future."

"Perhaps."

"Well, since we are both men of the moment, how about we discover from what secret place that smell is coming. My mouth started to water halfway into this conversation."

"Lead on royal investigator."

CHAPTER ONE HUNDRED AND THIRTY

Dawn was breaking over the sea when Aden was sighted. We had not been far from the Arabian coast for days now, but nothing we had seen prepared me for the vision of rising peaks surrounding the harbor. Our ship glided into the well protected haven. The rocky town beginning at the beach rose to the foot of the towering hills. Several ships bore Roman standards raising the curiosity of our two ambassadors and Gnaeus who determined to visit one of the vessels while our own was being stocked, to see what so many Roman soldiers were doing so far away from home. The rest of us stayed on board waiting for the ship to be restocked and returned to sea as soon as possible.

Most of my free time was spent throwing sticks at targets I had devised when not officially in class with Decimus. I was losing fewer and fewer over the side of the ship. I requested a supply of wooden knives from one of the merchants on board, dipping into my funds in order to have the proper tools for our practice. I was sure some would be lost overboard.

Supplies were ferried to us from the docks in flat-bottomed barges carrying fresh fruit, beer, water and foodstuffs. By evening, the boat's stores were replenished, I had a box of knives, and we were ready to sail at first light.

By midmorning, we were crossing the narrowest point between Arabia and Africa. The sight of my continent filled me with a profound sense of belonging. Though there were many leagues yet to travel, I had returned.

"It turns out that the warships in Aden are heading for the kingdom of Characene at the mouth of the Euphrates. From there the Romans are sending reinforcements against the Parthians at Ctesiphon," Septimus told me over our midday meal. "King Orabazes, from all accounts, though pretending neutrality, is caught between a rock and a hard place and is allowing us to use his kingdom as a southern staging ground against Vologases. On the northern front, Artaxata in Armenia has been captured and Lucius Verus is designing a new capital to be called Kaine Polis."

"Meanwhile, the Parthians have taken Edessa," Gnaeus said indignantly. "What is Verus doing designing new cities when what he should be doing is pressing the attack into Parthian territory!"

"That is just north of Palmyra, is it not?" I asked, suddenly feeling more connected to this back and forth war that had been playing itself out in the background our entire trip.

"A considerable distance," Gnaeus remarked.

"Otherwise, things seem to be at a standstill, neither side making much headway," Tatius said, summing up the gist of what was happening along the Euphrates.

"So Acacio and Anata's home is safe?" Zos asked, his expression having grown more and more serious as the conversation proceeded.

"Yes, for now Zos," I said.

The remainder of the day I spent reading and bringing my journal up-to-date with the most recent events and news of the war. Eventually, the coastline disappeared on both sides of us, and night began to fall. The air smelled differently, saltier and warmer.

By evening of the third day out of Aden, we were navigating the islands along the coastline of the city of Adulis. Alongside our ship were Egyptian barges, Greek merchant ships and least surprisingly, more Roman warships. The flat expanses of sandy terrain on both sides of us seemed to shimmer with heat. I half expected the shore to sizzle as hot sand met cool water. My heart was fairly thumping out of my chest with the thought of stepping foot on African soil in the city of my birth. I could never have imagined that the first visit to my native city would be from the sea to the south rather than from

Egypt to the north. I rubbed my freshly shaven head as I gazed from the prow of the ship at my dry and dusty homeland. Somehow, in my memory, it was greener.

ADULIS

Gregorian Calendar – January 14th, 164
Alexandrian Calendar – Tobi 6th, First Proyet
The Season of the Emergence
4th year of Marcus Aurelius

"As a bird that wanders from her nest, so is a man that wanders from his place."
(Solomon, *Proverbs 27:8*, ca 900 BC)

CHAPTER ONE HUNDRED AND THIRTY-ONE

Rather than wait till we could dock in the overcrowded harbor, I hailed a ferry to carry Septimus, Tatius, Zos and me to land. Gnaeus stayed on board with his troops until they could all disembark together, though he insisted on sending a quaternion along with us for the protection of the ambassadors.

The thought of seeing family after all of these years was disconcerting. Would I recognize them? Would they remember me? It had been almost twenty years since my family emigrated. So many things had happened since. My father and his younger brother who was also a scribe stayed loosely in touch through letters, but nobody had any idea that I was passing through. I had been out of contact with my family since the last letter I had sent home from Purushapura, months ago. It was useless trying to send letters back across the Parthia-Roman border, and what news could I send in any event? I was traveling the route the letters would have taken. I just prayed my family was not worrying too much about me since, barring the letter I wrote from the Kushan capital, they had not heard from me in almost a year.

Knowing my uncle lived and worked somewhere in the center of the city, I led our party to an inn situated near the administrative palace before setting out alone to find my family. This city, located in a well-watered valley between two hills was a bustling metropolis, much like Ecbatana yet more African with considerable Roman and Egyptian architectural influence, graceful stelae inscribed in Greek and Ge'ez rising like guardian angels from the four corners of the central plaza. For the first time since leaving Alexandria, I was unaware of my skin color.

My first stop was at the Royal Archives, housed in a building to the right of the palace but connected to it by a colonnaded portico. I was stopped at the door to the Archives by two guards in white linen kilts bordered in red, spears held horizontally to block my entrance. I held out my signet ring to show that I was from the Library of Alexandria. They returned to their stance, spears upright, eyes staring straight ahead, like Nubian guards of the underworld.

The cool air enveloped me, like an unexpected current in the warm waters of the Mareotis. My eyes took a moment to adjust to the dark interior. Right or left? I decided to begin my search by following the dimly lit hallway to my right. Pausing at the first door I came to, I stood silently, observing clerks at work in the crowded office. One of them raised his head, then his eyebrows. "Yes?"

Shaking off the hesitation I had felt, I entered, asking after my uncle, "I am seeking Scribe Ezana." The other clerks in the office had looked up to see who the visitor was. I smiled and nodded to them.

"There are three scribes I know here with that name."

"The man I seek is in his fifties and has been working here for many years."

"Follow this hallway to the third door on your left. Enter there and you will see a stairway. Go up the stairs and then to your left. Follow…"

"Oh for Aten's sake Aphilas, take him yourself. He'll never remember those instructions," the older clerk to his right said, gesticulating in my direction.

Flustered, the clerk named Aphilas stood, knocking askew a cup of tea which shattered on the tile floor.

"Go, go," said the clerk still smiling towards me, "I'll take care of the spill. Take this young man to Scribe Ezana before he turns to stone standing there."

Aphilas deferentially squeezed between the doorway and me, casting me sidelong glances as he did so. Once in front of me he started walking, so I followed. He never looked back or said a word.

Zos would be helpful here. I feared I would never remember my way out of this maze of offices, halls and stairways. My heart was beating faster, and I struggled to maintain the slow, methodical pace of my guide, the young Aphilas. Abruptly, he stopped. My mind, working out different scenarios of how I should greet my uncle, failed to register that we had arrived till I ran into Aphilas. He apologized. Before I could speak, a voice bellowed out of the office where we stood.

"Who is interrupting me now! Am I to accomplish nothing today?" Aphilas gave me a fleeting glance and hustled down the hallway in the direction we had come, his steady pace quickened by the sudden outburst.

I gathered my wits and entered the office. "I apologize for disturbing you Scribe Ezana. I am seeking my uncle, the brother of Scribe Yakub who now resides in Alexandria." Seated at his desk, he could have been my father but for the sprinkling of silver around his temples. He looked me up and down before breaking into a smile that took over his entire face.

"Nephew Kaleb, can it be true!" Before I could respond he had risen and was smothering me in an embrace. "What are you doing here? Are you here with your father, that scoundrel? How could he come without letting me know? Sit down, sit down; no, stand up. Let me look at you." He held me at arm's length, his strong hands gripping my shoulders. I grinned back at him, elated that I had so quickly connected with my family here, a sense of completeness washing over me. I was home. I had come full-circle. From this moment, a new circle would begin.

"I am here alone Uncle. No, not entirely alone. I am with the son of my parents' servants. His name is Zoskalis. He was born in Alexandria."

"How did you get here? When did you arrive? I have to take you home. Your aunt is going to be beside herself. You must meet all of your cousins. We must have a feast to celebrate your home-coming."

"Please do not trouble yourself on my account, Uncle. We are already installed at the Thebes Inn just around the corner."

"Nonsense. Idad!" he shouted. A young boy I had failed to notice when I entered jumped up from his seat behind me and stood to attention. "If anybody asks after me, tell them I have returned home. My nephew from Alexandria has arrived;" he smiled large and throwing his arm around my shoulders, pulled me against him, knocking me somewhat off balance. Taking my hand, he led me out of his office and back the way I had come, but this time, he pulled me into every office we passed and announced, "My nephew from Alexandria!" By the time we stepped past the guards into the dazzling sunlight, my cheeks hurt from smiling.

Our first stop was Thebes Inn to collect Zos who had occupied his time organizing our things in the room. Uncle Ezana wrapped him in a bear hug, welcoming the speechless Zos in true Aksumite fashion. I left a message with one of the centuria who were guarding the hall to tell Septimus and Tatius, who were napping, that I was going to see my family.

The three of us set out for the hills to the west of the city where my uncle's house stood. Trees lined the road as we climbed, about midway veering onto a narrowed path that followed terraces cut out of the mountain forming garden plots. We passed single storied homes built of stone and adobe with thatch roofs. Uncle Ezana, still leading me by the hand, called out as he approached a two-storied white adobe house that looked out over the city of Adulis and the sparkling sea.

A short plump woman in a shockingly white tunic came around from the back of the house. "Meet your nephew, come to see us from Alexandria!" he exclaimed, pushing me in front of him as if on exhibit. Her eyes flew wide, and she locked me in a warm embrace, kissing my cheek, all the time clucking endearments in Ge'ez. Children came running out of the house to gawk at the stranger. Zos, who had been following politely behind us came to stand beside me. I took his hand and presented him to my aunt.

"This is Zoskalis, son of my parents' servants who accompanied them to Alexandria."

"Of course, I remember them well," she said, taking Zos' face between her hands. "It will bring your family such happiness to meet you! Ezi, go fetch Nia and tell her to come quickly. Tell her a surprise awaits her. She'll never guess!" One of the children that were standing in the huddle watching us broke away and ran in the direction from which we had just come. "You, Yakub, run tell Shanla to prepare the pit. Tonight we will celebrate with a feast!" Another of the band of children ran in the direction of a small hut nestled between the garden and the wall of the terrace to the back of the house.

The rest of the day I felt that I was in the eye of a whirlwind. Aunts, uncles and cousins began to arrive, crowding the room where my uncle held court, showing me off to the family and telling what stories he had been able to glean from me in the short time we had talked on the way to his house. Zos had long ago been whisked away outside amidst shrieks of pleasure to his own reunion with extended relatives. Two young girls reminding me of Abebe and Abeba were continually refilling cups of tea and bringing around platters of sweetmeats and bowls of freshly cut fruit. Occasionally, one or more of the women, more cousins no doubt, who were in the back preparing the grand feast would poke their heads shyly into the room to see what was happening, giggling and darting back into the kitchen if our eyes met. Once my uncle had regaled everyone with stories of my father and his achievements in Alexandria and then reminisced about my escapades as a boy before we emigrated, the room grew quiet and everyone looked at me expectantly. "So tell us where you have been Kaleb and what brings you here," my uncle said.

I looked around at the eager faces, amazed that everyone in this room was related to me by blood. I had forgotten what it felt like to be surrounded by family beyond my own immediate family in Alexandria. "I am unsure where to begin," I said hesitantly. "There is so much to tell. The ship I just arrived on hails from the port of Barbaricum."

"Barbaricum," one of the young men whispered, eyes wide. Another asked how I had come to be in Barbaricum.

"Perhaps I should start at the beginning," I said. "The sky was clear and the Sea calm when I boarded a ship bound for Tyre two years ago in the month of Meshir, before the harvest…"

CHAPTER ONE HUNDRED AND THIRTY-TWO

Sunlight poured into the open window of the room where I lay. The air smelled of the sea, dust and grilled fish. I opened one eye and jumped, sitting straight up on the mat on which I had been lying. Two giggling boys sat staring at me. I stretched, reached out and rubbed their heads. "And who might you little rascals be," I said in Ge'ez. Breaking into outright laughter, they stood and ran out of the room.

The feast had gone till dawn, and my uncle had insisted I sleep here in his home. A mat was laid for me in this room that I suspected was his and my aunt's, but I was too tired to argue. I had not seen Zos since arriving. The house was alive with activity. I wandered out of my room to the source of conversation, the kitchen. A young girl squealed when she saw me, and my aunt looked up from the fish she was scaling.

"Kaleb, you're up," she said. "Come over here and give your auntie a kiss." She held her cheek up in my direction.

"I need a bath," I said.

"Bibi," she said, looking at the girl who had squealed, "fetch Ezi and tell him to come here." The young girl skipped from the kitchen out into the sunlight in the back of the house. "Ezi will take you to the river where we wash." Ezi, the young boy I last saw running to fetch Zos' aunt came bounding into the kitchen. "Slow down boy," she said, cuffing him on the back of the head as he panted and looked up at me. "Take your cousin to the river. He wants a bath. I'll have something for you to eat when you get back Kaleb," she said, directing her attention back to me.

Ezi took my hand and pulled me towards the front of the house and out the door. Once outside, he ran ahead of me in the opposite direction of the road we had taken yesterday. I lost sight of him but continued to follow the path down which he had disappeared. Before long, he returned with three other boys, all agape, studying me up and down. "This is my cousin from Alexandria," he said proudly. One of the boys came up and took my hand.

"Ezi says you speak twenty languages," he said.

I laughed but stopped when I saw Ezi's expression. I could not cause him to lose face in front of his friends. "Something like that," I said, winking at Ezi.

"Ezi says you met the king of Parthia," the second boy said, taking my other hand.

"Not the king of Parthia, the king of Kushan," I said.

"Say something in Kushan," the third boy said trying to gain a handhold as well. I said something in Sanskrit. They all howled with laughter. "Say something else," they all said in unison.

"That's enough!" Ezi said. "Cousin Kaleb is an important man. You can't be hanging all over him." They fell instantly silent, but none let go of my hands. "You should all go home now. Cousin needs some privacy." I could see they were disappointed, but I was not about to intervene. It was too early in the morning to deal with entertaining a bunch of boys with words in different languages.

Once they moped off in the direction from which they had come,
Ezi took my hand and continued to walk with me in silence.

The pool was full of children, and women were washing clothes
along the sides of the river where it grew rocky. I quickly gathered
that a quiet bath would be impossible here. "Is there not a more
remote spot where I can bathe privately?" I asked Ezi.

"I know where," he said, pulling me by the hand along a path
that led beside the river further up the hill.

CHAPTER ONE HUNDRED AND THIRTY-THREE

"And then they wanted me to say it in another language," Zos
excitedly recounted his reunion. I had not seen him for three days.
His family had treated him like royalty from the sounds of it, stunned
that he was going to become a scribe at the Library of Alexandria.
His cousins had paraded him around to all of their friends and
relatives showing him off.

Septimus and Tatius had invited all of my and Zos' family to a
huge dinner to celebrate our homecoming. Uncle Ezana gave an
invocation thanking Septimus and Tatius for watching over me and
Zos and then a lengthy prayer blessing all in attendance. "It seems
prayers grow longer with age," Tatius grinned.

Though the ambassadors meant for our families to be the guests
of honor, my uncle had them sit at the head of the table, and after
the meal bid everyone be quiet as he again thanked them for
everything. Two of my cousins who were also scribes in the Royal
Archives came forward bearing gifts, followed by six younger
cousins, each also carrying a gift in turn. Septimus and Tatius were
extremely gracious. The gifts, though humble compared to what the
ambassadors usually received at state affairs were representative of
what made Adulis famous: ivory carved into sphinxes, tortoiseshell
necklaces, a book on the history of Aksum and finally a rhinoceros
horn. Septimus had risen and thanked everyone for their hospitality
and for the friendship they had shown their Roman brothers.

Septimus and Tatius were growing restless to continue the
journey home. But they wanted to see the Nile, the pyramids and
Alexandria before returning to Rome. An idea occurred to me. My
plan was to sail to Berenice from where the shortest distance lay to
the Nile at Thebes. My Roman friends on the other hand were
anxious to see as much of the ancient civilization of Egypt as they

could. I proposed that we part ways until Thebes from where we could continue the journey together. That would give me more time with my family and them more time to see the sights along the Nile. Uncle Ezana arranged the caravan for the Romans. It was the coolest time of the year, so the trip should not be too uncomfortably hot, although a great portion of it would be through desert. I read a portion of *The Voyage around the Erythraean Sea*, a 100-year-old document I had brought with me providing background for where I planned to travel. It said of the route they were taking that *"Farther inland are the Berbers, and beyond them the Wild-flesh-Eaters and Calf-Eaters, each tribe governed by its chief; and behind them, farther inland, in the country towards the west, there lies a city called Meroe."*

"Let's hope by wild flesh they don't mean people," Tatius frowned.

Meroe was their objective. There were pyramids there as well as many historic sites further up the Nile towards Thebes. The journey sounded exciting. I was almost envious, but I loathed passing up this chance to spend more time with the family I had just re-encountered here in Adulis. Gnaeus wanted to leave me a quaternion for protection until we met again. Secure in the fact that I was once again in my element, I refused, little imagining that I would soon enough regret that decision.

CHAPTER ONE HUNDRED AND THIRTY-FOUR

As I was spending so much time with my family and getting to know my cousins, I hardly noticed that my Roman friends were gone. One morning, a week after arriving in Adulis and three days after Septimus and Tatius had gone, I found myself alone at my inn. Zos had gone to stay with his relatives until our departure. I sat at a table on the second floor terrace shaded by date trees that rustled in the breeze blowing in from the sea. Though the sky over Adulis was clear, clouds were gathering over the sea in the distance. Earlier, before coming out to break my fast, I had located the list of names and addresses my father had sent me, the list someone else had copied for him from his personal address book. I began to go through the names, sipping hibiscus tea while putting faces to the names on the list. It seemed I had met everyone he had listed in Adulis except one person, Sara, the woman whose name I did not recognize. I determined I would set out on my own to find her after my morning meal.

Mitsiwa lay a day's journey by boat to the north of Adulis. I left word with my uncle that I would be gone for two or three days, packed a bag and hired a boat in the harbor. The quiet and solitude calmed my spirit after the previous days of activity. Since the boat I had hired was little more than a glorified fishing vessel, we hugged the coast riding the wind that was slowly building bringing the clouds to shore. By the time we reached the small fishing village, the waves were dangerously rocking the boat, and I was employed in keeping the water that was accumulating bailed out. Lightning flashed across the sea, the sky ominous with roiling clouds rich with memories of the storm I had barely survived at the beginning of my trip. With my heart in my throat, I climbed thankfully out of the small vessel just as the storm broke over land. There was no warning for the deluge that was let loose. Immediately I was soaked to the bone, bemoaning the fact that all of my belongings were getting equally soaked in the bag I had slung across my shoulder. The pilot of the small boat had indicated where I could find shelter for the night, a small house near the shore where an old woman rented rooms. I made my way as quickly as I could to the house, lit by the now constant flashes of lightning, the sky roaring with thunder. As I stood rapping at the door under the awning that did little to protect me from the driving rain, I looked back across the beach and watched the boatman drag his boat onto the sandy beach out of the clutches of the rising waves.

The door opened and a tall white-haired woman with a lantern in her right hand stared out at me.

"I was told I could rent a room for the night here," I said, trying not to sound desperate.

"You were told correctly," she said, stepping aside to allow me entry. She shut the door on the storm leaving us in shadowy silence. Wiping the water from my eyes, I looked at her. Her stark white hair was pulled back into a bun revealing a beautifully sculpted face, ageless and smooth. She stood erect and with ease, unconsciously giving off an air of nobility.

"Scribe Kaleb of Adulis at your service," I said, running my hand across the back of my dripping neck.

"Sara of Mitsiwa at yours," she said, her voice clear and strangely familiar. "Follow me. I'll show you to your room." She led me down a short hall, one door on each side, the lantern casting shadows haphazardly across the walls as if we were underwater. Entering the door to the right, she lit a lamp from the lantern she carried, light and shadow rippling across the narrow bed and short table that made up the room's furnishing. "Are you hungry?"

"Terribly," I said. "But I do not want to be a bother."

"No bother," she said, "I was just going to fix myself something. You can join me. I will call you when the table is set." Her voice faded down the hallway. I pulled the curtain across the door and stripped off my wet tunic, ringing it out on the floor in the corner of the room. I fished my things out of my dripping bag and set them on the table to dry. Taking the sheet from the bed, I toweled off, and then, on impulse, wrapped it around my waist. Better to wear a dry sheet than a wet tunic. I peeked my head past the curtain into the hall. I had no desire to sit in this dark room until she called me. I took the lamp and barefoot, padded down the hall to the main room. Light flickered in the room adjoining this one, and I could see her silhouette bent over a table. Outside, I could hear the storm raging. The sea sounded as if it were at the very door of the house. I held my panic at bay, and opened the door a crack just as a bolt of lightning ripped across the sky illuminating the sea in the distance. Reassured I shut the door and turned to see Sara staring at me from the kitchen.

"I love storms," I said.

"Then tonight the fates favor you," she said, disappearing back into the flickering light. I sat on a stool in the corner of the room and gave thanks to God for protecting me and the pilot on the sea, for this safe haven in the storm, for his awe-inspiring creation, for bringing me to the home of the very woman I was seeking. When I opened my eyes, Sara was staring at me. "Shall we?"

"I see you like my sheets," she said smiling as I sat down opposite her at the table.

"Everything I have is soaked. I hope you do not mind."

"It suits you."

"I am flattered," I said returning her smile. "I brought a bottle of wine. I got it in Adulis."

"Are you offering it to me?"

"To share with you."

"It would go nicely with this fish."

"I agree."

"What brings you to this spot at the end of the earth on a night when the gods are battling?"

"I am searching for someone."

"Perhaps I can help."

"Your voice reminds me of someone."

"I hope that's a good thing."

"Disconcertingly so."

"Who is she?"

"Her name is Mihret."

Without warning, the cup in Sara's hand fell to the floor and shattered; her hand covered her mouth. Thunder rolled across the beach. I stared at her and in that moment knew. Her eyes. They were Mihret's.

CHAPTER ONE HUNDRED AND THIRTY-FIVE

I took another cup for Sara and filled it. Her hands had stopped shaking. "She is your daughter." I felt a gnawing in the pit of my stomach. Why would Sara's name be among my father's contacts?

"Yes. It has been many years since I last saw her, before she left for Alexandria. She was just a child then."

"How is it she went to Alexandria without you?"

"I was given an offer I couldn't refuse. The governor of Egypt was in Adulis. His entire court was there, on their way to visit Ctesiphon. I was working in the kitchen of the palace. Mihret was with me. She was twelve at the time. She was chosen as a server at the meals the governor and his court attended. She caught the eye of his secretary, a fellow Ethiopian, who offered me an enormous sum to take her back to Alexandria. He promised that she would be brought up and educated like a princess."

"She was. He married her."

Sara sucked in her breath, her eyes wide with disbelief mixed with relief. "I have wondered all these years what became of her. I had to trust the gods, that what he said was true, that she had risen above that to which she had been born. The gods be praised. My beautiful girl, wife of the secretary to the governor of Egypt!"

"You said that to which she had been born. What do you mean?"

"She had no father."

"What are you saying?"

The Ethiopian

"Exactly that. I was unmarried when she was born. I remain so still. After she was born, I swore I'd never lie with another man."

"Who was her father?"

"He was a scribe, but I didn't find out till later that he was married."

"What was his name?" I was feeling a bit dizzy.

"That I will never tell, but I do not fault him. He has provided for me all these years since Mihret's birth, sending me money two or three times a year. He doesn't know Mihret no longer lives with me. He left Adulis before she did."

I set my cup on the table, too stunned to speak. Could it be true? Could Mihret be my sister? "It is late, and I am very tired." I could barely speak. I had to get out of here, to walk off this burning in my stomach, to try to make sense of what I had just learned. It was too much information at once, too much truth to handle while seated.

"Yes, yes, of course. We'll talk more tomorrow."

"Yes, tomorrow," I said as I stumbled towards my room.

I stood in my room, unable to see clearly. The silence was deafening. The room became a prison. To flee this confined space became my only thought, to find an open space where I could think, could work this out in my head before the pounding became unbearable.

I could hear Sara moving around in the kitchen as I opened the door and stepped outside into the black night. The storm had passed as quickly as it had appeared.

A half moon reflected in the pools of water along the beach, stars blinking on as remnants of the storm clouds skidded inland. Warm wind, vestige of the gusts that had just been beating against the inn, ruffled the sheet wrapped about my waist. At the water's edge I stopped, staring out at the vast dark sea, a silent dread filling me, a primitive fear threatening to swallow me into the dark, watery abyss. Truth, like Janus, had two faces. This face was ugly to me. If I truly believed that truth must be revealed, it was my duty to tell Sara I was her daughter's half-brother, to tell my father I knew his secret, to tell Mihret we shared a father. But what good could come of it? What false beliefs would be rectified by that revelation? The words of Solomon came to me, "I, wisdom, dwell with prudence, and I find knowledge and discretion." Prudence and discretion, the bedfellows of wisdom and knowledge. This was not a truth that would save

313

anyone from harm, that would correct anyone's misconceptions. The possibility that it would cause harm was much greater than that it could produce any positive outcome. I prayed aloud that God would grant me wisdom, and prudence. A crab ran across my foot making me jump. My thoughts were becoming jumbled; exhaustion from the day and evening suddenly spread through my limbs as if an undertow had sucked my energy out to sea. I turned back to the house that now stood dark and lonely against the black horizon.

CHAPTER ONE HUNDRED AND THIRTY-SIX

"...they say, 'Come along with us; let's lie in wait for someone's blood, let's waylay some harmless soul; let's swallow them alive, like the grave, and whole, like those who go down to the pit...'"
(Solomon, *Proverbs 1:11-12*, ca 900 BC)

"Are you sure it was him?"

"It could be no other. The boy was with him, and both were wearing the ring of the Library of Alexandria."

"Then our contacts in the East have failed."

The rogue group of Pythagoreans sat huddled in an unlit interior room after meditation. The Greek high council, having gotten wind of the plot hatched in Alexandria, had condemned it in no uncertain terms, though word of the announcement had failed to filter down to Adulis yet.

The three sat in darkness. "Light the lamp," Talharqa said. "The master said to speak not about Pythagoric concerns without light."

The youngest of the Ethiopian cabal went for a candle returning almost immediately, careful to avoid spilling melted wax on the cleanly swept floor. The three sat in silence, their shadows still as murals on the walls around them, the air static, the flame unwavering.

"Only a fool acts without thinking. We must devise a plan. The task is now in our hands." Talharqa directed his piercing gaze on the two men sitting before him. He had no doubt what action to take. He had received a directive from the temple in Alexandria of what must be done if they spotted Kaleb. Surely this final opportunity to finish Kaleb for good augured Talharqa's chance to rise in the ranks of the priesthood. An enormous amount of trust had been placed in him, the emissary had told him, and his success in this mission could spell great things for him. Of course, they were instructed to act with extreme discretion. No one could know they were involved.

"Shabak, as the youngest, the first task comes to you."

"I am yours to command," the young acolyte looked on expectantly.

"Determine by what route Kaleb plans to complete his journey."

"Hekashta, you will recruit a fourth member. As four is the number of justice and retribution, we must, in all things, submit to the divine order if we are to meet with success."

"And you?" Hekashta asked, the edge in his voice betraying his contempt for Talharqa who had somehow been consulted instead of him, the eldest of the three and in his opinion, rightful leader of the group.

"You presume to question me?" Talharqa's eyes flashed.

"I was only curious," Hekashta quickly looked down.

"Enough. Each to his job," he said rising, the candle flickering with the sudden movement in air.

BERENICE

Gregorian Calendar – February 11th, 164
Alexandrian Calendar – Meshir 3rd, Second Proyet
The Season of the Emergence
4th year of Marcus Aurelius

"How I came to this place, and what have been my fortunes… would take up more time and words than there is at present opportunity for."
(Achilles Tatius, *The Adventures of Leucippe and Clitophon p. 18*, ca 160)

CHAPTER ONE HUNDRED AND THIRTY-SEVEN

It was the Hour of the Ghost World, the third hour of the Duat when the jagged peaks behind Berenice rose like mist out of the dark water. Unable to sleep, so close to the final port from where I would make my way to the Nile and Alexandria, I sat on a stool on the port side of the boat, my chin resting on the back of my crossed hands.

To my left, a priest of a temple in Thebes quietly chanted the poem for the third hour, tracing Ra's journey through the underworld. "How beautiful is Ra in the sight of those whose home is the dark west, how welcome it is to these to hear again…" His voice was carried aft on the wind. Yes, I was arriving home, in the dark west. "…row between these banks of death's river, travel through these fields of paradise… I have come here to see my own corpse, to examine my other self, my form that stays here in hell and I've come on a ship manned by the graveyard shift, whose arms grew strong at the shovel long before they touched oar." I shivered. I was not superstitious, but the words of the priest were unsettlingly apropos of our current situation. I stood and paced the deck.

Saying goodbye in Adulis was the most difficult parting to date. Like a tender vine torn from its tendrils on a trellis to be planted elsewhere, my heart was wounded. I was leaving behind pieces of my heart, and my joyous imaginings of the homecoming in Alexandria had been tainted on the beach in Mitsiwa. Zos and I both promised to return before another twenty years passed… best laid plans. My uncle had secured us passage on this Egyptian merchant ship, more luxurious and faster thanks to the expertly used sails than the Greek vessel we had come on from Barbaricum. In the end, the trip up the coast only took five days. I had scarcely noticed in Adulis, surrounded as I was by family, how much I missed my Roman friends. I said a silent prayer for them before lying down again. This was my last chance to rest before reaching land.

CHAPTER ONE HUNDRED AND THIRTY-EIGHT

Berenice was a small but dynamic Romanesque city, one of two port cities connecting the Sea with Thebes. Our vessel dropped anchor at a short distance from the wide expanse of beach, and we were ferried to the coast in small boats. I paid the pilot and loaded our things to be carried to the beach alongside us. I had chosen the overland twenty-day route, much of it through the desert, instead of the quicker option of continuing by ship for two reasons. The Roman road to Thebes was purportedly in excellent condition and famed for the ancient Egyptian carvings, statues and temples along the way, and I also planned to meet the Romans there.

My first order of business was to find a place to stay for the few nights we would spend here while making preparations for our journey. My uncle Ezana had given me the name of a colleague who he insisted I could trust to organize it. I hired two porters in the bustling port to carry our things, and Zos and I set out for the city center. The porters guided me through the hectic market, famous for the trade in emerald and topaz mined in the area, to an inn my uncle had recommended. Once settled, we made directly for the House of Trade, Tax and Exchange where I would find my contact. Tomas' tiny office was in the bowels of the building, a veritable anthill of narrow hallways, offices and activity. Italian by blood, Tomas had been born in Berenice and spoke Greek, Latin and the local Trogodyte. Wizened by age and the harsh sun of Africa, his once fair skin had turned to leathery parchment. He rose, as stiffly erect as his straight-backed chair. His head remained tilted to the left, and his arm shook as he reached for his cane. As he came around from behind the desk to greet me, I noticed that his right leg did not bend at the knee, lending him a curious gait.

"Scribe Ezana of Adulis you say?" he wheezed in a high pitched whine. "How many years, how many years." He took hold of my shoulder with his free hand and peered closely at me through rheumy eyes. "You seem younger even than last I saw you. And who might this be?" he asked patting Zos on the head. "Is your son accompanying you on this journey?"

"This is young scribe-in-training Zoskalis." I smiled as Zos bore the old man's attentions stoically. "And I am Scribe Ezana's nephew," I repeated more loudly this time. "My uncle told me you could possibly put us in touch with a party heading for Thebes."

"Sit, sit." He motioned us to the low stools facing his desk, the only furniture besides the shelves full of parchments jumbled haphazardly on the wall an arm's length from where he returned to sit. The one window to his back threw him into silhouette and his desk into shadow. I wondered how he ever saw to read or write anything. He rang a small bell and a boy appeared almost instantly. "Bring our guests tea," he coughed, "and a glass of wine for me," he added, almost as an afterthought. "It helps my digestion," he whispered, looking slyly in my general direction. I wondered if he could see me at this distance.

After what seemed like an eternity in his cramped office, catching him up on my uncle's activity in Adulis, listening to stories of his exploits and drinking several cups of tea until I thought I would explode, Zos and I stood and bid farewell. "Until tomorrow then," I said, backing out of the door just as he was ready to launch into yet another story.

"What a nice old man," Zos said, causing me to look at him in amazement.

"That is very gracious of you Zos."

"He had so many interesting stories. I could have listened to him all day."

"I am sure he would have been happy to oblige," I said, doubtful that I could have sat for another story myself.

After depositing three letters, one to Ptolemaios, one to my father and one to Silara, with the scribe in the front office where Tomas had instructed me, Zos and I set out to explore the city.

PART NINETEEN

THEBES

Gregorian Calendar – February 15th, 164
Alexandrian Calendar – Meshir 7th, Second Proyet
The Season of the Emergence
4th year of Marcus Aurelius

"There is nothing so wretched or foolish as to anticipate misfortunes. What
madness it is in your expecting evil before it arrives!"
(Seneca, *Epistoloe Ad Lucilium (XCVIII)*, ca 60)

You were born in the city of Thebes
As one who belongs to the followers of Osiris.
Its houses took care of you as a child
Its walls have received your old age.
(Inscription of Harsiese, 22nd dynasty, ca 800 BC)

CHAPTER ONE HUNDRED AND THIRTY-NINE

The morning of our departure, I rose before dawn and walked
alone to the beach for one last encounter with the sea. By the time I
felt sand beneath my feet, the horizon had gone from black to
luminescent blue. Enjoying the play of cool dry sand between my
toes, I made for the water's edge where the gently rippling waves
were smoothing the sands as if it would level them for a promenade.
The sea, restless even with the winds stilled, came up on shore with
waves crisped and cuffing, breaking against the soles of my bare feet.
Lulled by the rhythmic beating of the sea against the sand, I went
along silently, memories playing on the edges of my mind mimicking
the play of water against my feet, tracking the curve of the gently
bending shore. The sun's appearance over the horizon spurred me to
retrace the path I had followed with reverted footsteps. Coming
again to the dock, now lying dry and at rest on the beach with the
receding of the tides, I stopped for a moment to observe the play of

some boys, eagerly gesticulating as they played at throwing shells into the sea, the victor being he whose shell swam, glided and skipped the furthest along the rippled waves, a game I often played as a child on the edges of Mareotis.

My pace quickened as I returned to the inn to rouse Zos, break fast and connect with the party leaving from the depot at the edge of town, confident that Tomas had everything in order.

My hopes were not unfounded. Before leaving the inn, a young slave-boy of Tomas' arrived having been instructed to lead the two of us to our camels. Zos and I arrived with time to spare to load our camels and find an agreeable spot near the front of the caravan. Experience had taught me that the further down the line from the puller one found oneself, the dustier the journey.

Horns blew and the air was filled with the familiar groans and moans of the camels as they rose in unison. I lifted my hands in prayer asking God's blessing on the journey. By the time we said amen, we had begun to move forward. The road we were on was the Via Hadriana, a well-traveled highway that ran a thousand leagues north along the coast from Berenice before turning inland to Antinopilis on the Nile. Our route however turned inland within a league of the city, angling northwest through desert to Thebes, a little under two hundred leagues away.

My heart thrilled at this new journey. Once again, I was alone, dependant on my own wits, beholden to none; a heady sense of freedom washed over me. The caravan detoured left off the Via Hadriana towards a pass in the range of mountains separating Berenice from the desert beyond. I said a silent goodbye to the sea which quickly receded into the distance.

CHAPTER ONE HUNDRED AND FORTY

The caravan was forty-four strong, four pullers each leading a row of ten camels. Zos and I rode in the two center lines, three camels from the lead. The end of the first day we broke camp at the base of the mountains setting up tents along the roadside, our camels circling us forming a perimeter from which a night guard of randomly chosen travelers stood watch. My aching body, unused to the rigors of riding a camel all day, throbbed as I stretched out prone on the cot Zos had set up, and thankfully I slept quickly and deeply.

Morning dawned bright and clear. The small fire Zos was tending cut the chill in the air, and he handed me a cup of tea as soon as I emerged from the tent, my steps tentative and stiff from the soreness that had taken over my lower extremities. Our neighbor, who I took for an Ethiopian by his dress, shivered and blew into his hands to warm them as he battled without success to get a fire going. "Join us," I said in Ge'ez. "Would you like a cup of tea to warm your bones?"

"Beher bless you," he said, approaching our fire. Zos handed him a cup of steaming tea as he leaned into the fire.

"Are you traveling alone?"

"Yes, and as you can see, am quite helpless when it comes to building a fire."

"You are welcome to join our small party of two."

"You are very kind." A horn blew once, advising the travelers that we would be leaving within the hour.

"Nonsense, you will join us this evening when we break camp again."

"It would be an honor. If you will provide the fire, I will cook. That is one thing I *can* do."

Zos had already packed our things and was disassembling the tent when my new acquaintance returned to his tent.

The days passed slowly, and though the companion we had met the first morning spent subsequent evening meals with us and broke fast with us in the mornings, we saw little of him otherwise. It also appeared that the brief conversation the first morning we met was an anomaly since he rarely spoke more than a few words at a time after that. Nonetheless, it was pleasant to have company in the morning and evening, even if conversation was not up to the standard of our Roman friends.

The mountains gave way to a vast expanse of desert, more mountains rising in the distance like a mirage. Five days from Thebes, our companion began to speak of a massive complex of ruined temples half a day's journey from the road that he desperately wanted to see. "My brothers have spoken of it so many times that I almost feel I have been there. It would be the greatest pity if I, being this close, did not try to see them myself."

"You would have to separate from the main body of the caravan, not recommendable this far from civilization," I said, surprised that he would even consider such a venture.

"According to my brothers, there is a marker about three day's journey from Thebes. A seldom traveled path follows a wadi to the temple compound, and then continues on to rejoin the road to Thebes. We would not even be separated from the caravan for a full day."

"We?" I asked surprised. "Who said anything about we?"

"I just assumed you would be interested."

"It sounds unsafe," I said.

"What if I could convince some others to join us?"

"I would have to think on it." I could see from Zos' expression what his vote would be.

CHAPTER ONE HUNDRED AND FORTY-ONE

Though uneasy at separating from the safety of our numbers on the road, I could not deny that my body practically hummed with excitement at the thought of exploring a complex of temples that lay abandoned in the midst of the vast wastelands between Thebes and the sea. Our now more loquacious friend had found another party of three who were willing to join us in our adventure, and I had informed the dubious pullers of the caravan that we would rejoin them later that evening. They had confirmed for me that there were temples in the hills and promised to advise us when we reached the detour. I was encouraged that their main worry was that we would get lost, not that we would be waylaid by bandits.

Zos had filled our water skins at the last watering hole, and I had made sure we were stocked with food in the unlikely event we did get turned around. Soon after breaking camp, the caravan came upon the detour into the low hills to the north. Our party of six who had not tied up to a puller that morning broke away like a stream diverted from its path, and our companion eased any fears I had of being attacked since he informed me that the three Ethiopians he had recruited were practiced archers. They kept to themselves, following us at a short distance. I touched the hilt of the real knife that I now wore on my belt, vaguely comforted by the fact that my continued practice had improved the precision of my aim somewhat, though I still had a long way to go. Zos meanwhile had become something of a marksman.

The sun was at its zenith when, upon emerging from the narrow wadi, the temples came into view. There were three in all, the fronts facing each other, the rears seemingly growing out of the hills they butted up against. Massive columns supporting gigantic rectangular lintels lined the fronts, much of the roofing having caved in or disappeared altogether. Statues three times as tall as I stood between many of the columns. Forgetting the others, Zos and I led our camels to a shady spot in the courtyard of the temple to the right and dismounted. The inner row of columns was entirely inscribed in hieroglyphs. I dug parchment and a square of charcoal out of a bag on my camel. I instructed Zos to hold the parchment steady over a section of hieroglyphs that bore a list of proverbs, and I began to make rubbings of the engravings. Our companion joined us, complimenting us on our industriousness.

"There is so little time. I would like to take something to remember this place by." I said, rolling up the rubbing I had just made and handing it to Zos to store in my bags.

"Perhaps in Thebes you would make a copy for me." He reached out his right hand and leaned against the column on which I had been working. The sun was in his face and lit up the small tattoo of a triad on his inner wrist. I quickly looked away and smiled, but my stomach had gone into knots.

"Of course. It is the least I could do after you have shared this priceless treasure of a place with me." I hoped that my expression, hidden in shadow as it was, had not betrayed my shock. My mind was a blank. I had no idea what to do. Of course, the archers. I could appeal to them for help. "You know, it occurs to me that I have never asked your name," I told him. It is difficult to believe that we have been on the road together for over two weeks, and I still do not know it."

"Proximity is not a guarantee of knowledge. There are many things you do not know about me. My name is Talharqa," he said. "Talharqa of Adulis."

"Would you care to join Zos and me as we continue to explore?" I asked, praying he would say no, giving me time to get as far away from him as possible.

"I think I'll join our other fellow adventurers for a moment to see what they are up to."

"Of course," I said smiling.

As soon as he was out of earshot, I told Zos to take his camel to the furthest recess of the temple and then hide. "And do not come out till you hear me call you," I said. I took my bag from my shoulder and passed it to him. "Take this."

"What is wrong Teacher?" he asked, fear replacing curiosity in his eyes.

"I think our friend is out to kill me. I have to enlist the help of our archer friends over there," I said, nodding with my head towards the group that were now engaged in an animated conversation.

"I should stay to help you Teacher."

"Nonsense! Do as I say, immediately," my voice hushed but harsh.

Zos was already leading his camel into the dark interior of the temple when I started walking toward the group of men in the courtyard. They turned as one to watch me approach. I began to suspect this was worse than I had anticipated. They were all in this together. I stopped, only a few passus from the steps of the temple I had exited, wondering whether to continue or to turn around and flee. But Zos was in the temple, and if I ran, he would be at their mercy. I stood rooted to the spot, not knowing what to do, lifting up a silent prayer that God deliver me yet again from this situation into which I had fallen through my own stupidity.

"Kaleb of Adulis," Talharqa shouted, "you have stolen and profaned the writings of our revered father Pythagoras. Now you have also stolen and are on the verge of profaning the sacred writings of Zoroaster. We are here to exact justice."

"You call this justice?" I answered, my voice sounding more confident than I felt. "Who is the judge that condemns me?"

"You condemn yourself, through your lies and deceit, your disregard for what is sacred."

"If you believe Pythagoras is true, why hide his teachings? I do not lie or deceive. I bring what is in the darkness to light. Do not all men deserve to know what is true, or do you fear your truth cannot stand the light?"

"Blasphemy!" he shouted. The three men to his side pulled up their arches and aimed at me. "Execute him!"

I fell to the ground as three arrows whizzed over my head, then jumped up and ran back towards the temple I had come from. Before I reached the shadow of the front columns, I was knocked to the ground by the second volley, one of the three arrows finding its mark in my back. I stood and stumbled forward, leaning low, running in zigzag as I had read to avoid making an easy target. There was a humming in my ears, and I did not hear anyone behind me till the four of them were upon me. "Propitious for us, you chose the right temple to run to."

"Why is that?" I said, turning to face them, backing up as I did so. My heart was beating so fast, I found it hard to breathe.

"You will understand shortly."

"Understand what?" I asked, stepping backwards into thin air. I reached out instinctively to grab one of my attackers, but they stepped back and watched as I plummeted into a pit.

CHAPTER ONE HUNDRED AND FORTY-TWO

"Teacher, Teacher!" I awoke, disoriented and in pain, to Zos' frantic calls. "Teacher! Where are you?"

"Zos," I called out, my voice much weaker than I had intended, a sharp pain shooting across my back and chest as I drew in my breath to call out more loudly. "Zos!" I shouted, this time my voice echoing off the walls of the black dungeon I had fallen into.

"Teacher! Is that you? Call out again. I think I hear you."

"Zos! I am here," I called, coughing, again pain shooting through me. A circle of light appeared above my head, like a giant moon on a starless night. But this moon flickered. "Careful Zos, there is a hole in the floor!" I called, suddenly remembering my fall. Zos' head appeared at the edge of the circle.

"Are you down there Teacher?" he called, his voice trembling.

"Yes Zos. Are the men gone?"

"They left before dark. I have been searching for you since the first watch."

"What hour is it now?"

"By the moon, I would say it is the Hour of the Depths. I have been terrified Teacher. I thank God that you are alive."

"We have both survived Zos. Now we must find a way to get me out of here. Did they take the camels?"

"No Teacher, they only took the books from your bag." My heart sank. They had taken my books. But the one book they expected to take was safe with Tatius where I had hidden it. They had one Greek copy, which I hoped would satisfy them that they had succeeded in their mission, thinking me dead at last. The second copy, my journal and the Sanskrit translation of John was still in my bag that I had given to Zos. We had our camels. We were only three days from Thebes. It was not as bad as it seemed at this moment.

"Prepare a torch and throw it down here, so I can see where I am."

I sat up, stifling my moans so as to not frighten Zos any more than he already was. I dragged myself from directly under the hole. I did not want the torch to land on top of me adding burns to my other copious injuries. In the process of moving, I discovered that my left arm was either broken or dislocated, and any pressure on it caused excruciating pain. The arrow that had pierced my back had been jammed through me entirely by the fall, and now protruded from my chest. "Here comes a torch Teacher," Zos called, dropping the flaming branch from his perch on the edge of the hole. It fell where I had been lying just before, and the narrow confines of my prison lit up like a box lantern. The floor was littered with the skeletal remains of animals and what might be humans nearer the corner, but I was not in the mood to investigate.

"Bring the rope from the camels, Zos." How I expected to climb out of here with a broken arm and an arrow sticking out of my chest, I had no idea, but I was sure we would figure something out.

Before long, Zos was back with the rope, had tied the lengths from each of the camels together and lowered it down into the pit. It did not reach. "Use my woolen cape to add length," I called up, judging that it should be just enough to allow me to reach it. While Zos was preparing that, I stood, clenching my teeth at the pain, picked up the torch and investigated the corners of my cell. In one corner, there was a stone cube, the size of a step. I pushed against it with my bare foot in an attempt to roll it to the center of the room. It barely moved. I tried again. And again. Finally, it rolled over one time. A black snake that had been hiding underneath hissed at me. I jumped back. This was just what I needed now, a snake. I jabbed at it with the torch and it slithered off into a far corner. One more reason to get out of here as quickly as possible. I touched the arrow sticking out of my chest. Unbelievable. I began again to work on the rock.

By the time Zos was ready with the extended rope, I had managed to roll the cube to the center of the room. I had also determined that my arm was dislocated, not broken, but I was not relishing the thought of setting it back in place, though I knew I had to do it. Between the stone and the cape, I could be rescued. Now the trick was how to climb out of here. There was nothing to tie the rope to up top, and even if there were, I could not climb with my dislocated shoulder.

"I've got it Teacher! I'll tie the rope to the camels and walk them forward which will pull you out of the pit!" I could hear the excitement in Zos' voice, but I imagined reaching the top only to plummet back to the bottom when the rope slipped or the camels stumbled or the cape tore. And this time I would surely smash my head open like a melon on the cube of granite I had rolled into place. But it was the only way. Meanwhile, I was going to have to pop my arm into place. I warned Zos not to be frightened at my scream, explaining what I was about to do. I had seen this done once before and read of it in the medical journals I had studied, but it was a very different issue to do it to oneself. I woke up after my first attempt to Zos' frantic calls. I had fainted. I felt my shoulder. I moved my arm. I had done it! My arm was in place. I tentatively held out my arm, then lifted it above my head. It was still extremely painful, yet it was functional. God be praised.

"Send down the rope Zos. I am ready."

CHAPTER ONE HUNDRED AND FORTY-THREE

Zos and I sat on the steps of the temple and watched the sky turn pink. "We should get moving Zos. The caravan will be gone by the time we reach the road. We will have to follow the road to the next town. God will watch over us. He always does. See?" I said raising my hands and shrugging. Pain shot through me. I grimaced. "Here we are, safe and sound… well, not completely sound, but sound enough. And we have our camels, food and water." Zos had dressed a wound on my head that I had not even noticed. My fingers played with the arrowhead sticking out of my chest. "I need to get this thing out of me."

I instructed Zos to break off the tail end of the arrow and file it down smooth. Every jolt and movement was an agony, but it had to be done. He had built a small fire to cauterize the wound once the arrow was extracted. I sat on the steps and braced myself as Zos slowly pulled it through me, hoping to God that no artery had been pierced. It was a strange sensation having the arrow drawn through me, and once it was done, I realized I had not breathed during the entire episode. I was not spurting blood which I took to be a good sign. I let the blood run free for a moment to clean out the wound before Zos cauterized it. I fainted again at the searing pain.

I woke to Zos leaning over me whispering prayers. When I spoke, my voice was husky and pinched. "Next we should take up medicine Zos. I think we have done quite admirably." Zos laughed nervously.

We reached the main road well before midday and followed it till nightfall. Every inch of my body hurt, but I did not want to stop till we had reached a town. I could feel a fever coming on, and I did not want Zos to carry the responsibility of caring for me alone in this wasteland. We stopped for a moment while Zos dismounted and prepared water and food for us. I felt dizzy and wanted to press on. The water was sweet and cool on my lips. I wet a cloth and held it to my head, wiping away the sweat that was breaking out on my face.

Later Zos recounted to me the details of the rest of the night. By the time we reached the village, a day's ride from Thebes, I was delirious. We arrived in the morning on the Lord's Day. The arrival of two lone strangers, one young and the other hallucinating, drew the attention of everyone in the tiny village. Zos says I was praying loudly in Ge'ez, Greek and other languages he did not recognize when a man approached asking me if we were Christians. Zos affirmed we were, and he immediately took us in to his home. Several days passed, and Zos thought more than once that I would not make it. Since we were only a day's journey from Thebes, Zos borrowed our host's donkey and rode into the city searching for Tatius and Septimus. He feared that they would continue up the Nile if they did not find us, and we were already a week late.

I awoke in the dark. "Water," I whispered, feeling so weak I wondered if I were dreaming.

"Teacher, you're awake," Zos answered softly, close to my ear, his hand on my forehead. He gently lifted my head and put a cup to my lips. I drank deeply and lay back exhausted.

Sunlight streamed through the open window of the room where I lay. I sat upright and was momentarily overwhelmed by a wave of dizziness. A pitcher of water stood on a low table by my bed. Shakily, I dragged myself off the bed, stood and poured a cup of water, drinking it down without stopping for breath. I walked to the window, still disoriented, wondering where I was and how I had gotten here. The last I remembered was riding a camel with Zos, the sky growing steadily darker, my grasp on consciousness ever more tenuous.

As if responding to the growling of my stomach, Zos entered the room carrying a small bowl of water and towel. "You're up!" he shouted, quickly putting down the bowl and running to me. He took my hand in his and kissed it. I prayed that you would awaken this morning. After asking for water during the night, I felt sure you were coming back to us."

"Coming back?" I asked withdrawing my hand. "Where have I been?"

"You have been asleep for ten days Teacher."

"Ten days? How is that possible? Where are we?" I felt suddenly weak. I returned to the bed and sat. "I am starving Zos. Can you bring me something to eat?"

"Immediately Teacher. Rest. I'll tell you everything when I return with food."

Left alone, I looked at the hands that lay on my knees in front of me. They looked old and gnarled. I felt my arms. They too were thin, the bones standing out on my shoulders. I had lost much weight. No wonder I was weak. Over a week unconscious. It did not seem possible. I took the bowl of water and towel Zos had left and disrobing, bathed myself. I had just finished donning my kilt when Zos returned with a steaming bowl of soup and a loaf of bread. My mouth responded by watering, my stomach by turning joyful yet painful somersaults. "Master Bes says this will bring back your strength." Zos moved the table with the pitcher beside the bed where I sat, removed the pitcher of water and set the bowl before me. I was barely able to wait long enough to offer a prayer of thanks for the food before biting into the bread I had dunked in the soup, hardly chewing before sending it down to my stomach that was by this time fairly screaming with impatience.

"Start from the beginning Zos," I mumbled between bites.

Zos related the story of our arrival, of Bes our host and of his own solitary trip to Thebes to find Tatius and Septimus. Bes, whose name appropriately meant protector, was not a Christian but a worshiper of Ra; however, he had dreamed only a few nights before our appearance that a Christian in need of help would come to his village and teach him more about God. The first three days, I had burned fiercely with fever alternately mumbling or shouting incoherently in any number of languages or groaning in pain. A few times I had apparently awoken and spoken lucidly, but I had no recollection of it.

The fourth day, my fever broke, but I did not awaken. The fifth day, a new worry overtook Zos. We were already a week late to Thebes where we were to meet our Roman friends, and Zos feared they would leave without us if we failed to show on time. After the near miss in the desert, he did not want to risk traveling up the Nile alone. The sixth day, he took one of the camels we had arrived on, packed lightly and made for Thebes alone.

"That was foolhardy, Zos." I interrupted.

"I had no choice Teacher. I didn't know when you would wake up, and I was terrified we would miss the Romans. We are less than a day's journey away."

"Was there no-one our host could send with you?"

"There was no-one Teacher. Bes lives alone, and I was not sure who to trust. I felt safer alone."

"Go on."

Zos had spent the better part of his second day on the road riding through the villages situated among the temples of the once mighty Thebes looking for any sign of the Romans. At long last he came upon one of the centuria who, recognizing him, took him to their inn. The Romans had already gone ahead, but had left instructions with a quaternion to accompany us until we reunited in Alexandria if not before. Zos spent one night with the Romans before coming back the next day together with the small guard that Tatius had left with orders to watch over us.

"It is a spooky place Teacher."

"Why spooky Zos?"

"It's like a vast city of the dead where the ghosts of the past outnumber the living who remain behind."

"Where are the guards now?"

"Downstairs."

"What does our host think about that?"

"I think he's enjoying the fame it has brought him in the village."

"So you have been back two days now?"

"Yes."

"Where is our host?"

"Tending his garden."

"A garden will grow in this desolation?"

"Yes, I know it seems incredible. These people live off what they can grow and trade with the caravans that pass through."

"I need to rest Zos. I can barely keep my eyes open, ridiculous since I have been asleep for ten days."

"Rest Teacher," Zos said as he came and put his hand on my forehead. "No more fever. I'll prepare something more solid for you to eat when you wake next."

I was asleep before Zos left the room.

CHAPTER ONE HUNDRED AND FORTY-FOUR

The next time I awoke it was night. I could hear Zos' easy, measured breath on the floor beside my bed. Again, I felt hunger pains before sitting up. Scanning the moonlit room, I spied a loaf of bread and cheese on a tray on the table. I rose as quietly as I could and helped myself to the simple feast. I walked to the window and looked out at the half moon. It cast the entire town in an unearthly blue. The low hills in the distance glowed like grave mounds, the tallest the throne of Osiris in his realm of the dead. Like Bes' Ra journeying nightly to the underworld and back, I too was rising from the grave of a ten-day journey.

My thoughts went to Alexandria, to my family who would be expecting us sooner than we would arrive. For the first time I remembered the wound in my chest. My fingers carefully searched the scar, already healing with Zos' and Bes' ministrations. I stretched out my arm then raised it above my head to test its range. Besides a slight pain that made me wince, it was fully functional, a miracle really. Suddenly, I was ready to be on the road again, away from this place, away from memories of this desert, of my brush with death. I needed to see the sky above my head. In silence, I ascended the steps to the roof where I stretched out prone on my back to look at the stars. I extended my arms palms up and lost myself in the heavens. Weightless, I floated towards the bottom of the inverted bowl of the sky, myriads of stars surrounding me on every side, swallowing my existence into eternity, becoming just one more light hung in the heavens by the hand of God.

A raspy voice brought me plummeting back to the roof, the collision as silent as the breath I expelled on impact. "Pardon my intrusion scribe."

I sat up, wiping tears from the edges of my eyes. "It is I who intrude on you," I said quietly. "I owe you my life, and the life of my servant and student Zoskalis."

"But for the time he left you to find your friends in Thebes, he has not left your side. He kept you dry and warm through the fever, and your forehead was never free of a cool towel. You never asked for water but that he was there with a full cup. I have rarely seen such devotion. Only when he knew the fever was past did he dare leave you to find your friends."

"May I tell you a story?"

Bes sat beside me as I propped myself up on one arm. "There was once a man traveling from Jerusalem to Jericho," I began. "On the way he was attacked by robbers. They took his clothes, beat him up, and went off leaving him half-dead. Luckily, a priest was on his way down the same road, but when he saw him he crossed to the other side. Then a religious man showed up, but he also avoided the injured man.

A Samaritan traveling the road came on him. When he saw the man's condition, his heart went out to him. He bandaged his wounds, pouring wine and oil on them. Then he lifted him onto his donkey, led him to an inn, and made him comfortable. In the morning he took out two silver coins and gave them to the innkeeper, saying, 'Take good care of him. If it costs any more, put it on my bill; I will pay you on my way back.'"

We were both quiet.

"Zos told me that you were the only one in the village that approached us when we arrived. The rest either peered past half-closed doors or just stood and watched, as if waiting to see if we would disappear back into the desert from whence we had come."

"I had a dream."

"Yes."

"Tell me about God."

"The story I just told you is one he told when he was on earth in human form." And thus began our first conversation. We had many more before I was strong enough to continue on to Thebes. Bes our protector. On our departure, I left him a small carved box I had brought from India. In it, I placed a single gold aurea.

CHAPTER ONE HUNDRED AND FORTY-FIVE

Like a mirage, the green trees of Thebes rose from the desert floor. As if a line had been drawn, across which the desert could not pass, we crossed from sand to a garden of grass and trees. The air turned cooler, and the dusty air was replaced by the perfume of flowers and the promise of water. The Romans led us to the courtyard of a massive yet deserted temple complex. A small collection of adobe huts lay huddled against the outside walls of the temple like so much debris blown into a corner of a room. I regretted missing our reunion with Tatius, Septimus and Gnaeus but was grateful they had left word of their whereabouts and a rearguard. Little could they know how reassured I was even though I was sure we were finally safe.

Though anxious to reunite with my Roman friends, I wanted Zos to see some of the more important sites before moving on. We spent a morning exploring the Temple of Luxor before crossing to the west side of the river to visit the Valley of the Kings and Queens and a myriad of other sites that, though abandoned, still maintained their grandeur and sense of permanence, as if the temporary absence of people were of no concern to them. Zos stood silently before the Colossi of Memnon where a poem had been inscribed in Greek below hieroglyphs.

"It is like magic Teacher."

"What is Zos?"

"To be able to decipher script."

"But not always edifying."

"If we only wrote what was edifying Teacher, we would be out of business."

I laughed. "Well said, young scribe in training. Loquacity is no crime, but doubly rewarding when edifying."

"Who wrote this?" Zos ran his fingers over the etched glyphs.

The poetess Julia Balbilla. These poems are in homage of the emperor Hadrian and his wife Sabina."

"They look new."

"They passed through here a few years before our families immigrated to Alexandria."

"That is almost twice the span of my life Teacher."

"But a grain of sand in the vast hourglass that is the history of this country. Some of these monuments are two thousand years old."

"Perhaps we could add our own inscription here," Zos smiled, pointing to an empty spot just below the recent inscriptions of the Greek poetess.

PART TWENTY

BOUND FOR ALEXANDRIA

Gregorian Calendar – March 25th, 164
Alexandrian Calendar – Paremhat 15th, Third Proyet
The Season of the Emergence
4th year of Marcus Aurelius

"It has been related that dogs drink at the river Nile running along, that they may not be seized by the crocodiles."
(Phaedrus, *Fables, I, 25, l. 3* ca 8)

"...we shall suppose that the whole of Egypt, beginning from the Cataract and the city of Elephantine, is divided into two parts and that it thus partakes of both the names, since one side will thus belong to Libya and the other to Asia; for the Nile from the Cataract onwards flows to the sea cutting Egypt through the midst..."
(Herodotus, *The Histories: Cambyses, Book II, 16,* ca 526 BC)

CHAPTER ONE HUNDRED AND FORTY-SIX

The placid waters of the Nile reflected the columns of a temple as we glided past. We rode in the center of the river where the current was quickest. Our pilot stood at the bow with a pole, plumbing the river to ensure we did not run aground on a shoal, the river being at its seasonal low point.

Zos and I rode with our guard in a comfortable barge, spacious enough for the six of us, the pilot and two servants I had hired for the journey to handle the cooking and cleaning. I had purchased a small table that would serve as my desk, for there was much to record before reaching home, not least of which regarded my encounter with the nefarious Pythagoreans. A pang went through my chest. Those four were still out there, but I imagined myself safe now since they most assuredly thought me dead. I had been on my guard the entire time in Thebes, fearing lest we run into one of the attackers there alerting them to my survival and inviting further attempts on my life.

Along with my Greek copy of the Avesta they had stolen a few other books I kept at hand; my Ge'ez book of the Gospels and letters of Paul, which I hoped they would read, my book of medicine, my maps of the area. But thankfully, my other books were in a pouch of Zos' camel since, that very morning, my bag of personal items had ended up on his camel by mistake. Zos was slowly rolling his way through a scroll he had picked up with his own money at one of the markets we had visited in Thebes. Setting my pen to parchment, I began sketching the scene. While in Adulis, I had been impressed with the drawings on the walls of the home of my Uncle Ezana. He had done them himself. He also illustrated the books he transcribed. Where he had added color, the effect was stunning. I determined to try my hand at it as well, but until now had not had the chance.

Acting as guide, I recounted Herodotus' journey down the Nile almost 700 years before. I bid our pilot stop at Tentyris to view the temple and visit the baths there. The temple traced its beginnings back into the mists of time, but successive rulers had added on to it up until Trajan's final addition less than a century before. Though we could have spent the night there, I was anxious to catch up to the rest of the Roman party, so we continued upriver till nightfall, only a day's journey from Panopolis.

The next morning, we continued north. The river carried us through the familiar landscapes of my adopted country. The time of harvest was close at hand, and the fields were busy with workers, darkened by the sun, clad in short linen kilts if anything at all. The brilliant red poppy fields around Thebes had given way to corn, wheat and barley, endless fields of gold and green, broken only by the dikes and dams that blocked and directed the flooding only a few months away. We passed small towns clinging to the edges of the Nile, shaded by palms and date trees swaying in the gentle breezes like feathered crowns. As I sketched, Zos was hard at work writing letters for the guards.

Rounding the final curve before Panopolis about an hour before sunset, we were suddenly blinded by the giant yellow disk of the sun directly ahead, as if our destination were the very resting place of Ra rather than home of the serpent demon. I had been here on my first mission, so long ago now. Zos and the four centuria gathered round as I told them the story of Asmodeus, the demon of lust who jealously seeks to destroy those who fall under his spell, purportedly bound for eternity by the angel Raphael in the waters of the city. The story was an amalgam of ancient Egyptian superstition, Greek Pan worship, Avestan lore and writings from the Book of Tobit, but it made for a great story. One of the centuria stared out at the water, his eyes fairly popping out of his head. He raised his hand to his lips and kissed it murmuring "Serapis preserve us."

"Be vigilant centurion, you would do well to stay on board tonight." Zos suppressed a smile.

The next towns of any note were where the Via Hadriana terminated in Antinopolis on the eastern side of the Nile and opulent Hermopolis on the west bank. Though named for the Greek god Hermes, it was actually the seat of the worship of Thoth, god of magic and writing. His temple was surrounded by numerous buildings, some as tall as seven stories. Arriving around midday, we had time to roam the wide boulevards of the city before retiring to our boat for the night.

At Memphis, we were three days from Alexandria, and I could already feel a tingling sensation all over my body at the thought of being home. We had yet to reunite with Tatius and Septimus, and at this point, I knew we would not overtake them till Alexandria. This however, was the place Zos had dreamed of seeing ever since he heard we would be returning this way, and I had to confess, I was not against the idea of seeing the monolithic structures one more time.

"How old is this city Teacher?"

"Until Alexandria became the most important city in Egypt, this was the capital for 3000 years. It is perhaps the oldest city in the world."

"Older than Sippar?"

"Right. I guess Sippar could be older if it was really founded by Noah. But Memphis probably comes in a close second."

"And how old are the pyramids?"

"When Solomon began construction of his temple, the pyramids had already been standing for over a millennium."

On our day trip to the pyramids, we stayed on the main thoroughfare since much of the outlying area had been deserted and was now falling into ruin.

Zos wanted me to sketch him seated on one of the long catlike legs of the Sphinx. The centurion competed to see who could climb the highest up the smooth surface of the largest of the pyramids. Suspicious priests peered out at us from the protective shade of their temple porticoes. Our servants from the boat set up a tent and laid out our midday meal while I led Zos around expounding on the history of the place. Just as we were heading for the table to eat, a small party of travelers arrived, Tyrians by the look of them.

"Good day," I called in Punic.

"Good day to you Ethiopian. What a joy to meet someone who speaks to us in our own tongue."

The man who addressed me seemed to be the one in charge of the small group which consisted of four men and two ladies. The veiled women carried parasols to protect them from the sun which by this time had risen directly overhead.

"Come in out of the sun, and join us under our tent," I motioned for the servants to prepare more food.

"We cannot intrude. Thank you for your hospitality."

"It is no intrusion. Where do you hail from?"

"We have come from Alexandria, three days by boat. We are on a pilgrimage to the Temple of Isis on the Isle of Philae."

"You have quite a journey ahead of you. Please, do not refuse our table. I would like to hear news from my city from where I have been absent far too long." He looked at his companions who nodded agreement. "Excellent! It is a pity you missed the tour I just gave my young Zos here," I said, putting my hand on his shoulder. Perhaps he could regale you with his newfound knowledge."

"We would be delighted."

"But first, allow me to give God thanks for our food, and we can exchange information over our meal."

CHAPTER ONE HUNDRED AND FORTY-SEVEN

"The news is good and bad. The war with Parthia is at an end."

"Do you speak Greek? I am sure our centurion here would be interested to hear news of the war."

"Of course," he obliged, switching easily to Greek. Zos breathed a sigh of relief. Punic was not yet part of his repertoire. The Romans also looked in our direction for the first time.

"Seleucia has been destroyed, and the palace at Ctesiphon has been burned to the ground." I immediately lifted up a silent prayer for Anata, Acacio and Tano.

"Was the city razed?"

"Not entirely. Vologases fled to the interior of the country and from a safe vantage point sued for peace."

"God be praised."

"But it does not end there," he continued. "Now for the bad news. Though the Romans pushed towards Media, many of the army began to fall ill, so Lucius Verus was unable to continue his push into Parthian territory, not that there is anything between Ctesiphon and Ecbatana worth pushing for."

"What of the ill soldiers?"

"Many have died, so Lucius and Cassius are now making their way with their troops back to Rome. I have heard rumors that disease follows in their wake, but we left before they began their march back, so I cannot confirm anything."

"That is terrible news."

We sat in silence for some time. "Zos, perhaps you could enlighten our guests with some of the history of this site," I said in an attempt to dissipate the dark cloud that had fallen over our meal.

For the rest of the afternoon, Zos delighted them with the stories he had heard me tell only hours before.

CHAPTER ONE HUNDRED AND FORTY-EIGHT

Beyond Memphis, there was little of note, and nothing that could surpass the pyramids. We only stopped now to sleep at night. The river wound its way torturously north, splitting at irregular intervals, a frayed stylus reaching towards the Great Sea. Before nightfall, we would pull up at a dock, secure the boat, and Zos would set about tying long cloth slings to trees along the bank for the two of us to sleep in, keeping us off the ground and away from venomous snakes, aggressive hippopotami, six meter long crocodiles and lethal scorpions. The Romans preferred to stay on the boat, but I had had enough of boats. We rubbed ourselves constantly with basil which seemed to ward off most of the mosquitoes. During the day, we would doze or engage in languid conversation with each other. Evenings found either Zos or me reading aloud from some of the books I carried to entertain ourselves and the others.

HOME AT LAST

Gregorian Calendar – April 20th, 164
Alexandrian Calendar – Paremoude 11th, Fourth Proyet
The Season of the Emergence
4th year of Marcus Aurelius

"The days that are still to come are the wisest witnesses."
(Pindar, *Olympian Odes, I, l. 51,* ca 500 BC)

"What is more agreeable than one's home?"
(Marcus Tullius Cicero, *Ad Familiares, IV, 8,* ca 60 BC)

CHAPTER ONE HUNDRED AND FORTY-NINE

The morning of the final day of our journey dawned clear. The air tasted crisp and green. By midday, the monotony of our days since Memphis came to an abrupt end as the branch of the river we had taken emptied into Lake Mareotis. Sea gulls circled and screeched above us, bringing the smell of the Sea on their wings.

By evening, we could make out the shoreline of Alexandria, of home. We would reach it before dark. I felt tears running down my cheeks, wondering why I was crying. I pointed to the dock that jutted out into the water, the one that I had jumped from every morning of my life for my morning swim and bath. There were heads bobbing on the roof of my house. The light was getting dimmer, but I could just make out my father, waving to me. I could hear their shouts. I could wait no longer. I jumped out of the boat, Zos behind me, and we swam to the dock. The doors along the street emptied out, and we were suddenly surrounded not only by family but by the neighbors, all of whom had been watching for our return since my letter arrived weeks earlier. The boat pulled up along the dock. My father called for the servants to unload our things. Zos, his scribe's hat knocked askew, was being smothered in the embraces of his mother and sisters. His father stood to the side smiling from ear to ear, a look of pride beaming on his face.

The four centuria stood to the side kicking at the cobbled stones wondering what to do with themselves. I asked my father if he knew of a party of Roman ambassadors that would have arrived a few days earlier. They had left word with Ptolemaios regarding where they were lodged, and Ptolemaios had told my father. Seth was sent to guide our guard to where the rest of their company was staying. I thanked them profusely and sent word with them that I would seek the ambassadors out the following day.

The feast to which we were treated exceeded anything I had imagined so many times. That night, I lay in my bed, incredulous that I was actually back in my own home, in my own bed, looking up at the window that glowed softly in the moonlight. It was as if I had never left this place. I inhaled deeply, breathing in all the smells I had forgotten I missed, the hibiscus outside the window, the lingering odors of familiar food, the completely distinct smell of my home. I thought of Zos, of how he was dealing with being back in his home, in his own bed.

The next morning, just as the shade of darkness changed almost imperceptibly in the window, I awoke, my eyes wide, wondering if I were dreaming. I threw my right arm out slamming it into the wall and stifled a yelp, having forgotten that my bed was in an alcove. I felt around me, wondering whether or not to believe that I was actually in my own home or if I had just dreamed it.

"Teacher," I head Zos whisper. "Are you awake?"

"Yes, Zos."

"Would you like to take a swim in the lake? I brought towels."

"Lead on, Zos, lead on."

We went outside in the dark, careful to open and close the door quietly. No one was about. We were the only souls on the cobbled street. We went to the end of the pier, stripped and jumped into the warm water, laughing and splashing each other.

Before going to the Library, I needed to find Tatius. He did not know that I had hidden the Avesta among his things, and though I was sure it was safe, I would not feel entirely at ease till it was in my hands. I knew the Director was expecting me, so I had no time to lose. I made straight for the wing of the palace where I knew the governor had housed the ambassadors. I was stopped at the outer gate by guards who were not inclined to listen to my explanations of why I needed to see the ambassadors. Zos put his fingers into his mouth and let loose the loudest whistle I had ever heard.

"Where did you learn to do that?" I asked, shaking my head. The guard frowned menacingly at Zos.

"Ahoy there," Tatius leaned his head out the second story of the palace. "Let them in," he called to the guard who grudgingly let us through. We were met at the door by another guard who refused to let us pass till Tatius actually opened the door and waved us in.

We embraced and greeted each other enthusiastically.

"Septimus is out right now, but if you will wait, he'll be back before midday."

"I fear I am in a bit of a hurry myself," I said. "We just got in yesterday, and I know the Director of the Library is expecting me first thing this morning."

"Well, I'm honored that you thought to come see me first when you are in such a hurry."

"Yes, about that. I trust you will forgive me for not having told you, but I hid something of mine among your books." A sly smile grew on Tatius' unshaven face.

"You sly bastard. Let me guess. It's that precious book you have been carrying halfway across the world."

"You guessed it. And it is the reason for my entire trip. I cannot appear before the Director without it."

"Well, you may have to. Every book I had on me was taken from me the minute I came into the palace."

"Of course they were!" The realization of what had happened came to me in a flash. I had to go immediately to the Scriptorium at the back end of the Library. Who knew what would be done with the Avesta when no one recognized the language. I was already backing up towards the door. "I will explain everything later, but right now I have to go. Forgive my haste, and hello to Septimus when he returns."

"But..." I was out the door before Tatius could finish, walking as fast as I could along the harbor, unable to enjoy my first views of the Sea and my beautiful city, entirely intent on finding the Avesta before it became known what it was. I must keep my promise to Aschek. No one could know I had it. I was walking so fast, I even forgot that Zos was behind me. I crossed the avenue to pass between the Theater and the Forum in order to avoid the front side of the Library, in case someone saw me. Though uncomely, I broke into a mild jog once I had passed the Forum and turned right on the narrower street that would take me to the rear of the Scriptorium.

Panting, I reached the back entrance, showed my ring to the guards and was let through, the air cool on my sweat as soon as I crossed into the thick-walled, well-lit room. It was enormous, like the forum but with a roof, the entire space filled with geometrically placed islands of desks where copyists even at this early hour were sitting working on manuscripts from the four corners of the empire. I walked purposefully to the desk of the Superintendent of Temporary Acquisitions, a colleague and friend of mine who had been promoted to his position around the same time I had risen to mine.

"Scribe Kaleb! What a surprise. When did you get back? I heard you were roaming the globe searching for new acquisitions for your department."

"You heard right Ngozi. But I returned yesterday. I have not even seen the Director yet, and I have a bit of an emergency."

"What can I do?" A boy brought a tray of tea for the two of us. I noticed Zos for the first time. "Sit. Catch your breath." Ngozi slid a chair out for me to sit down. Zos stood to my right behind the chair.

"I cannot tell you the whole story now because the Director is expecting me. Suffice it to say that three of the books that were collected from the Roman ambassadors who recently came into the city belong to me. I hid them among their things for the protection of the documents, but now I need them back in order to present them myself to the Director. I cannot stress enough that this whole matter is highly confidential. The purpose of my mission has not been made public yet, if it ever will."

Ngozi made a clicking sound with his tongue. "This is all very unfortunate. No wonder you are at your wits end. What can I do?"

"What do you mean, what can you do? Everything that enters this Scriptorium passes by your desk. I just need you to locate who now has those three books and bring them to me."

"Kaleb, you make it sound so easy."

"Ngozi, it is easy."

"Let me see if I understand," he said, his cup of tea poised as if he were about to take a drink. "You hid three of your own books among the books of one of the Roman ambassadors, and now you want them back."

"You clearly understand."

"There is only one small problem."

"Which is?"

"I have signed a Bill of Receipt to the effect that every book I took will be returned to said ambassador. If I give three of the books to you, I will be in breach of the receipt and could be in serious trouble."

"What if I had a signed letter from the ambassador giving you permission to release the books to me?"

"The entire problem would evaporate like the dew from a hibiscus," he said, finally bringing the cup of tea to his lips.

"Zos, you know what to do," I said turning and looking at him. Zos took off before I finished speaking.

"Your servant boy? You seem quite familiar with him."

"He accompanied me on my journey, and is now a scribe in training."

"More tea?"

CHAPTER ONE HUNDRED AND FIFTY

Reaching the top step of the Library, I turned and gazed out over the harbor, at the Pharos, the clean white lines of my city, the blue of the sea. My bag hung from my side, filled with letters for Ptolemaios, my journal, manuscripts and what maps remained after the robbery that I had copied over the past two years from libraries I had discovered among my hosts and thankfully, the Greek Avesta. Zos carried the prize. Ngozi had packaged it for me in plain brown sackcloth which I then wrapped in a fine gold cloth I had brought from India for that very purpose.

I heard my name called from the open doorway behind me. Recognizing the voice of the Director, I turned. My father had let Ptolemaios know we were coming, and he had stationed a slave on the steps to let him know the minute I arrived. We embraced, and he slapped me repeatedly on the back. He led me to a large anteroom where I proceeded to lay everything out on the long marble table, from least to most important. Ptolemaios shooed everyone out of the room except Zos and me. Zos set his parcel carefully at the end of the table. Ptolemaios picked up a map and studied it. "You must tell me everything. I want every detail."

"It is all in my journal Director."

"Bah, I want to hear it from your lips. Then I will read it."

"It is a very long story."

"I will speed you along if it gets boring." He proceeded to ask me countless questions about each paper, each manuscript, each book.

"And what is this?" he asked, holding up the Sanskrit copy of the Gospel of John.

"While in the Kushan Kingdom, aided by a Buddhist monk, I translated the Gospel of John to Sanskrit and left a copy with the head monk and the prince there. I made one extra copy to add to our translations of this book."

"I say, that was quite industrious of you. Sanskrit, eh? You are going to have to tell me more about how that language works. What an interesting alphabet, quite beautiful really."

Finally, he reached the pièce de résistance. He proceeded to slowly unwrap it, appreciating the fragile texture of the finely woven cloth. "It is beautiful," he said, holding one leather bound copy in his hands. "We must begin the translation immediately."

"Not to worry Director. I have already taken the liberty of translating it." I held out the copy of the translation I had made in Purushapura and finished on the Indus. "I could not have finished it without Zos' help. The copy I made was stolen, but we made a second before that happened. This one is in Zos' own hand." Zos looked at the floor.

"Indeed. Extraordinary!"

"I was going to talk to you about it later, but I would like to enroll Zos in the school for scribes to complete his education."

"Complete it you say?"

"Yes, he has studied under some of the best tutors and teachers in the Parthian and Kushan Empires. I believe he is more than capable of holding his own and even excelling."

"As you wish Kaleb. Today you could ask me just about anything, and I would grant it you." I rubbed the top of Zos' freshly shaven head.

EPILOGUE

It is the sixth year of Marcus Aurelius. Today is the anniversary of my return. I have now been back as long as I was gone. My wife Silara and I have a one-year-old son named Yakub after my father. Zos is now fourteen years old and has already surpassed all of his peers in his classes. When he is not studying, he works for me in the Department of Religious Archives. Though I have not heard back from Aschek, Ptolemaios has guaranteed that he will keep the Avesta under lock and key for one more year. If by then I still have no word from Aschek, it will be made public.

No further attempts have been made on my life. I have heard nothing from Mihret nor did I ever tell my father what I learned about Sara.

A ship arrived in the harbor yesterday, and everyone on it, crew and passengers, was either dead or dying. It is a miracle they made it into port. The plague has reached our fair city. The ship was quarantined, but it is only a matter of time before it spreads through our streets like it has already done in Rome and Tyre.

My father called our whole family together last night. He prayed, we ate, and he prayed again. He has written his brother, my uncle, in Adulis. We are leaving Alexandria next week, at least until this plague is past.

I have just left the Library from a meeting with Ptolemaios. He has commissioned me to obtain a copy of the Buddhist sutras I told him about. He has already funded my trip. The timing could not be better, but in truth, I believe Ptolemaios chose this moment purposely, to get me and my family out before the worst.

May God have mercy on this my beloved city.

THE END

GLOSSARY

acnua	a measure of land 120 yards square
acusmaticus	exoteric disciple who listened to lectures that Pythagoras or a mathematicus gave out loud from behind a veil
aft	rear of a ship
apodyterium	Dressing room at the entrance of the baths, or in the palestra, where one stripped
arpent	120 Roman feet
as	denomination of money worth 4 quadrans or 1/16th of a denarius
aureus	gold coin worth 25 denarii
ayvan	a high arched ceiling that serves as a kind of reception hall
barbat	lute-like instrument played with a quill for a pick
bark	a ship
bhavana	meditation
bulwark	a solid wall enclosing the perimeter of a the main deck for the protection of persons or objects on deck
caldarium	round domed room in a public Roman bath with a hot pool usually in the center
capsaria	Servant in charge of clothes in the bath
centuria	Roman military contingent of 100 soldiers
Centurion	head of a centuria
contubernium	tent groups - groups of 10 soldiers
crutch	a forked apparatus where the mast or oars are supported on deck
cuirass	breastplate
Delphi, oracle	Greek priestess who delivered obscure messages as advice from Apollo
denarius	half a denarius was equivalent to a good day's salary
diptych	re-usable wooden and wax tablets on wooden leaves which were strung together; there was a shallow recess in the wooden leaves which was filled with wax and was used as the writing surface. This allowed for the leaves to be closed and bound together without damaging the

	writing on the wax surface.
dromedary	Arabian camel with one hump whereas a Bactrian camel has two
fibula	brooch resembling a safety pin
fore	front of a ship
forestay	a piece of standing rigging which keeps a mast from falling backwards
Gades	the modern Cadiz, port city in the south of Spain
Ge'ez	language of the Kingdom of Axum
greave	a piece of armour worn to protect the shin from the ankle to the knee
hawser	thick cable or rope used in mooring or towing a ship
jhana	a meditative state of profound stillness and concentration in which the mind becomes fully immersed and absorbed in the chosen object of attention
kalak	traditional raft or bargelike vessel for downstream transportation on both the Tigris and Euphrates
lappet	decorative flap or fold in a ceremonial garment
Mare Nostrum	Our Sea, Roman name for the Mediterranean
mathematicus	cult member who had gone through years of study and training
Necropolis	City of the Dead, common name for city graveyards
ney	an end-blown flute
nka	ancient Egyptian diminutive inserted before a name
pace	5 feet (Roman measure)
palaestra	exercise ground
palette	a writing box containing pigment for making ink and writing utensils, reeds and stylus
perch	10 Roman feet
quadran	denomination of money worth 1/64th of a denarius
quaternion	a group of four soldiers
Ra / Re	Egyptian god of the sun
rigging	term which embraces all ropes, wires, or chains used in ships and smaller vessels to support the

	masts and yards and for hoisting, lowering, or trimming sails to the wind
sestertii	unit of money (see chart)
stadion	approximately two and a half Roman miles
stelae	obelisk
stern	the rear of the vessel
stertor	snoring
strigil	a small, curved, metal tool used in ancient Greece and Rome to scrape dirt and sweat from the body
stupa	A dome-shaped monument, used to house Buddhist relics or to commemorate significant facts of Buddhism
subligaculum	loincloth
tackle	pulleys for raising and lowering cargo or the mast of a ship
Tanakh	The complete collection of Jewish holy writings, also the Old Testament of the Christian Bible
tepidarium	a room in a public Roman bath with heated walls and floor
Tetrapylon	an ancient type of Roman monument of cubic shape, with a gate on each of the four sides
Teuton	of Germanic or Celtic origin
yard	a spar on a mast from which sails are set

HIEROGLYPHS TRANSLATED

ABOUT THE AUTHOR

JP is the author's initials, O'Connell the name his grandfather
dropped when he ran away from home as a teenager to join the
cavalry where he fought on the Mexican border before eventually
marrying his Cherokee Indian bride in Georgia. A 27-year veteran
teacher by trade, JP holds a masters in Spanish Language and Culture
from the University of Salamanca, Spain and a degree in TESOL and
has spent his life teaching English abroad and at home, first as a
foreign and now as a second language. He spends his summers
visiting new and faraway places, volunteer teaching and learning new
languages.